Praise for Anne Holt

"Fast-paced and involving . . . Holt knows psychology as well as she knows the ins and outs of police work. She quickly draws the reader into the minds and lives of half a dozen disparate characters—none more interesting than Inspector Wilhelmsen herself. . . . Holt's visions of societal and ethical decay are balanced by glimpses of great poignancy, human consolation, and love."

—*The Wall Street Journal*

"Wherever Hanne shows up next, my advice is to follow that wheelchair."

—Marilyn Stasio, *The New York Times Book Review*

"When you think of Scandinavian noir, names like Stieg Larsson, Henning Mankell, and Camilla Läckberg probably come to mind, not Anne Holt. That may be about to change. . . . Hanne Wilhelmsen is a character who's going to get in your head—and stay there."

—*Entertainment Weekly*

"This is a series that demands to be read, and the more quickly, the better."

—*Bookreporter*

"Holt proves a masterful plotter. Unexpected twists hold up to scrutiny, loose ends are tied up, and the finale leaves readers wanting more."

—*The Cleveland Plain Dealer*

"An ideal read-alike for fans of Jo Nesbø's Harry Hole and Karin Fossum's Inspector Sejer."

—*Booklist*

"Powerful . . . nuanced characters and a strong sense of place make for an immersive tale that packs an emotional punch and offers incisive commentary on the failings of the criminal justice system."

—*Publishers Weekly*

"What a delight it is to read Anne Holt! Few succeed in being so thrilling as they discuss contemporary society's greatest issues."

—*Dagens Nyheter* (Stockholm)

In Dust and Ashes

A Hanne Wilhelmsen Novel

Anne Holt

Translated from the Norwegian
by Anne Bruce

SCRIBNER

New York   London   Toronto   Sydney   New Delhi

Scribner
An Imprint of Simon & Schuster, Inc.
1230 Avenue of the Americas
New York, NY 10020

This book is a work of fiction. Any references to historical events, real people,
or real places are used fictitiously. Other names, characters, places, and events are products
of the author's imagination, and any resemblance to actual events or places or persons,
living or dead, is entirely coincidental.

Copyright © 2016 by Anne Holt
English translation copyright © 2017 by Anne Bruce
Originally published in Norwegian as *I støv og aske*
Published by agreement with Salomonsson Agency

First Scribner hardcover edition May 2018

SCRIBNER and design are registered trademarks of The Gale Group, Inc.,
used under license by Simon & Schuster, Inc., the publisher of this work.

For information about special discounts for bulk purchases,
please contact Simon & Schuster Special Sales at 1-866-506-1949
or business@simonandschuster.com.

The Simon & Schuster Speakers Bureau can bring authors to your live event.
For more information or to book an event, contact the Simon & Schuster Speakers Bureau
at 1-866-248-3049 or visit our website at www.simonspeakers.com.

Manufactured in the United States of America

1 3 5 7 9 10 8 6 4 2

Library of Congress Cataloging-in-Publication Data has been applied for.

ISBN 978-1-5011-7478-0
ISBN 978-1-5011-7480-3 (ebook)

Therefore I despise myself, and repent in dust and ashes.

Book of Job 42:6

In Dust and Ashes

FRIDAY, JANUARY 1, 2016

Only a couple of weeks left, and then it would all be over.

And everything could begin.

Their new life, he and his wife in Provence. She was the one who had insisted on a move. He couldn't speak French and didn't drink wine, but at least the climate down there was appealing. He had been in the police since 1978 when he had entered what they had then called Police College, and it was high time he found something else. Dog breeding—that was what he and his old woman had decided on.

A whole lifetime had gone by since the end of the seventies—a couple of generations of Norwegians and thirty-nine sets of trainee officers. Or police students, as they had snootily come to be called over the years. He himself had started in the police force when they used pen and paper and the odd IBM golf ball typewriter and the youngest officers were more than content to be known as constables. A few months ago, he had been promoted to the rank of superintendent, less than six months before everything came to an end. Having turned fifty-eight in the middle of January, he could pack up the odds and ends in his office and walk out the doors at Stovner Police Station for the very last time.

Kjell Bonsaksen was a contented man in most areas of life. He had no intention of looking back; after all, it must be possible to get a decent beer down there in Provence. His son was an only child and their two grandchildren half French, so it actually hadn't been too difficult to persuade him to move closer to them. They had sold their terraced house in Korsvoll following a furious round of bids for a sum that had caused him to blush. A good chunk of money was left over, even when the little house outside Aix with the sprawling, overgrown garden was paid in full.

He wouldn't be able to eat so many hot dogs down there, when his wife could keep an eye on him all the time.

Placing a fifty-kroner note on the counter, he received some change in return and dropped it into his pocket. He zigzagged a generous portion of ketchup over his hot dog, shaking his head when the assistant pushed the bottle of mustard toward him.

Through the large windows, he glanced at the gas pumps. The weather was horrendous, as it had mostly been all through Christmas. Plump, wet snowflakes melted before they reached the ground, and everything was in shades of gray. A parked trailer truck blocked his view of the E18. It would probably be red once it was washed.

A man came walking toward the automatic doors. Tall, he had most likely been good-looking at one time. Bonsaksen was not a particularly adept judge of that sort of thing, but there was something about the wide mouth and the extremely straight, symmetrical nose. As the man entered, he looked up and straight at him.

Kjell Bonsaksen froze in the middle of chewing.

There was something about those eyes.

The man stopped for a moment, so briefly that it was actually more a matter of slowing down midstep, before resuming his pace. He was holding an empty cup in one hand, and without a word to the fellow behind the counter, he filled it with coffee from a dispensing machine on a table by the window.

Bonsaksen was a dependable police officer. Never exceptional, and this final promotion had probably been the police chief's way of saying thanks for long and faithful service rather than real acknowledgment of his suitability to be in charge of very many subordinates. His forte was working hard and according to the book, being honest and exact, and he was never tempted to take shortcuts. He was a workhorse. Policemen of his ilk were a dying breed. It had bothered him for some time, but now he couldn't care less. He had only thirteen days left of his solid, if somewhat nondescript, career.

As a police officer of almost forty years' experience, what he was proudest of was his memory. A policeman had to be able to remember: names and cases; relationships and faces; crime scenes; perpetrators and victims. You had to have some glue up top.

Although the man at the coffee machine had lost most of his hair and was also much thinner than the last time they met, Kjell Bonsaksen recognized him as soon as they exchanged glances. His big eyes were unusually deep-set in his skinny, almost gaunt face.

They radiated nothingness. Neither curiosity nor evil. No trace of pleasure, not even that the stranger had also recognized him. They contained not a sliver of reproach as the man placed the lid on his cup and, with steady steps, approached the hot dog–munching policeman. He stopped a few feet away from him.

"You knew I was innocent," he said softly.

Kjell Bonsaksen did not answer. He had more than enough to do, struggling to swallow an oversized chunk of hot dog, roll, and ketchup.

"You knew it," the man repeated. "And yet you did nothing."

He let his gaze linger on Kjell's face for a second or two before giving an almost imperceptible shrug as he turned on his heel and headed for the exit.

Kjell Bonsaksen stood lost in thought, a half-eaten hot dog in his hand, until the stranger climbed into the trailer truck that might have been red and drove out onto the highway in the direction of Oslo.

"Maybe so," he said, so quietly it was possible he only thought it. "Maybe it's true that I knew you were innocent."

MONDAY, DECEMBER 3, 2001

O ne extra cup of coffee would cost him everything.

If only he had left it there. Then the day would have progressed like every other December day, and they would have celebrated Dina's third birthday the following weekend. As a matter of fact, it might just as easily have been his fumbling with the bunch of keys that proved so fatal. Earlier, he had cut his thumb on a can of mackerel. Dina had been allowed to be his nurse. She had used a whole roll of gauze bandage, loosely fastened with a Donald Duck adhesive bandage. He should have done it himself. That would have saved the necessary seconds, suffi- cient time to let the day follow its customary, safe course to evening.

It might also have been something else entirely. Anything at all, really, of all the inconsequential things that took place on that ordinary, rain-sodden, Advent morning: any one of a number of things that hap- pened or didn't happen. If he hadn't overslept, for example. If he hadn't taken that third cup of coffee, or even if he hadn't drunk the second one down to the dregs. A couple more gulps would have been enough for them to reach the road a bit later, and maybe he could also have resisted checking the mailbox because he knew they were running late.

He did the calculations later, when his whole head was swarming with reflections about time and he spent a whole day ensconced in the mas- sive spruce tree in his neighbor's garden. It grew right beside the mail- box that he had torn down that same morning and smashed to smithereens with a sledgehammer. He sat there, just before Christmas, on a sturdy branch, aloft and unseen by passersby, counting the cars that drove past the little exit road from seven o'clock in the morning until seven o'clock at night. He arrived at a total of sixteen. If he calculated five seconds for each, five seconds when a potentially dangerous situation could arise when a soon-to-be-three-year-old child ran out into the road while her father was opening the mailbox and crossly starting to sort out

4

the junk mail, it totaled no more than eighty seconds. Twelve hours, those twelve hours when it was feasible for Dina to be outside, beside the mailbox, while something distracted her father and she, for a fleeting millisecond of time, was not properly supervised, amounted to 43,200 seconds. So, in eighty of those seconds, something could happen.

In less than two-thousandths of that time.

0.185185185 percent—something he would always remember.

If only he had taken some time to return the milk carton to the fridge, nothing would have happened.

It was Jonas who screamed. Dina made not a sound.

He yelled the moment before, when his life had not yet fallen apart, and he saw her stumble. It was Jonas who roared so loudly that the driver braked abruptly. It was Jonas who desperately tried to shove the car back, away from Dina, who was still lying wedged under the left front wheel. It was Jonas's scream that made the baffled driver roll down his window, without understanding any of it, until he finally let his BMW trundle on a few feet or so.

In the years that followed, the scene never released its grip on him. Dina's fall in front of the winter tire. The look she gave him as her open mouth drained of color and turned almost white under the dim street-light. The seconds when he stood with Dina in his arms, realizing what had happened, without yet possessing any capacity to comprehend it. All of it, image by image, turned into a horror film that kept him awake when he ought to be sleeping and exhausted him so much that he fell asleep when he shouldn't.

He would remember that tableau forever. The blue snowsuit and the pink hat he had attempted to straighten before the police arrived. Dina's eyes that stared through and past him. The day care bag on the ground and what was inside it. The Donald Duck bandage and the bloody gauze that had fallen off when he picked her up. The smell of feces as they leaked from Dina's diaper before the blue lights approached. Jonas would never forget the driver who kept talking on his phone while he sobbed endlessly in a nauseating cloud of aftershave.

"It was my fault," Jonas shouted at him, over and over again. "It's not your fault."

That was the only thing he said on that morning when he lost his only child.

"It was my fault."

THURSDAY, JANUARY 7, 2016

H is hand warmed her shoulder through the flimsy sweater.
Hanne Wilhelmsen could not stand being touched by anyone
other than the people she lived with—her little girl and her wife,
whom she would have called her family if she had ever spoken about
them to others. This hand, narrow and tentative, felt strangely welcome all the same. A lifeline, she thought, a flicker of something familiar and stable in a situation she had been forced into and had dreaded
for days on end.

She screwed up her eyes against the unrelenting camera flashes. The
photographers were so persistent that she had enough of a problem
maneuvering her wheelchair, and that was no easier when she was
blinded.

"Move yourselves," she said sharply, and felt the man behind her
release her shoulder and take hold of the chair handles instead.

"Let me push you for once," Henrik Holme said, bending into ear-
shot. "We have to get out of here."

"Were they convicted?" a journalist called out. "All of them, I mean?"

"What did you think of the prosecutor's arguments?" another one
asked, thrusting a phone into her face.

"Get out of the way, won't you!"

Henrik Holme's voice rose to falsetto as he resolutely steered the
wheelchair through the crowd. Just before they reached the heavy
doors leading from the courthouse, it was as if Moses had intervened.
The journalists, probably twenty in number, were suddenly preoccupied with checking their phones and turned aside. The photographers,
at least some of them, confused by the abrupt change in atmosphere,
lowered their cameras. Henrik stopped for a second, taken aback to see
a clear route to the door and the waiting police car outside.

"What's going on?" Hanne asked, grabbing hold of the wheels.

"No idea. Let's get out of here."

The winter weather met them head-on. It had begun to snow at last, following a gloomy Christmas. It was not yet cold enough to turn the city white, but damp, downy flakes were falling thickly, making Hanne scrunch up her eyes.

"My goodness," Henrik said, coming to an abrupt halt.

The police car, which had been parked a few yards away, rolled slowly up to the steps, and a uniformed woman emerged from the driver's seat.

"What is it?" Hanne asked Henrik in annoyance as she wrapped her jacket more snugly around herself.

"Iselin Havørn is dead."

Hanne looked at him. He was holding his phone so close to his face that a faint, bluish light was reflected off his glistening cheeks.

"If you're now going to tell me that she's been murdered, now that we've just done our best to get twenty-two right-wing extremists put behind lock and key at long last, then . . ."

The policewoman approached them, obviously unsure of how to negotiate Hanne into the vehicle.

"It doesn't exactly look like murder." Henrik scrolled down with his thumb on the screen. "They don't spell out that it's suicide," he went on, "but it does in fact look as if she voluntarily kicked the bucket." Stuffing the phone into his pocket, he walked halfway around the wheelchair.

"Would you allow me the honor?" he said with a smile, holding out his arms. "It's easier that way, you know."

"I'll have to put up with it for once," Hanne muttered, raising her arms sluggishly, like an unwilling child.

He carried her to the car. For such an unusually small-boned man, he seemed strong, Hanne felt, even though her aversion to being carried made her feel physically ill.

"Would you see to the wheelchair?" Henrik said to the woman in uniform, who had already begun to fold it up.

He deposited Hanne on the backseat.

"Iselin Havørn," Hanne said in an undertone. "What a stupid name. But to be quite honest . . ."

Henrik carefully straightened her legs.

". . . hardly a single person in this country has more reason to feel ashamed now than . . ."

She used both hands to push him away before snatching at the seat belt.

". . . Iselin Havørn. What a name. And what a deplorable harridan."

If the police were taciturn and subdued in their attempts to play down Iselin Havørn's death, the media went berserk. Even on a day when the most far-reaching criminal case in Norwegian history brought right-wing extremists to court, the sixty-two-year-old woman's suicide was headline news everywhere.

"Three weeks ago, hardly anyone had any idea who she was," Henrik said as he picked up the remote control to reduce the volume on the TV. "And now there's a real hullabaloo about her."

"Well," Hanne answered, "lots of people have known her by her pseudonym. Difficult to avoid it, for one thing. At some time or other, that sort of thing was bound to be exposed. It just took an unusually long time in this instance."

"I thought press ethics stipulated that suicides should not be reported, at least at the outset?"

"That no longer applies, apparently. And anyway not when they've been all over her in recent weeks. From that point of view, there may well be some paradoxical connection between the media's hounding of her and their now having a suicide to gorge themselves on."

"Do you think she was hounded?"

Hanne shrugged nonchalantly.

"In fact she certainly was. After her identity was revealed, she's hardly ventured out of her apartment, from what I've read. And it's clearly been more or less under siege."

"Yes, I suppose so, but hounded? After all it was her own fault that—"

"Were you thinking of moving in here?" Hanne interrupted him, glancing demonstratively at the clock.

Henrik blushed and touched the side of his nose.

"No, of course not. But hounded? Do you really think that?"

Hanne did not reply. She switched off the TV and nodded at the door.

"Iselin Havørn wasn't stupid. Ergo she was evil. I don't shed a single tear that she's dead, but there are probably a few others who do. What she's had to endure in the past few weeks would have been enough to tip the greatest stoic into depression and suicidal thoughts, but now you have to leave. You don't need to come back or get in touch until another cold case turns up."

"Not even when sentence is passed, you mean?"

"You don't need to. They'll be convicted, one and all."

"Do you really think so?"

He had stood up and was heading for the door when Hanne began to trundle to the kitchen. All of a sudden she stopped and looked at him.

"Thanks to us, they most certainly will. Or in actual fact . . ."

An almost imperceptible smile crossed her face.

". . . thanks to you, Henrik. All thanks to you."

Henrik had been allocated his own office.

It was far from spacious, but it was his. For several years, he had been shunted into impersonal shoe boxes he was allowed to keep for a few days, a few weeks, or, in one case, a month and a half. This one, however, he had kept ever since several days after May 17, 2014, when sixteen people were killed by homemade bombs hidden in a tuba and four big bass drums during the two-hundred-year anniversary of the Norwegian Constitution. The total number of deaths would have been far greater if it had not been for Hanne Wilhelmsen and himself. They were too late to prevent the attack, but just in time to reduce its scale and have two people arrested and, later, twenty more in a network so terrifying that it had given him sleepless nights for ages afterward. Since Hanne had downright refused to move into Police Headquarters at Grønlandsleiret 44 for the duration of the subsequent intense and lengthy investigation, he was upgraded to a deputy of sorts. And errand boy, as he already had been for a while.

He loved that office.

His mother had called only a few days after he had moved in. She hated the curtains, which in her opinion looked like municipal issue, and had mailed him new ones. At first he had hesitated to hang them; after all, there could be some sort of proscription against adding any personal touches to government property. When one of the older female civilians in the Violent Crime Section had come across the bundle of fabric on the spare seat in his office, she had insisted on helping him to hang them. Along with a couple of posters he had bought at IKEA and a potted plant at the window that he contented himself with watering every Monday and Thursday, the curtains made his office look very nice, to tell the truth.

Henrik arrived at work every morning at 7:15 and seldom went home before 10:00 p.m. He headed for Hanne's whenever she asked him to come and returned to Police Headquarters when she ordered him out of the apartment in Kruses gate. For the first six months following the terrorist attacks, he had, for the most part, worked every weekend without exception. Eventually, when the case was close to being submitted to the public prosecutor, they had once again been given a couple of old unsolved cases to keep them busy. They never managed to figure out one of these, and the other, an ancient homicide case, was solved only a couple of months before the time limit expired. The killer turned out to have been dead for sixteen years, but the aged mother of his victim could at least rest more easily in the knowledge of what had actually taken place.

Now it was 8:30 p.m., and Henrik was staring despondently at the empty in-tray on his office desk.

They had no cases in progress.

Nothing to do. No excuse to visit Hanne.

In fact, he ought to report to the Chief Inspector: Police Chief Silje Sørensen had given him a roving commission on the assumption that he would inform his superiors whenever he had time to spare.

"Do you have a minute?"

A burly man with a broad smile stood in the doorway, knocking lightly on the doorframe. A small bag was slung over his right shoulder.

"Quite a few," Henrik answered. "Come on in."

"Bonsaksen," the man said, holding out a huge hand. "Superintendent Kjell Bonsaksen, Stovner Police Station."

His stubby fingers touched the police badge suspended on a blue cord around his neck.

"Henrik Holme," Henrik reciprocated, trying to avoid grimacing at the overly firm handshake. "But of course you knew that. Since you . . ."

He smiled sheepishly, tapping his forehead with his fist before he sat down.

"Since I'm the one who looked you up," Bonsaksen said, nodding, as he sat on the empty chair.

"Yes."

"You're starting to make a name for yourself, Holme."

Henrik did not answer. He had enough to cope with as he battled with increasingly flushed cheeks and struggled to tuck his hands safely under his thighs.

"People talk about you. With respect. The way they once spoke about Hanne Wilhelmsen."

He smiled again.

"Or . . . you've got some way to go before you reach that stage, I suppose. I worked here in the bad old days, so I know what I'm talking about. We never worked together, Wilhelmsen and I, but my goodness, what a reputation she had. Queen of them all near the end. Before that—before she was shot and became a bit . . ."

His index finger rotated slowly above his forehead.

The room fell silent. The sound of a siren in the backyard finally penetrated the walls and floor.

"Much to do?"

Bonsaksen ran his eyes over the almost clear surface of the desk. They stopped at the wire basket, empty of its contents.

"Not right now."

"Excellent. I'd actually like to—"

The older policeman lifted the bag from his lap and pulled out a blue ring binder. It was so crammed with paper that it was bulging open. He placed it on the desk with a dull thud.

"I'd really like you to take a look at this case," he said.

"We . . . It's the Police Chief who gives us cases. We can't just—"

"I know, I know."

Kjell Bonsaksen ran his finger thoughtfully along the ridge of his nose.

"You've been here for only three years?"

"Five this summer."

"Five."

Bonsaksen nodded. "I retire on full pension in exactly one week," he continued. "I'll be fifty-eight on January 14. I've been in the police for nearly thirty-nine years."

Henrik stared intently at the blue ring binder that looked terribly worn and faded.

"And in so many years, making the occasional mistake can't be avoided," Bonsaksen went on. "Even though I may have made fewer than most. But as I said . . ."

He glanced around the room and caught sight of Henrik's coffee machine on a table in the corner.

"Could I have a cup?"

"It's been standing for a while, I'm afraid."

"That makes no difference," Bonsaksen said as he got to his feet. "I just told you, I've spent more than a lifetime in the force."

He crossed the room, picked up a clean cup from the tray beside the coffee machine, and poured himself a cup. Lifting the cup to his nose, he sniffed loudly and swallowed a mouthful.

"Absolutely fine," he said tersely, resuming his seat.

"You were saying?" Henrik reminded him. "You started to—"

"As I said," Bonsaksen broke in, lifting the cup to his mouth once more before changing his mind and putting it down again, "it's inevitable to have made one or two mistakes. Letting people go too easily. Maybe not putting everything into solving a case. It can't be discounted that now and again, you haven't been able to remain as objective as you should, according to the book. All the same, Holme, it's true that . . ."

He sniffed slightly and ran his finger several times under his nose.

"There's nothing I can't live with. Nothing that's going to niggle me when I put my belongings in a box in a week's time and trudge out of my office to get on the first plane to France. There's nothing I've done in all these years, or nothing I haven't done, that's going to cost me a minute's sleep in all the years that lie ahead. Not one single minute."

He emphasized the point by slamming his fist on the desk.

"Except for this one," he added, tapping the blue ring binder. "This has rankled like a stone in my shoe since 2004."

"I see. I know how exasperating it can be when an offender gets away with it."

"This one didn't get away."

"What?"

"He certainly didn't get away. He was charged, tried, and convicted."

"Then, then—in that case . . ."

Henrik swallowed. He could still feel a slight tenderness around his larynx, where, at the beginning of December, he had undergone an operation to have his Adam's apple reduced in size. Considerably. Now he went about in high-necked sweaters or with a scarf around his neck, dreading the warmer weather to come. It was true that the operation incision was made so precisely in the spot between his neck and his chin that it was barely visible, but everyone would notice the great change in his neck itself. That of course had been the intention, when he came to think of it.

He fiddled with the collar of his army-green sweater.

"Hanne Wilhelmsen and I work on unsolved cases," he said, trying to give the impression of firmness. "Cold cases. I'm afraid we can't . . . and anyway, as I said earlier, we're subject to the Police Chief and no one else."

"I dare say," Kjell Bonsaksen said, "there's probably nobody else here at headquarters with any hope of keeping any sort of control over Wilhelmsen, right? But this case . . ."

He laid his hand on the binder and pushed it insistently across to Henrik, who sat back a little, as if the collection of documents scared him.

"This has to do with an error," the older policeman went on. "A miscarriage of justice. Or . . ."

Leaning back abruptly in his chair, he fished out a half-smoked cigar from his breast pocket and stuck it into his mouth.

"Only sucking on it," he murmured reassuringly. "I won't light it."

"A miscarriage of justice," Henrik reiterated in a monotone. "If you mean that a wrongful conviction occurred, then the Criminal Cases Review Commission is the place to take that up."

"Yes, I know. If the guy had been interested in doing so, yes. The problem is . . ."

Kjell Bonsaksen gave a slight groan as he stood up. He was at least forty pounds overweight, and the cigar had obviously found its customary place at the corner of his mouth, in a tiny crevice between his lips formed by decades of habitual pressure. Henrik, who thought the cigar resembled a dry puppy turd, cast his eyes down.

"I've consoled myself that he never fought back," the soon-to-be-retired policeman said, staring out into the darkness. "For nearly twelve years now, I've tried to placate myself with the fact that he was never willing to fight. Could anyone like that be innocent? I wonder."

Henrik did not reply.

"I think . . ." Bonsaksen spat out invisible tobacco flakes without removing the cigar from his lips. "All the evidence pointed to him. He told an obvious lie. Two courts of law found him guilty. Damn it, not even the poor guy's own defense lawyer believed him!"

He turned to face Henrik and flung out his arms.

"Do you understand?"

Henrik wanted to say no. Instead he stared intently at the ring binder in front of him.

"In fact, I was the only one who doubted it," Kjell plowed on. "I was the chief investigator in the case. Of course, that could have been a fucking advantage for the guy, that the chief investigator wasn't entirely convinced that he was guilty of killing his wife, but—"

"Killing his wife?"

Henrik looked up.

"Yes. He was sentenced to twelve years in prison for murdering his wife."

"So he's . . ."

Henrik did a rapid mental calculation.

"He's out now, then? He didn't serve his whole sentence, did he?"

The other man nodded and sat down again.

"He was released after serving eight years. I know that now. Did some digging, you see, after I bumped into him recently. On New Year's Day, in fact, at a gas station out on the E18. Completely by chance. He had lost his good looks, to put it mildly. Emaciated. Nearly bald, and the few wisps of hair left on his head were totally gray. In the past, he was quite a guy. A real show-off, with a brilliant job at Statoil. Now he drives a trailer truck between Norway and Sweden and looks like it too. Pale and drawn and so full of coffee that you're knocked wide awake just by looking at him. Absolutely unrecognizable. But his eyes, Holme . . ."

He placed both strong hands on the desk and leaned forward unexpectedly.

"They were exactly the same as that time. Absolutely identical."

"I see," Henrik said meekly. "Eyes probably don't change so much in twelve years."

"Yes, they can. But not these ones."

Henrik could detect a sharp, cloying smell from the cold cigar and drew his chair even farther back.

"Do you know what my wife says is the worst thing about me after all these years in the police force?" Kjell asked, deadly earnest.

"No."

"That I've become so damned cynical. She says it's as if I don't believe in anybody, that I come out with objections and reexamine everything that's said. It's probably true. An occupational injury, that's what it is."

Finally he took his cigar from the corner of his mouth and tucked it back inside his breast pocket.

"But do you know what Bjørg-Eva thinks is the *best* thing to emerge from all these years?"

Henrik shook his head energetically.

"That I can tell—just from people's eyes—when they're lying."

Henrik sat quiet as a mouse.

"Of course, I can't really," Bonsaksen said. "But almost. And the problem at that time was, I saw no trace of a lie in his eyes when he said he hadn't done it. But there was no spark behind them, that sort of thing. No indignation at being unfairly treated. Just . . ."

He used both hands to snatch up the ring binder and stood it edgeways on the desk. Henrik could see that the man's wedding ring was disappearing into his ring finger and recognized an equally tight Odd Fellow ring on the other hand.

"Resignation," Bonsaksen completed his sentence. "The guy seemed totally resigned. As if he had no energy left, in a sense. So I've tried to allay my concerns by telling myself that justice was up to the mark at that time. As I said, the case has been like an irritating stone in my shoe: uncomfortable but far from dangerous. A nuisance, but something I can live with."

He set the bulky ring binder down again, and yet again shoved it across the desk to Henrik.

"But not now," he added, with a heavy sigh. "That look he gave me out there at the gas station . . ."

"What's the guy's name?" Henrik asked, merely to say something rather than through genuine interest.

"That look told the truth, Holme. And then . . ."

Kjell Bonsaksen got to his feet, grabbed his almost empty bag, and hooked it over his right shoulder before heading for the door. The ring binder was left on Henrik Holme's desk, as if he had already accepted responsibility for it.

"... then he really does qualify for the title of the most anguished soul in the country. That man lost everything. Absolutely everything, and in such a short space of time. Take a gander at the case, please. Give the man the chance I should have given him twelve years ago."

"What's his name?" Henrik repeated.

"Jonas," Kjell Bonsaksen said as he opened the door. "Jonas Abrahamsen, and I hope to God the two of you can help him."

FRIDAY, JANUARY 8, 2016

"This is a gift. Despite everything. A gift."

Halvor Stenskar, general manager of the health food firm VitaeBrass, gave a loud sigh and placed his hand over hers. She pulled back, just slowly enough to appear dismissive rather than downright rude.

"I mean . . ."

He stood up and walked to the window, where the accursed weather cast the fjord in shades of dark gray beneath a sky that seemed only slightly paler. The Nesoddland peninsula lay like an oppressive predator on the other side of the water, only just visible in the low clouds above the city of Oslo.

November weather in January.

"Of course, suicide is a tragedy," he said.

It dawned on him that this was probably the fifth time he had said that since his arrival. He cleared his throat and began over again.

"Nevertheless, suicide is a voluntary act. I'm sure it isn't undertaken lightly. Not by anyone. Not even by Iselin. But despite all that, it is a choice, after all."

He turned again to face the living room. Although the apartment was located in an eye-wateringly expensive area of Tjuvholm, it was not impressively large. Besides, there was too much furniture here, which made it all seem cramped. Furniture and bric-a-brac and strong colors—completely different from the strict minimalism his wife favored. A gigantic painting above the fireplace of a sea eagle in flight was the only picture in the entire room. Otherwise there were only curios, made of ceramic and wood, of copper and wrought iron. And brass. There were objects made of brass everywhere. Admittedly, the pale-yellow metal was the key to the company's success, but there had to be a limit as to quantity. He had counted candlesticks and arrived at fourteen before he had given up. The room reminded him of a boudoir most of all, with its dark red sofas, countless soft cushions, and the scent of incense that was making him feel slightly queasy. Boudoir was appropriate to some extent, since two lesbians, getting on in years, had lived together here.

But he had never set foot inside a boudoir, so what did he know?

He caught himself staring at Maria.

The sofa she sat on was so deep and low that her legs, when stretched out, were almost parallel with the floor. She was clutching a cushion to her stomach, holding on to it as if for grim death. It could not possibly be to hide her paunch. Despite her age, she was slim, healthy, and relatively fit. She seemed neither tear-stained nor devastated, at least not the way he would imagine his own wife to be if he had been the one to die.

"The most important thing is to pour oil on troubled waters," he said. "It's been an unpleasant time for all of us these past few weeks. It's not particularly advantageous for the company, all this . . ."

His hand waved uncertainly in the air, as if he was bothered by an insect.

". . . media interest."

Finally Maria glanced up. They had never enjoyed a close relationship; they were far too different for that. He did not understand her. To him, BrassCure was a business idea. An exceptionally lucrative one, but he had never felt tempted to swallow a single one of the pills they sold at such an extortionate price. Iselin was the one who had belief in the product. She was the one who could mesmerize a whole room full of agents and sellers with explanations about BrassCure's active ingredients and effects on the human body. The theories would not have taken her very far in a medical institute, but they had laid the foundations of a small fortune for her, as well as several others.

It was less clear where Maria fit in to all this.

She had always appeared loyal to Iselin, sometimes bordering on self-effacing. Whereas Iselin could fill a room with her mere presence, Maria was a wide-eyed admirer who seldom spoke in her spouse's company. He had warned her before she had brought her lover into the firm. And handing over half of Maria's shares to Iselin as a wedding present, with no conditions stipulated, had been sheer madness. Halvor Stenskar had spoken up, both indirectly and eventually more bluntly and boorishly, but it had been to no avail. A matter of months after they met, the two turtledoves were registered partners. And Halvor Stenskar had to admit that it had been with Iselin's introduction to the company that VitaeBrass had really taken off.

Maria had seemed totally enthralled by Iselin. Endlessly.

"Media interest," he repeated, mainly to break the painful silence.

"You're always claiming that all PR is good PR."

"But by that I mean *relevant* PR."

He placed exaggerated emphasis on *relevant*.

"Such as articles stating that we promise more than we deliver?" she asked. "That we have no scientific proof that BrassCure has any effect whatsoever? About the Consumer Council having slaughtered our ads time after time?"

"Whenever someone writes something along those lines, we can cite umpteen patients who claim the opposite. And the right of reply, Maria, is not to be sneezed at. The right of reply has given us a lot of free publicity over the years for both VitaeBrass as a company and BrassCure as a product. Iselin being unmasked as . . ."

He was not quite sure about his choice of word. After all, this was a brand-new widow seated in front of him.

"Extremist," she offered helpfully. "That's what they call it. But I can't recall you ever expressing disagreement with what Iselin stood for."

"Socially, no! We're all agreed that these immigrants are getting out of hand, aren't we, and that something drastic has to be done to prevent . . ."

He used his fingers to comb his thick, gray hair and discreetly brushed away flakes of dandruff from his jacket shoulders before sitting down on the arm of the only chair in the room.

"Healthy skepticism about this flood of dysfunctional illiterates and prospective benefit claimants is one thing. It's another thing entirely to preach that pure . . ."

"Racism," she helped him again when he hesitated.

He blinked hurriedly, but did not answer.

"Iselin, or, more correctly, Tyrfing, was not racist in the tabloid sense of the word. She was more of a modern nationalist. She wanted to free her country from its multicultural yoke. Racism builds on certain people being inferior to others. Iselin's ideas were not based on any ranking of races. She simply meant that our ethnicity, identity, and culture are important, so important that we must protect them from the completely unwarranted influence that Islam has had. You said before that you agreed with all this."

"No. What she wrote in that damned blog of hers is something very different from what she voiced in social settings. As I said, it's some way from—"

"You've never expressed reservations about anything Iselin said on this subject. Neither have I, for that matter, but that's because I quite simply wasn't too bothered. About politics, I mean."

"Not too bothered?"

He stared at her in disbelief.

"You picked Iselin up out of nothing," he said, far too loudly. "You've financed this entire . . ."

He flapped his hands distractedly. Now it seemed as if he had been attacked by a whole swarm of insects.

". . . blog business of hers. You've made this crusade possible. You're the one who gave her half your shares, and you're the one who—"

"You seem to have forgotten that the company doubled its turnover in ten months once Iselin joined the management team. Anyway, Iselin could have been Tyrfing without me. A blog costs two kroner and fifty øre to set up. But forget it. I can't stand all this."

Maria Kvam got to her feet with more difficulty than usual, he thought, as if she was weighed down by something almost intolerable. The angry, almost aggressive expression in her eyes was gone. Maybe it was her way of grieving.

"Despite everything, this is also a gift," Halvor Stenskar said, lifting his backside from the soft chair arm. "As I said. With all due respect, Maria, now that the worst has happened, with Iselin given a thrashing and deprived of every last shred of dignity as she was, despite it all, this is best for . . ."

He hesitated, just long enough for her to give him a smile he had never seen before.

"For the company," she declared. "It's good for the company that the storm around Iselin is calming down. And, of course, that is the most important thing. The most important thing of all."

"Your company," he said sharply. "Very much yours. Especially now. After this, I mean . . ."

His hand swept over the room in an imprecise gesture, as if Iselin's suicide lay hidden somewhere between the velvet cushions and knick-knacks.

"Mine," she said, with a nod. "Now it's almost all mine."

He saw that she was crying. Absolutely silently and almost unnotice-ably, with only the tears running down her cheeks giving him to under-stand that it was high time he left.

Henrik Holme had been greatly in doubt about whether he should dare to visit Hanne at all. His dismissal yesterday had been just as peremp-tory and imperious as ever, and strictly speaking, this was not a new cold case he had tucked under his arm.

It was not a case at all.

The papers inside the worn ring binder did not contain a mystery. No unknown perpetrator lurked there, no blind alleys as in the cases they had previously investigated and in some instances solved. Quite the opposite. Henrik had spent the past night and morning skimming through most of the documents, and Jonas Abrahamsen's conviction seemed far from unreasonable. In the bargain, the poor man had accepted the judgment on the spot when it had been pronounced, admittedly with one conspicuous and somewhat uncommon reserva-tion: when the convicted prisoner had been permitted to speak, he had repeated his assertion of innocence despite accepting his severe pun-ishment. It happened now and again that people expressed such reser-vations when it was a matter of a minor case, but to agree to twelve years' imprisonment without admitting guilt seemed remarkable. His lawyer had immediately intervened and advised his client to take some time for reflection.

That had not helped one iota.

"Obviously the correct judgment," Hanne Wilhelmsen said, slam-ming the ring binder closed after leafing through it in silence for less than a quarter of an hour. "This Superintendent Bonsaksen has obvi-ously just had an attack of pension blues. It's never easy for these old guys when their time in the police force is up."

Henrik felt a certain inclination to remind her that she was only two or three years younger than the Superintendent. He resisted the temp-tation.

"Bonsaksen seemed pretty convinced," he said.

"No doubt."

"And he is immensely experienced."

"No doubt."

"He said it was the only case in nearly forty years that has plagued him with doubts."

"Then he's an idiot. As for me, I had doubts in every other investigation. Why have you adopted that high-necked style? And do I see the suggestion of a beard, Henrik? Have you become a hipster, or what?"

Touching his neck and hesitating slightly, he said: "Haven't you noticed?"

"Yes, of course. Your Adam's apple is much smaller. You can see that even through your sweater. Congratulations. Is it still sore?"

"No, just a bit tender."

"That will pass, I'm sure. And it was about time you did something about that monstrous lump. And since the scar . . ."

She angled her head to squint at his neck.

". . . is placed so neatly and tidily in the fold right under your chin, I don't understand the point of that sweater."

Henrik did not answer. He took hold of the table edge to deter his intense compulsion to touch the side of his nose.

"It's noon," Hanne said. "Time for lunch. If you're not hungry, you can go."

Henrik still sat in total silence. His gaze was fixed on the ring binder between them, and he still clutched the edge of the table. But his left leg, which until a few seconds ago had been vibrating so violently that his heel had beat a muffled tattoo on the parquet floor, stiffened.

"Henrik?"

There was something he had spotted last night. Something he had not quite caught, perhaps because it was already past two o'clock and the collection of documents was so extensive. So convincing. So full of damning evidence.

"There's something about this case," he said suddenly in a loud voice. "Something that doesn't quite add up."

"What's that?"

Hanne's tone was a touch more forceful than usual, as always happened when she was impatient. Henrik raised his eyes and peered out the picture windows at the bleak day outside, where the streetscape was distorted by raindrops clinging to the windowpane, and the light from a floor lamp adjacent to the sofa was reflected in the dark glass.

This was exactly what he required.

He remembered one peculiarity. A detail. Of course, it did not have to mean anything.

But it could, in fact, be significant.

"Nothing," he said with a defensive smile after pondering for a fraction of a second. He wedged the ring binder under his arm and departed.

When anyone occasionally asked him how he was, he always gave the same answer: "Can't complain."

Jonas Abrahamsen could not complain.

He had lost his only child because he had not taken good enough care of her.

Their marriage was already on the rocks when Anna died two years later, and he had served eight years in prison for something he had not done. His job in Statoil went up in smoke when he was sentenced. Since Anna had sole ownership and her application for a legal separation had been approved, he had lost the house and most other things with it.

He no longer had any friends.

It was true that a surprising number had been supportive during the trial, but the majority melted away when he was found guilty. A cousin, a colleague, and a couple of childhood friends had visited him in prison during the first year. All except his cousin had abandoned him after a while. He hardly encouraged them to come back, sitting there in clothes that grew increasingly baggy and eventually giving up all efforts at personal hygiene.

But he could not complain.

He was the one who should have taken care of Dina. He was the one who had allowed himself to be distracted by the junk mail in the mailbox, and it was his fault that Dina was gone and his whole life had been shattered.

He did not complain.

It was chilly in the spartanly furnished living room. Jonas tossed a couple of logs into the cast-iron stove in the corner before it crossed his mind that he had not eaten since breakfast. It was years since his body had stopped telling him it was hungry. It had stopped telling him most things. The only thing he could not do without was coffee: it was rare for more than half an hour to elapse between each cup. All through the day and the evening too. Sometimes he woke about 3:00 a.m. and had to brew himself a cup or two. If he was lucky, he could have a nap afterward for an hour or so.

As a rule, he was not lucky.

But he was never tired either.

That was just as well, given that he was a long-distance driver—normally only to Sweden, but once in a while he had also driven to Germany. It was his cousin who had found him the job, six months after he had been released from prison. Guttorm had even paid for his truck driving HGV license. Jonas had insisted it was a loan and had repaid in full.

He earned reasonable wages and his needs were few.

The house he rented in Maridalen was tiny. The total floor area was barely four hundred fifty square feet, and the basement was so damp that it could not be used for anything. He had insulated the door with polystyrene on the inside and sealed it off. The ceiling of the attic was so low that he had decided to close it off as well, and the narrow staircase was nailed up to save heat. The ground floor included an old dining room he had transformed by simple means into a kind of bathroom, a bedroom measuring a bit over a hundred square feet that used up an unnecessary amount of space, and an open-plan kitchen-cum-living room. It was a furnished rental, and the majority of the furnishings harked back to the fifties. The most flamboyant exception was a colossal TV screen for which he had needed to block one window to make sufficient space. The house in the woods was not connected to broadband, but he had splurged on a subscription for TV, which gave him six channels through a roof antenna.

Jonas Abrahamsen watched a lot of TV.

Drank coffee and watched TV. Used the Internet for an hour each day, but never more than that. He had to connect via 3G, and that was expensive.

Most of all, he thought about Dina. She would have just turned seventeen now. In his mind's eye, he pictured what she would have looked like and wondered whether her hair—that beautiful fair hair shot through with electricity from her winter clothes—would still have been so blond. At nights, he dreamed of her, and he found himself increasingly often talking out loud to her during the day. She would have been almost grown up and graduating from high school next year. Of course, it was

impossible to say what a youngster who had not even reached the age of
three would have chosen to study, but Jonas had decided on agricultural
economics. She would have attended agricultural college and maybe
even married a farmer.

Dina was so fond of flowers.

Sometimes, but increasingly infrequently, he also thought about
when Anna died. On his arrest, the shock had been so great that he
quite literally had been unable to speak for two days: his vocal cords
went on strike. Even when the investigator who called himself
Bonsaksen had explained to him in a fairly friendly tone how difficult
he was making things for himself by not answering any questions, it
was barely possible for him to open his mouth. His jaw was locked, his
hands and feet numb, and he had not slept for more than forty-eight
hours. In the end, he received medication and was able to cope, but by
then it was too late.

Apparently those two days of silence had cost him eight years in
prison.

It seemed as if they had made up their minds. Bonsaksen had made
good use of the time while Jonas was curled up in a fetal position in a
bare cell at Police Headquarters, Grønlandsleiret 44. He had realized
that only half an hour into his interview, when one compromising snip-
pet of information after another was presented to him.

Nothing he said could change anything.

Anyway, the first words he had uttered were a lie.

He was certain of being convicted, and so he gave up. This had
brought him a peculiar sense of peace. He would never admit anything
he had not done, but denying his guilt was about the only thing he had
the stamina to do. Days and weeks in jail eventually felt quite comfortable: predictable and completely lacking in responsibility for anything
whatsoever. He could dream about Dina every night and talk to her
under his breath during the day, at that time still with a slightly affected,
childish voice that Dina's grandmother had considered detrimental to
the little girl's speech development.

Nowadays he spoke to her as an adult.

He could have had a grown-up daughter, and the sorrow and sense
of loss over her death had never been assuaged. A psychiatrist they had
fobbed off on him at the approach of his release date was of the opinion
that his grief reaction was pathological. Not that the doctor had said so

directly to him. Far from it. On the contrary—the guy had mostly fixed him with a resolute stare, holding a pen in his hand that he never used on the blank sheet of paper in front of him. A couple of years later, however, and most definitely without requesting it, Jonas had received a copy of the entire file in the mail. It stated in black and white that Jonas was not really healthy, that he was tormented by "uncontrolled, intrusive memories about the deceased even almost ten years after the accident." It said that he displayed "a conspicuous lack of interest in anything other than his sorrow" and a whole pile of other guff that Jonas had put straight on the fire.

That psychiatrist could not possibly have had any children.

He could never have known the joy of holding a newborn in his arms for the very first time, only seconds old and so beautiful that the world would never be the same again. He could never have felt the wafting fragrance of a newly bathed one-year-old in pajamas. That damn doctor had never held his dearest, most precious person in his arms as the light in her eyes faded and she breathed her last breath.

The doctor was wrong. Guilt about Dina's death did not prevent Jonas from living.

Grief at Dina's death was the only thing that made it worthwhile for him to stay alive. Sorrow, and those fleeting moments when he felt blessedly guilt free. They were what gave Jonas Abrahamsen the strength to live yet another day, yet another month, and perhaps yet another year: eternal sorrow and the occasional, sporadic glimmer of intense hatred.

SATURDAY, JANUARY 9, 2016

The murder of Anna Abrahamsen, née Hansen, had been handled in exemplary fashion by the police, prosecution service, and courts. Henrik Holme had already arrived at that conclusion on first reading the case notes the night before last. Nevertheless, the stark reflection in Hanne Wilhelmsen's living room windows had given him an idea that made him take the thick ring binder home with him for the weekend.

Now it was 4:00 p.m., and he had been through the almost five hundred pages again, far more thoroughly this time. Considering that the case seemed so conclusive and the court case had not taken more than three days in each instance, it was impressively well documented.

Anna was killed on New Year's Eve, 2003.

It was difficult to establish with any precision whether she had died before or after midnight, and she was not found until the morning of New Year's Day. All the same, the forensics team had decided it was unlikely that she had managed to see anything of the new year. Late evening, in other words, and since there are always a lot of people who jump the gun with fireworks, it was not difficult to understand how the sound of a pistol shot behind closed doors could be drowned out by all the noise.

It turned out that the murder weapon had probably been her own.

Anna had been an enthusiastic competitive markswoman before her only daughter died in a tragic accident. That had occurred a bit over two years before Anna herself was killed. This scrap of information had escaped Henrik's attention on Thursday, as the accident was mentioned only in passing in the papers pertaining to the criminal proceedings, first in a report from the Oslo Pistol Club, which gave an account of the deceased's relationship to the club. It had lasted from her early teenage years, and Anna had served two periods on their committee. When her daughter died, she dropped all activities. Not until four months prior to

her own homicide had Anna turned up again for the occasional training session.

She had stopped taking part in competitions.

The second time the child was mentioned was in the actual court
case.

Defense counsel had made subsidiary reference to the tragic death as
a mitigating circumstance. The judge had alluded to this briefly before
rejecting it.

Anna Abrahamsen died as the result of a shot to the head. It had
been fired at close range, without killing her immediately. The ammunition was the most common in the world, a 9-millimeter Parabellum.
She had four boxes of cartridges, stored strictly in accordance with regulations. They belonged to a Glock 17 that she owned, in addition to
three other pistols and a saloon rifle. They were all in their regular
places, in a locked cabinet, as laid down by the rules—apart from the
Glock, which was missing and never subsequently found.

The police had tried to find the bullets fired by the gun at the firing
range she had visited that same day in order to conduct a ballistic comparison. This had turned out to be impossible for countless reasons, so
it was far from certain that Anna's own Glock had been the murder
weapon, but it seemed likely.

Only two people knew where the keys to the gun cabinet and the
locked ammunition were kept.

Anna herself and Jonas.

Henrik had taken all the documents from the ring binder and
sorted them according to his own system. The judgments from the
district court and the court of appeal lay on the far right of the coffee
table. All the interviews conducted lay stacked beside them. Five were
of Jonas Abrahamsen, all carried out by Kjell Bonsaksen, then the
chief inspector. A total of eleven friends, neighbors, and colleagues of
both spouses were also questioned in the course of the weeks and
months after the homicide, in addition to Anna's sister, Benedicte.
Their parents were dead, and no other family members survived. In
addition, there were several special reports made by police officers
who had talked to other neighbors, including a group of guests at a
New Year's party near the Abrahamsen house. The party had lasted
until the opening notes of the first Strauss waltz at the New Year's
Concert in Vienna chased the staggering guests home. One of the

partygoers had apparently been in possession of a profoundly interesting piece of evidence. It was included on top of the bundle of interviews, and Henrik Holme, with arm outstretched, held a photocopy of
it out in front of him.

The guests at Anna's neighbor's house had been the impatient sort
and had already streamed out to the terrace an hour or so before midnight. One of them, a young man who later ended up at the emergency
room with a broken arm after tumbling down from that terrace, was
able the next day, now considerably more sober, to show the police a
photograph he had taken.

The display gave the time as 22:58.

The picture was pretty indistinct.

In the first place, the weather was far from the best. Admittedly, the
low clouds had cleared slightly during the course of New Year's Eve, but
light drizzle and a suspicion of mist filled the air. A young woman in the
center of the photo was waving a gigantic sparkler that made the rest of
the picture even darker than it otherwise would have been. To make
matters worse, the photographer was very drunk.

Nevertheless, in this not-entirely-ideal photograph, you could still
see a garden lamp just above and behind the woman's right shoulder. It
was later identified as part of the lighting in the driveway leading to
Anna Abrahamsen's house. Since the young woman in the picture had
tilted her head sideways, so much so that it almost looked as if she was
about to topple over, a figure was visible beneath the lamp. A man, it
looked like, on his way up from the brick building in the little cul-de-
sac in Nordberg—Jonas Abrahamsen, in fact, as closer analysis of the
photograph demonstrated.

It was a shame, Henrik thought, as he replaced the picture on the
table, that the man had started his very first police statement with a lie.
Bonsaksen had not managed anything more than a run-through of the
introductory caution before Jonas explained that he had not set foot
anywhere near Stugguveien 2B since December 28.

In addition to all the documents from 2004, Bonsaksen had included
a summary of the case as he saw it. Henrik had read this twice already,
but snatched up the bundle on the far left of the coffee table and headed
into the kitchen. He preferred to work at the little dining table beneath
the window with its view of street life below, but the table was too small
to hold all these documents. Now he poured tea into a big cup already

sitting there, before lighting the candle in a Christmas candlestick his
mother had brought a few weeks ago. He should have packed it away
last weekend, but he liked the jolly Santa Claus who sat on the sled with
the candle placed inside. It offered some kind of company.

Henrik read the document for a third time.

Anna and Jonas's marriage had completely broken down before the
homicide took place. Only three days earlier, Jonas had picked up the
last of his belongings. The separation application had been signed that
autumn, and Jonas's new address for the last two months had been a
temporary one-room apartment in Grünerløkka.

Marriage on the rocks.

Check, Henrik mumbled.

Anna Abrahamsen had sole ownership of the house, a cottage in
Hemsedal, and a part-share of a small summer house outside Arendal.

Sole ownership of almost everything. The house was her childhood
home, and her parents had given her and her sister each a generous
sum of money when they sold the family business—with conditions
attached, naturally, such as sole ownership. Following a divorce, Jonas,
in his mid-thirties, would be left high and dry. He could not have known
that he would also be disinherited if Anna died. Judicial authorization
for the separation had apparently been granted as early as December
28. It had reached Anna, and investigators had found it in a kitchen
drawer in the course of the investigation. Jonas's copy, however, had
gone astray in the slow delivery of Christmas mail and did not turn up
until he was in custody. The motive held water, then: it was about
money, a story as old as time itself.

Check, Henrik said. Louder this time.

Only a few days after the murder, during examination of the couple's
finances, the police had discovered that Jonas had siphoned money
from a joint savings account on more than one occasion. In the course
of the last two months he had transferred a total of 200,000 kroner to a
local bank located in western Norway, in a small village where neither
of them had ever set foot.

There was little to indicate that Anna had known about these trans-
actions. DnB NOR, the bank they normally used, would have complained about a lack of paperwork if she had not sanctioned it all, as the
conditions of the joint account specified.

So Jonas had misappropriated money from his wife.

Moreover, he had lied to the police as soon as he opened his mouth.

Check and check and double check, Henrik thought, sounding discouraged.

Jonas had more than enough reason to wish his wife dead. He was a thief in the bargain. Also, he had been present at the crime scene when the homicide took place, and he later refused to admit to that until proof was thrown on the table in front of him.

His defense lawyer had definitely been faced with quite a challenge.

Henrik drank some of the boiling-hot tea. It had already grown dark outside. He was not very fond of winter, at least not here in the big city. Not primarily because of the darkness—that could actually be pleasant, in fact—but because the endless slush and rain made walking so disagreeable.

Henrik Holme was a walker.

He walked up and down the streets and in the forest. He walked to go to places and in order to think. Most of all, he walked because he liked to walk. To use his body. He had never been fond of sports, and running made his knees sore. His slim figure, bottle-shaped shoulders, and pale complexion, even in the six months of summer, all contributed to give an impression of a man who spent hardly any time outdoors. Just as most people mistook most things about Henrik Holme, neither did they appreciate that he was actually in good shape—in excellent shape and very careful about using sunscreen because his mother had always felt that his skin was delicate.

He also walked in winter, but spring was nevertheless the best time of year as far as he was concerned. He never walked as much as he did in spring. He loved the spring. He could clean the windows then, he thought, just as his mother always did as soon as the low March sun revealed their true condition. He was annoyed by his own windows, which even in the dark were obviously dirty. They never looked good in winter, no matter how much he rubbed and polished. Either the cold temperatures drew frost roses with the cleaning water, or else it rained outside and everything became speckled again almost at once.

All the same, he had noticed yesterday that the recently cleaned windows in Hanne's apartment had been sparkling. Not only were they shiny and the reflection of the floor lamp disturbingly distinct, but there had also been a faint odor in the room that Henrik had not been able to identify at first. Only when his thoughts strayed to how clean and tidy it had been in Anna Abrahamsen's house on the day she was murdered had he realized that Hanne's apartment smelled of vinegar water.

The rinsing water used after window cleaning the old-fashioned way.

Only in one place in the crime scene report was there any mention of Anna's house seeming thoroughly cleaned. No one had seen the point of it, in one direction or another. The report writer had simply made passing reference matter-of-factly in his attempts to write an objective description of what it looked like inside Stugguveien 2B.

But there were plenty of photographs.

Most of them were of the bathroom, of course, where she had been found. In the case file, there were pictures of the deceased before she was moved and also of the room afterward: close-ups and wide-angle photographs in which almost the whole of the bathroom was included.

Naturally, it was not particularly tidy in there.

But the remaining rooms looked as if they were about to participate in an interior design competition. The house was attractive—inviting, as it usually says in that kind of article in weekend magazines. The house seemed large for only two people, but after all, they'd had completely different plans for how their lives and family would turn out. The furniture was appealing, and everything was well matched, but Henrik Holme did not know very much about furnishings. He did not recognize any items from IKEA, anyway, though he was there fairly often. IKEA had cheap candles, good meatballs, and it took exactly an hour and a half to walk there.

It bothered him that everything was so tidy inside Anna's house.

However, it had not bothered any of the investigators in late winter 2004.

No one keeps things so tidy all the time, Henrik Holme reflected as he stood up. Not even him, and he was very particular about it and on his own to boot. As soon as he had finished the Friday cleaning, suddenly a dirty cup appeared here and a newspaper was tossed aside there.

He returned to the living room, teacup in hand. He stood and looked out at the street through the grimy windows. The serried ranks of Christmas stars shed their pale light on the street all the way along Markveien. They had hung there ever since November, and the season seemed to extend with every year that passed.

He noticed his cactus was in need of water. It sat on the window ledge and had survived for nearly three years now. He saw that the soil was so dry that it had shrunk from the sides of the pot.

There had been no flowers in Anna's house either. No plants. No Christmas stars or centerpieces of the type almost everyone had on display during the festive season. In fact, there had been nothing reminiscent of Christmas in the house. No Christmas tree or angels, Advent candles or star in the window.

She could have celebrated Christmas at someone else's house. When he thought about it, he knew that this could not be right. In Bonsaksen's summary of the case, it had emerged that Anna had spent Christmas at home alone. On Christmas Eve, just before the Sølvguttene boys' choir concert was shown on TV, her neighbor had seen her returning home from something or other. And the day after Christmas, she had been spotted disposing of a bag of trash and an old backpack in the trash bins. On the morning of New Year's Eve, in fact, her neighbor had spoken to her when she was on her way up the driveway in her car.

The very last person who had seen her alive was her sister, Benedicte, elder by seven years. She had called in to see Anna on New Year's Eve around 5:30 to wish her Happy New Year before she headed off to a party. Anna was also invited, but she had turned down the invitation.

All of a sudden, Henrik put down his cup and turned to the coffee table. He grabbed the bundle of photographs and began to flick through them. There: photos of the kitchen, just as perfect and immaculate as the rest of the house. He could see the fridge in the left corner. An immaculate white door. Not a single magnet—no souvenirs or children's drawings or Christmas cards with pictures of children wearing elves' hats.

He simply could not get it to make sense. Of course, the lack of Christmas spirit could have something to do with her daughter's death. After all, the accident had happened two years before these pictures were taken.

Henrik would have liked to have a picture of the opened fridge. He had looked through the sheaf of papers and knew it was no use looking for one. Nevertheless, he browsed through everything one last time.

If the shiny white fridge matched the rest of the house, it would be virtually empty.

The house actually looked as if the occupant was about to move out. Or, to be more precise, as if she intended to travel somewhere, quite soon and for some considerable length of time.

There was absolutely nothing to that effect in Kjell Bonsaksen's cumbersome ring binder.

In not a single instance in all the more than five hundred pages of exemplary police work was there any mention whatsoever that the victim's house seemed so obviously scoured clean for someone who lived alone at home, despite no indication that the dead woman had intended to leave.

That specific point was really impossible to apprehend.

"What are you watching?"

"The debate."

"On a Saturday night?" Nefis asked, bewildered, stopping short in the middle of the room.

"Recorded," Hanne said. "I didn't manage to see it on Thursday. Pizza?"

"Yes please," Nefis answered, plopping down beside Hanne on the enormous sofa. "What are they discussing?"

"Themselves."

"What?"

"They're discussing the power of the media. To what extent the media witch hunt Iselin Havørn was exposed to drove her to take her own life."

"Glory be," Nefis murmured as she grabbed a slice of pizza. "If anything good is ever to come out of a suicide, then it might as well be this time. And hopefully we'll not hear any more either from or about that woman."

"Now you're being unkind."

"I guess so. I've a lot of unkindness in my favor, actually. In this marriage of ours."

Hanne smiled as she wiped her mouth.

"True enough," she said, nodding. "But as you say yourself: everyone is loved by someone."

"I've never said that. Because it's quite simply not true."

Hanne leaned forward and picked up the remote control.

"Boring self-laceration from some individuals," she summed up with her mouth full of food as she switched off the TV. "Idiotic, stiff-necked self-defense from others. Plus the usual media critics hammering away at journalists as soon as they get the chance. The truth about this case probably lies somewhere in the middle, in my opinion."

"And where is the middle?"

"Iselin Havørn deserved more than most to be unmasked. *VG* did a solid piece of journalism: apparently it was impressive the extent to which this woman used the very latest computer technology to conceal her true identity. Fist bump to *VG*, I think."

She pushed her clenched fist lethargically out into the air.

"That doesn't exactly sound like a point of view from the middle," Nefis objected. "Are you pouring?"

Hanne lifted the bottle of red wine and poured a generous amount into the glass Nefis had brought from the kitchen, where she had been playing Monopoly with their soon-to-be-thirteen-year-old daughter Ida and her sleepover guest.

"The problem isn't that such things are discussed. They ought to be. You can say whatever the hell you like about freedom of speech and all that, but people should damn well stand up for their shit and express their opinion under their own full name. We must all be held accountable—for whatever we say, as well as anything else."

"I still don't see any 'middle' in this," Nefis said, drawing quote marks in the air.

"The problem is the usual one—that everyone jumps on the bandwagon. This was actually *VG*'s story, but it was so juicy that none of the other media outlets could keep their hands off it. They poked their noses into everything. Her apartment was virtually under siege. I think that's a real invasion of privacy. Just think—the magnitude of it all. The pressure, you might say. And if she'd been a very famous person, a politician, for example, then it might have been . . ."

"But she *was* famous!" Nefis protested.

"In the past, yes. But anyway, that was before you came to Norway."

"That's a long time ago now," Nefis said, putting a hand on Hanne's thigh. "You really mustn't get any thinner, sweetheart."

"I do eat. Look!"

Hanne grabbed another slice of pizza.

"Do you remember her?" Nefis asked.

"Yes. I remember her programs. It must have been in the mideighties. About then. Before the NRK monopoly was ended, at the time when the whole of Norway sat and watched exactly the same thing every single night. She came to NRK from a post as a journalist in the culture section at *Dagbladet* and became the presenter for some sort of infotainment show. Current affairs with entertaining guests, that sort of thing. With breaks for music and so on. I've lost count of the number of formats like that that NRK tried out, but Iselin Havørn was actually pretty okay. By the way, that was before she was called Havørn. At that time her name was Solvang. Iselin Solvang."

"Did she get married?"

Hanne rolled her eyes. "Havørn, Nefis! Nobody's called Havørn! It's a made-up name. Or . . ."

She bit into the pizza and went on talking as she chewed.

"Of course, there *is* something called 'havørn': a sea eagle. So it's the name of a bird rather than a person. She changed her surname in 1989, according to what I've read, after she'd completely withdrawn from everything and everyone."

"1989? She can't have been very old then?"

"No, born in 1953, so she must have been . . ."

"Thirty-six at that time," Nefis said quickly. "What happened?"

"Don't you read newspapers?"

"Slightly different newspapers from you. And slightly different pages in those newspapers, for that matter."

"She was . . ."

Hanne swallowed and took a mouthful of wine.

"She got mercury poisoning," she said with a broad smile, "and contracted electromagnetic hypersensitivity."

"Oh no," Nefis said softly. "Not one of them."

"Yep. In fact she's taken a path that's not entirely unusual. Comical, perhaps, and pretty tragic, but not really out of the ordinary."

"What do you mean?"

"It started in the seventies. With the great awakening visited on our country."

"What?" Seeming a bit annoyed, Nefis pulled ever so slightly back from Hanne, and straightened up.

"A slightly distorted book title," Hanne rushed to explain. "Iselin Havørn, or Solvang, was highly active in the Marxist-Leninist movement, in other words, AKP, the Workers' Communist Party. Real left-wing radicals."

"Aha," Nefis exclaimed slowly. "Communists."

"Marxist-Leninists," Hanne corrected her. "Total idiots. Maybe there weren't so many of them, but my goodness, what a song and dance they made. Many of them went on to do well in later life. Most of them came to their senses and distanced themselves from what they had thought and done, while others have resorted to 'context' and 'well, those were different times' . . ."

Now she was the one who sketched quote marks in the air.

". . . as if there weren't many of us others in the seventies who could see quite easily what terrorist regimes they supported and stood for. Even me, and I was only a teenager then."

She rearranged her lifeless legs and tucked a cushion behind her back.

"You can be glad you weren't here at the time."

"Glad? Do you think I preferred being a really young lesbian Muslim living in Turkey in the seventies?"

Hanne gave her a big smile and clasped her hand.

"Touché."

"But what was this journey you mentioned?"

"From the AKP to cultural radicalism to alternative lifestyles and on to what might be called pure unadulterated nationalism. And often racism too. Some of this also has a lavish sprinkling of fairly blind hatred of the United States, which actually brings us back to what it all started with in the first place. The Vietnam War, for one thing. A completely absurd circle, if you ask me. All the same, surprisingly large numbers have trotted around it in some variant or other. And what most of them have in common is that they acquire a propensity for conspiracy theories. Which isn't so strange after all, since . . ."

Hesitating slightly, she set down her wineglass.

"There's a weird connection here," she said slowly. "When I was working on the major terrorist case, I had to read up a great deal on right-wing extremists—both the violent ones and the ones who seemingly stick to the keyboard but share many of the same opinions. And, to put it bluntly, it's striking how many of them become alternative."

A narrow furrow appeared between Nefis's eyebrows.

"You look so much younger than me," Hanne said sotto voce, using her thumb to smooth the frown.

"And by 'alternative' you mean . . ." Nefis ventured, turning away.

"It usually begins with one of these bizarre illnesses. You go around with some allergy or reaction to something for which there's not a scrap of scientific evidence. Electricity and suchlike."

"There's a great deal that science still can't explain, you know. That doesn't mean it won't be explained when we have more knowledge."

"For heaven's sake! You're a professor of mathematics and should be agreeing with me here. You know what I'm referring to. There's probably a lot of that sort of thing in the Middle East as well. When I was a child, all of a sudden everybody was supposed to drink ash extract. It was meant to help cure everything from cancer to rheumatism. When I was a young teenager, there was an epidemic of candida. Everyone who felt unwell in the slightest was suddenly able to buy all sorts of wonder cures to counteract a fungus . . . a fungus! One we all have inside us whether we're healthy or sick!"

Nefis's frown had returned.

"But what on earth does all this have to do with right-wing extremists?"

With a sigh, Hanne leaned over to her wheelchair and extracted paper and pen from the pocket under the seat.

"This is right-wing extremism," she said, drawing a circle. "And this is the people who have a predisposition to conspiracy theories." She drew another circle so that it only partially covered the first one.

"What do you mean by 'conspiracy theories' in this context?"

"Chemtrails, for instance. A theory that says," she said, laughing softly, "that vapor trails from aircrafts are actually—"

"I know what chemtrails are, Hanna."

After all these years, Nefis had still not learned to pronounce Hanne's name correctly.

"Then I don't need to explain it. You know what I mean. That the moon landing didn't actually take place. That it was, in fact, Jews who were behind 9/11. That all the Muslims in the world have a secret plan to take over Europe and drive out all the rest of us."

"Aren't we actually supposed to kill you all?"

"Or kill us. That's right."

Although Hanne was still smiling, she suddenly grew serious.

"The people claimed to be behind these conspiracies are many and varied, but what they have in common is that they are either the authorities, such as the CIA, ethnic groups, or immensely wealthy organizations. The medical industry is one example, at which all the nonsense spouted by the opponents of vaccines is directed. But worst of all, the ones with the most sinister intentions and the greatest power, they are . . ."

"The United States, the Jews, and Muslims."

"Exactly. And this here . . ."

Hanne drew yet another circle. This one also only partially covered the other two.

"This, roughly, is what we can call the alternative."

She used her pen to shade the middle area of her sketch.

"My contention is that there are a surprising number of people who end up here," she said.

"That's called a subset."

"Whatever. They've been left-wing radicals, become terrified of Islam, are often alternative and in the bargain believe so many weird conspiracy theories that it would make you dizzy. Either simultaneously or subsequently, they move around from one circle to another. I'll show you what I found on the Internet, on the blog written by someone who was actually at the forefront of the Marxist-Leninist movement at one time. I . . ."

She snatched her laptop from the wheelchair and opened up the screen.

"No," Nefis said, shutting it again. "I can't put up with that right now."

"But it's absolutely crazy," Hanne insisted. "He insinuates that it's actually the Americans who are behind the Paris terrorist attacks! That the whole of ISIS is a fabrication, a . . ."

"It's Saturday evening, Hanna."

Hanne paused before putting the laptop back in place.

"As you wish. But while working on the terrorist case, I was able to read a lot of what Iselin Havørn wrote on the Internet under her alias, Tyrfing. And what's quite odd, in fact, is that . . ."

She heard laughter from the kitchen and the sound of dice rolling across the table.

"What?" Nefis asked when Hanne demurred too long.

Ida gave a cheer from the kitchen and her friend groaned noisily.

"It's unbelievably strange that a woman like that took her own life," Hanne said in an undertone. "On reflection, I mean. At first it struck me that her suicide was understandable, but . . . no. Not for her in particular."

"Why not? After all, you said yourself that she'd been driven so hard that—"

"Because she's convinced, Nefis. Because she knows she's right. She simply *knows* that what she writes, and the battle she's fighting, is the most important thing in the world. A number of times she's written that she's taking part in a war of resistance, at least as important as the one that took place during World War II. People like her . . ."

She glanced at the black TV screen and touched her forehead.

". . . don't take their own lives. No matter what. Setbacks give the fanatic strength. It's unbearable pain and a completely different conviction that leads to suicide—a conviction that all the world and your nearest and dearest will be better off without you and that this terrible pain is not going to subside."

Nefis picked up the remote control.

"But she did feel that, didn't she? She actually did take her own life. Shall we watch a movie?"

She looked questioningly at Hanne as the youngsters entered the living room. Hanne did not answer. She said next to nothing for the rest of the evening.

Jonas Abrahamsen could remember the very first time he had seen Christel. The little girl had been eight years old then, and only four months had passed since Dina died.

He had still been on sick leave.

Anna was already back at work, a fact he used against her for all it was worth in the progressively uncompromising quarrels between them. In the beginning, in the days and the first weeks after the accident, they had tried in some way to comfort each other. At least Jonas had tried to comfort Anna. Most of all, he wanted it to be just the two of them. He wanted to browse through photo albums. To be in Dina's room, that princess pink room he often crept into at night to lie on a narrow divan bed with Dina's favorite teddy bear in his arms and wait for morning to come. Anna wanted to see other people. Friends. It was as if she needed to fill every single waking hour with noise and distraction, conversation and meals, and, as far as Jonas was concerned, increasingly unfamiliar people who came and went in the house at Stugguveien 2B. She began to attend church, and the pestering clergyman with the gentle expression paid so many visits that Jonas wondered for a while whether Anna had embarked on a relationship with him.

At night, she took two sleeping pills and burrowed down into her side of the bed.

She was lost, to both him and Dina.

Anna had never reproached him. Not once, even during their most poisonous arguments, had she blamed Jonas for not taking better care of their daughter.

That provoked him.

He deserved to be blamed. It was even more difficult to bear his sense of guilt when it failed to be nourished by the only other person in the world who had loved Dina just as much as he had. If only she had screamed accusations at him, he could have defended himself. He could have refuted them. Screamed back at her. She could have been just as inattentive herself, and wasn't she the one who had turned away for a fatal second when Dina at the age of one had upset a cup of coffee and burned her arm so badly that they had to rush her to the emergency room?

But there never was a reproachful word, and Jonas was left to pass judgment on himself.

On one of those spring days in 2002, he had visited Christel's address for the first time. She lived only a half mile or so away from their house. He had been standing there for more than half an hour when she appeared, in new sneakers and with her schoolbag slung over her right shoulder, carrying a bunch of coltsfoot and bluebell flowers in her left hand.

She was singing.

Jonas did not want anything of her. It was just one of those periods when he couldn't sleep, even after lying awake for two nights in a row. He never drove the car in that state and had walked to the low-rise functionalist house. He had cut out alcohol long before, following one evening when Anna had thrown a poker at him after they had sobbed their way through three bottles of wine. Nevertheless, he felt intoxicated as he stood there beneath a weeping birch that had not yet sprouted any pale green leaves.

He had no idea whether watching her felt good or bad.

It was something, though—something other than sorrow.

Every feeling that was not sorrow was welcome. And so he continued. Sometimes frequently, while at other times several weeks could pass between the occasions when he felt the urge to see Christel. As years went by, he got to know her. She played soccer until the age of twelve. She was not particularly good, he had discovered, though from a fair distance. When the coaches were eventually able to select the best players and she ended up on the bench, she transferred her allegiance to dancing classes. When Jonas was jailed, Christel was no longer accessible to him for a lengthy period, but as soon as he was granted spells of parole, he found his way back to her. She had become a dancer by then and attended Bårdars Dance Institute in the city center almost daily. Once he had bought a ticket for one of the performances held at the end of the spring term. When he arrived to watch, at the last minute, so that he could sneak in after the lights had dimmed, he caught sight of Christel's father and Jonas had turned on his heel and fled.

But she was a good dancer. He could see that from the way she walked. There was a spring in every step. A rhythm, in a sense, as if she were always actually dancing. From having been small and compact, almost plump, puberty increased her height. At sixteen, Christel was a beautiful, slim, and athletic girl, with the same blond hair as in her younger days.

Now she was twenty-two years old and a mother herself.

Jonas knew that her three-year-old daughter was called Hedda. She was so like Dina that it was a shock to set eyes on her for the first time. The child was a year old then and was being carried by her mother from the car into the apartment at St. Hanshaugen, where they lived. Prior to that, the baby had been a bundle, invisible to Jonas, tucked up inside a stroller.

Hedda was wearing a blue snowsuit and a pink hat, and the wisps of hair that had escaped around the edges were so blond and fine that they would almost certainly stick out in every direction when the hat was removed.

Christel had become famous.

At the start, it was only among young women aged twelve to twenty. Her blog was among the most popular in the country long before she was seventeen. Now she was an outstanding, top exponent in a world Jonas knew little about and understood even less: Christel's blog was the only one he ever read. And he did so often. It had begun as what they called pink blogs, with subdued images of interiors, clothes, and, most of all, Christel. Gradually she added material about films and TV programs, and when as an eighteen-year-old, she posted a perfectly timed initiative opposing the breeding of animals for the fur trade, she was immediately called in to take part in a TV debate. She came across exceptionally well on screen, and the blog had reached fifty thousand unique daily readers before the year was out.

Christel had become a professional celebrity.

The fact that she became a single mother at the age of nineteen boosted the wind in her sails. Contrary to what all her readers had expected, she never posted pictures of the baby. Far from it. In a contribution to the *Dagsnytt 18* news roundup on TV the day after Hedda's second birthday, she elaborated on a fiery blog post in which she stated that all children needed to be protected from the Internet until they were old enough to understand what it was.

Just after that, she was offered the leading role in a drama series for NRK.

It was now shooting and being discussed almost daily in the online newspapers. And Jonas followed them all.

He noticed she had dyed her hair.

He was not happy about that. It looked dark brown, with a glimmer of reddish chestnut, possibly; it was difficult to be certain in the twilight. Maybe it was for her TV role.

She did not have the toddler in tow. Hedda was probably asleep at this time of day, and her grandfather would be looking after her. Christel had talked about that, time after time, in both her blog and interviews. For a long time, it had been only her father and her. Her parents had divorced when she was a mere six years old. Her mother had returned to New Zealand, where she came from. Now there were three of them again.

Her father, Christel, and Hedda.

Without her father she would never have made anything of herself, she had declared, and he had welcomed his grandchild with open arms, even though she had arrived somewhat inconveniently and totally lacking a daddy.

Noise could be heard when she emerged from the apartment. Blaring music and boisterous laughter, despite all the windows being closed. Half an hour ago, he had seen her up there, leaning toward the window with her hand above her eyes, as if looking for something outside. It was just after midnight when she opened the heavy door and took a right turn. Her footsteps were determined and fast, not as rhythmic as usual, and there was something tense about the way she held her shoulder bag close to her body, as if it were a weapon.

Or something she was very fond of, perhaps, and afraid of losing.

Jonas considered for a moment whether to follow her, at some distance, as always, as he was unwilling to make her feel more anxious. He took a step onto the sidewalk from the small entranceway where he had stood huddled for more than an hour. Christel looked back unexpectedly, and Jonas turned his back on her with indifference.

He could hear her boots behind him, tapping on the wet asphalt, picking up speed now. Jonas Abrahamsen had followed Christel's life from a distance for nearly fourteen years but had never allowed her to catch sight of him. He had not done so tonight either.

Calmly, he began to walk in the opposite direction.

It had never been his intention to frighten her.

Nothing was her fault, and now Jonas was anxious to go home.

SUNDAY, JANUARY 10, 2016

Maria Kvam had made up her mind to replace the furniture. The energy in the living room was all wrong. It was Iselin's life that vibrated throughout the apartment, between all the nuances of red and orange, among all the ornaments and furnishings and soft cushions.

And all that infernal brass.

Now Maria flitted from one shelf to another collecting objects in a big cardboard box. It grew far too heavy even before it was half-filled, so she put it aside and sank into the deep sofa.

It crossed her mind for the very first time that she really hated this room. In fact, she was fond of cool colors, straight edges, and right angles. From the time she was little, she had drawn imaginary lines between all the objects as soon as she stepped into a new room—like a chess player across the board, she thought, and the pattern had to work out. She sought symmetry and restfulness on the eye.

She had decided the previous evening that everything would have to go. She had scarcely slept since Thursday. At night she had surfed the net and watched the occasional film, the contents of which she barely took in. The night before last, she had inadvertently smashed a ceramic jug from Morocco on her way to the bathroom. When she stooped to pick up the pieces, she was overpowered by such a sudden rage that she threw several other items on the floor. She had left the mess lying there until yesterday evening, when she had finally pulled herself together sufficiently to clean it up.

More changes had to come in the wake of all this change.

After the funeral, she had decided, and carried the half-filled box of candlesticks and small sculptures to the massive closet inside the bedroom.

Iselin had wanted to be cremated, expressing a wish to have her ashes scattered to the winds. Years ago she had applied to the authorities for permission to use the sea beyond Reine in Lofoten, where she had spied a sea eagle for the first time. The response had been positive, and the relevant papers were kept in the safe inside the closet.

That's where they will stay, Maria thought, as she set down the cardboard box in front of the metal door.

Although the authorities in the north had been well disposed to the idea of scattering Iselin's ashes on the sea, Maria could not imagine that any obligation was implied in the application. After all, people sometimes changed their minds, and bureaucracy probably had far more to do than follow up to what extent people had their wishes respected in the hereafter.

Iselin did not deserve to have any wishes fulfilled, and everything would be arranged with great simplicity, as appropriate following a suicide. The police had given the green light for Friday, when the formalities regarding the autopsy would certainly be completed. Maria hoped that no one would turn up. The obituary would not be printed until Saturday, including text that "a private funeral has taken place in accordance with the deceased's request."

Maria had chosen the cheapest casket. The man at the funeral home had raised his eyebrows almost imperceptibly when she had pointed at it, an unpainted coffin made of particleboard, costing less than 4,500 kroner.

Iselin and Maria had been an item for so many years now. They had been lovers and sweethearts, business partners and the closest of friends. Maria had taken Iselin into her life when Iselin needed everything. She had made Iselin healthy. Given her a fresh start when otherwise she would have gone to the dogs. They had promised each other so much. Maria had kept her promises, but Iselin had chosen to disappear.

Maria was now entirely on her own, and when she suddenly grew aware of Iselin's perfume wafting from a silk poncho on the hanger above the safe, she burst into tears. She dropped to the floor, where she was convulsed by sobs. Snatching the multicolored garment, she rolled it up into a ball that in the end she tried to hurl at the wall. It collapsed into fronds of feather-light fabric as soon as she let go and fell softly on her legs.

Maria screamed. She forced air out through her throat and gave a long-drawn-out howl, yelling over and over again until she lacked the strength for any more; her chest was aching and her voice trailing into nothingness. The sudden silence impelled her to open the top drawer of a chest and grab a pair of scissors. Quickly and methodically, she attacked Iselin's side of the closet and refused to stop until she stood in the midst of a heap of rags, and all the racks and shelves on the right-hand side were empty.

The scissors made a soft landing on the pile of remnants.

She struggled to breathe evenly. Her hands lightly smacked her thighs, and she opened her eyes wide, lifting her face to the ceiling to stop her tears.

"Pull yourself together," she whispered through gritted teeth, well aware that this was exactly what she had to do.

Otherwise everything would go awry.

MONDAY, JANUARY 11, 2016

Hanne Wilhelmsen caught herself looking at the time.

He was late, something he had never been before. It made her incredibly anxious, and she glanced yet again at her watch. Ten minutes past eleven.

Henrik Holme was a gift.

Nefis was the one who had first said that, in the days that followed the terrorist attacks on May 17, 2014, and Hanne had objected at first. It was true that she liked him a lot—if not at first sight, then certainly after a couple of meetings. He had been foisted on her even though she had not asked for anyone and did not see any point in having an errand boy.

She had been wrong.

In the first place, it was practical to have an assistant who could take care of most of the work outside her spacious apartment in Kruses gate. Besides, he was the smartest police officer she had ever met. Henrik Holme was brilliant, and Nefis had been right: he was a gift.

The young policeman came and went at her command. Gradually he had become a sort of friend of the family. Ida idolized him and had suggested to her parents several times that he might as well just move in with them. Nefis had shrugged and looked at Hanne, who for her part had put her foot down emphatically. At first Ida had not given in and had argued enthusiastically how wonderful it had been when Mary had lived there. The prostitute whom Hanne had stumbled over in the course of a police investigation in the nineties and later took under her wing had died when Ida was nine years old. The grief had been almost unbearable for Ida and Nefis.

Hanne had taken it far more lightly.

While the others had been genuinely fond of old Hairy Mary, Hanne's emotional repertoire had not been able to extend quite so far. Mary had barged in on her at a time when she had neither Nefis nor Ida, and it had been difficult to throw her out. Little by little as the aged whore began to make herself useful with housework and food preparation, Hanne eventually made peace with the idea of having a limping scold as a lodger. When she had met Nefis and the cramped apartment in Tøyen was replaced by a shameless number of square yards in the best area in Oslo's city center, Mary had simply followed as part of the furniture. *Like a dog, in a way*, Hanne had sometimes thought, without ever daring to say so out loud. A street mongrel you didn't have the heart to throw out.

Hanne Wilhelmsen herself acknowledged that she had a limited amount of love within her. Throughout her childhood, she had expended all her efforts on trying to be loved for the person she really was. By her parents, who regarded this unwelcome afterthought of a daughter with irritation, and later almost with revulsion. By her siblings, a brother and sister who were so much older and had never paid her any attention at all.

Throughout her first eighteen years on earth, what Hanne Wilhelmsen had wished for more than anything else was to be acknowledged and loved. All through her adult life, she had tried to hide away from everyone. Both of these efforts had drained her of energy, and she had no more love to offer than what she felt for Nefis and Ida.

That was sufficient.

She had not grown fond of Henrik Holme, but she liked him well enough. Even admired him, without ever mentioning that to anyone.

Now he was, in fact, a quarter of an hour late, and Hanne was weighing up whether to phone him when at last she heard a key inserted in the front door lock. It was Ida who had given it to him; the little girl could not understand why he should have to ring the doorbell when for one thing he was here so often and for another he was a policeman and therefore, as everyone knew, entirely trustworthy.

Hastily and without a sound, Hanne rolled toward the massive dining table and began to read. A book and three stacks of printouts sat on the table in front of her.

"Hello," she said nonchalantly without looking up from the papers. "You're late."

"Sorry," he shouted back from the hallway. "Something turned up at the last minute."

"What was that?"

"Just some things at work. But I'm here now!"

He hovered in the doorway, in his stocking feet as usual. It was unusual to see him in uniform. Hanne glanced up and noticed that his shirt was sitting better. His shoulders were still so narrow above his skinny body that he bore a resemblance to a bottle of Rhine wine. Nonetheless, it seemed as if his sleeves were straining over muscles where previously they had unforgivingly revealed that his upper arms were barely any thicker than his wrists.

"Did you come on foot?" she asked superfluously.

"Yes," he replied, tugging slightly on the shirt fabric at the armpits. "Fast as I could too. What was it you wanted?"

With a smile, he rapped his knuckles on the doorframe before entering the living room.

Hanne gave no answer. Once again she was hunched over the literature in front of her.

"Have we been allocated any new cases?" she asked when he drew out a chair and sat opposite her.

"No. Odd, really. There are plenty of unsolved cases here in Oslo. Should I go to the Police Chief and ask?"

"Not yet. What do you know about suicide?"

"About suicide?"

"Yes."

"What do you mean?"

With a sigh of resignation, Hanne stared at him.

"I mean exactly what I say. What do you know about suicide? Or taking one's own life."

"More men than women," Henrik answered swiftly. "Nearly three times as many."

Hanne nodded and waited for more.

"In Norway, the suicide rate is slightly higher than ten per one hundred thousand people," he went on. "And the majority who take their own lives are between twenty and seventy years old."

"What?" Hanne looked quizzically at him.

"From a purely statistical point of view," he explained. "If you look at those graphs, you know . . ."

He drew a zigzag pattern with his narrow index finger.

"The ones that are divided according to age. Then you'll see that there are relatively few very young or very old who commit suicide, but otherwise there's a pretty even distribution among all the age groups."

Hanne shrugged and looked down again. "More?" she said. "Method, history . . ."

"Women are overrepresented when it comes to use of medicines, that is to say, poisoning. Men when it comes to the use of guns. They shoot themselves. Not only them, of course, but more often than women. On the other hand, women drown themselves far more often than men."

"More?"

"The suicide rate has remained reasonably stable for the past fifteen years. And then . . ." He reflected for a moment. "I don't know very much more than that."

"Heavens. I thought you knew everything."

"What are you working on, specifically?"

"Reading, as you can see."

"About what?"

She peered at him above the rims of her glasses. "What do you think?"

"About suicide."

"Exactly."

She let her gaze rest on him. The habitual red roses had appeared on his cheeks where he was definitely in the process of cultivating something resembling a beard. Unbecomingly wispy, she felt. The hairs seemed soft, like on a teenager, and just below the corner of his mouth on the left side, there was a totally naked area about the size of a twenty-kroner coin.

"That beard of yours is a bad idea," she said, and now his whole face turned puce.

"Apologies," he replied, despite the fact that for almost two years now she had tried to rid him of his bad habit of apologizing for everything. "I'll shave tomorrow."

"Don't worry about that scar under your chin. It really doesn't show at all."

A fleeting, shy smile made him seem even younger than he was.

"I can't comprehend how Iselin Havørn could have taken her own life," Hanne said. "She's definitely not the type."

Henrik repeatedly ran his tongue over his bottom lip.

"I understood that it's an open-and-shut case," he said softly. "Also, it's not a case that concerns us in any shape or form. Strictly speaking. Was it because of this that you asked me to come?"

"Yes."

"I see. Why?"

"I just wanted to play catch. Are you hungry?"

"No."

"I am. Could you be bothered making me a sandwich? Cheese and ham, no butter, and with a slice of red pepper on top?"

Henrik stood up and padded out into the kitchen. Hanne placed the printouts in a single bundle that she pushed to one side as she adjusted her glasses and opened her book. The title was quite simply *On Suicide*. The work had been written by an American authority on modern psychiatry and ran to more than eight hundred pages. It had been at the back of her mind somewhere, meaning a box of professional literature in the basement she had spent an hour struggling to find before getting Nefis to get it.

Henrik rummaged in the kitchen, and Hanne found herself smiling. She heard some rattling in the silverware drawer and the fridge door being opened and closed twice. Henrik had grown familiar with her home; she had come to know him. To put it bluntly, the sounds from the kitchen indicated that he was annoyed. There was a sharp edge to them—purposeful movements, quite different from the circumspect and unassuming, almost hesitant, way he normally behaved.

"Here," he said peremptorily as he placed a plate before her.

"Thanks. Why are you annoyed?"

"I'm not annoyed."

She smiled again, more broadly now.

"I shouldn't have asked you to make me something to eat. But I'm pleased you came. What makes people commit suicide, Henrik?"

"That's a very big question."

"Yes, and I'd like an answer. At least the beginnings of one."

"Suicide is probably best explained as . . ."

He mulled it over, as if trying to recollect something he had once read.

". . . an unfortunate interaction between external and internal factors," he concluded. "Where the internal factors can be anything from serious mental illness at one extreme . . ."

His left hand drew a line at the far side of the table.

". . . all the way to low self-esteem at the other."

His right hand indicated another line on the opposite side.

"And fear of loss of reputation," he continued. "As we've also seen before, unfortunately. After the type of media pressure that poor Iselin Havørn was subjected to in the last few weeks of her life, I mean. In 2009, for instance, there was an increase in the number of men who took their own lives. Could that have had something to do with the financial crisis? No one knows, as far as I understand, but you can speculate, of course. The risk for suicide is higher among people who are mentally ill, but you definitely don't need to be ill to take your own life."

Hanne nodded with her mouth full of food.

"I was right," she said with satisfaction. "You do know everything."

Henrik plopped his elbows on the table and leaned closer to her, more enthusiastic now.

"Physical illness is also a risk factor," he added. "Terrible, chronic pain. Degenerative illness when you slowly shrink to nothing though your mind remains clear. Was Iselin Havørn unwell?"

"No idea."

"How did she take her life? Do we know that?"

"Not us," Hanne answered. "But you're going to find out."

"How?"

She took another bite of her sandwich and munched steadily, glancing at him over the edge of her glasses and smiling.

"No," he said with a note of determination.

"Why not?"

"I can't go and take a look at a case that's got nothing to do with me."

Swallowing, Hanne gazed at him for a few seconds before shaking her head gently.

"You can ask," she said. "There isn't a single rule on earth to prevent you from going to the office of the investigator responsible and asking nicely. It's a suicide case, Henrik. An open-and-shut case, as you said yourself. It's probably sitting tidily in a folder waiting for the final papers from the pathologist prior to being sent to the archives. Ask. You can surely go and ask."

She turned her gaze to the hallway, and he obediently got to his feet.

"Why are you so interested in this case in particular? The woman was awful, and she chose to take her own life!"

He threw his arms wide. Hanne pushed her plate away.

"Do you know anything about sea eagles, Henrik?"

He stared at her in confusion without giving an answer.

"Come on," she insisted. "What do you know about sea eagles?"

He took a deep breath.

"The largest bird of prey in Northern Europe," he said quickly. "The fourth largest in the world. It belongs to the hawk family and was almost eradicated in Norway in the sixties. It became a protected species, and now it is found along extensive areas of the coast, even though there are still few of them. Most commonly in northern Norway."

He gulped. Hanne noted that his Adam's apple had really become much smaller.

"Period," Henrik said. "That's all I know about sea eagles."

"A walking encyclopedia," Hanne said brightly. "Have you ever seen a sea eagle?"

"No."

"It's a magnificent sight. The females—they're the ones that become the largest—can sometimes have a wingspan that's more than eight feet. Fantastic fliers. They can live to be as old as Methuselah. In truth, a glorious bird altogether."

Henrik straightened his uniform tie and headed for the hallway.

"What does that suggest about someone who chooses such a name—Havørn?" she asked loudly.

Henrik wheeled around to face her. Now his irritation was obvious.

"Tell me," he said.

"Iselin Havørn was strong. Her self-image was of enormous proportions. She was a holy warrior, Henrik, a soldier behind a keyboard fighting for her native country. That was how she saw herself. Being exposed as Tyrfing was probably inconvenient for her and certainly terribly embarrassing, but it was not earth shattering. She was right, Henrik. She and everyone like her believe they're right. They don't doubt any of it. Iselin Havørn was an exceptionally intelligent and far better-educated version of the notorious far-right blogger Fjordman, and folks like that have no shame. To her, there was no loss of standing involved in being

Christel was already an established blogger when Hedda came into the world, and in recent years she had earned around 1.5 million kroner a year through her activities as a writer. When interest in her blog among young readers waned rapidly throughout 2015 and the more instant forms of social media took over, Christel had already succeeded in attracting women twenty-five years and over. The business was still a roaring success. Her father took care of the finances and managed her money, without deducting as much as a single krone in payment. As for himself, he got by exceptionally well on his pension, and if he ever needed any extra, he had a substantial sum of money invested in an equity fund following the sale of his childhood home in Nordberg.

Christel was happy with her life.

Now she was at home on her own with Hedda for once. Her father had allowed himself to be persuaded into going to the movies with an old colleague who had recently become a widower. Usually Bengt Bengtson turned down the dwindling invitations he received for social occasions. This time too, but Christel had almost forced him out of the house.

He should have arrived home a quarter of an hour ago, she thought. Ever since her parents had divorced and her mother had moved back to New Zealand, she had depended on knowing where her father was at all times. The movie finished just before 9:30. She had just checked that on the Internet. It took no more than twenty minutes to walk home from Klingenberg unless he had gone for coffee afterward. But that would be unlike him. He had difficulty sleeping if he took any caffeine after eight o'clock. He seldom drank alcohol; that was something he had given up when Christel was pregnant and he wanted to be able to pick her up and take her home at any time of the night or day.

She could phone him.

It was silly to make a fuss if he was actually having a good time. She would call him in half an hour.

Christel muted the volume on the TV and crossed from the sofa to one of the large picture windows overlooking the street. She had closed the curtains earlier in the evening. Using the back of her hand, she pushed one of the curtains aside ever so slightly and peered outside.

The street was almost deserted.

A man in a hooded top under a quilted jacket was out walking one

unmasked. It was just damned unpleasant. No one commits suicide because their life is unpleasant for a short time."

She could see that he was turning this over in his mind, taking his time to consider it.

"That," he said in the end, "that is what you would have called . . ."

With a heavy sigh, he approached her and leaned on the table with both palms before starting over again.

"In the first place, it's not your case. Second, you know nothing about Iselin Havørn apart from what has been printed in the newspapers. She might have been ill, had a broken heart, lost someone, been far more . . ."

Hesitating, he straightened his spine and put his hands on his hips.

"You're the one who always tells me that we mustn't form hypotheses. That instead we should examine the facts and build a case piece by piece. That we should never ask, 'What if?' Questioning a self-evident suicide on the basis of having chosen a curious surname and a somewhat fanatical attitude to immigration policy is . . ."

He paused once again.

"Far-fetched, is what you'd have called it, if I'd been the one coming out with such crazy ideas. Far-fetched!"

He spat out the words before turning on his heel and marching to the hallway. Hanne's eyes followed him. She liked him well enough, and more and more with the passage of time. He was a wonderful policeman.

He could become even better than her if he continued in this fashion.

"Find out how she's meant to have taken her own life," she shouted at his retreating back. "As soon as you can, please!"

She could have sworn that she heard him mutter an "Okay."

Christel Bengtson could not really remember how long she had felt like this.

She could not pin down a starting point. This feeling of being watched had been present all her life, she now and again thought, but at the same time she knew that could not be correct. Presumably it had started when she was older and able to move independently out into the world: at elementary school, perhaps, or when she began to walk the short distance to and from school by herself. She had once told her father about her feeling of unease. About how she sometimes suddenly felt the urge to turn around because she was convinced that someone was following her, even though she did not dare to do so. He had taken her on his knee, so she could not possibly have been more than thirteen or fourteen then, and smoothed her hair. Comforted her and told her that it was far from unusual to feel like that. Not for anyone, and especially not for a woman, as she was growing up to be. It was quite a sensible anxiety, he had declared. Women should always be on the alert. Most people were good, but unfortunately not everyone could be relied on. She was old enough to hear about that sort of thing now, he felt. The world was not a safe place, and life provided no guarantees, but if she was self-reliant, made good choices, and was cautious, there was nothing out there to be scared of.

Although the conversation actually frightened her a little, it helped too. At middle school, everything had improved. Sometimes she might turn around all of a sudden without catching sight of anything suspicious whatsoever—not in the city, or en route to school, or in the evenings on her way to and from visiting her friends. She had almost forgotten what it had been like when the feeling returned toward the end of tenth grade.

Over the years, she had grown accustomed to it.

Nothing ever happened, and maybe her father was right. Feeling under observation could be good because it made her attentive and helped her to make the right decisions. Now and again she had to walk alone after dark, but in the main, she was careful to have company. A girlfriend or boyfriend, or her father, who always gave her a lift anywhere she wanted if she asked as long as he was able. He worked in a bank, and even though he worked a lot and sometimes had to take whatever overtime he could get, he had put Christel at the top of his list of priorities ever since the divorce.

That list actually contained only her.

Christel and, later, Hedda was added.

When Christel fell pregnant following a two-year relationship with a classmate, her father was the person she had tearfully approached. The prospective parents had ended their romance a few weeks before the eighteen-year-old stood in front of the mirror in the bathroom with a pregnancy test, convinced that the world would collapse

around her ears. It didn't. Quite the opposite: Bengt Bengtson, after a pause for thought so brief that she had barely noticed it, declared that every child deserved to be welcomed with delight. Even this one. He was approaching the age of sixty-two and would soon be able to take early retirement. It would mean slightly less in his paycheck, but that too was something he could afford. The house in Nordberg that he had always jokingly called his piggy bank could be sold for at least 15 million kroner. The property needed renovation, but it was on an unusually large piece of property. That same afternoon he had sat down at the computer and found an apartment with a bit more than sixteen hundred square feet in St. Hanshaugen with a price tag of 8 million.

Six weeks later, Bengt Bengtson and his pregnant daughter moved in to Geitmyrsveien in the middle of Oslo. Christel had long dreamed of moving into the city center, and her father's enthusiasm about their new situation soon infected her too. Single-handedly, he redecorated the smallest of the bedrooms in five shades of pink, as soon as Christel had been given confirmation of the baby's gender. When Hedda arrived in the world, it was Bengt Bengtson who had sat in the waiting room at the hospital for nearly thirty hours without a wink of sleep. He was the one who got to hold the infant when she was only ten minutes old and was totally overwhelmed by the miracle that life had revealed to him. For the past couple of years, he had grown increasingly melancholy, almost depressed, at the thought that Christel was making her way out into her life and he was going to be left entirely alone.

Hedda was Bengt's grandchild, and he loved her like a daughter.

The little family in Geitmyrsveien was doing well.

Christel's father did not poke his nose into her life, apart from being there for her and being the dad for Hedda that her biological father was not much interested in being. Martin might have been the best-looking boy in the school and pretty good company in the bargain, but becoming a father at a young age formed no part of the plans he and his parents had made for him. When Hedda was born, Martin was in the United States, where he had been awarded a soccer scholarship at a top university. Every month, the minimum contribution was promptly paid into Christel's bank account, but Martin had not once laid eyes on his own daughter.

It did not matter.

of the dogs Christel could not abide. A pit bull, she decided it was, even though that breed of dog was forbidden in Norway. Several weeks ago, the fellow had moved in with his mother on the ground floor, and Christel had phoned the police. They arrived at the pale-gray apartment building at St. Hanshaugen surprisingly quickly, took a closer look at the dog, and then attempted to reassure Christel that it was in fact a Staffordshire bull terrier, which was legal.

Christel could not see the difference and did not believe it.

The thought of Hedda living on the same stairway as a pit bull was the only thing that had ever made her want to move from the attractive, practical, and now completely renovated apartment she shared with her father.

The young man and his dog disappeared into the park.

A delivery van, driving from the east, drew up at the curb. It was light-colored, probably white, with no company logo emblazoned on the side. Christel could see the driver fiddling with something, without making any move to get out of the van.

She would call her father soon. She really could not understand what had become of him.

Hedda was sleeping soundly. There was no reason Christel shouldn't go to bed as well. Filming would start again at nine o'clock the next morning, which meant that she would have to be at the little makeshift film studios in Sørkedalen as early as 6:30. In the first scene, she had just been involved in a car accident, so the makeup would take ages. Fortunately they would be finished by noon at the latest, because the director had to fly to Sweden, and they would have a welcome day and a half off. She had arranged to meet a girlfriend who also had a child. Christel could not remember the last time she had had time to do nothing other than just spend some time around Løkka. She had been looking forward to it for days on end despite the hellish weather.

From this height, Christel could not see whether a man or woman was driving the vehicle. She could only see the person's thighs and the hands that looked as if they were assembling something. It crossed her mind that it might be a camera, even though the light was too dim for her to say for certain.

Once again this familiar unease at feeling she was being gawked at. She tried to shake it off; whoever was down there did not even look up. When she peered to both the right and left along the street and then scrutinized the bare trees in the park, she wanted to reassure herself that, as usual, she was merely imagining things.

No one was looking at her.

It turned out to be a man who was driving the van.

He had stepped out and now stood gazing up at her window. He had a reflex camera hanging from a strap across his right shoulder. Christel stiffened and dropped the curtain, but remained standing there. She could scarcely be visible from the street. The window was almost entirely covered now, as she peeped out with only one eye at a narrow chink.

The man below raised his camera.

This was not a figment of her imagination. The guy took a step back and stood calmly with his legs apart, letting the camera lens zoom in on her.

All of a sudden she withdrew into the room, her pulse racing so fast that she felt dizzy. She ran across to the door and flicked off the light switch. All was in darkness now: it was connected to all the light sources in the room. Even the silent TV went black. She gasped for breath and tried to compose herself.

"Paparazzi," she whispered into the gloom. "They're not dangerous."

Despite her ever-increasing popularity, she had never experienced being photographed against her will. A number of years ago, her father had advised her to turn up voluntarily whenever she had to. Not to drink too much. Not to make a fool of herself in the public arena, and definitely not to do anything illegal.

Until now that had kept them away.

"Paparazzi," she tried to convince herself yet again.

What any photographer wanted with a picture of the apartment where she lived was beyond her comprehension. She could not be entirely certain whether he had directed his lens to the precise window where she had been standing. She struggled to breathe evenly, but her ears were ringing, and her heart was thumping so violently that it made her even more terrified. A key slid into the front door lock, and she let out a scream so loud that she quickly put a firm hand over her mouth.

"Christel?" she heard a voice ask from the hallway. "What on earth is wrong, my princess?"

"Dad," she answered through her tears, running to greet him.

When she had related the story, sobbing all the while, and he firmly pulled the curtains aside to check who was loitering outside in the street, he found it deserted.

"I didn't see a photographer when I arrived," he said, giving her a quizzical look. "Strange. You must have been mistaken. I would have noticed a photographer, my dear."

Christel could not recall the last time her father had not believed her. It felt absolutely awful.

TUESDAY, JANUARY 12, 2016

"Come in!" The policewoman's invitation sounded friendly. Henrik Holme tugged at his high-necked sweater and tried to be discreet when he tapped the knuckles of his right hand three times in quick succession on the doorframe before responding to her encouragement by stepping inside the small office.

"How can I help you?" she asked.

Henrik was easily knocked off his perch by many people, but especially by women. Most women, but worst of all were ones like this. Probably no more than thirty-five years old, she was already a chief inspector. Her hair was blond, long, and glossy, just like a TV ad, and her teeth were even and brilliant white. When she smiled, something she had still not stopped doing, her dark-blue eyes became narrow slits in her apparently ecstatic face.

"Lovely to meet you," she said, getting to her feet. "Amanda Foss!"

He shook her hand: warm and dry, and the firmness of her handshake was just right.

"We've met before," she said. "But we've never been properly introduced."

"Henrik Holme," Henrik muttered. It dawned on him that he should release her hand.

"I know that, of course," Amanda Foss said, resuming her seat. "Your reputation precedes you, you know. Coffee? I've just filled my thermos."

She picked up a Marimekko-patterned thermos and brandished it in the air, as if it was a triumph to be able to offer relatively freshly brewed coffee. "I have a sort of little . . . special arrangement!" She smiled even more broadly and leaned toward him, as if disclosing a secret.

Henrik could easily understand why this chief inspector would be granted special arrangements.

"No, thanks," he said. "Yes, please. I mean . . . yes, please."

He inhaled loudly as she poured the coffee into two cups she had produced from a drawer. The coffee aroma combined with the scent of fresh flowers. It must be her perfume, because he did not see any sign of a plant anywhere. The office was attractive. The windows faced southwest, and even though the interminable gray weather had still not capitulated to snow and real winter chill, it was brighter than his office. A poster he recognized, a black-and-white photograph by Robert Capa taken during the Spanish Civil War, hung on the wall. On the shelves behind her were displayed three framed children's drawings between neatly arranged folders and books.

"What can I do for you?" she asked, carefully moving a steaming cup toward him. "Here. Have a cookie too."

"I don't know whether you can do anything at all," Henrik began. "It's to do with one of your cases."

"I see. I thought you dealt mainly with old, unsolved cases, though. As far as I'm aware, I don't have any old cases. Unsolved, yes, but that won't last long once I get stuck into them!"

Her laughter was just as beautiful as the woman herself.

It seemed that Chief Inspector Amanda Foss really did have a cheerful disposition.

"It's about this suicide," Henrik said tentatively. "Iselin Havørn."

She was still smiling, but her eyes widened ever so slightly.

"It's not especially interesting. It's clear-cut—she took her own life."

"How?"

"Why do you ask?"

Henrik reached his hand out to the small dish of cookies but changed his mind. He would only make a pig of himself and drop crumbs, and they were coated in chocolate.

"Because . . ."

Before he met Hanne Wilhelmsen, he had never told a lie. At least not since he had been a really small boy. Henrik was an honest soul, and deep down he thought everyone ought to be the same. Hanne, however, had a far more pragmatic relationship with the truth. That was what she called it herself, pragmatic, as if there were something positive about lying. If it was easier to arrive at something of merit by twisting reality a little, then she considered that not only acceptable but also morally justified.

In Henrik's experience, she was absolutely correct as far as results were concerned. They materialized more smoothly if you didn't always feel the need to tell it like it was. He found following her example in practice more problematic.

"Hanne Wilhelmsen and I are working on a minor . . . research project."

A blush rose from his neck at such speed that it would suffuse his entire face in a matter of seconds.

"Oh?"

"We'd like to take a closer look at hidden suicides. Accidents. Involving cars and boats, as well as in the mountains. Falls and drownings and that sort of thing. We really know remarkably little about that kind of thing. Did you know, for example, that each year around six hundred Norwegians die abroad without the Norwegian authorities ever getting to know the cause of death?"

"No," she said, and her smile had vanished.

He had no idea how he had dug up all this information, but his appetite was whetted. He hoped she would interpret his red face as a sign of enthusiasm.

"Many of these may be suicide."

"I guess so. And this has . . . and how has this anything to do with Iselin Havørn?"

"Extending the scope," he said desperately, raising the cup to his lips.

His hand was shaking so badly that he had to put the cup down.

"Extending the scope?"

"Yes. From the obvious suicides at one extreme . . . Did you find a suicide note, for instance?"

"Yes."

When she nodded, tiny sparkles flashed from diamonds on her ears.

"Precisely. An open-and-shut case, then. We want to try to examine the entire range, from obvious to concealed suicides, and by learning more about the former, we hope to be able to recognize the latter more easily."

"That sounds like an extraordinarily ambitious research project," she said, and now there was little sweetness and light left in her manner.

On the contrary—the laughter lines had disappeared to make way for a highly skeptical frown between her well-groomed eyebrows.

"And wouldn't that be a more appropriate subject for psychologists, anyway? Or even psychiatrists?"

"We're working in cooperation with them," he said, closing his eyes. "Hanne and I are looking at the more police-oriented aspects. The others..."

He waved vaguely at the door, as if a whole pack of shrinks waited outside in the corridor.

"... deal with the psychological facets, so to speak."

He was about to bite his tongue. Quite literally.

"Ouch," he said under his breath as he opened his eyes again.

Amanda Foss studied him for a few seconds before she gave a shrug.

"I haven't heard anything about that," she said. "And I can't hand out photocopies without the express permission of the Police Chief. But if you can..."

A manicured finger pulled back her left cuff and she glanced at her watch.

"I have a meeting down the hall in two minutes flat. It won't take long, I hope."

Letting her chair spin 180 degrees, she opened a cabinet and removed a slim, green folder and set it before him on the desk.

"There are still a few formalities missing, but most of it should be there. You can sit here and look at it while I'm gone. As long as you make all of it anonymous, I don't see any reason why you can't take notes for this..."

Once again an unbecoming furrow appeared between her eyes.

"... research project of yours."

"Thanks. Thanks a million."

Henrik yanked the neck of his sweater so hard that he heard a seam rip.

"Thanks," he repeated.

And before he had composed himself, she was gone, trailing a faint fragrance of some kind of flower behind her. He breathed slowly, mouth open and eyes shut, before sitting up straight and opening the folder.

It took him no more than six or seven minutes to skim through all of it.

Not so strange, then, that the police, only hours after finding Iselin Havørn, had hinted that the woman had taken her own life. It was the most cut-and-dried suicide he could think of, with an indisputable suicide letter, referring to the witch hunt of the past few weeks, as she chose to call it. The deceased had been discovered in bed, neatly dressed in immaculate clothes, lying on her back with her hands folded over her chest. *Like a macabre lying-in state*, Henrik thought as he scrutinized the photograph. She had been found dead by her wife, Maria Kvam, who had rung the emergency number exactly forty seconds after she had chatted with the receptionist on the ground floor, a facility that was no longer totally foreign in Norwegian apartments of the more exclusive type. Maria had been on a business trip to Bergen since the morning thirty-six hours earlier. The death had occurred at some time the previous evening, in any case no earlier than 9:50. At that time, Maria had phoned home to say goodnight from her suite in the Hotel Norge. Iselin had seemed depressed, but no worse than she had seemed ever since the notable unmasking of the right-wing radical blogger, Tyrfing.

The cause of death was cardiac arrest.

Provisional blood analysis showed a blood alcohol count of 0.9. Not excessive for a mature woman, but considering that Iselin Havørn seldom or never drank alcohol, she must have been excessively intoxicated when she died. Apparently what had caused her heart to flutter before eventually coming to a stop, however, was a considerable overdose of a tricyclic antidepressant.

Henrik could well understand that Iselin Havørn was down in the dumps. It was nevertheless odd that she had persuaded a doctor to prescribe antidepressants after only three weeks of being hassled by the media.

Maybe she had already been depressed.

He glanced at the clock on the gable wall. Amanda might come back at any moment. Henrik would really have liked to read the folder more thoroughly. Most of all he would prefer to have a copy. More than likely, Hanne would have thousands of questions and get wound up about something he had forgotten.

Without giving it another thought, he produced his cell phone from his back pocket. With rapid and surprisingly calm dexterity, he placed every document in front of him, zoomed in with the camera on his phone, and clicked—a total of twenty-four pages, five of them pictures. When he was finished, he heard Amanda's black pumps approach on the corridor floor. As fast as he could, he returned all the papers to the green folder and lifted the coffee cup to his mouth, feigning nonchalance.

"Did you find anything of interest?" Amanda Foss asked, a heartfelt smile back in place. "Or do you need more time?"

"It's fine," Henrik said. "I'll talk it over with Hanne Wilhelmsen. If she thinks it might be of interest in connection with our . . . project, I'd prefer to ask the Police Chief for permission to take a copy. Thanks for your help."

Henrik downed yet another generous mouthful of coffee before setting down his cup.

"I didn't do much," Amanda Foss answered.

Henrik took a chance on getting to his feet. He was no longer shaking. Quite the opposite—he felt unexpectedly calm and even remembered to proffer his hand for a quick farewell handshake before exiting the door and closing it softly behind him.

His delight at achieving something Hanne would accord a nod of acknowledgment was so intense that he had to resist the temptation to break into a sprint and phone her from his own office. At the thought of what his mother would have said about his actions, though, he came to a sudden halt. And remained rooted to the spot.

It was incredible that he had allowed himself to be tempted into breaking the rules, if not actually committing a crime, and he made up his mind not to phone Hanne at all.

He was already thoroughly ashamed of himself.

Jonas Abrahamsen was to drive to Linköping with a cargo of salmon.

In fact, it would be a pleasant trip. He was to load up in Vinterbro, and the roads to Sweden through Østfold via Ørje were becoming acceptable. From the border, it was mostly a straight road all the way to Marieberg, before a couple of tricky hours on narrower roads lay ahead. He usually took less than six hours for the journey, including stops to fill his stainless steel thermos with coffee and perhaps eat a banana or two.

His truck was having an oil change and would not be ready until four o'clock.

Jonas sauntered aimlessly in Grünerløkka. He did not like being in the city center and mostly avoided going there apart from when he felt the need to see Christel. Now his needs lay in a totally different quarter: he required new pants and a couple of shirts. At the Storo shopping center, he had found what he wanted in record time. When he saw that he still had an hour or two to kill before he could pick up his truck, he had turned up his lapels and headed to the city center, no particular destination in mind.

He was ready for coffee. Actually he preferred boiled coffee, and at home had a coffee pot so old that it was almost black. Once he had walked a good stretch down Thorvald Meyers gate, he stopped in front of the Godt Brød bakery, where the smell of freshly baked bread and cakes wafted from the low yellow stone building every time the door opened and closed. Jonas saw shelves of bread and cakes through the huge windows and a coffee machine. Two women were parking strollers beside the door, and the interior was crowded with people. They placed the strollers with hoods facing the street and handles close to the windowpane and pulled on the brakes.

"That'll be fine," one of them said. "We can watch the whole time. Come on, then."

She had long, dark hair beneath a blue hat trimmed with leather. Although she was smiling, Jonas could detect a trace of irritation as she impatiently waved at her friend with extravagant, almost angry gestures.

"They're both sleeping like logs," she said in dismayed tones, just as Jonas realized the identity of the other woman. "We'll be standing only six feet away from them! Honestly, Christel!"

Jonas turned away slightly. Calmly. He took out his cell phone and began to surf at random. When he spotted from the corner of his eye that the door had slammed behind the two women, he leaned resolutely against the yellow stone wall, still with his phone in hand, only ten inches away from his face.

But he was watching the child.

Hedda was the one lying nearer him. She had acquired a new three-wheeler stroller: bright red and wheels bigger than her old one. The toddler was dressed in a snowsuit—he thought he could make it out under the woolen blankets tucked around her. Although the hood was up, he could still see her soft, sleeping face from where he stood.

She wore a pink hat and slept with her mouth open.

Jonas took a step closer. Stuffing his phone into his pocket, he thrust a hand down into the stroller. He threw a rapid glance over his shoulder, but the two women were standing in a chaotic line inside, Christel on tiptoe to keep an eye on the stroller. When an athletic guy in a sheepskin jacket opened the door, she was momentarily out of sight.

Jonas ran the back of his index finger over the little one's cheek.

It was warm and soft. At the same time, he felt a slight roughness against his finger, the typical winter complexion of Norwegian kids. He felt a jolt in the pit of his stomach as he remembered: Dina's face that was given a lavish application of cream after her evening bath but was just as dry and frostbitten again after the next day's outdoor activities at day care.

He withdrew his hand and started walking.

Tears had begun to roll down his cheeks, combining with sleet that gained momentum from a north wind forecast to be gale force by that evening.

He had never touched Hedda before.

His finger burned inside his jacket pocket and he wept, heartbroken.

WEDNESDAY, JANUARY 13, 2016

As Henrik Holme let himself into Hanne Wilhelmsen's apartment in Kruses gate, he felt an absence of anticipation so strong that he froze to the spot in surprise.

This was something entirely new. For almost two years now, he had arrived here at her least command and dutifully left again whenever she ordered him to. Their unwritten contract applied to both work and leisure time: Hanne decided when he should come and how long he could stay.

He always looked forward to his visits. No matter whether it was just the two of them and they had hours of work ahead, or Ida was going to bake pizza and a Friday evening was to be spent playing cards and maybe watching a movie—visiting Hanne's had become the very meaning of his life. At least, it was the part he liked best of all.

Now he felt no pleasure whatsoever. Far from it. He peered at the key with something reminiscent of reluctance. He had managed to stay away yesterday. He had not phoned her, which had been his initial, exhilarated impulse after securing a copy of the contents of Iselin Havørn's folder by illegal means.

Of course, Hanne had called him only a couple of hours later.

Now he was standing here and could hardly do anything other than turn the key.

"You're late again!" he heard her shout as the door opened. "Don't make it a habit."

He did not answer. Instead, he flipped off his sodden boots and grabbed a newspaper from the bundle of old ones beside the door, waiting to be thrown out, and stuffed each boot full of paper before setting them aside on a shoe rack. Today he paid special attention to arranging his laces so that they lay exactly parallel beyond the toe and hung down at the wall. As usual, both were of equal length.

70

"Are you coming in?"

"Yes, of course," he whispered, as he picked up his bag and padded through to the living room.

"Are you in a bad mood?" she asked, deadpan. "Let me see!"

Henrik sat down opposite her at the dining table with his bag on his lap.

"What's the point of that chic office of yours if we always sit here in the living room?"

"You and Nefis are the only ones who think that office is chic. I'm more comfortable in here. Let me see!"

Extending her hand to him, she waved her fingers impatiently.

"Here," he said curtly as he handed her a sheaf of papers. "The quality's not the best, but you can read the most salient points. I used photo paper to make the images as sharp as possible."

"Very dark," she mumbled.

"Yes. After all, they're copies of photographs of a photocopy."

Hanne had already immersed herself in the bundle. Henrik was left sitting with his hands dangling on his knee, now and then letting his right forefinger touch the left side of his nose and vice versa. No longer annoyed, he did not entirely know what it was he felt. Guilt, perhaps. Or pangs of conscience.

It dawned on him all of a sudden that he felt offended.

"Relax," Hanne said, as if she were a mind reader. She did not even look up.

"These papers will stay here with me, and I assume you've deleted the photos from your phone."

"Yes."

"No one will find out anything about it. Besides, what you did wasn't so wrong. No harm done."

"But what do you actually want with all this?" he said more sharply than intended. "What on earth was the point of getting me to break a whole pile of regulations just so that you could have a look at a really obvious case of suicide?"

"It's not obvious, as I said."

For once, Henrik felt his face turn pale. The blood drained from his head, and the resulting dizziness forced him to cling to the table.

"It doesn't matter!" he said so sharply that Hanne looked up in surprise, pushing her glasses on top of her head. "It doesn't matter how interesting you might find that flaming bundle of papers. *It's still not our case!* The Iselin Havørn case isn't yours to investigate!"

"Good heavens," Hanne said, canting her head to one side.

"I can't be bothered with all this!" He raised the palms of both hands as if disclaiming all responsibility before he got to his feet. "Keep all of it. Don't ever mention this case to me again, please. I really can't stand the idea of being in on this."

"Sit down."

He made a move to leave.

"Henrik. Please. Sit down. I'm really sorry for sometimes treating you . . ."

While she searched for the right words, he wheeled around.

"Badly?" he suggested. "Disrespectfully? Do you need any more suggestions?"

Hanne took on the expression he never quite understood. Her face became blank and inscrutable, but there was a glimmer in her eyes, as if she was amused.

"I think that's enough," she said in the end. "Sometimes I treat you badly. Lacking in respect, if you like. But you should take it as a compliment. If it means anything, of course. What I think of you."

Henrik shook his head dejectedly without uttering a word.

"I treat you as I do because I always believe we're on the same page," Hanne went on. "I think something, and then I automatically believe you think the same thing. That you're wondering about the same thing as me, that you find the same facts interesting. Significant. I do that because you're clever, Henrik, and because I can be fairly lacking in consideration. People skills, as you know, are not my strongest suit."

She gave a tentative smile, as if she was, in fact, sincere. Henrik refrained from returning her smile, but did at least continue to stand there.

"You're amazingly good on people," he said. "But only in theory."

Now she burst out laughing. Her laughter was so infrequent that he nearly jumped out of his skin. The first time he had heard it, it had brought to mind ice cubes in a glass of lemonade on a summer's day. Now it was darker. More natural, in a sense; it was as if he had finally been honored with some totally genuine laughter.

"You're right," she said at last. "I'm best on theory. When I met you nearly two years ago, I thought you were exactly the same as me. Smart up top but no people skills. I was mistaken. In the first place, you're sharper than I am, and second, you're something incredibly rare, a real humanitarian. Maybe you're not always so good in human company either, but you do like people. You care about them. I only like you and my two girls, Henrik, and I truly hope that my hopeless behavior doesn't drive you away."

"No, of course not," he said, embarrassed, and felt his face turn bright red.

He struggled to restrain himself, but his right hand rose of its own accord and tapped his forehead seven times in succession.

"Please sit down."

He obeyed.

"I'll try to explain why this case interests me," she said. "And I hope you can bring yourself to listen. Here." She pushed a thermos and mug toward him. "Have some tea."

Henrik did as she asked and crooked his fingers around the red-hot mug to keep them under control.

"Do you know the worst thing about suicide?" she asked.

"Someone feeling so terrible that they choose to relinquish life. So many people left behind with sorrow, unanswered questions, and feelings of guilt."

"Yes, true enough," she dismissed him abruptly, already exhibiting impatience. "Suicide is awful, of course. But entirely from a police officer's point of view, Henrik? What's the worst thing about suicide for an investigator?"

He gave a slight shrug.

"Finding out whether it is in fact suicide," he suggested. "Rather than homicide. From that standpoint, this case doesn't present a particularly great challenge. It's clear-cut."

He let go of his mug and pointed at the papers in front of him.

"Why is it clear-cut?" she asked.

Henrik began to count on his fingers. "One: it's easily explained in terms of the deceased's difficult personal circumstances. Two: a suicide letter was present. Three: no indication of anything other than yet another tragic suicide."

Nodding, Hanne put her left hand on the book, *On Suicide.*

"Your points are valid. But at the same time, Henrik . . ."

She picked up the book with both hands and stood it on edge. It seemed as if she could not quite make up her mind what she wanted to say; she opened her mouth and then shut it with an almost inaudible sigh.

"Suicide is in itself a mystery," she ventured hesitantly. "As far as I know, we humans are the only species on earth who sometimes choose something in direct contravention of every single theory of evolution: we kill ourselves. Some suicides are . . . expected? Can we say that? At the very least, not entirely unexpected. Deep depression. Psychosis. Anxiety. Other serious psychological illnesses. At other times, a severe shock or a chronically deteriorating personal situation can make this definitive solution to the problem virtually . . . understandable. Is it too excessive to use the word *understandable*?"

Hanne leaned forward a little, the thick book still in her hands, and gave him a quizzical, almost pleading, look. Before he got as far as giving her an answer, she added: "I mean, if Nefis were to die . . ."

She let go of *On Suicide* and knocked on the wooden tabletop.

". . . I would be devastated. I've gone through it before, losing my life partner, and believe me . . ."

Henrik could have sworn that Hanne's eyes were moist. He hardly dared to breathe.

"I know what I'm talking about. You never know whether you'll be able to get through the day. If Nefis died . . ."

Once again she knocked hard on the wood.

". . . my heart would break. I'd be in a dreadful state. But I would never consider taking my own life."

"You have a child."

"I didn't have a child when Cecilie died. I freaked out completely. Ran away from everything and everyone. I lived in a convent outside Verona, did you know that?"

"No."

"I did. For months on end. I felt more or less dead, to be honest, but not for one single moment . . ."

Her gaze melted away. It looked as if she had fallen asleep with her eyes open. Henrik was about to rise from his chair. It could be an attack of some kind, maybe she needed assistance, but he was only halfway up from his seat when she suddenly continued: "I decided never to take my own life. But if Ida died today, I would follow her without hesitation."

Henrik dropped back on to his chair and shoved his hands under his thighs.

"You don't know that."

"Yes, I do. I know it very well."

The old Hanne was back. She sniffed, rubbed the small of her back, and once again peered at him over the rims of her glasses. Like a teacher before a promising but obstinate pupil.

"And that's what I mean when I say that some suicides can be understandable. Someone loses a child. Or you face total social ruin."

"Exactly," Henrik said. "Just as Iselin Havørn did. Or . . . as she had just done."

"She was not ruined."

"What?"

"That's precisely my point, Henrik! You really must listen to what I'm saying! Iselin Havørn was unmasked as the blogger Tyrfing. That led to a great deal of awkwardness, as I've said before. But for Iselin, that exposure certainly didn't involve social ruin. On the contrary, you might say. The traditional press has been hard on her, and the chorus of condemnation from pundits has been resounding. No more than expected. When Fjordman, the right-wing terrorist, Anders Behring Breivik's great role model and inspiration, fled abroad with his tail between his legs after Breivik's killing spree on July 22, Tyrfing seized her chance and rose in all her majesty."

Hanne's eyes narrowed.

"Tyrfing was more capable than he was. More knowledgeable. Wrote better, even though she could have done with a basic course in grammar and spelling. In point of fact, she'd been active for a number of years, but prior to the tragedy that summer, few people had heard of either Fjordman or Tyrfing. She hurt many people, Henrik. Only a few days after that gruesome Friday, she began to receive public attention for spreading ideas that had cost seventy-seven people their lives. It's not strange in the least that so much revulsion has been directed at her now."

Henrik opened his mouth to say something.

"But have you followed the comments?" Hanne continued abruptly. "Have you delved into all those online sites where Tyrfing was purveyor to the royal court of anti-Islamic articles and analyses? We're no longer talking about the occasional website run by loonies. We're talking about popular, professionally edited online newspapers, and we're talking about loads of them. Before she seems to have taken her own life, Iselin Havørn was being acclaimed like a queen. To her own folk, Henrik, she was more distinguished than anyone else as a result of being unmasked! She was supported and praised and applauded. When she died, she became a martyr. The greatest savior since Jesus, that's the impression you get."

"Yes, I suppose so, but—"

"Have you learned nothing from the May 17 terrorist attack? Didn't you see Kirsten Ranvik during the trial we've just stopped attending? The woman was behind seven fucking bombs that killed forty-five totally innocent people, but in court she sat there smiling. She was smirking, Henrik! Immaculately dressed and with that damned smile—"

"Kirsten Ranvik was crazy."

"She was found to be of sound mind by the court psychiatrists."

"In my eyes, someone like that is completely off their rocker, no matter what the psychiatrists think. Iselin Havørn, on the other hand, was not crazy in the slightest. She ran a major business and led a quiet, normal life in the bargain."

"Didn't Kirsten Ranvik also live an apparently quiet and normal life? With a half-wit of a son and a job as a librarian?"

Henrik fretted over the use of the word *half-wit* but—once bitten, twice shy—said nothing.

"The only difference between Kirsten Ranvik and Iselin Havørn," Hanne plowed on angrily, "is that Ranvik threatened violence. She began to kill for 'the cause.'"

Her cheeks were flushed, and she used both arms to draw ostentatious, invisible quote marks.

"Incidentally, they're both very similar. They have exactly the same opinions. They're equally dangerous. And more important than anything else, they're completely convinced that they're right. People like that don't take their own lives, Henrik. *They don't kill themselves!*"

She slammed the flat of her hand on the table six times to emphasize her words. Henrik sat bolt upright and felt his narrow shoulders lift.

He had never seen her behave like this.

Occasionally he had felt Hanne to be dismissive, cold, and contemptuous. Warm and loving to her daughter, and measured and punctilious as a witness in court. She could be grouchy, almost misanthropic. Sarcastic or attentive, encouraging and sometimes verging on enthusiastically complimentary. He had even seen touches of frustration, but only once or twice.

Never before had he seen her so furious.

She was speaking to him far too loudly, and he noticed that her words were accompanied by a fine spray of saliva, almost as if she were gasping for breath.

"I think it's not been terribly good for you, studying these right-wing extremists for such a long time," he said cautiously, adding a tentative pause.

When she did not object, he added: "It's not an entirely unknown phenomenon, you know. Police officers who work on public morality and deviant behavior sometimes have to take a break from it. Especially the ones investigating child abuse. The cases eat them up; they—"

"Don't lecture me on the effects of police work," she broke in sharply.

"No, of course not," he said hastily, swallowing.

It felt as if his Adam's apple had become enlarged again. To double its original size.

"All the same, maybe you should realize that you might harbor prejudices, just the same as everyone else," he nevertheless plucked up the courage to say. "To be honest, you have a tendency to regard right-wing extremists as nothing else. People with no capacity for shame. Lacking the ability to show remorse. Depressed. Suicidal, for that matter."

"Not at all."

"You seem remarkably sure of yourself. On very thin ground. It's not really like you. And since it's true that you've just had an overdose of right-wing extr—"

"Drop it."

"But how do you explain the suicide letter?" he insisted. "It's handwritten, and the preliminary handwriting analysis concludes that it's genuine. That is to say, written by Iselin Havørn."

Hanne poured more tea and took time to screw the lid back on the thermos. She lifted her steaming mug without drinking from it.

"I hate suicide letters," she said.

"Uh . . . why's that?"

"Because those damned letters make us draw rapid conclusions. Because all killers who use suicide as their method know that's what we do, of course. Because there's barely a murder disguised as suicide where a false letter isn't found."

"But this one is genuine!"

"Do you think so?"

"It doesn't matter what I think. The handwriting specialists—"

Hanne raised one hand, and he quickly shut up. She leafed through the bundles of paper he had given her and located the photograph of the suicide letter.

"To hell with handwriting analyses," she said, pushing it toward him. "By now, this . . ."

She glanced down at one of the other pages.

"Amanda Foss," she read. "By now, this Amanda Foss has had this case file in her office since Thursday, but I'm willing to bet that she hasn't gone to the bother of reading this letter. It took me three minutes. I mean *really* read it, Henrik. Do it, now."

Henrik had already read it twice before.

"Why?" he asked without looking at the letter.

"Because until now it's just been treated as a document, as a piece of evidence in the case. But try to read it as text, Henrik, as a written expression of a person's thoughts."

"Why?" he said again.

"Because I'm convinced that a smart guy will see the same as me."

"Which is what?"

"Which is that this letter was probably not written by Iselin Havørn at all. It doesn't matter what all the handwriting specialists in the world might say. It's bogus. And if it's been forged, then we're not faced with a suicide, but a—"

Now her smile was broad and encouraging, and he knew what he had to do.

"A homicide," he completed, with a note of resignation. "If the letter is a forgery, then Iselin Havørn was probably murdered."

Jonas Abrahamsen never received visitors.

He had not even gone to the trouble of having a doorbell. If, contrary to all expectation, anyone should turn up, something that had happened only once before in the two years he had lived there, he would be able to see them from the kitchen window long before they arrived at the door. Besides, the track from the narrow asphalt road was still deserted. The sound of car tires on the gravel could be heard through the drafty walls.

Now someone was knocking even though Jonas had not heard or seen anything.

He was standing bare-chested after taking a shower in the makeshift setup he had built in the old dining room. The coffee was ready—he had made a full pot. It was only a couple of hours since he had arrived home from Linköping. The trip had gone well, even though the return journey had been made with an empty truck. Jonas was not happy driving empty trucks. It was a waste of diesel, and the old girl was less stable on the road. Now he sipped scalding-hot coffee while he considered whether to open the door. It was five o'clock and dark outside, and he needed to sit in peace in his own home.

But it might be something important.

Not that he could think of anything. In the worst-case scenario, it could be the owner of the house standing out there; he was the only person who had been here before. A reasonably jovial sort, but he had reservations about the somewhat idiosyncratic shower arrangement. Jonas had installed a plastic water tank on the ceiling. He could fill it from a little hot water tank with a hand pump and thus have exactly enough water for a quick shower. The house owner had pointed out that the tiny dining room was by no means a wet room. He had kicked away the tub Jonas was in the habit of using to collect the gray water, grunting something about having to put a stop to this.

It might possibly be him.

Refusing to open the door would just be asking for trouble. It would be best to get the inconvenience over and done with, and Jonas snatched up a T-shirt from the back of the kitchen chair and slipped it on.

"Guttorm?" he said in bewilderment when he opened the door and saw his cousin standing there.

"Hello, Jonas. Can I come in?"

Jonas stood, momentarily silent and confused, before pulling himself together and opening the door wide.

"My goodness, yes, of course. Come in."

The porch was so small there was no room for them both. Jonas retreated into the open-plan living-room-cum-kitchen.

"Coffee?" he asked. "I don't have much else to offer, I'm afraid, but at least it's freshly boiled."

"Boiled coffee," Guttorm said, with a smile. "I don't think I've tried that before."

"Sit down, won't you?"

Guttorm Abrahamsen was a big, stout man, more than six foot two,

and he gazed skeptically at a chair beside the sofa before he sat down
warily.

"How did you know I lived here?" Jonas asked as he poured an extra
cup from the scorched black pot.

"Barbro in the accounting department. But I got lost. I parked too far
up the road and rang their doorbell."

"I couldn't afford to rent that house up there," Jonas said, setting a
cup of coffee in front of him. "Far less own."

"No." Guttorm scratched the back of his hand. "I don't suppose you
could. A woman pointed out a path leading straight down here. Through
the woods. My car's still parked up there, but I expect it's safe enough."

Jonas sat down on the sofa. He felt remarkably uncomfortable without quite understanding why. His cousin was a great guy. They had seen
a lot of each other in their childhood, when they had both spent summer vacations with their grandparents in Solør. Admittedly, three years
separated them, with Jonas the older of the two, but beggars can't be
choosers. The small farm belonging to their grandparents was idylli-
cally situated just beside a large mountain lake, but some distance from
the nearest neighbor and even farther from anyone closer to Jonas in
age, and the two cousins had enjoyed a lot of fun together.

When Jonas was released from prison, Guttorm was the only person
who got in touch. He loaned him money and got him a job. Guttorm
was a kind man, and it should be pleasant to have a visit from him.

But it was not.

His cousin was still scratching the back of his hand, and his coffee sat
untouched. The silence began to feel awkward. Jonas felt increasingly
worried, even though he could not think of anything that might actually affect him. He had not done anything wrong, and since he had
obtained the job at Kirkeland Transport, he had not shirked a single
day. Not even a day off through illness, and he complied with every
single rule to be found in the transport business, both written and
unwritten.

"Was there anything in particular?" Jonas eventually asked. "If you'd
told me you were coming, I'd have done some shopping. As a matter of
fact, I think I might have a few oat cakes, I . . ."

He was halfway up from the sofa when Guttorm said: "No thanks. Sit
down, please."

Jonas did as he was told.

"It's about . . ."

Guttorm stopped scratching at last. Instead he took a firm grip of both armrests, as if preparing for a jump.

"The boss," he added, gazing down at the floor.

"The boss?"

"Yes. Georg Kirkeland."

"The owner, yes."

Guttorm nodded and looked down again. He still seemed to be clinging to the chair. Jonas could feel his pulse accelerate and tried to dismiss nagging thoughts about where this conversation was headed.

"What about him?"

"He has . . . Georg has heard through the grapevine that you . . . that you have a criminal record."

Jonas said nothing. A loud whistling noise suddenly sounded in both ears. Inside his head, somehow, and he swallowed three consecutive times to get rid of it.

It was no use.

"I've been told to fire you, Jonas."

Guttorm did at least feel enough shame to bow his head.

"I see," Jonas said in an undertone. "After two years with an unblemished record driving for the guy, without as much as a speeding ticket or late delivery, he's suddenly decided I'm not good enough."

"Well . . ." Guttorm squirmed in his seat. "He didn't know about your jail time before now. I had to . . . I kept that close to my chest when you were hired. I probably should have . . . you understand . . ."

He slapped one hand on his face and rubbed hard. His face was red and blotchy when he finally made eye contact with Jonas. "I'm sorry, Jonas. Really sorry."

"It's okay. You can go now."

"I'm really fucking sorry. You've lost everything, I know. First Dina, and then that business with Anna—"

"You can go, I said. Just go." Jonas's voice grew gradually softer.

"Your child, wife, house, car, job, friends. You've lost everything, Jonas. I really wish I could . . ."

He straightened up and thrust a hand into the inside pocket of the jacket he was still wearing.

"Here," he said, handing Jonas a thick envelope. "Here's fifty thousand kroner in cash. I'd have liked to give you more, but this is what I've . . .

had in reserve, you might say. Money the wife doesn't know about. I know it won't last long, but at least you'll have something until you get things sorted out with unemployment benefit and suchlike, and—"

"Would you please go?"

Jonas was still speaking quietly. His voice was gentle, as if speaking to a small child. He sat bolt upright on the sofa, with his legs slightly apart and his hands on his lap.

Guttorm put the envelope down on the table and got to his feet, zipping up his jacket before turning up the collar.

"I'm really sorry. If there's anything more I can do for you, you've got my number."

Jonas did not say a word. He would not say anything for some time to come.

He was thinking of Dina. Of the daughter who would have been seventeen if he hadn't become so annoyed by the clutter of junk mail in their mailbox. As Guttorm crossed the room, the rough floorboard, with deep cracks that had made the draft from the damp basement extra troublesome this winter, creaked loudly.

As the door slammed behind his cousin, the words of an old song drifted into Jonas's head.

Freedom's just another word for nothing left to lose.

Now he was certainly free, and it felt just the same as being dead.

Henrik Holme sat crouched over Iselin Havørn's last words.

The handwriting was regular, without a single deletion or correction. The ink had run in a couple of places, he noticed, but apart from that, all the writing was straight as could be, neat and tidy.

"I've read it three times now," he said to Hanne with a note of dismay, "and I still don't understand what you mean."

"Read it aloud," Hanne told him.

Puffing out his cheeks, Henrik slowly let the air escape. Hesitating slightly, he began to read:

Dear Maria,

Before I leave now for the land of darkness and deathly shadows, never to return, I must explain. It should never have turned out like this. I had hoped for good things in life, but evil came instead, I expected light, and everything grew dark. My days are futile, and I want no more.

The fight against Islam and the destruction of everything that is Norwegian and European goes on. At any rate I have done my share, but the witch hunt of recent weeks has cost me too much. My friends, even the ones I know are in total agreement with me, have turned their backs. I can scarcely leave the apartment without being engulfed by journalists, not to mention the fucking left-wing activists and the multicultural mafia that assailed me with spitting and verbal abuse the last time I ventured out to the supermarket to do some shopping. What is said and written about me is so unjust, so wrong, and so offensive that it's unendurable. I have devoted my life to saving our fatherland. Now it's no longer within my power to continue. They have stolen my life and my natural right to express my opinions, and I can't bear it any longer.

Iselin

He looked up as he put the copied printout aside.

"Well?" Hanne said. "Can't you see it?"

"See what?"

With a sigh, Hanne trundled her wheelchair across to his side of the table.

"How would you characterize the opening paragraph?" she asked.

"What do you mean?"

"Good God, Henrik. You went to school for years. You must have done some textual analysis?"

He tapped his forehead and snatched up the sheet of paper.

"Beautiful," he said once he had mulled it over. "Almost biblical."

Hanne grinned and rolled back to her usual place.

"You're exactly right with that," she said. "It's actually taken from the Bible—to be more specific, the Book of Job. If my memory doesn't fail me, the first paragraph is a loose collection of quotations from there."

Her hand blindly rooted around under the seat of her wheelchair. She produced a laptop and opened it.

"In my office, there's a bundle of Internet printouts," she said, pushing her glasses back up her nose. "In the middle of the desk. Would you mind getting them, please?"

When he returned with the papers, she raised one fist triumphantly in the air.

"Yep. The opening paragraph of Iselin's letter is a little bit of cut-and-paste from the Book of Job right enough. And of course, you know what this part of the Bible is about?"

"Well . . . Job is a dreadfully afflicted man, is he not?"

"You can say that again. It all begins with God sending for his sons."

"I thought God had only one son."

"In all probability, this means angels. Of which one is Satan, or the Adversary, as some translations have it. Satan has been absent for some time, and when God asks where he has been, he is given the answer that Satan has ventured into the human world."

Henrik stared at her in fascination. "How do you know that?"

"By reading," was her terse response. "What do you think I've been up to in all these years of self-imposed isolation?"

"On the Internet," he muttered.

She ignored him and pressed on: "The Book of Job is a fantastic story. It's said to be the very oldest part of the Bible, even though it doesn't appear first and it's impossible to understand it completely. Lots of people have tried, of course, but there are countless different interpretations."

"What happened between God and Satan?"

"They quarreled, about Job, the richest and most powerful man in the land of Uz. God boasted of what a God-fearing man he was. Satan said, *Not at all; anybody would be God fearing if they had received such great gifts from God.* They entered into some kind of wager, no less."

"A . . . wager? Between God and Satan?"

"Yes. Satan was given permission to remove everything Job owned, because God was confident he would retain full trust in him all the same."

"So it was Satan, rather than God, who tested Job?"

"Yes, I suppose so." Hanne shrugged and closed the laptop. "You could say they were both in on it. But enough of Bible stories. The point in this connection is that Job was a God-fearing man. He begged for an answer as to why he had been so sorely punished and even pleaded to be allowed to die, but he never doubted God's existence. Never questioned God's omnipotence, not even when Satan brought down a plague of boils on the poor man because it had not helped in the least to rob him of everything he possessed."

Her eyes were sparkling with eagerness, and her tone of voice softer than usual, the way she always dropped it a notch or two when she was really passionate about something. This was how Henrik liked her best: when she was teaching without becoming too domineering, when she drew him into a discussion instead of suddenly shutting him out, as she still did all too often.

"Since I've tracked down the primary source for the first paragraph, what would you say about the letter now?" she asked.

Henrik reflected for a few seconds as his eyes absorbed the suicide letter once again.

"Resignation," he concluded. "It's quite a resigned piece of writing, I'd say. Fairly . . . elegant, in a way too."

He glanced up at Hanne. Her face was almost expressionless, but he thought he could detect a trace of skepticism in the way the corners of her mouth curved down ever so slightly.

"Maybe a bit melodramatic for someone of our times?" he ventured one more time, but she did not seem any more satisfied. "Or . . . what do you think?"

Hanne put her hand around her neck and angled her head to one side.

"Resignation and melodrama might not be too crazy an interpretation. After all, great chunks of the Bible are pretty melodramatic when read by modern eyes, so I wouldn't place too much weight on that particular point. But resignation? Well, maybe so. Perhaps you're right. At least the wording seems to come from someone facing death with . . . equanimity? A sort of . . ."

She released her neck and took a gulp of coffee.

"This text sounds as if it comes from someone who has really suffered. Who has struggled with life for a long time. Like Job, for that matter. What about the other part?"

"The second paragraph?"

"Yes."

Henrik raced through the letter one more time. "Self-justification," he said firmly. "Anger and self-justification."

"Right! You can see it too!"

She leaned over the stack of papers Henrik had brought from her office.

"These are printouts of some of the worst articles Tyrfing posted on various websites," she said, lightly slapping the top sheet of paper. "The day she was outed, I dashed onto the Internet and secured them. Smart thinking, because they were nearly all deleted in the course of the first twenty-four hours following her exposure. And these . . ."

Once again she smacked the bundle of papers.

"These articles provide evidence of the same cocksure, self-justifying, and hateful writer who could have written the second part of this letter. Apart from one thing."

"What's that?" Henrik asked when she paused, before using his fingers to beat out a little drumroll on the table.

"Are those tics, or are you expressing eager anticipation of my answer?"

"Tics. Sorry."

"Iselin Havørn could never have written a suicide letter."

"But she clearly has done," Henrik said glumly.

"I greatly doubt that. In a suicide letter, you don't talk about 'fucking left-wingers' and spitting at the supermarket. Have you ever read a genuine suicide letter?"

"Er . . . no."

"You will eventually. They are terribly sad. During my time in the police, I read maybe fifteen to twenty of them. There was no reason to suppose any of them were forgeries. Some were hopeless, many downright confused. Some were well written, bordering on being absurdly rational. What they had in common was that they were . . ."

Now she leaned all the way across the table, maintaining lengthy eye contact before she finished her sentence.

". . . brimming over with pain."

Her voice had dropped so low that he could not avoid leaning closer.

"Unbearable pain," she added. "And pleading for forgiveness and understanding. I've never read a suicide letter in which the writer has not reassured their loved ones that it's not their fault that everything has gone wrong. That it's best for everyone that he or she disappears. It can be absolutely heartbreaking, Henrik. Believe me."

All of a sudden she turned her back. Henrik automatically drew away. Hanne picked up the copied suicide letter and flung it across the table.

"Not a word to her wife. Not a single sign of affection."

"It opens with 'Dear Maria.'"

"Dear? I send letters to the tax authorities with 'dear'! Common courtesy, it's known as. Even though teenagers as a whole seem to have forgotten what that is these days. By the way, you look so much nicer now that you've shaved. Excellent."

Henrik touched the sides of his nose four times as she went on: "Where is the pain in this letter, Henrik? Where is the overwhelming feeling that everything is insurmountable and there's no way out apart from death?"

"Maybe a bit . . . at the beginning?"

"Exactly. I just can't see that this letter here has been written by one and the same person. It looks as if the first paragraph was written by someone who really is up against things, maybe even a religious person. Someone who has been brooding and reading and struggling to find some kind of meaning in a dreadful existence. Paragraph two?"

She sighed noisily. "In many ways it looks as if it was written by Iselin, even though, as I said, she never—"

"Could have taken her own life," Henrik added in a voice that suggested he was very far from being persuaded.

"Don't you agree? Surely you agree with me, Henrik?"

He moistened his lips and clasped his hands. Parted them again and pushed them under his thighs.

"Let's say that I see your point," he said. "The letter seems quite odd. And Iselin Havørn was maybe not the world's best suicide candidate. But then, can you tell me . . ."

He looked at the letter now lying askew on the tabletop.

"How can it have taken two different people to write a suicide letter? And why? And why on earth could the writing so obviously belong to Iselin Havørn all the way through? And what's more . . ."

Fortunately this time, she did not take the opportunity to interrupt him when he paused for thought before continuing: "Iselin Havørn was a damned racist who incited hatred, conspiracy theories, and antagonism. She stood for everything you despise and oppose. Now she's dead. Why . . . why are you so intent on showing that a bitch like her did not take her own life but was . . ."

Now he hesitated too long.

"Murdered," Hanne finished for him. "I believe she was murdered. And no one should be murdered. No one. No matter who. I don't have any answers to those other questions of yours. But we'll find the answers. You and I, Henrik. And the first thing you're going to do is to investigate Iselin Havørn. Dig up absolutely everything you can. In the meantime . . ."

She drew the thick bundle of printouts closer.

". . . I'll delve even more thoroughly into Tyrfing's realm. Somewhere in Iselin's life lies the answer to why she was killed. If we find that, we'll find the perpetrator. Elementary, my dear Dr. Watson. Elementary."

The fact that Sherlock Holmes had never said anything of the sort, and strictly speaking it was the Oslo Police Chief who decided what Henrik could and could not do, were points on which he wisely kept his own counsel.

"Okay," he said and, rising from his seat, he left for home.

FRIDAY, JANUARY 15, 2016

When Christel Bengtson finished the first recording of the day at 11:40, she checked her cell phone for the first time since breakfast. There were four new text messages, three of them from her best friend. The messages all exhorted her to get her hands on a copy of that day's edition of the gossip magazine *Se og Hør* as fast as she could.

It turned out to be not too difficult.

Piles of weekly magazines were scattered through the largest of the buses parked in Sørkedalen that was used as a really cramped break room for the film crew. Christel had never quite known why, until one of her more experienced colleagues explained it to her. The production company had an arrangement with most of the magazines. They provided exclusive interviews with actors and received positive reviews of their series and free magazines in exchange.

Only then did Christel understand why the producer had been so unbelievably annoyed when she had refused to be interviewed. *Se og Hør* had also dangled the inducement of a free trip to Bali for her, Hedda, and her father as soon as filming was over, but Christel had stood her ground. An in-depth interview in the *VG Helg* weekend supplement would suffice, she said. The producer had made a fuss for several days before finally giving up.

Se og Hør lay at the top of the pile, and Christel Bengtson was today's front-page headline.

Making Millions was splashed inside a bright yellow star above a portrait photo taken three months ago in connection with the start of filming. Diagonally above the lower part of the picture, big red letters screamed: *Christel Bengtson—Blog Queen Moves to TV Screen.*

Groaning aloud, she began to leaf through it.

Over a five-page spread, the magazine had stolen comments and photographs, some from one source, some from another, and cobbled

it together into what passed for an article. Incredibly enou…
appeared perfectly seamless, Christel concluded with a sigh afte…
reading. You would have to be a terribly critical reader to notice t…
a couple of instances, it was clear that the quotes had not actually b…
given to *Se og Hør*. One of the double-page spreads was dominated …
a picture of the apartment in Geitmyrsveien, taken after dark—in the
evening, obviously, since most of the windows were brightly lit. She saw
that the curtains at her own living room window were closed. When
she held the magazine all the way up to her eyes and at a particular
angle to get the best possible light, she detected a tiny gap in the curtains. And a hand. She knew it was her hand.

The man in the white delivery van had only wanted a photograph of
the apartment. The guy who had scared her witless had been a wretched
Se og Hør photographer. She felt relieved, quite literally. Her breathing
was easier, and she noticed her shoulders drop.

She could live with this article. The fundamental tone was positive,
and none of the content was specifically wrong. As for herself, she
found the reporting pretty innocuous, but if that was what they wanted
to use to fill their columns, then be her guest.

And it contained no photos of Hedda.

Christel tossed the magazine into the wastepaper basket and left the
bus. She could manage a walk down to Røa for lunch before the next
scene. As she strolled across the parking lot, taking deep breaths of the
raw, cold air, she made a decision: she would stop feeling watched.

Everything had an explanation, and that creeping sense of being followed was only her imagination. Probably it had something to do with
her mother leaving her when she was small, just as a psychologist had
once tried to explain to her. She had become so well known that she
had to live with the reality that there would always be photographers
around. At the end of the day, they did not mean her any harm.

No one was out to get her, she decided then and there.

And felt immensely relieved.

Only four people turned up in addition to Maria herself.

Thank God.

And not a single journalist, despite Iselin Havørn's life and suicide still
being a hot topic in the public arena. That day's *Aftenposten* published a
feature full of stinging denunciation of the brutal campaign against the

sixty-two-year-old immigration critic. The writer shared many of Iselin's viewpoints but used a slightly different turn of phrase and, moreover, had never made any attempt to hide his identity. That had given him free access to the country's newspaper columns in recent years. In the beginning, Iselin had followed him with interest, but she had lost faith in him along the way. He was too wishy-washy, in her opinion—far too wishy-washy. She would not have thought so today, it had struck Maria Kvam as she skimmed the article over the meager breakfast she had managed to force down before leaving for the chapel. His fulmination against the Norwegian authorities in general and the tyrants of sweetness and light in particular had been allocated three full pages in the newspaper. The author concluded that the treatment of Iselin Havørn had constituted an even more excessive and acutely worrying curtailment of freedom of speech in Norway. Furthermore, the witch hunt would lead to increased numbers of a large, expanding, and totally legitimate group of anti-immigration commentators feeling hounded into expressing themselves under a cloak of anonymity. They would simply have to do a better job of hiding their identities than Iselin Havørn had done.

It crossed Maria's mind that Iselin would have liked the article as she folded the newspaper and dropped it into the bag of papers beside the fireplace.

Apart from herself, only Halvor Stenskar and three employees from the VitaeBrass administration section had gathered to accompany Iselin Havørn to her grave.

They had all succeeded in keeping their mouths shut about the time and place, and the funeral directors were obviously trustworthy. The man who had expressed a scintilla of disapproval when Maria had chosen the casket pranced discreetly around them in the minutes before the organ music struck up and Iselin Havørn's final journey began. The chapel was decorated with candles, but only a single wreath of flowers. Enormous, it was composed of red and white roses, and the wording on the broad silk ribbon was printed in gold letters on a white background: *With eternal gratitude from colleagues and friends.*

Maria had ordered it and VitaeBrass had paid the bill.

Halvor Stenskar was the only person in the front pew with Maria. Near the end of the eulogy, he leaned close to her.

"I had the distinct impression that Iselin wanted to be cremated. We once talked about it, on a boat trip—"

"She's to be buried," Maria said so loudly that the pastor stopped in surprise for a moment before expertly picking up the thread again and continuing.

Soon it was all over.

Halvor Stenskar and his employees carried out the coffin. Maria walked immediately behind them. On the way to the open grave, she stared down at her own feet and concentrated intently on putting one foot in front of the other without keeling over. Not until the casket was lowered into the dark, wet earth that even in January was soft and crumbly did Maria lift her gaze. The very last she saw of the great love of her life was a box of the simplest particleboard.

At last it was over and done with.

Hedda had slept well ever since she had been tucked in at around seven. She frequently woke again about midnight, mainly because for the past week, she had been trying to do without a night diaper.

Without much success so far.

Bengt Bengtson had patiently changed bedclothes and washed her sheet every morning without fail. Even though the little girl went to the bathroom in the middle of the night, she slept so soundly near morning that it all went haywire. Every time. Her grandfather consoled and encouraged and washed the sheets, still persisting in his delight at being able to stay at home with a totally unexpected toddler in his old age.

He loved this child.

In a way, it was even better this time around.

When Christel had been born, he was already past forty, but still becoming established in life. It had cost him a fortune to take over his childhood home in Nordberg. Although both his sister and his much younger half brother had been generous in terms of how much they were willing to accept for their share of the property, he and Eleonora were left with a mountain of debt. He had taken all the overtime he could get, and days would pass between the times he came home before his daughter had gone to bed. Eleonora soon had enough of being mother to a toddler. She discarded the little family, the house, and the remainder of the debt, and Bengt was left alone with Christel. So much of his time since then had been spent taking care of his daughter's material needs that he had lost out on far too much. All the same, things had gone well, he often comforted himself, and Christel had turned into a mature, responsible young woman who, on top of everything else, provided well for herself and her daughter at the age of only twenty-two.

With Hedda, everything was different.

It was true that she attended the day care center in St. Hanshaugen at Christel's insistence. For his part, Bengt felt that a few hours a day was more than enough of socializing with other children. He dropped her off late and picked her up early on four out of five days in the work-week: Thursdays belonged to Christel. In addition, he frequently gave Hedda a day off without Christel having any knowledge of it. Now the toddler had become so proficient at speaking that he had to admit to his own daughter what was going on. Last week she had been annoyed with him when Hedda told her how they had spent the day. Grampa and the little girl had visited the Oslo Reptile Park, baked buns, and then watched Disney's *Frozen* for the umpteenth time. A brilliant January day for them both.

It was now well past eleven on a Friday night, and he sat reading John Grisham's latest thriller. Jazz was playing on the radio, and he had lit two scented candles on the coffee table. On Fridays, he always spent Hedda's time at day care making the apartment shining clean. Christel thought they should employ a house cleaner, but he had never capitulated on that point.

People should clean up their own dirt, he thought. You should never be too grand to do that.

His teacup was empty, and he wondered whether to treat himself to a glass of whisky. Because Christel was at a party, he had not touched any alcohol. The habit had persisted since the time of Christel's high school graduation that she had spent with a huge belly and been rein-forced for a while when Hedda had suffered two attacks of false croup within a short period. It had scared them witless. Bengt Bengtson wanted to be in a permanently fit state to drive unless everything was shipshape and everyone was at home.

However, maybe he could make an exception tonight.

The NRK jazz station was playing Chet Baker, and he decided to pour himself a nip to savor before going to bed. Whenever Christel was at a party, he let Hedda sleep in his double bed. That was the safest way, both he and Christel felt. By the grace of God, he was a sound sleeper, and a number of times he had failed to wake when Hedda began to toddle around, slightly confused and fast asleep. She was far safer sleeping by his side.

The phone rang.

Bengt was in the process of pouring from a bottle he had held on to since before his granddaughter's birth. He looked up at the telephone, half in surprise and half in annoyance. Of course, it might be Christel, and most of all he felt worried as he put down his glass and crossed to the armchair to take the call. He did not recognize the number. It was far too late to phone anyone you didn't know well, and he was almost angry when he picked up the phone and barked: "Bengt Bengtson!"

A woman's voice answered at the other end.

"Good evening," she said. "This is Turid Belsvik from Hamar. So good of you to take the call, Bengt. I'm really sorry for phoning so late."

"Yes, it's nearly 11:30."

He did not know anyone in Hamar. He could not bear the idea that someone he had never met should call him by his first name just like that.

"Yes, of course," the cheerful voice answered. "But we up here thought you might like to hear this news straightaway. Are you on your own at home?"

"Yes. Not really, as a matter of fact. What's this about?"

"I'm calling from Norsk Tipping, the Norwegian National Lottery, you see. And we'd like to ask if you've submitted a few ticket lines in this evening's EuroJackpot?"

Bengt felt unusually hot.

"Yes. Yes, I have. Ten regular lines that I place for five weeks at a time. On the Internet, you know. I have one of those . . ."

He began to feel faint. He was lightheaded, and his feet felt heavy as lead. He sank down into the chair.

"Did you say you had someone with you?" Turid from Hamar asked him; her voice suddenly sounded very distant. "Or are you on your own?"

"I'm . . . my grandchild is sleeping, but my daughter will be home soon. What . . . what's this all about?"

"You've probably already guessed. I'm phoning to tell you you've won."

"I've . . . have I won, did you say? The EuroJackpot?"

"Yes. When will your daughter actually get home?"

"I don't know. But she's not usually late. What prize have I . . . I mean, this week it's the maximum sum, isn't it? I surely haven't—"

"Yes, you have, Bengt."

The woman was unable to hold back a burst of cackling laughter.

"Norwegians have won the main prize in the EuroJackpot before, but never when it's been at its highest."

Once again she laughed with delight.

Bengt rose gingerly from his seat. His legs held. As he walked slowly across the room to his whisky glass, he heard someone enter the front door. From the hallway, he heard Christel whisper a hello: she didn't want to wake Hedda. Bengt listened for a long time to Turid from Hamar, punctuated only by a couple of minor questions from him. Christel came into the living room and, taken aback, stood watching him until the conversation was over. Bengt let the hand holding the phone drop slowly. He put the glass of whisky to his mouth and drank it all down in a single gulp.

"I've won the star prize in the EuroJackpot," he said. "We're rich, Christel. We are 763 million kroner richer than we were only an hour ago."

He lifted the bottle of thirty-year-old Glencadam and indulged himself with a bit more.

SATURDAY, JANUARY 16, 2016

The frost had arrived at last. When Jonas woke around 6:00 a.m. with a thumping headache, it was still dark outside. Nevertheless, he could see that the trees in the forest on the other side of the yard were glazed with frost. The sky had cleared, and the ice crystals glistened in the moonlight.

Winter was finally here.

Not that it made any difference.

For once, he had a hangover. On Friday evening, he had watched five episodes of *The Walking Dead*. He had seen them before lots of times, and he had no idea why he had decided to view them again. It was at least somewhere to fix his eyes while he drank. When an old bottle of red wine was empty, he attacked a half-bottle of vodka he had bought in Sweden a long time ago. He had drained that too by the time he tumbled into bed.

His body was screaming for water and more sleep.

Fortunately he had some cola in the fridge. He drank a bottle in record time and chewed down three aspirin lying loose in an eggcup on the shelf above the stove. Naked, he stood staring down at his skinny milky-white torso.

He could play a part in *The Walking Dead*.

Anyway, he felt more dead than alive as he stumbled across the ice-cold floor to make some coffee. After two or three cups, he had hopes of falling asleep again, as sometimes, paradoxically enough, a dose of caffeine was the only possible way for him to calm down.

His headache was still excruciating. He grabbed a pair of jogging pants from the back of a chair and pulled them on without bothering with boxer shorts. A sweater lay on the floor beside the stove. When he slipped it on, he held his breath to fend off the pungent smell. He did not have a washing machine, and it had been some time since he was able to muster the energy for a trip to the laundromat in Thorvald Meyers gate. The bag of dirty laundry beside the bed was so overflowing that it had begun to stink too.

He switched on his computer while he waited for the water to boil. His eyes were so dry that he had to squeeze out tears by screwing them up several times in order to see.

At least that old crow Iselin was no longer headline news.

Blogger Christel's Father Wins Three Quarter Billion! VG shrieked at him.

Uncomprehending, Jonas clicked into the story and began to read. All of a sudden he stopped.

Bengt Bengtson had won 763 million kroner.

The man was on top of the world, it said. It certainly looked like it in the accompanying photograph. Bengt was grinning from ear to ear with a shy, pajama-clad Hedda in his arms and a smiling Christel by his side. The three-year-old's face was hidden in the crook of her grandfather's neck, probably on Christel's instructions. The picture must have been taken during the night.

Jonas read the article several times over. His headache had gone.

Everything was gone. Slowly he got to his feet and stared at his own hands. These were his hands, he realized, attached to arms that must also belong to him, though it didn't feel that way. He took an abrupt, forceful, and involuntary breath. He had forgotten to breathe. His bare feet on the floorboards suddenly felt red-hot, as if he were standing on glowing embers.

The kettle of water was boiling.

He must have stood there for some time. When he finally approached the stove, the kettle had almost boiled dry. He switched off the hot plate and stripped off his clothes. Without a stitch, he walked around, flicking off every light in the tiny house. Then he walked out the door and closed it softly behind him.

The frost enveloped him.

It felt blessedly painful, and he trudged slowly across the gravel to the little woodshed at the edge of the forest. Minute stones pierced the soles of his feet; he had not walked barefoot outside since Dina died. When he reached the shed, he turned to face the house and stood transfixed.

It was a beautiful morning.

In the subdued light from the new moon, it seemed as if the world had turned silver. A pale, shimmering gray glitter clung to the trees, to the tufts of grass alongside the house, to the tiles on the roof that he should have asked the house's owner to replace long ago.

He glanced up. Out here in Maridalen, some distance from Oslo's perpetual light, the stars were so much brighter. The Big Dipper looked crooked up there, and he pinpointed the North Star. In the shelter of the woodshed, he turned to face north and lay down on the ice-cold undergrowth. His feet were bleeding, and the sharp thorns of dead bushes punctured his skin as he stretched out on the ground.

After a while, his teeth stopped chattering. He saw a shooting star above the Maridal Alps but did not make a wish.

There was no longer anything to wish for.

SUNDAY, JANUARY 17, 2016

It was so cold that even the dogs did an about-turn at the door.

Henrik had barely met a single person on his long walk. Admittedly, it was just after nine o'clock, but with the capital city as beautiful as it was this morning, he found it remarkable that not even kids had pestered to escape outdoors. The white frost on the vast grassy incline sloping down from Muselunden went some way to compensate for the snow that had not yet made an appearance. It was fine weather for a walk, Henrik Holme thought, at least until some point later that day. He tightened his scarf as he headed into the pedestrian tunnel under the Sinsenkrysset intersection.

The stench of stale urine hit him, in stark contrast to the fresh, dry air he had inhaled as he strolled through the city streets. When he had set out from his apartment in Nedre Grünerløkka, it had still been dark. He had fallen asleep with the window open and woke freezing at the crack of dawn. The best idea would have been to close the window and sleep on, but he felt remarkably wide awake. The previous evening, he had drawn up a list of questions he wanted to ask Amanda Foss. His plan had been to go to Police Headquarters on Monday morning, but after feeling annoyingly restless for half an hour or so, he decided it would be worth paying her a short visit. She lived in Risløkka, an Internet search had told him, and he had planned a circuitous route that took him all the way up to the lake at Maridalsvannet before it really began to grow light. He had followed the entire length of the Akerselva River. When he veered southeast to cross Grefsenplatå at an angle, he had walked into the embrace of a magnificent sunrise.

Once through the disgusting tunnels, he headed for the local public housing below Aker Hospital. The decay was unmistakable—windows were broken, and attempts had been made to patch them with chipboard and cloth. Garbage was scattered everywhere, and just as he was leaving the area, a gigantic fat rat ran across the path immediately in front of him. It was incredible to think that only a mile and a half or so west of here, on the other side of Trondheimsveien, lay one of Oslo's most expensive districts, lined with luxurious homes.

Distance could not always be measured in miles, Henrik thought as he passed the refugee reception center at Refstad and took a left turn. He checked the GPS on his phone twice and was soon standing in front of a red terraced house that could have done with a coat of paint.

The mailbox informed him that Amanda and Marius Foss were indeed the owners who had let themselves down in the house maintenance department and also that they had three children: Fredrik, Christian, and Margrethe. Judging by the toys strewn across the little patch of frozen lawn facing the entrance, the children were pint-sized.

Then at least the family would be awake at this hour.

Henrik removed his cap and loosened his scarf to make himself more easily recognizable. He tried to seem purposeful as he walked the few steps from the low gate to the canopy above the front door. This had seemed a really good idea before the sun came up. He would be able to look back on an enjoyable hike and maybe obtain some of the answers he needed. From Amanda Foss's point of view, it would be helpful to avoid being detained by Henrik's questions tomorrow morning, since her time at work was probably already busy enough.

Hanging back, he stopped at a big toy tractor missing its back wheels.

Since he had met Hanne Wilhelmsen, he had improved in his dealings with other people. He had made a virtue of necessity. Given that the retired Chief Inspector mostly sat at home and also behaved in a sullen and dismissive manner on the rare occasions when she ventured out among people, Henrik had adopted new habits. In fact, he was no longer shy, and in the past couple of years he had gained the distinct impression that he now encountered more kindness and respect from his colleagues.

He liked his new, more self-assured self much better. The problem was that it did not come entirely naturally to him. He knew he was good at understanding other people, but mainly from a theoretical point of view. Exactly like Hanne. The difference between the two of them did not lie in the ability to understand or interpret the actions of others, but in their attitude toward them. Henrik liked people. To be honest, Hanne could not stand many of them. Henrik desired more than anything else to be able to fit in, to be like others, and to be part of a social circle. He just could not quite succeed at it, even though he was no longer so socially inept, and, what's more, had gained greater control over those blasted, alienating tics of his.

Hanne isolated herself, shut people out, and got on absolutely excellently that way.

Over the years, Henrik had begun to regard interaction with people as a complicated arithmetic problem and had gradually become skillful at mathematics. If he included himself in the equation, it all fell apart.

It was possible that Amanda Foss had absolutely no wish to be disturbed by work issues during a Sunday family breakfast. Quite the opposite, it suddenly dawned on Henrik. She was off duty. She was a busy career woman with probably thousands of irons in the fire and three small children in the bargain. Most likely a visit from a colleague harboring questions about a suicide was the last thing she wanted on this beautiful, ice-cold morning.

He wheeled around and was on the point of fleeing from the tiny front garden when the door opened.

"Henrik Holme," said an enthusiastic voice, and he turned around again. "I thought it was you! Spotted you from the kitchen."

Amanda Foss pointed at the window. She was wearing a vivid-yellow college sweater with LSK in large letters across the chest. Her jogging pants were gray, and she had socks made of coarse wool on her feet, squeezed into a pair of pink Crocs that looked too big for her.

She was just as beautiful as ever.

"Come in," she said, beaming. "We were just about to eat. Are you hungry?"

"No, thanks," Henrik said, with a gulp.

He smelled bacon cooking, and all of a sudden was so ravenous that his mouth ran with saliva.

"Oh, I'm sure you can manage a little bite," Amanda said, ushering him in. "Sorry about all the chaos, by the way."

It was the messiest home Henrik had ever stepped into. The porch was a jam-packed storeroom, overflowing with snowsuits and soccer balls, boots, and quilted jackets. The floor was sprinkled so thick with sand and gravel that he felt it stabbing into his feet when he slipped off his own winter shoes. He would have to forget about arranging them neatly with parallel laces, and he tapped his forehead in desperation.

Amanda had to move a pair of children's skis that had toppled over before he could walk through. That gave him the opportunity to rap his knuckles lightly on the front doorframe all of ten times before he crossed the threshold into a hallway equally untidy and grubby.

Inside the living room was even worse. Leftover food and toys were littered everywhere. Dolls and cars, teddies and other soft toys, and a huge pile of Duplo bricks. He stepped on one of them. It was painful, and he wished he had dared to keep his boots on. Two boys aged three or thereabouts, so alike that Henrik had to blink, sat on the sofa, arguing over an iPad, and one of them burst into tears when the other won the battle for ownership rights by hitting his brother on the head with a hefty police car.

"Do you have twins?" Henrik asked, the question so superfluous that he wanted to bite his tongue.

"Triplets, actually." Amanda laughed as she rumpled a little girl's hair.

The third child had come toddling downstairs. She was wearing a traditional sweater in green and white over blue knitted wool tights. Over her warm clothing she wore a shocking pink tutu, full and ruffled. On her feet she had a pair of rubber boots that were far too big for her and threatened to fall off with every step she took.

"I want to go out," she declared firmly. "I want to go for a walk."

"After breakfast. Go to Daddy, won't you? Are you sure you don't want to eat with us?"

This last question was directed at Henrik, who shook his head vigorously.

"I just have a couple of questions. It'll only take ten minutes. Max. I'm really sorry for coming here and disturbing you. We can do this tomorrow. At your office."

"No, of course not," she brushed him off, gesturing for him to follow her downstairs. "Marius!"

Her head disappeared as she leaned into a room Henrik assumed to be the kitchen, because of the smoke from the grill belching out of the doorway.

"Hold the eggs for ten minutes," she said to her husband. "I'm just going to have a chat with Henrik, a colleague of mine."

"He can eat with us," Henrik heard the man answer. "We've plenty of bacon."

"He's not hungry. Just ten minutes."

Now she headed for the stairs. She used her foot to push aside a pink pedal car plastered with Barbie stickers. Henrik followed obediently down into the basement, where she led him into a sitting room turned into an attractive home office for two.

It was immaculate in here. Tidy, clean, and well organized.

As Amanda sat down on an ice-blue sofa along the gable wall, she pointed encouragingly at the solitary armchair.

"How can I help you?" she asked cheerfully. "As you can probably see, this room is kept child-free, but I don't have a lot of time, I'm afraid."

"Iselin died of cardiac arrest," Henrik said quickly, having pushed his hands extra-far under his thighs. "Apparently caused by a hefty overdose of antidepressants."

"Yes," she said, drawing out the word. "That's what it says in the case documents you were allowed to read, and—"

"She had swallowed them down with a vegetable smoothie."

"Yes. The pills were probably crushed and mixed into the drink, and almost all of it was consumed. Spinach, broccoli, nuts, and carrots, all mashed up, as far as I recall. And some lemon. Cabbage too, I think. Doesn't sound especially tasty, to be honest."

"No. But a drink like that might well camouflage the taste of the pills. They're quite bitter, apparently."

Amanda's face took on a guarded expression. "Yes. I guess so. The pills would probably be easier to swallow that way, I suppose."

"Do you know where the pills came from?"

"The case isn't concluded yet. As I told you, there are still a few formalities to attend to. It's only a week or so since she died."

"Yes," Henrik said, trying to smile disarmingly. "I really do understand."

"Understand what?"

"No, I mean . . ." His fingertips twitched, and he had to press his thighs down hard on the soft seat. "I understand that the investigation into the case isn't complete, I mean. But you might be able to answer me all the same. Where did the pills come from?"

"They came from . . . Well, I suppose they came from a pharmacy."

"Exactly. I realize that. Do you know what brand of tricyclic antidepressants they were?"

"No, I'm still waiting for the final analysis results. But anyway, the case is absolutely straightforward. Suicide letter and all that. As you

must have seen from the preliminary autopsy report, she died of cardiac arrest following fibrillation. Which was of course self-inflicted. By
an overdose of those tricksicklick—"

"Tricyclic," Henrik rushed to correct her, and was immediately filled
with remorse. "But were they hers? I saw nothing in the documents
about where the pills had actually come from."

"Oh, is that what you mean?" Amanda Foss tucked her hair behind
both ears. "As far as I remember, there was no box found in the apartment. Or blister pack, or whatever these pills come in. No packaging."

"But you must have looked into whether Iselin Havørn was actually
taking antidepressants? You've checked the national database to find
out whether the medication had been prescribed for her?"

She hesitated precisely one second too long. "It's on my list for
tomorrow," she said brightly. "In fact it'll be the very first thing I do.
According to the plan I have. For tomorrow."

She flashed him a brilliant smile as she stood up. "But you know," she
said, "cold bacon's not much fun. If you have anything else you want to
ask me, could we leave it until we're back at work?"

Without waiting for a response, she headed for the stairs. Henrik
began to guess why Amanda Foss had been given responsibility for
what seemed the simplest police case in the world. Three-year-old triplets took their toll, he assumed, and an open-and-shut case of suicide
was the least risky assignment to give her.

"I'd be obliged if you'd phone me with the results," he said on the
way up.

"Results of what?"

"If you find anything in the national database," he answered, struggling to keep his tone light.

"Yes, of course. As I said, first thing tomorrow."

The chaos hit him between the eyes again when they came back
upstairs. The boys had put on weatherproof mittens and were using
the coffee table as a boxing ring. Amanda darted forward and just
managed to catch one of them after an impressive uppercut from the
other. Little Margrethe was standing, red and perspiring, at the window, daubing a very colorful abstract picture on the glass with finger-
paints. He heard a loud bang from the kitchen followed by a loud
stream of swear words.

"I'm off," Henrik said. "Sorry for disturbing you."

Amanda Foss, already making hell for leather for the kitchen with a toddler under each arm, did not reply. Henrik cleared a way through the masses of winter clothing and a whole shoe shop full of footwear, stumbling over toy goalposts before he finally emerged into the open air.

If Hanne Wilhelmsen was correct that Iselin Havørn had been murdered, the mother of three in there presented a serious challenge. She really didn't have any inkling, Henrik thought as he took deep breaths of the fresh air. The advantage of her incompetence, however, was that she had willingly answered his questions and she was clearly easily led. If she really came to grips with the problem of where Iselin's overdose had in fact come from, he would be first to know about it.

He was so hungry that his guts were burning. He decided to buy bacon and eggs on his way home, treat himself to a real Sunday breakfast, and pay Hanne a visit.

He would offer her an exchange. Horse-trading, pure and simple. The mere thought of it sent him into ecstasies.

Jonas Abrahamsen was woken by the sound of voices.

Without opening his eyes, he tried to figure out where he was. A terrible anxiety shot through his body when he discovered he was attached to cables: on his chest, arms, and fingers.

. . . dangerously low core temperature . . .

The voices were not too far off, but Jonas could make out only fragments of conversation.

. . . alcohol count of 1.2 . . .

. . . stinking and feces on . . .

. . . that was on his hair, you see . . .

. . . possible suicide attempt, maybe just a drunken accident . . .

. . . and totally naked, then . . .

He was the one they were talking about. All of a sudden he opened his eyes wide. The harsh light caused him to pull a face, and a nurse dashed across.

"There, there."

The man in white gripped his arm reassuringly. His hands were warm, dry, and soft.

"Everything will be all right now," the soft voice said. "Just take it easy. Relax. We're looking after you."

Jonas closed his eyes again. The heat from the nurse's hand spread through his whole body. Since New Year's Eve 2003, no one had touched Jonas, apart from a handshake now and again.

Perhaps he was dead. It felt as if he had wet himself, but his crotch wasn't damp.

"You must lie still," the friendly nurse said. "We have you connected to a host of machines to be on the safe side. You also have a catheter inserted. You're peeing into a bag, in other words."

Jonas was not dead. He was in the hospital.

The tears began to roll.

"You were dreadfully cold," the nurse said. "It was your neighbor who found you. Or her dog, in fact. An elkhound, the woman said; she phoned to find out how you are. We can't say too much, of course, as I'm sure you know, but I let her read between the lines that everything's fine. Do you know Tassen? Your neighbor's dog?"

Jonas had not even succeeded in taking his own life.

Neither had he succeeded in watching over Dina, nor had he been able to keep hold of Anna, despite that being the only thing in the world he wanted. He had never learned to live with his guilt, but he hadn't managed to shake it off either. Or diminish it; in his darkest moments, he had asked the God he did not believe in to help him. If only it could all turn into something he was capable of dealing with, he begged, so that it might be possible for him to build some kind of existence on the ruins of what had once been a life.

He sobbed so violently that the nurse grabbed a remote control to raise the mattress into a sitting position.

"There, there. I realize this hasn't been easy for you. We're looking after you now, you see. Do you want us to phone anyone? Your neighbor wasn't entirely sure whether you had—"

"No," Jonas whispered.

"Sure?"

Jonas nodded and turned his head away. The light from the ceiling lamps was excruciatingly bright, and he closed his eyes again.

"Now I'm going to talk to the doctor," the nurse said. "I'll find out whether you can have a sedative. This must have been a terrible strain, and it's absolutely understandable that you—"

"I just want to sleep," Jonas said, his voice barely audible.

"Back in a minute," he heard her say.

Jonas went on weeping. He had wept through more than sixteen years, but this was different. Unfamiliar warmth spread through his body, and he had to open his eyes to examine his own hands. He thought his tears tasted of vanilla and raisins, and they ran copiously, as if emanating from an inexhaustible source. Jonas inhaled, more deeply with every breath he took. It was as if he could breathe again at last, really breathe with his whole being, for the first time since one December morning in 2001.

He could not bear any more. He had not even managed to take his own life, but the sorrow and guilt he had carried on his own for all these years had finally grown far too heavy.

It was time to share it.

The thought ran through Jonas's mind before he fell asleep that he would do that at last.

"A what?" Henrik smiled as he repeated: "What did you say it was?"

"Tyrfing was a magic sword," Hanne reiterated. "Odin's grandson Sva . . . Svala . . ."

She had to cheat by glancing down at her notes.

"Svafrlami," she articulated with a rolling and overly distinct r. "He forces two dwarfs he had captured to forge a very special sword. It was to strike anything it was aimed at and cut through steel and stone. The dwarfs fashioned this fantastic sword, but they were pretty annoyed at being forced into it, and so they put a curse on it."

"And what was that, then?"

"That it would kill Svafrlami and also commit three crimes."

Henrik poured Coke Zero into a glass full of ice cubes. Ida had just come into Hanne's home office with refreshments before leaving for riding lessons with Nefis.

"Why are we sitting in here now that the others have gone?" he asked, looking around. "I've somehow become used to working at the dining table."

"Don't get into any habits in my house. I can't be bothered moving all these papers."

Henrik raised his glass a bit too abruptly and knocked it against his front teeth.

"Sorry," he let slip.

"You can safely say that the name Tyrfing was a rather unfortunate choice by Iselin," Hanne said, taking no notice of him and giving a lop-sided smile. "She met the same fate as Svafrlami. Tyrfing cost the woman her life."

"But that's what you're not entirely convinced of, surely?"

"Yes, I suppose so. Even though she didn't commit suicide, it's still reasonable to hold the possibility open that these writings of hers cost Iselin her life."

She helped herself from the cola bottle.

"And as far as Tyrfing's crimes are concerned," she said, taking a swig, "we're well past three and counting. Let me hear what you've discovered."

Henrik took a folder from his bag.

"Iselin Havørn," he began slowly, running his eyes down the top sheet before glancing up. "She was buried on Friday, did you know that?"

"Yes. It's been in all the newspapers, Henrik, even though that crazy Lotto prize was given most column space yesterday."

"EuroJackpot."

"Same thing."

"No—Lotto's the Norwegian lottery, VikingLotto is all the Nordic countries, and EuroJackpot is—"

"Henrik."

"Apologies."

Hanne gave an almost inaudible sigh before rotating her hand in a pleading gesture.

"Iselin Havørn," Henrik began again. "Born November 3, 1953, in Oslo. At that time her name was Iselin Solvang. I've found hardly any information about her childhood, except that she attended Lilleborg School as a child and, later, Hartvig Nissen's School. Which she only just scraped through, is my impression, even though she began studying law in Oslo when she left high school in 1972."

"Law was open to anyone then."

"Open? What do you mean?"

"Anyone at all could enter, regardless of exam results."

"What? For law? But that's one of the most difficult faculties to enter!"

"Now, yes. But not then. What happened after that?"

"Following two years of study, she dropped out and got a job as an industrial worker at the Christiania Spigerverk steel company. Incredibly odd, if you ask me."

"She was joining the proletariat."

"What?" He looked up in confusion.

"It fitted with her becoming part of the Marxist-Leninist movement, don't you think?" Hanne asked impatiently.

"Well, I haven't exactly found any kind of membership lists," Henrik said. "But I was at the university library yesterday. Have you ever been there?"

"There was a time before the Internet, Henrik. A pretty *long* time before the Internet, in fact. Of course, I've been there."

"Unbelievable number of books!"

"It's a university library. And this is going to take an unbelievable length of time if you're going to head off in all sorts of different directions."

"Sorry. At the university library, I found a fair amount of literature about the Marxist-Leninist movement in Norway. And, yes, by all accounts, Iselin Solvang was quite a central character in it. Did you know they used code names? I mean . . . code names! As if they were at war or something!"

When Hanne raised her eyes to the ceiling, he rushed on: "She stopped working at the steel company in 1978 and started at journalism college. She went to classes there for two years without ever taking any exams. Nevertheless, she got a job at *Dagbladet*, and at this point the sources multiply. Not exactly dealing with her life, as such, but the newspaper has digitized a lot of her material from that time. It's pretty easy to find a huge amount of what she wrote throughout the eighties. She started as an ordinary journalist, that is, writing more day-to-day material. Eventually she was able to write articles that were more like features, as well as some in-depth interviews. Quite good, in fact. In 1985 she started working for NRK."

Producing a picture, he placed it on the table in front of Hanne.

"You looked a bit . . . freaky in those days," he commented, with a smile.

"Don't look at me," Hanne said. "I was walking about in a police uniform!"

The photograph showed Iselin Solvang in front of a colossal NRK logo that Hanne assumed was made from polystyrene with a coat of blue paint. A tall, slim woman dressed in flowing robes, layer upon layer, all in blue and purple. Her hair was long on one side of her head and slightly shorter on the other. The short part was dyed a shade of blue, and the long side was bleached. What at first glance resembled huge salmon flies were hanging from her ears.

"She was given her own program in 1986," Henrik added. "It was called *Tivolini.*"

"I remember it," Hanne said absentmindedly as she studied the earrings to see if they were in fact fishing hooks. "A popular entertainment program of the type that was really trendy then, with a suitable dash of controversy. It ran for three seasons, if I'm not mistaken."

"Yes. Then Iselin became ill."

"Mercury poisoning," Hanne said. "So-called. I know all that."

"Well, it turned into more of a search for a diagnosis. Iselin subsequently wrote a lot about it. She felt listless and lacking energy, and at times it was so bad that she had to lie down in a dark, quiet room for days on end. Something like chronic fatigue syndrome patients nowadays."

"Chronic fatigue syndrome isn't a genuine diagnosis."

"Maybe not. But it's definitely a condition. A really distressing condition."

"Which obviously has a psychological origin," Hanne said stubbornly before returning the picture to the bundle. "People feel it's a matter of life and death for them to find a physical explanation for their symptoms. I can't fathom why."

"Maybe because it feels very physical?" Henrik ventured.

"There's no difference between physical pains and conditions on the one hand and psychological problems on the other. Physical and psychological are closely linked. Have you never had a stomachache when you were dreading something? Pains are not imaginary because they arise from a psychological condition. Far from it—they can be really authentic."

"Yes, true enough. But I think chronic fatigue syndrome might be a bit more complicated than—"

"Where did she end up?" Hanne interrupted him.

"With a bit of everything," Henrik went on. "Candida, for a while. A whole heap of food allergies. She was treated at one of those clinics, you know."

"Quacks."

"They came to the conclusion that it was mercury poisoning. Later, when computers became increasingly common, it turned out that she was hypersensitive to electricity. She had a whole host of her own protective gadgets made so that she could use a computer and a cell phone."

"Is that possible? There's no such thing on earth as—"

Henrik squeezed the cola bottle so tightly that the plastic crumpled.

"Hanne! Could you please stop spouting so many opinions? I've done exactly what you asked me to do. Now I'm telling you what I found out about Iselin Havørn. I'm not the one who believes all these things! You're splitting hairs with someone who's dead, Hanne, and I find that downright counterproductive."

"Okay. Do go on."

Hanne crossed her arms over her narrow chest and kept her mouth demonstratively buttoned. Henrik stared at her for a few seconds to make sure he would not be interrupted.

"During the period from 1989 to 1995, Iselin Havørn was certainly ill. She had also changed her name following what she later called . . ."

His skinny fingers riffled through the documents now perched on his lap.

". . . 'spiritual contact from the cosmic universe' was what she wrote. She had seen a sea eagle. Outside Reine in Lofoten."

Hanne pressed her lips even more tightly together. Henrik pretended not to notice.

"And even though she spent years trying to find out what was actually wrong with her, she claims that the sight of this huge eagle was the beginning of her long journey back to health. It was also at that time she came into contact with what you might call more conspiratorially inclined circles here on earth."

He shook his head gently.

"Conspiracy theories as a phenomenon are probably just as ancient as humanity itself," he continued. "But heavens above, the Internet has made it easier for those people. For Iselin, it began with a battle against the doctors who thought there was nothing wrong with her and against the pharmaceutical industry that she claimed was exclusively intent on creating ever-increasing opportunities to earn money from gullible and naive sick people. Her skepticism, or paranoia, call it what you will, developed further into something that can be briefly summarized as that Americans are behind most of what is wrong with the world. The rest is taken care of by Muslims. Moreover, they are also ruled by Americans, in fact. It is pretty difficult to follow her line of reasoning, to be honest."

"And Jews?" Hanne asked with a note of resignation. "Aren't they out to get us too?"

"Yes," Henrik said. "But then they're American! Whether they are Israelis, Norwegians, or British, the Jews and the United States are tarred with the same brush. At what time Iselin moved from general dissatisfaction with academic medicine to a belief that the CIA is Satan himself is difficult to pin down. All we know about Iselin from this period was actually recorded in retrospect. She was apparently really ill and did not work. Wrote nothing. At least nothing that has been made accessible to the public."

"Off her head," Hanne mumbled, only just audibly.

"In 1995 she was better. What she lived on during this period is anyone's guess. There are limits to how long you receive medical benefits. Maybe she was declared incapacitated for a time. Anyway, there's a lot to suggest that she was hard up. She didn't own her own apartment, and she moved around frequently. Until she got a job at a refugee reception center."

"A . . . what?"

"A refugee reception center. At Tanum in Bærum. It's closed now, but it was one of the first reception centers to be established."

Hanne opened her arms wide, taking in the paper printouts now stacked in four separate bundles before her.

"I've followed Tyrfing's writings for two years and gone all the way back to the first time that blog name appeared. But I've never seen any allusion anywhere to her ever working in a refugee reception center!"

"Seeing as Iselin Havørn had no wish to be identified, it's maybe not so strange that she made no reference to her CV, don't you think?"

He could not resist a smile.

"Touché," Hanne said. "Go on, then."

"But here, on the other hand . . ."

He fished out two sheets of paper in a red plastic cover that he set down on the table.

". . . is an article she wrote in 1997. Under her own full name, in fact. The job at that reception center was nothing but undercover journalism.

And now she was able to write about what it was *really* like in a reception center. You can read it at your leisure, but the short version is . . ."

With a sigh, he squashed the already damaged empty bottle. A brittle sound of shattered plastic provoked Hanne into pointing at the waste-paper basket.

"Asylum seekers are ungrateful. Filthy. Demanding and far too alien. They are not actually being persecuted. They are fortune hunters, and only the strongest of them travel here. The weak ones, the really desti-tute, never leave their respective homelands. We should help the ones who are truly distressed where they are and not admit any of them to Norway."

With a shrug, he dropped the bottle into the basket. "Along those lines. You know the script."

"That could easily be printed today," Hanne said. "But in 1997? The climate was quite different at that time. Was it really published in a Norwegian newspaper as early as that?"

"No."

"No? But—"

"It was turned down. By *Aftenposten* at any rate, I know for a fact, but whether she tried to get it published anywhere else, I've no idea. It's not available on the Internet."

"If it was turned down, how did you get hold of it?"

"Surplus information," Henrik said, smiling. "Easy as pie. This article was left over from the work done on the May 17 terrorist attack. As you know, we undertook a pretty thorough search of all possible racist, nationalist stuff over the past twenty years. Since so many of the sus-pects were getting on in years, we had to go pretty far back in time."

"To huge protests from press organizations, as far as I recall. We wanted to get our hands on unpublished material."

"Something the Supreme Court felt we had no need of," Henrik added. "More or less as expected, but it was worth a try. This article, though, was something one of our colleagues at Police Headquarters found. Or, more accurately, got hold of. From a now retired . . . night editor, I think it's called these days. At *Aftenposten*. He'd been so shocked by the content that he held on to it. And when half of Oslo was blown sky high, he secretly went to the police with a pretty cool stash of rejected articles he had collected in the course of a long career in Akersgata."

"And this was one of them?"

"Yes. I was given the task of going through the pile in the summer of 2014. I came across it yesterday when I was doing some research on Iselin as you asked me to and found this in the archives. Or . . . it's a copy, of course."

"Okay. Then we know that Iselin Havørn's attitude goes back to quite an early period. The blogger Tyrfing did not appear until 2007. What was she doing in the meantime?"

Henrik pushed his chair slightly to the left and fixed his eyes on the enormous painting on the wall. Hanne could not stand it, he knew. It had been a gift from Nefis and was tolerated for that reason. The night scene in Las Vegas was so realistic it could easily be mistaken for a photograph. He leaned forward a little and studied the two police cars in the foreground.

"After a few years of this and that in her working life," he said, sounding preoccupied, "she met her wife. Maria Kvam. They were obviously head over heels in love because they entered into a civil partnership only a few months later. Maria Kvam managed and held the majority of shares in a health food company, which at that time was relatively small. Annual turnover of around 20 million kroner and four employees. When Iselin came on the scene, they began to make headway."

"And they changed their name, I see?"

Hanne glanced at the chronological overview Henrik had constructed of Iselin Havørn's life and work.

"Yes. I need more time to make a more detailed summary, but from the company's web pages, it's clear that it was called PureHerb until Iselin became chairman of the board. An uncommonly active one, from all accounts. That happened only a few weeks before they got married. The new company name was VitaeBrass, and the name change coincided with the launch of the product they're best known for nowadays. BrassCure."

"Brass. An alloy of zinc and copper."

"Yes. BrassCure is a dietary supplement that contains brass."

"Heavens above—"

"In homeopathic quantities, of course. Which strictly speaking means next to nothing. The pill also contains a whole heap of vitamins and minerals we *do* need."

"And do *get* from the food we eat rather than exorbitant pills that are nothing but sheer—"

Henrik raised both hands.

"Hanne. Let's not discuss this. We're in agreement, okay? This cunning cocktail apparently has a miraculous effect on the skeleton, joints, and muscles. In other words, the physical ailments that to a large extent everyone suffers from with advancing age. The whole world is bamboozled, and VitaeBrass now has an annual turnover of 350 million kroner. In recent years its operating margin has been about 15 percent. Whatever you might think about Iselin Havørn, she certainly had a head for business."

They both fell silent.

Henrik took advantage of the opportunity, drumming his finger on the side of his nose, tapping his forehead, and banging his heels together three times in succession. Then he silently counted his shirt buttons from bottom to top and then back down again.

"To be honest, I don't see any homicide here," he said finally.

Hanne looked at him with that distant gaze of hers he had gradually learned to recognize all too readily. Hanne was well on the way to withdrawing into herself, and he had to speak quickly if he wanted to forestall her.

"I mean . . . I see your point with that letter. Of course I do. It's a bit weird. On the other hand, Iselin was almost certainly upset when she wrote it: hurt, angry, and depressed. It's maybe not so strange that—"

"That letter's a forgery," Hanne broke in scathingly. "A forged suicide letter nearly always suggests murder."

Abruptly, she began to rummage through the piles of documents in front of her and snatched up a newspaper cutting Henrik could not read from where he was sitting. Once again there was stony silence. The two of them often sat in silence, deep in thought, but this time the pause lasted so long that it began to feel uncomfortable.

"Iselin Havørn was buried," Hanne said all of a sudden, in an undertone, as if actually talking to herself.

"Er . . . yes. On Friday."

"It doesn't add up."

"What? Yes it does. The death notice was printed yesterday, and in the newspapers—"

"The Østre Gravlund cemetery," she cut in.

"Well?"

"You must go there. Talk to the custodian. Or a grave digger or who-ever it is these days can tell you something about the circumstances surrounding a burial."

"I think the best idea would be a church official," Henrik said. "But now? On a Sunday afternoon?"

Hanne tugged her sweater back from her wrist. "Half past four," she muttered. "It can wait until tomorrow."

"But what should I inquire about?"

"Everything. How many came to the funeral. Flowers, eulogies . . . the lot. And now you can go."

Henrik did not move a muscle.

He felt no need to touch his nose or drum his fingers. On the con-trary, he felt a warm weight in his body that made him sit deathly still. It was anger, as he had learned from experience. The first time he had felt it had been in a similar situation. Hanne had been sitting in the very same place, in her home office, with Henrik on the spare seat. Then as now, she had quite suddenly, in the middle of a conversation, clammed up and asked him to leave. The sense of his veins filling with molten lead was so unfamiliar and new that for a second, he thought it was the prelude to an attack. Something dangerous.

Now he knew better.

"Four days," he said, struggling to keep his voice steady. "That was what it took. Four days ago, you sat in there . . ."

He pointed his finger accusingly at the living room.

". . . and said you were sorry for how you sometimes treat me. It took just four days for you to forget the whole business. That apology wasn't worth . . ."

He was searching for a suitable word.

"You're right," she said before he found one. "You're absolutely right."

"*I'm not leaving*," he said, immediately aware that his voice was threat-ening to rise to falsetto. "And I certainly can't be bothered rooting around over there at Østre Gravlund searching for something I haven't a clue about, in a case I don't even think *is* a case. Just can't be bothered!"

Now his voice was shrill, and he felt tears brimming in his eyes.

"I understand," Hanne rushed to say. "Of course, I'll give you a better explanation of what—"

"On one condition." He was almost shrieking now. "I'll listen to you and do as you say, on one condition!"

"Whatever. You can calm down. You're perfectly right."

"You have to look at these," he yelled, crouching down for his bag and withdrawing a bundle of photocopies. "These!"

The bundle slapped down so hard on the table that the pictures scattered everywhere. One of them slid past the edge and fell on the floor.

"Sorry," he said meekly as he bent down to pick it up.

Hanne laughed softly. "Good grief, you've got quite a temper," she said. "That's good. So at least I've taught you something. What am I looking for?"

Henrik blushed to the roots of his hair and pushed the last picture closer to her.

"Just look," he said mildly. "These are the photographs from the crime scene in Stugguveien, where Anna Abrahamsen was murdered."

Hanne gave him a totally baffled look, before it dawned on her.

"Old Bonsaksen's case!"

"Right. Just look."

They heard a door open in the hallway. Ida was laughing loudly at something Nefis had said. A cupboard opened and closed, and footfalls could be heard on the way to the living room. Hanne paid no attention. She scrutinized each image carefully. First the photographs from the bathroom where Anna Abrahamsen had been killed. Then she studied every single one of the other pictures just as carefully, of the kitchen and the living room, the bedrooms and the little exercise room in the basement. Of the hallway, which could be considered almost a foyer, and the guest room in the basement, a room dominated by a huge billiard table with a green baize surface. When Hanne had perused the entire bundle, she scanned the pictures one more time.

Henrik thought he could smell fried onions.

"A brutal murder," Hanne said.

"Yes."

"You can see that she bled to death."

"Yes."

"If she'd survived, a plastic surgeon would have had a challenging task. Her chin is almost gone."

"Yes."

"And then there's another thing," she said, shoving the bundle aside slightly. "I've never seen a tidier crime scene in all my life. It's astonishing. Either Anna Abrahamsen was an obsessive bordering on mental illness, or else . . ."

Her eyes narrowed and she took hold of the cola glass, pale brown now from the melted ice cubes.

"Or else she was setting off somewhere," she said, slightly quizzically, as she stared straight at Henrik. "Or . . . was there to be an open house for the sale?"

"On New Year's Eve?"

Leaning back in his chair, Henrik placed one foot on the opposite knee. His rage seemed to have blown over. Quite the opposite now; he felt fired up, almost elated.

"I knew it," he said, clenching his slim hand in triumph. "I just knew it! That you would see it exactly as I had. And as nobody, absolutely nobody, did at the time."

He dropped his foot to the floor and leaned across the table, using his lower arms for support.

"Anna Abrahamsen was not selling her house. She wasn't planning an open house. She wasn't holding a New Year's party. Far from it—she was going to be entirely alone on this, probably the most festive of all the days in the year. In the kitchen, there's nothing to suggest that she was going to make herself something nice to eat. Or any kind of food at all, for that matter. If she died just before midnight, she had sat there all evening without a morsel of food. The dishwasher was empty. The garbage can the same. The counters were spotless. And as you see here . . ."

He swiftly produced a picture of the kitchen, where the fridge was visible on the far left.

"If the photographer had opened the door, the photo would show that the fridge was bare."

"How do you know that?"

"I called Bonsaksen. You said it yourself when I showed you this case for the first time: it was exceptionally thoroughly investigated. Bonsaksen has gone around mulling over it for years, and he remembers it well. The fridge was empty, he was certain on that point, apart from a couple of bottles of water. And not only that . . ."

The enticing smells of Sunday dinner being prepared in the kitchen made his stomach rumble. Noisily. He touched his abdomen apologetically.

"The fridge was sparkling clean. It stank of bleach, Hanne. Bonsaksen was positive on that point. He just hadn't placed much importance on it at the time. It didn't appear to have the least significance for the homicide case, in his opinion."

"But you think it does?"

"Yes."

"How?"

There was a knock at the door, and Ida popped her head in without waiting for an answer.

"Dinner is served in half an hour. You're staying, aren't you, Henrik?"

"Yes, please" was his rapid response.

"Good," Ida said as she closed the door.

"What relevance does a clean fridge have for the murder of Anna Abrahamsen?" Hanne repeated.

Henrik held eye contact with her for some time, as if he needed to test his theory on himself one more time before daring to air it to her.

"There are very few reasons to clean your house like that," he ventured and picked up the bundle of photographs. "One is that it is to be shown to other people prior to being sold. We can exclude that. There's no sign that a sale of any kind was imminent. I've checked the house-for-sale ads for the time in question, and it's not—"

"Have you really?" Hanne took on a surprised, almost dubious, expression. "Have you really checked the house sales ads for Christmas 2003?"

"Yes. There are plenty of archive services on the Internet. It cost me a bit, but it was well worth it."

Hanne gave an inscrutable smile; he had to put down the photos to sit on his hands again.

"Another reason could be leaving on an extended journey," he continued, more eagerly now. "Not that everyone goes to the trouble of making their house immaculate before going on a trip, but I make sure always to empty the fridge at least."

Hanne nodded gently.

"But nothing suggests that Anna was going away. In fact, it emerges from the case documents that she had two important meetings at work immediately after New Year's. She was a sales director for Bilia car showrooms. Specialized in fleet sales, meaning company cars and major contracts with various businesses. One of her meetings was with the police.

The Emergency Squad was to have thirty new vehicles and had chosen Volvo. An important contract, in other words. One of the investigators was excessively ambitious and had written down the tiniest details of what Anna's closest subordinates had said during the interview."

"Okay," Hanne said. "So she wasn't going anywhere, and she wasn't selling the house. Why was the house so immaculately clean and tidy, then?"

"There's another possible reason," Henrik said.

Now he hesitated again. Hanne's smile broadened, and he chose to interpret that as a form of encouragement.

"Suicide," she suggested, beating him to it.

"Yes," Henrik squeaked. He cleared his throat and repeated loudly: "Yes. Suicide."

Hanne burst into that new type of deeper laughter that seemed so genuine. So inclusive, Henrik felt, and he smiled back sheepishly even though he had no clue why she was laughing so heartily.

"So you believe," she began, trying to be serious, "so you believe that . . ."

Henrik had never seen her like this. Tears of laughter were running down her face. She wiped them away with the back of her hand, over and over again. Her mascara had run a little, he saw, and he knocked his heels together at such a neurotic speed that the table began to shake.

Hanne dried her eyes yet again and cleared her throat. "So we're faced with one case that looks like a suicide," she began over again, "but which I'm convinced is actually a homicide." She put her left hand on one of the bundles on the table. "And then another case, in which a man has served eight years for murdering his wife, which you believe might actually be a suicide." She put her right hand on the photographs of Anna's house.

"Yes," Henrik said, "and the worst thing is . . ." Now he was the one who began to laugh. He opened out his arms and exclaimed: "We've absolutely zero authority in either of these cases. They're quite simply not ours, Hanne. So what on earth do we do?"

"We behave like the good citizens and the outstanding police officers that we are. And as far as this vacuous hypothesis of yours about Anna Abrahamsen is concerned, I'd suggest . . . Let me see the whole folder."

Henrik bent over and picked up Bonsaksen's blue ring binder. It was a touch slimmer now, since he had extracted all the photographs. He slid it across to her, and she opened it. For a few seconds, she browsed through the by now pretty dog-eared documents before tapping her index finger repeatedly on one page.

"Just as I recall it," she said, sounding satisfied. "An unusually well-investigated case, this here. Even the victim's personal details are uncommonly thoroughly written down. Here . . ." She turned the ring binder and pushed it back across to him. "Anna's GP."

Henrik looked at the page and then up again. "Er . . . yes?"

"With the story of suffering related in this binder, it would not surprise me if Anna went to a psychologist or a psychiatrist. The normal way to do that is through your GP. Contact her, this doctor . . ." She tilted her head and read. "Sivesind. Christine Sivesind. Ask her where Anna finally got help."

"Why?"

"Henrik, come on. You've invented a theory that Anna Abrahamsen committed suicide, exclusively based on her home being so clean and tidy. Don't you think that's a bit thin?"

"I suppose so—"

"So try to put more meat on the bones. Talk to Dr. Sivesind."

"Doctors have a duty of confidentiality," he commented in a subdued tone. "Even after death."

"When they're dead, it's a bit difficult for them to speak."

"I mean . . . after the patient's death."

"They're usually impressed by a police badge. And after twelve years, it can't be so damn harmful. As I've told you countless times, Henrik, it's never illegal to ask. Asking people is the most important tool in every policeman's box of tricks." She folded her hands behind her neck and smiled. "Ask. Maybe Anna Abrahamsen really was suicidal."

"But why . . ." Henrik smacked his heels together three times before going on: "We're agreed that the case was investigated well. That Bonsaksen was painstaking and conscientious. Why hasn't he spoken to the doctor or a possible psychologist?"

Hanne let go of her neck and rolled her wheelchair across to his side. It seemed as if she had lost weight. Her pale-blue V-neck sweater looked baggier than before, and her knuckles could be seen clearly though her transparent skin when she put her hand on his thigh. Her touching him, voluntarily and without being in need of assistance, was something that had rarely happened before. Aware of her fragrance as she leaned against him, he began to blush.

"Bonsaksen saw a homicide," Hanne said slowly. "Everyone who came to the crime scene saw a homicide. For a number of reasons, as the ring binder emphatically shows, but, of course, first and foremost because there was no gun to be found. The assumption was understandable, but nonetheless it could have been a mistake. Personally, if I'd been the one to take a closer look at this case, I'd first look for another possible perpetrator. Why don't you start there instead of looking more intently at the possibility of suicide?"

"Because I can't find a shred of evidence pointing to any other perpetrator. Not in the entire case. Whatever way you twist it and turn it, Anna died behind locked doors some time before midnight on New Year's Eve. She was not sexually assaulted. Nothing was stolen from the house, as far as the police could ascertain. The only things missing were the gun and Anna's cell phone. If one of the partygoers at her neighbor's house sneaked out for some absurd reason and killed her by somehow miraculously entering and exiting a locked house without leaving any traces, it must have been totally lacking in motive. They were all checked out of the case, every single one of them."

Henrik gave a sigh of resignation.

"The only person who could have had any trace of a motive for killing her, apart from Jonas, was her sister, Benedicte. She had keys, it was their shared childhood home, and she had kept one of the storerooms. Later it turned out that she inherited from her sister, and the legacy was not inconsiderable. The problem was—"

"She had an absolutely 100 percent watertight alibi," Hanne said. "Something that can hardly be said for Jonas."

"Exactly. Jonas was on the scene at an extremely critical point in time. He had every reason to kill his wife. Disappointment. Rejection. Hate, perhaps, God only knows there can be powerful emotions between couples who separate. Money too; he didn't yet know that the separation had been granted and that he wouldn't inherit anything from Anna. No . . ."

He pursed his mouth and took a deep breath. Unaccustomed to having Hanne so close to him, he caught himself pushing his chair back a little.

"If Bonsaksen is right that Jonas did not kill his wife, then she must have done it herself," he said, sounding discouraged. "And got rid of the gun postmortem, somehow. Something of a task trying to unravel that mystery. What I'd most like is to . . ." He tossed his pen on the desk. ". . . give up."

Hanne smiled. "You never give up, Henrik. You're made of sterner stuff. If you really have decided to find out whether Anna Abrahamsen died by her own hand, then you ought to start with her psychologist."

She raised her hands suddenly and rolled back her chair. "But first you're going to speak to that chapel custodian at Østre Gravlund cemetery," she said. "Tomorrow without fail."

MONDAY, JANUARY 18, 2016

Jonas Abrahamsen had slept all through Sunday and well into the following day. At some time the previous evening, his sleep had been slightly disturbed when the catheter and various monitoring devices had been removed while he watched with apathy. Someone said something about being stable, and he slipped back into a blessed, dreamless slumber.

When he awoke at 5:30 on Monday morning, he felt a sense of peace so unfamiliar that it made him ravenous. The hospital had little to offer at this early hour, but a night nurse had shared her bag meal with him. When the white-clad nurse in clogs left, he wolfed down everything she had given him. Then he pulled the cannula from the back of his right hand and planted his feet on the floor.

He wanted to go home.

It dawned on him that he had been driven here stark naked. The washed-out pajamas they had put on him were hardly suitable for wearing outdoors, especially if it was as cold outside as it had been when he lay down near the woodshed barely two days ago.

Jonas tried to walk across the floor.

His legs held. He felt weak and quite dizzy, but had no difficulty reaching the bathroom. The worst of his hunger had been allayed, and he felt an intense craving for coffee. But first of all he had to pee.

The yellow stream sang against the toilet bowl. When he straightened his back, he already felt better. The shower in the corner looked so tempting that he peeled off his pajamas and turned on the water. The scalding hot spray lashed his back like a whip. He soaped himself twice, from head to toe, and stood so long on the white tiles watching the foam disappear down the drain that his skin turned scarlet.

Putting on the used pajamas did not seem tempting, but Jonas had no choice. As he pulled them on before he was properly dry, clouds of steam made it difficult for him to breathe.

"You can't . . ."

The nurse had returned.

Jonas had just emerged from the bathroom. The nurse retreated to the open door leading into the corridor, as if she feared he would take off.

"Have you yanked out your cannula?" she asked in alarm, quite unnecessarily: a thin trickle of blood still oozed from the back of his hand where he had forced it out.

"I want to go home," Jonas said quietly. "You have to sign me out."

"It's far too soon, my dear. Come here, now, and I'll give you a new cannula."

She crossed to the bed and smacked it with enthusiasm, as if encouraging a dog to jump onto the white bedclothes.

"I'd appreciate talking to the doctor," Jonas said in a determined voice. "Of course, I'm grateful for you taking good care of me after my . . . my little accident. But now I want to go home."

The nurse's eyes flickered. She looked worried, and Jonas tried to squeeze out a smile. The woman grew noticeably more alarmed as she walked sideways to the door.

"If you lie down, I'll bring the doctor on duty."

"I also need some clothes," Jonas said, walking obediently to the bed. "To borrow, please."

When she returned fifteen minutes later with a corpulent, completely bald doctor, Jonas had vanished. He had arrived at the hospital without a stitch and without a single possession.

He left nothing behind either.

For once Henrik had taken a taxi.

Admittedly it was not just as cold now as it had been two days earlier, but it had started to snow. During the night, a blanket of snow a foot and a half deep had enveloped Oslo, and the biting wind forced the snow to form impassable steep drifts all over. The journey in the white Mercedes had taken three-quarters of an hour. On a good day Henrik could have arrived faster on foot.

The taxi left him outside the main entrance to the Østre Gravlund cemetery in Tvetenveien. Farther along the road, a truck with foreign license plates had jackknifed, leaving half its trailer in the ditch. The cabin stretched across the traffic lane, and the taxi driver was muttering a string of juicy oaths. Henrik hardly had time to pay and secure a receipt before the taxi began to turn in order to drive back the same way it had come.

Someone had just cleared the couple of hundred yards of straight road leading up to the chapel. It would be necessary to do so again fairly soon. Henrik fished out a cap from his pocket and pulled it well down over his ears, shivering as the wind caught him from the side. He could barely see the long rows of gravestones through the whirling snow flurries. Also, some of the markers were completely buried in all the whiteness.

Henrik was already freezing by the time he reached the doors of the austere chapel, a typical sixties building. Brushing snow from his jacket, he kicked the wall with his feet and crammed the cap into his pocket again. As he made to step inside, the door opened.

"You're punctual," said a man in a suit with smoothed-back strands of black hair that looked as if they had been glued to his scalp one by one. "Well done in this weather!"

It crossed Henrik's mind that his hair must be dyed, and it was also so sparse that his pink scalp was visible in narrow, straight lines between the black stripes. It made the man look like a peculiar insect. He held out his hand: it was slim, bony, and dry as dust.

"This way," he said, leading Henrik along two corridors and into an office. "Take a seat. Coffee?"

"No thanks."

Henrik sat down. The room was bright and neutral, and it showed no sign of belonging to a house of God apart from a big Bible allocated a shelf all to itself. A framed map of the graveyard hung on one wall, but apart from that, the room was fairly bare.

"It's to do with what I mentioned on the phone, that funeral last Friday," Henrik said with a friendly smile. "Iselin Havørn."

"I appreciate that."

The chapel custodian, Mauritz Bolle, had sat down on a substantial pale-brown office chair. He made a steeple with his hands and put his elbows on the desk.

"We've had a lot of inquiries," he said, nodding, as if agreeing with himself. "The press, you know. No one had been able to find out where and when the ceremony was to take place. Not until it was too late."

He kept nodding his head.

"But my lips have been sealed. When it comes to you representatives of the police, though, that's another matter. Another matter entirely. What can I do for you?"

Before Henrik got as far as answering, Mauritz Bolle began to speak again.

"Dare I ask what is of interest to the police? Regarding a small burial service, I mean?"

"I can't really divulge any of that," Henrik told him, leaning forward with a reassuring smile. "I'm sure you understand. But I'm very grateful for you agreeing to see me. Just a couple of questions."

"Go ahead," the custodian said, smiling with teeth so pearly white and brilliant even they must have been bought at a knockdown price. "Ask away."

"Were there many participants . . . uh . . . mourners at the funeral?"

Henrik set up a new notes page on his phone.

"No. Only four or five people. Five, I believe?"

The custodian cocked his head in an exaggerated gesture of contemplation: with his elongated neck and sharp elbows, he looked more and more like a praying mantis.

"Five?" Henrik exclaimed. "Did only five people attend Iselin Havørn's funeral?"

"Yes. Certainly no more than that. I exchanged a few words with the funeral director, and as far as I understood, they had gone to great lengths to keep it all sec . . . discreet. You know. With all these writings and that sort of thing. Probably not too easy for the wife. Yes, they're all called wives these days, even in these equal-sex relationships."

"Same-sex," Henrik said, smiling. "So the wife was present?"

"Maria Kvam," Mauritz Bolle said, with a nod. "Good-looking woman. Didn't look in the slightest like . . ."

His hands lost their steepled pose and he put them on his lap.

"You know," he said. "She didn't look at all like that. Devastated, poor woman. On her way out to the burial, she seemed on the point of fainting, I thought. Quite ready to drop. Not that she was weeping so terribly much, but she was pale, and as I said, she was almost staggering. Anyway, it must have been someone else who made the arrangements with the funeral directors. It really must have been."

"Why is that?" Henrik asked without glancing up from his phone, where he was busy taking notes.

"It's simply not done to be buried like that," the man answered stiffly. "Not by anyone who's fond of you."

"What do you mean by that?"

"One wreath. Just one wreath. It was grand enough and beautiful too, but the mourning ribbon was unusually lacking in . . . warmth? Yes. It wasn't exactly very personal, to put it that way."

"What did it say?"

"I don't quite remember, but it was something about being from friends and colleagues. Nothing from the wife. And that coffin . . ."

He smacked his lips meaningfully and raised his eyebrows.

"What about it?"

"It's not for me to judge," Mauritz Bolle said, showing the flats of his hands. "It's absolutely not for me to judge!"

"But?" Henrik gave him some encouragement when the man in the pale-brown chair pressed his lips firmly together.

"It was of the very simplest kind, to be honest. Of the type that . . ."

Now he was wringing his hands before suddenly laying them on the desk in front of him. They were unusually well manicured for a man, Henrik noticed: perfectly rounded, clean, and so shiny they must have nail polish on them.

"You know," he said after yet another pause. "There are some among us who don't have any family or especially many friends. If anyone at all. The lonely. The extremely poor. The chronically ill—usually in the mind, if you get my drift. They too have to be laid to rest. Then they usually use the very cheapest kind of coffin. After all, it's the public authorities that pay in those instances."

Henrik had no idea that there were price differences even in death.

"I see. And what kind of coffin is that, then?"

"Particleboard."

Mauritz Bolle leaned forward to add in a whisper: "I call it cardboard, to be honest. You get them for next to nothing."

"Which means?"

"Four, five thousand."

Gulping, Henrik looked up from his phone.

"I see. And what do the most expensive ones cost?"

"Oh, there's really no upper limit. When your nearest and dearest sets out on their last journey, it's normal to spend fifteen to twenty thousand. At least."

"Is dying so expensive?" slipped out of Henrik. "After all, that coffin's just going to be burned!"

"In this case, it was going into the ground," the custodian corrected him. "And we're only talking about the price of the coffin now. In addition there are flowers and other decorations, the funeral programs . . ."

He counted on his fingers. They were really fascinatingly long.

". . . and usually a performance of some kind. A soloist. Also there's a reception of some sort, of course, with food and drink and . . ."

He broke off by running his left hand over his greasy hair.

"I don't think that happened in this case either. On the whole, I must permit myself to say, and only because it's the police asking, and absolutely for that reason alone, that it was fairly . . ."

Now he obviously had grounds for weighing his words with care.

"Dismal," he declared. "It was a dismal little ceremony. I've been following the newspaper reports in the past few weeks, and it certainly wasn't the case that the deceased was without means. Not the widow either. And even though there were rumors of suicide, and you can, of course, understand that the relatives did not exactly wish . . . anything extravagant, it was very striking. We were all astounded. All of us."

He surveyed the room, as if the employees in question at Østre Gravlund cemetery were assembled there.

"But we said nothing, of course," he added.

Henrik's phone gave a little growl. "Sorry," he said quickly and used his thumb to open the text message.

Checked in the database. The pills were not prescribed for Iselin. She has never had any medicines that have had to be registered. Is this of any significance? Amanda

He read the message and quick as a flash keyed in a response.

Maybe. If I were you, I'd check if any of Iselin's friends/fam/colleagues use anti-depr. Henrik

". . . hostile," Bolle concluded.

"What did you say?" Henrik asked. He had been lost in thought.

"I said that somebody else must have taken care of the practical arrangements for this funeral. Because if it had been my wife who had given me such a service, I would have interpreted it as hostile, not to put too fine a point on it."

"Hostile?" Henrik repeated in surprise.

"Yes. I would definitely say so. Well, I couldn't see anything if I was dead, of course, but you get my point. I've worked here at Østre Gravlund for twenty-three years and have seen most things. There can be great dignity in the smallest funeral. With a cardboard coffin and no one present apart from the clergyman and myself. Every person's meeting with God should be prepared with the decency and the . . . holiness such an occasion calls for. But when you actually have family, friends, and are well off on top of all that . . ."

Once again he smacked his lips in disapproval.

"Then I'd simply interpret it as a punishment. Of the deceased. Yes. A hostile act and a punishment."

He flashed a smile, as if to take the edge off his words.

"But as I said, it's not up to me to judge. And it probably wasn't the wife who was behind it. I just can't imagine that it was."

He stared at Henrik for a moment, before tilting his head to one side and grimacing with his row of pearls once again.

"But what do you think?"

It had been easier to leave the hospital than Jonas had feared. Only ten yards along the corridor, he had come across an outdoor jacket and a pair of Wellington boots in a cleaning cabinet that was left open. A net shopping bag with three brochures for charter vacations was also hanging on a hook by the door, and there was a thermos on the floor, the contents of which he did not take any time to examine. Presumably he was helping himself to a cleaner's belongings, and his pricking conscience had made him hesitate. When he heard someone approach in the corridor, however, he had pulled the door closed and struggled into both the jacket and boots.

The jacket was far too big, and the boots smelled foul.

The smell was particularly noticeable when he hauled himself into one of the taxis idling not far from the main entrance. The driver had fortunately not managed to catch sight of his pajama trousers before Jonas was ensconced in the backseat.

Only when they arrived at the snowed-in track in Maridalen did it come to light that Jonas had no money. Following a tirade of swear words in both Norwegian and Urdu, the driver finally realized it would be simpler to let Jonas find his way up to the house through the snow to get some money rather than call the police. In these road conditions, it was doubtful whether they would take a trip up to Maridalen for a measly unpaid taxi fare anyway.

It was now one o'clock.

Jonas was still shivering with cold, especially his feet. Wading through the snow with bare feet stuck inside a pair of old rubber boots had taken its toll, and the situation was not improved by the temperature in the little house having dropped to just above freezing in his absence. He had fed the round stove in the corner before putting on his own clothes. Now at least he had an area around the stove in which the temperature was tolerable. He had dragged a chair across and massaged his bare feet energetically for some time before pulling on his thick woolen socks and perching them on a stool only a foot from the flames.

It was a long time since he had felt so calm.

He was not happy. Not even content. Far from it—he did not feel much at all. It was liberation. He let himself be filled with the emptiness he had woken to the previous day, the great nothingness that had made it possible for him to sleep for nearly twenty-four hours at a stretch. He was still breathing more deeply and effectively than he could ever remember. The intermittent cramps, the stabbing pains in his heart, and the grumbling aches that had shifted around his body ever since Dina died were gone.

Only the frost had settled deep inside him.

He had kept the stove going for several hours and put on two woolen sweaters, one on top of the other. All the same, it was only here, really close to the dancing flames he could make out through the half-open air vent in the stove door, where his teeth did not chatter.

Since he'd shared the night nurse's packed meal at the hospital, he had eaten only a can of baked beans and drunk so much coffee that he had run out. He ought to excavate the thirteen-year-old Golf parked in the yard outside, now almost completely snowed in. It was possible that the intense cold had finished off the battery, but he had a battery charger on the kitchen counter.

First, he would have to clear the track.

He struggled to stand up and made for a cabinet beside the front door. He counted out six hand and foot warmers from an old plastic box. Unpacking them, he rubbed each one between his hands to activate the warming chemical effect and put two of them in each of his rugged hunting boots. He pulled on his quilted jacket, cap, and scarf. Finally, he inserted a hand warmer in each of his mittens.

It helped. He was no longer freezing. He stood, wrapped in wool and down, gradually thawing out. The stove was crackling furiously, but nevertheless he trudged across and threw on another log. He left the stove door open, knelt down, and peered into the flickering flames. They scorched his face, and he had to screw up his eyes to protect them.

He felt an unaccustomed twitch around his mouth.

Slowly, he drew on one mitten and put a wary hand to his face as he got to his feet and crossed the room to a black-speckled mirror at the kitchen sink.

He saw that he was smiling.

A sort of smile, at least. His teeth were visible, and the wrinkles between the sides of his nose and the corners of his mouth were deep and distinct.

Suddenly he grew really serious. He used his fingertips to examine his face, the stubble scraping his skin, and for the first time, he noticed that his eyebrows were growing bushy. Steel-gray devil's horns like an old man's.

Truly, life had given him a real beating. It had torn him to rags, crippled him, and knocked him to the ground time after time. In the end it had driven him out, naked, in below-freezing weather, without even giving him permission to die.

He had endured it all.

Always.

But no longer. It was time to get his own back, and deep down, behind that blessed emptiness that made it possible to stretch his spine and breathe freely, he had an inkling of how to do it.

As the reflection in the mirror grimaced back at him, he went out to clear the snow.

"When will sentence be passed?"

The man in the doorway was so tall he had to dip his head when he walked through doors. Now he leaned on the doorframe with his hands in his pockets and his neck at an angle. He had a bag packed with what looked like a bundle of documents clamped between his arm and his body.

Henrik glanced up: he was so absorbed in his own thoughts he had not even noticed the Superintendent's presence.

"Have you been standing there long?" he asked in bewilderment.

"Well, long enough to see that you're pretty engrossed in something. When's sentencing?"

"It's still unclear. Hanne Wilhelmsen reckons the end of the month. Major case, you know. Several accused. A lot for the judge to write up, that sort of thing."

"Yes."

Henrik Holme's boss took his hands from his pockets and stepped into the room. He perched on the edge of the desk and set the bag down at his feet. He half-turned to face Henrik, who drew back.

"What are you working on?"

Superintendent Ulf Sandvik nodded at one end of the desk, where the illegally appropriated copy set of Iselin Havørn's case was fortunately below the worn, bulky ring binder containing documents from the criminal case against Jonas Abrahamsen.

"This and that," Henrik muttered, tapping the side of his nose three times.

"I bumped into the Police Chief along there." Sandvik nodded in the direction of the corridor. "She says you're at a loose end at the moment."

"Well, yes, I suppose."

Henrik attempted an exercise Hanne had taught him. He filled his lungs, and with all the strength he could muster, he forced the air down into his abdominal cavity. It gave him a sudden headache, and his eyes looked as if they would pop out of his head.

"I'm keeping busy with some . . . *hic* . . . minor matters. They're Hanne's, those over there. You could say that I'm . . . helping her."

Ulf Sandvik straightened up. Henrik had heard that he was almost six foot six in height. From where Henrik sat, reclining tensely in his chair, the man looked more than seven feet tall.

"Great that you're helping out, Henrik, but Hanne Wilhelmsen has to manage on her own if the Police Chief hasn't ordered you to assist her. We can't have you kicking your heels, you know. After all your wages are paid by taxpayers."

"*Hic.*"

"I received these today." Sandvik opened the plastic bag and, as suspected, drew out a sizable bundle of papers. "Statistics," he said tersely. "There's guidance at the top here . . ."

He slapped the biggest hand on earth on top of the bundle.

"And it's all to be completed by Friday afternoon. That's barely enough time, I think, so you'll have to put your back into it. If you want to help Wilhelmsen, you'll have to do so in your free time. There won't be much of that this week."

Henrik, who had held his breath for so long that his face was now crimson, hiccupped noisily. Sandvik gave a crooked smile.

"Water," he suggested. "Drink a glass of water. Backward. From the opposite side, I mean. Like this."

He held an imaginary glass of water in his hand and took a deep bow with his hand under his chin. Henrik understood none of it.

"Yes," he said weakly. "*Hic.*"

Sandvik gazed at the blue ring binder and took a step closer. "Can I take a peek?"

Hanne would have been able to deal with this. She would have thought of something. Something quite credible, probably a lie as black as coal, but something that would make the Superintendent leave the office, cheerful and content, without having given the blue ring binder as much as a glance.

Hanne would have had ready answers.

"Yes," Henrik squeaked.

Sandvik hesitated. "Has Bonsaksen paid you a visit?" he asked.

"Yes. *Hic.*"

"I thought I recognized that ring binder. It bothers him, that case."

"Yes."

"But it has no business here with you, Henrik."

A huge forefinger ran across the worn blue ring binder with dog-eared corners and old stains left by coffee cups. Henrik closed his eyes and tried to picture how you drank water backward. It was impossible. When he opened them again, Ulf Sandvik had slipped one hand back into his khaki trousers.

"In your spare time, okay? Only in your spare time?"

Henrik nodded energetically.

"And you won't have any of that before Friday," Sandvik said as he disappeared out the door, giving him a thumbs-up as he left. "The statistics have to be ready by Friday at noon. Understood?"

He was gone before Henrik came up with an answer.

Maria Kvam was in serious doubt.

She had already emptied the apartment of ornaments, knickknacks, brass, ceramics, and glass and carted off the colossal painting of a sea eagle to the auction company, Blomqvist, for an appraisal. The man there who had spoken to her had not expressed great hopes, but she wanted to sell it regardless.

In the worst-case scenario, give it away, she had declared and then gone home.

The various items of furniture were still positioned exactly where they had always been. Bereft of all Iselin's trappings, the extremely deep sofa and the dark, shabby-chic coffee table looked out of place. After all, this was a modern apartment, only two years old, and Maria had come to the conclusion that she would have to get rid of absolutely everything if she were ever to have things the way she wanted.

Clean lines and cool colors and no trace of Iselin.

Now Maria sat on the coffee table, resting her elbows on her thighs.

Maybe it was time to move out.

For the first time since she had met Iselin, she felt a longing for her own childhood home. She still owned it. For years, she had rented it to the Russian ambassador, a tenancy agreement that paid handsomely and brought extremely few problems. They took care of cleaning and redecoration between every family that moved in, and there was never any nonsense with the rent. The last time Maria had been there, less than six months ago, the place had been in tip-top condition. The garden too: the embassy employed its own gardeners who obviously knew what they were doing. The property had never looked better.

She got to her feet and headed for the capacious wardrobe inside the bedroom. Iselin's torn clothes still lay piled up at one end of it. She paid no heed and began to turn the dial on the safe in accordance with the code she knew by heart and had not written down anywhere.

Iselin had also memorized the code, but she did not use the safe for anything apart from silverware and jewelry when they went on vacation. Maria let the heavy door swing open, and her eyes caught sight of the big plastic container on the top shelf. It was empty. This was what Iselin used to stow her bric-a-brac, and Maria grabbed it and threw it on top of the bundle of rags in the corner. With care, she lifted out her own belongings and placed them on the floor.

A photo album from when she was little.

Bank statements and stock certificates for VitaeBrass and tax returns for the last ten years. Her divorce papers from 2006: she and Roar, childless and amicable, had finally dealt with the formalities only three months before Maria met Iselin. An exquisite box with a pair of diamond earrings she had inherited from her grandmother. Papers, objects, and memorabilia. Iselin had been unable to grasp the purpose of such a large safe, but it had been filled fairly quickly. What Iselin had never known was that the thick steel walls, in addition to being secure, also made it possible to construct a secret compartment in the base.

Iselin had been everything to Maria.

They had met at a function during the Alternative Trade Fair one cold September evening in 2006. Maria was deeply skeptical about PureHerb, as it was then still called, of spending money on a booth there. Trying to outstrip all the others by renting as much as a hundred thousand square feet at Vallhall, an indoor sports arena in the east end of Oslo, seemed even more of a waste. Halvor Stenskar had been the one who insisted on it. The company was operating fairly well, but it seemed that the customer base was too restricted—mostly older people. Ordinary people without any real belief in either herbs or sunflower oil, but who thought at least they couldn't do any harm. To be on the safe side, so to speak, was the reason most had given when the company, only six months earlier, had conducted a customer survey.

They had to extend their scope, Halvor had insisted. Cater to people who were true believers.

Everything indicated it was just a matter of months until the promising new product would be ready to be launched on the market. It had been included when the firm had bought a company in Peru, from the time when PureHerb was nothing more than a few lines in the company registry at Brønnøysund. Unfortunately the formula had contained ingredients that Norwegian regulations defined as medicines. It would never be accepted, and it had taken time to change the formula. Not only because the rights holders in Peru proved particularly obstinate—they had based their concoction on an old Inca recipe and felt it disrespectful to alter—but also because it all cost money. A lot of money, and that was something PureHerb did not possess.

However, most of that was accomplished now, and Halvor had been eager to make an impression on the alternative health market.

In the gathering of some of the weirdest people Maria had ever seen and met, the idea of an old-fashioned reception seemed totally absurd. At any rate, Halvor had had the good sense not to offer alcohol at their stand when the trade fair was over and the function began. They offered sixteen types of herbs; extract of ash, birch, and juniper; and charcoal-filtered lukewarm water. The food was organic and vegetarian and, to Maria's great surprise, quite delicious.

And so it all took off.

The party was a huge success and subsequently became a highly esteemed tradition at every subsequent Alternative Trade Fair. It seemed as if all the exhibitors came to the PureHerb stand to celebrate yet another successful fair: soothsayers and angel whisperers, arche-type experts and exorcists, astrologists, crystal therapists, and the occasional yoga instructor.

Maria had not caught sight of Iselin until it was all nearly done, which was strange, considering what she looked like. Iselin Havørn was a woman who was far from ashamed of her six-foot frame. Quite the opposite. She had adopted a stately, almost laid-back gait, with her chest and chin jutting forward as if she were about to engage in sword-play. Although her big shoes were sensible enough, she had chosen a pair with soles at least two inches thick. Later that night when they had been kicked off and lay in a corner of her bedroom, it ran through Maria's mind that they were more or less platform shoes.

Iselin had never given up the loose garments she had become famous for in the eighties. On that marvelous evening in the autumn of 2006, when for the very first time Maria met a woman she could fall in love with, Iselin was dressed in red. At least eight shades of red, from pale ashes of roses on top in the form of a voluminous shawl, through darker shades down to a deep, blood-red tunic that reached to her ankles.

No one else could have carried off such clothes and colors.

Iselin became the one for Maria, and they moved in together forty-eight hours later.

In the years just before they met, Iselin had written an anonymous blog. She was not particularly secretive about it, and most of the party-goers that first evening were aware she was the one behind it. It was called *skepticism.no* and generated quite a lot of traffic because her readers misunderstood the name. She was not a skeptic in the normal sense of the word—quite the opposite in fact. It was the pharmaceutical industry she mistrusted. Doctors too. She also lacked confidence in the health authorities, and she had spent two years of her life getting people to appreciate that these three groups formed a highly unholy trinity. A triad, she called them, a criminal, capitalist conspiracy with international ramifications.

It all centered on money, she asserted. Not illness. Not suffering. Not pain relief. And certainly not human beings. Money was the root of all evil and, furthermore, something Iselin did not have very much of. Surprisingly enough, it soon turned out that she had remarkable abilities as a capitalist as soon as she had the opportunity. She had excellent connections with people suffering from conditions that academic medicine neither acknowledged nor understood. Already established as something of a character—also in a physical sense—among vaccine opponents and others with an alternative view of science, she maneuvered PureHerb in record time into a new and far more profitable direction.

Eighteen months later, the company had multiplied its turnover under a new name. The ancient Inca remedy with the new name BrassCure became a huge success, not least thanks to Iselin's talents in marketing strategy. She was a star at what she despised most in the world and looked as if she enjoyed it enormously.

Iselin was the aspiration Maria had never dared to dream of. But Iselin could never get to know everything. That was why Maria had ordered a double-bottomed safe.

When the upper part was empty, she pressed her forefinger along the base plate, all the way into one corner. A narrow slit opened, and eight black keys appeared. It took her only seconds to tap in the correct combination.

The plate came loose with a muted click.

Lifting it out, she propped it against the wall behind her. The hidden compartment was no deeper than five inches, but that was more than enough for what she could never show to anyone.

No one must ever be allowed sight of this. For reasons she did not entirely understand, she had also chosen to store the deeds to her childhood home in this concealed compartment. They were inside a plastic pocket with the Russian embassy's rental contract. She picked up the folder, gave one final glance to what was left in the bottom of the safe, and replaced the false base plate. With the plastic folder between her teeth, she filled the safe again before closing and locking the steel door.

She sat on the floor with her back to the wall.

The tenancy agreement was as she remembered. Three months' notice on either side, with no specific reason required. One or two photographs of the house were included among the documents. As Maria peered at them, she was seized by an emotion she could not quite figure out. Wistfulness, perhaps, almost a sort of yearning.

Aware of a sudden, uncomfortable stab of shame, she tucked the picture back into the plastic folder. The house was hers, and nothing could change that.

She sat for a while staring into space.

It was warm in there, inside the windowless wardrobe, and Iselin's scent still lingered in the air.

Maybe it was time to move.

Move home.

It was 10:30 at night, but Hanne Wilhelmsen was not at all as bad-tempered as she usually was at this time of day. On the contrary, she seemed absolutely delighted as she sat behind her massive desk with Henrik directly opposite.

"That's brilliant!" she exclaimed. "That Ulf Sandvik gave you the thumbs-up like that is exactly the same as saying go ahead, you know! Now you can use all the resources the police force can provide, Henrik, without sneaking around in corridors and taking clandestine photos of case folders with your phone. Since that Iselin Havørn case was actually underneath Bonsaksen's ring binder, I would say most decidedly that it is also included in Sandvik's approval."

"You can't mean that," Henrik said in disbelief. "Sandvik gave me sanction, with some reservations, to take a look at Bonsaksen's case in my free time, but that doesn't in any way extend to the other one! I think you're being—"

"Be a bit creative," Hanne said, with a mocking smile.

Hanne never gave mocking smiles. It disturbed him.

"You and I have already arrived at the conclusion that these cases have a remarkable connection," she went on. "A suicide that's a murder and a murder that very poooossibly . . ."

She paused dramatically.

". . . is a suicide. If that's not a connection, then I don't know what is."

"Hanne. You can't really think that."

She laughed. Henrik had never seen Hanne like this. Even so, after all the time he had spent with her over nearly two years, he could still discover fresh facets of this mysterious person. It was as if she were a huge number of personalities wrapped up in one. Only with Ida was she always the same. Friendly as a rule, often affectionate, always firm. With Nefis, she seemed just as changeable as she was with him.

It must be quite trying for Nefis, he sometimes thought. But congenial too.

He had to admit increasingly often that he would have liked to change places. But only for his own sake. After all, who else would he be able to confide in? After so many years in Oslo, Nefis and Ida were still the closest he had come to having friends. What Hanne was to him was something of which he was still not entirely sure. At least, not what he meant to her.

And now she was a completely different person.

"Think about it," she said eagerly. "Now that Amanda Foss has established that these antidepressants did not belong to Iselin, my theory about it actually being homicide is reinforced."

"How on earth do you arrive at that conclusion?"

Hanne paid no attention to his doubts. "You have to find out where the tablets came from."

"And how am I going to—"

He broke off when she put her hands on the locked wheels of her chair and used her arms to propel herself up. Hanne was so enthusiastic and different that for a moment he expected her to stand up and walk around the room. Then she simply sat down again in a more comfortable position.

"The whole point of this case is that it's never been investigated," she said. "This damned letter was found right away. The police knew her history and all the pressure she had been under. Her death was put down to a massive overdose. Then they jumped straight to the seemingly obvious conclusion."

She snatched up the Havørn papers and waved them in the air.

"There's only one single interview here, Henrik! And it's of Maria Kvam. Only one! If this Amanda woman had held open the possibility of murder, then there would be at least ten comprehensive interviews here already. Twenty, maybe. We could have read what friends have to say, what her colleagues thought and had heard. We would have known an incredible amount about Iselin Havørn's life and lifestyle if the police hadn't been convinced, after only three minutes at the scene, that the woman took her own life. All that resembles an investigation in this skimpy folder are the inquiries into Maria's statement. It was confirmed that she had been in Bergen since the morning prior to Iselin's death. The phone conversation she claims to have had with Iselin from the Hotel Norge at ten to ten also actually took place. It lasted seven minutes. The time that elapsed between Maria's arrival at the apartment block in Tjuvholm and her phone call to the police emergency line was measured at precisely forty seconds with the help of the CCTV camera in reception and our log."

She tossed the folder on the desk. "And that's about it!"

Henrik had picked up a ceramic figure from the desk. Cobalt blue, it was probably meant to represent an animal. A horse, perhaps. Or a cat, since a few bristles of cut piano wire had been inserted on either side of what might be said to be a nose. He clutched Ida's work of art as he struggled to gain control of his hands.

"But now you can find out so much more," Hanne said with relish as she picked up paper and pen. "Friends."

She wrote the number 1 and circled it, followed by "social network."

"Finances," she continued as she jotted this down as point number 2.

"But, Hanne . . ."

Henrik began to regret working like a madman since Ulf Sandvik had left his office. He had completed the violent crime statistics, which the Superintendent had intended to take him until Friday to finish, in six hours flat. Thoroughly and conscientiously and entirely in accordance with the accompanying guidance. Henrik had placed it all in a

drawer and did not propose to deliver the finished work until Friday at
11:59 a.m. His efforts had rewarded him with three and a half clear
working days he could use for whatever he wished.

Which was to take a more meticulous look at Bonsaksen's ring
binder.

That was why he had phoned Hanne. It was Jonas Abrahamsen's case
they had talked about on the phone when Hanne had quite unexpectedly asked him to come, even though it was then already 9:30 p.m.

Not Iselin Havørn's.

"Wait now," Hanne said. "Let's watch our step here. From what
this . . . chapel custodian, what was his name again?"

"Bolle. Mauritz Bolle."

"From what he told you, which by the way was terribly interesting,
you will also have to find out who took responsibility for the funeral."

"That can't—"

"Wait!"

The pen raced across the paper. Henrik was unable to make out anything other than the number 3.

"When you were here yesterday," Hanne said without looking up, "I
actually had good reason to be immersed in thought. I shouldn't shut
you out every time I'm struck by something, I know that, but there was
something about this funeral that I couldn't get to add up, you see."

She slapped the pen down on the paper and folded her hands behind
her neck. "Iselin Havørn actually did not want to be buried," she said.

"I've really not been given permission to look more closely at this
case," Henrik said, trying to seem adamant. "What you want me to
investigate requires authorization, Hanne. I can't use my authority as a
police officer in a case that in the first place is not mine and second is
about to be wrapped up as an obvious suicide."

"Don't you hear what I'm saying? Iselin Havørn made it clear to anyone who would listen that she did not want to be buried! Or . . . Tyrfing
made it clear. In an article in Gates of Vienna only four months ago."

Henrik got to his feet. "Now I'm telling you for the last time," he said
deliberately. "I can't do this. There's nothing I want more than to get
your help to investigate whether Jonas Abrahamsen is a victim of a miscarriage of justice. That's a case I've been given a green light of some
kind on from the boss to take a closer look at. This case here, on the
other hand . . ."

He nodded at the picture of Iselin Havørn from her time in NRK, which Hanne had pinned up in the middle of a bulletin board directly behind her. ". . . I've already gone much too far into. I say stop. Here and now."

"Don't you read mystery novels?"

"No. I suppose so, but—"

"These things are always linked. At the beginning, the reader is presented with two seemingly unrelated cases. But it turns out eventually that they are linked. Always, without exception."

Now Henrik was the one who burst out laughing. Discouraged and fairly reluctant, but he laughed all the same. And sat down again.

"It's absolutely certain that nothing here hangs together," he said. "This isn't a novel, Hanne. I'm not going to do any more stunts like the ones I did by visiting Amanda Foss yesterday and the chapel custodian, Bolle, today. I can help you with open Internet searches, discussion, and that sort of thing, but it's out of the question to do anything whatsoever that requires me to show my police badge or use resources only the police have authority to access. Okay?"

"Four months ago, she wrote that she wanted to be cremated and have her ashes thrown to the wind."

"Hanne—"

"No further details, I admit. Tyrfing, as you know, treasured her anonymity. All the same, she posted an entire article about the ethical immorality of using up space in a graveyard. About how burning corpses is an ancient, honorable tradition in Nordic culture. She was equally supremely convinced that she was right in this point of view as in everything else. And so it's quite remarkable . . ."

Henrik had given up. He hammered his heels together and stared blankly into the distance.

". . . that she was buried," Hanne continued. "In that regard, I'm actually partly in agreement with Bolle, the chapel custodian. It's maybe not either humiliating or hostile to bury someone who has expressed a clear preference for cremation, but it is at least pretty lacking in respect. Lacking in love. When Tyrfing was so definite on this point, it's difficult to believe Maria wasn't aware of Iselin's wishes. As I said, you must find out who arranged the funeral."

"Haven't you heard a word I've said?"

"Yes, of course I have. But you can find this out without using your authority as a policeman, Henrik. For instance, you can call your friend the chapel custodian. He'll know for sure."

Henrik rose from his seat. Without a word, he grabbed the blue ring binder containing the criminal case against Jonas Abrahamsen and stuffed it into his backpack. He slung it over his shoulder and headed for the door into the hallway.

"Good luck with your case," he said without turning around. "I'm taking mine and I'm out of here."

TUESDAY, JANUARY 19, 2016

Jonas had cleaned everywhere.

A major clean, as he had never cleaned the little house in Maridalen before. It was true he had not polished the windows, since the water turned to frost on the glass whenever he made an attempt. But otherwise he had scrubbed everywhere. When he had finally managed to fire up his old car yesterday, he had done some food shopping before driving to the laundromat, where he spent four solid hours. Now he had nothing but clean clothes and had changed the sheets on his bed too. He could not remember the last time he had done that.

Catharsis, he thought when he awoke at 6:00 a.m., feeling completely rested. It seemed as if his unsuccessful encounter with death had nevertheless led to something worthwhile. As if something had torn inside him and thus restored him in some strange way. Unburdened him, at least, as the psychologist they had foisted on him prior to his release had prattled on about. Jonas had found his own absolute rock bottom, and it felt liberating. He no longer had anything to fight either for or against. No more guilt or pain left to endure.

It was someone else's turn.

In the years following Dina's death, he had kept himself alive to punish himself. He had never viewed it like that before, but on that ice-cold morning as he knelt down, scrubbing the rough floorboards until they shone, he realized that was how it had been. When, two years after the catastrophe, he had been accused of murdering Anna, he had undoubtedly been terrified by the thought of going to jail—so petrified that he had automatically lied to the police. If he had told the truth at once, everything might have gone differently. He had visited Anna one hour before midnight on New Year's Eve 2003 to talk to her. To get her to withdraw the papers for legal separation. To beg her for one last chance to find their way back to each other in something other than mere sorrow over Dina's death. To wish her a better New Year than the one they had just put behind them.

Anna had not been at home.

At least that was what he had thought then. The house was almost entirely in darkness, and no one came to the door even though he rang the doorbell three times. For a while, he had stood staring at his key. He still had it and could have let himself in. A party was in full swing in the neighbor's house, and he could hear laughter, shouts, and loud music as he stood there, overcome by doubt. In the end, he reached the conclusion that letting himself into a house that was no longer his home would hardly be an auspicious start to any reconciliation. He thrust the bunch of keys back in his pocket and left.

That was what he should have told the police.

The truth.

When he first let slip the lie about not having visited Stugguveien since December 28, it turned into an unruly beast that followed him thereafter. He had realized that almost immediately. They did not believe a word he said and attacked him from all sides. Matters weren't improved by his fiddling with their shared bank account, something it did not enter his head to mention to the police because it had quite simply got lost in his shock at being arrested for homicide. Since he had not managed to mention any of this in the first few days, the police had the upper hand and he lacked the emotional capacity for any attempt to fight back.

As the days in custody passed by, he reconciled himself to the idea of being imprisoned for something he hadn't done. He had more than enough guilt in his life to justify an eternity of punishment and therefore accepted his sentence without demur. That his lawyer had insisted on two rounds in court had only added insult to injury, and Jonas should really have protested.

He had not even possessed the strength to do that.

When after four hours he was able to look around in a miasma of green soap and cleanser, he was beset by hunger pangs. The cupboards, now both clean and well stocked, contained so many ingredients that he began to prepare food at random. He fried three eggs and bacon and slid a frozen pizza into the oven. He threw together a salad with lashings of Thousand Island dressing, and for dessert he decided to eat chocolate pudding with vanilla sauce. On opening the silverware drawer, he stiffened momentarily at the sight of Guttorm's envelope.

He should not have accepted it.

At present he did not need the money. He had a little more than 18,000 kroner in his account, and the rent for the next three months was already paid. That should be enough. He would return the money later. It would be best to send it back to Guttorm at his work address, though, because Jonas was reluctant to cause more trouble for his cousin by risking his wife's opening the envelope and realizing that her husband was doing some double-entry bookkeeping.

But in the meantime he would keep it.

Even though a plan was taking shape, a great deal was still unclear. Maybe he would come to need the extra money.

What happened to Jonas was of no consequence to him. His life was nearing the end of the road, no matter how short or long. Fate had denied him the ability to take his own life, and whatever happened to him now was immaterial. The only important thing in Jonas Abrahamsen's life now was the execution of a plan he should have concocted years earlier. Maybe as early as the moment he had clapped eyes on Christel for the first time, in spring 2002, in her new sneakers and with a bag slung over her shoulder.

He still recalled the flowers she had picked, a bouquet of bluebells and coltsfoot held in her chubby, sweaty child's hand, on her way home from school.

It had all gone so smoothly that Henrik grew worried.

It had eventually dawned on him that he had become some sort of celebrity.

Hanne, in the days following the terrorist attack on May 17 nearly two years ago now, had persuaded the Police Chief to let Henrik speak to the press. Silje Sørensen had been deeply skeptical for a number of reasons. Henrik was of low rank and did not have responsibility for the ongoing investigation. The top brass would feel offended at not being given the chance to shine on TV. Besides, Henrik Holme occasionally had a somewhat unfortunate manner, as the Police Chief chose to word it.

Hanne stuck to her guns. If Silje wanted Henrik and her to bring everything they had to the table and, what's more, continue their exceptionally successful collaboration, it was Henrik's turn for a share of the limelight. After a superintendent had made an idiot of himself with

one-syllable answers during a live interview on *Dagsrevyen*, the daily
evening news program, Henrik got his chance to prove himself at last—
scared witless and with hands discreetly fastened behind his back with
a rubber band, to be on the safe side. It soon became apparent that the
involuntary tics vanished like dewdrops in the sun at the sight of a
microphone. Just like when a stammerer sings, as he had animatedly
tried to explain to Hanne later.

He had not exactly become a household name, but Anna and Jonas's
family physician, Dr. Christine Sivesind, was friendliness personified
when he phoned and introduced himself. With no further argument,
he immediately learned that Anna Abrahamsen had in fact been
referred to a psychologist. He was given the name and address in the
course of ten minutes of conversation, and only three hours had
elapsed since he had called the elderly psychologist to request an
appointment.

Her office did not much resemble the picture he had conjured in his
mind's eye in advance of their meeting. There were no couches and no
winged armchair where the psychologist could listen, unseen by the
reclining patient. No diplomas were displayed on the walls. Not even a
desk to be seen. Instead, the room was reminiscent of a modern living
room. A seating area consisting of four comfortable chairs upholstered
in deep-red velvet formed a quartet beside the huge picture window
overlooking the bay. At the opposite end of the room, a small kitchen
with glossy black cupboard doors was separated from the rest of the
room by a tall kitchen island. Almost a bar counter, Henrik thought,
jumping to the conclusion that it served as a work area when he spotted
a closed laptop and document folder beside a barstool. A floor-to-
ceiling bookcase ran the length of one wall; an impressive number of
specialist books were all that disclosed the occupant's profession.

The psychologist herself, Herdis Brattbakk, looked like an aging
Hollywood actress. Henrik had googled her before he arrived and knew
that she was sixty-nine years old. However, she looked younger than his
mother, who had just turned fifty. Considerably younger and far pret-
tier as well. Her steel-gray hair was cut in a short, almost boyish style.
Her face was broadly heart-shaped, with slanting narrow eyes above
high cheekbones. Her wide mouth had full lips, and when Henrik
warily sat down in one of the red chairs, it occurred to him that Herdis
Brattbakk resembled an older version of Cate Blanchett.

It made him feel extremely awkward.

"I suggest," Herdis Brattbakk began when she sat down so graciously that Henrik wondered whether Google had been lying about her age, "that we skip the part where I declare my duty of confidentiality and you argue that it's of exceptional interest with regard to a serious criminal case in order to get me to talk."

Henrik gave a faltering smile and risked a brief nod.

"After all, since it's almost thirteen years since Anna Abrahamsen was my patient, and more than twelve years since she died, we can simplify matters. Section 24 of the Health Personnel Act applies in this regard, so I'll ask you one question: Are there important reasons here for me to break my duty of confidentiality?"

"Er . . . yes."

Henrik nodded enthusiastically before tucking his hands under each thigh. He had prepared himself for having to persuade her and felt increasingly unsure of himself when she came straight to the point.

"I'm old enough to think for myself without being hidebound by rigid regulations. I choose to trust you."

Henrik went on nodding until, realizing that it looked idiotic, he stopped abruptly.

"Anna came to me in late autumn of 2002," the psychologist said, crossing one leg over the other.

It was so long and slim that Henrik had to compose himself and look away.

"Almost a year after she had lost her daughter," she continued. "It would have been better for her if she had come sooner. As is well known, there is no formula for the grieving process, but as you're probably aware, it's not at all unusual to go through an initial phase of denial."

Henrik kept on nodding without giving any response.

"However, Anna got stuck there, in that phase, for far too long. She was heartbroken, understandably, but in a way that reminded me more of a . . ."

Herdis Brattbakk smiled, raised her chin, and looked diagonally across at Henrik.

". . . man. There was something masculine about the way she seemingly managed to move in and out of grief. She went back to work extremely soon after her daughter died, and from what I understood, that actually went well. One of many problems was probably that she didn't spend time dwelling on what had happened. Instead of grieving and absorbing the reality of the situation, she went on living in a condition of denial. At work she took on more and more responsibility. She filled her free time with friends and . . ."

For the first time since his arrival, she hesitated. But only for a moment.

". . . an excessive amount of alcohol. She used sleeping pills too. When she was finally referred to me, her friends had disappeared, and all that was left were alcohol and tablets. Neither of them particularly reliable friends in a time of crisis."

"But she still went on working?" Henrik asked, and he was so annoyed for asking about something he already knew that the timbre of his voice grew tremulous.

"Yes. She still had some sort of hold on her existence. But only to a degree. You see . . ."

Now she was leaning closer to him. Her purple silk blouse was buttoned so low that he caught a glimpse of a black bra. He tore his eyes away and stared straight out through the window.

". . . children also move in and out of grief. But they do it properly. A ten-year-old can be devastated at the loss of his mother one minute and take delight in a new iPad the next. Only to start crying again. And then the next day have a great time at an amusement park. It does them good to be like that. It doesn't make their sorrow any less and doesn't indicate that it's any less genuine either. It makes life easier to live, that's all. Adults, on the other hand . . ."

She straightened her back at last, and Henrik was able to tear himself away from the view across the Oslo Fjord, where the Danish ferry was plowing a pale furrow on the dark-blue water.

". . . can become ill from that kind of behavior. Or it can be a sign that they already are."

"I see. What kind of illness?"

She smiled.

"I would be happy to give you a lecture on it, but I'm sure that's not why you've come. Anyway, I'm convinced that Anna wasn't ill. Not then, at least. Later, however . . ."

She stopped herself.

"Don't let me anticipate," she said. "I'll come to that shortly. Anna was healthy, I believe, but simply not very good at grieving. Losing a child is the most challenging thing a person can be subjected to, and few of us are equipped to deal with it. Do you have children, Henrik?"

"No."

"Me neither. I've never dared."

The blush took off from the depths of his knees. It came rushing through his body and reached his face far faster than he had ever experienced before. It felt as if a gigantic hand had grasped his body, and he broke into a sweat.

"Here," she said in a friendly tone, pouring a glass of water from a carafe on the circular glass table between them.

Henrik took hold of the glass and guzzled all the water.

"Thanks," he whispered hoarsely as he poured himself another. Unfortunately he missed the glass, and a puddle of water spread slowly across the tabletop.

"There's been a great deal of research into parents who lose their children," Herdis Brattbakk said, as if nothing had happened. "Into the surviving family members after the massacre on Utøya island, for example. Tragic reading. Without a doubt, things are not going especially well for very many of them."

Henrik saw that the puddle of water had taken on the shape of Africa. He glanced up at her and thought he could see her eyes welling up. She took a deep breath and fiddled with her wedding ring.

"When Anna's friends began to abandon her, she sought solace in God. That's not unusual either. Especially since what she was probably struggling most with, quite apart from eventually having to accept that her daughter was gone for good, was . . ."

Henrik glanced at the kitchen section, in two minds whether to go for a paper towel.

". . . her sense of guilt," Herdis Brattbakk rounded off after a moment's thought.

"Guilt?" Henrik repeated in surprise. "Surely it was an accident! And she wasn't even there; it was Jonas who probably should ha—"

"Guilt is a fascinating phenomenon," she interrupted him. "We humans totally depend on feeling guilt in order to be able to adapt to society. In a family. In a workplace. When we've done something wrong, we ought to understand that and feel it. Guilt, or conscience, if you like, spurs people into good or desirable behavior. And it can make us throw in the towel if we make a wrong move. The problem is that it's often misplaced. We feel guilt when we haven't done anything wrong. And what's more, it can be too late to put things right. As in Anna's case."

"What do you mean?"

"Anna didn't have a high opinion of her own abilities as a mother" was Herdis Brattbakk's forthright response. "And once Dina was dead, there was very little she could do about it."

"Could you . . . elaborate?"

"In a way, Anna and Jonas had reversed gender roles. It was Jonas who loved the child above all else. He was the one who took care of most of the broken nights during the first year, and Anna stopped breast-feeding her daughter very early. He was at home with their daughter for nine months. Anna could barely hold out for three months as a full-time mother. Jonas was their daughter's primary caregiver, on the whole."

"There's nothing wrong with that."

"No. And if Dina were still living, it probably wouldn't have bothered Anna in the least that she was a successful worker who found greater pleasure in selling cars than changing diapers. Also, she could rely on the fact that the child had an absolutely outstanding, ever-present father, just as men have relied on their children's mother from time immemorial."

"But Dina died," Henrik said softly.

"Exactly. And when Anna entered her religious phase, she began to regard her daughter's death as a punishment."

"Of her?"

"Yes. She really never reproached Jonas, I believe. Far from it—she defended him. Before you arrived, I went through my notes from that time . . ."

She nodded in the direction of the kitchen, as if her archives were stored in the fridge.

". . . and she mentioned an episode when Dina was quite small. Anna's attention was distracted for a moment, and her daughter knocked over a cup of freshly brewed coffee. She sustained a serious burn, and they had to take her to the emergency room. To tell the truth, she surprised me with her repeated insistence that Jonas was not to blame for Dina's death. We humans are actually pretty poor at that. As a rule, we believe that catastrophes are easier to handle if we can find someone to blame. Anna never fell for that temptation."

"For how long did she come to you?"

"Not long enough. She came once a week from September 2002 until March the following spring. So, six months."

"Did she not want to continue?"

"No. Unfortunately. And the break was sudden. She didn't turn up for an appointment, and the following day I received an email saying she had decided to stop."

"Did she give any reason?"

"Not really. She wrote something about coping better now, but I knew that was sheer nonsense. In fact she was getting gradually worse. But she didn't come back."

Henrik could not stand it any longer.

"Can I get a paper towel?" he asked weakly, staring at the water, where Africa had turned into an immense Antarctica.

"Of course," she said, with a faint smile. "You'll find a roll of paper towels next to the fridge."

"When did she come back?" he asked loudly, halfway across the room.

"At the end of September 2003. So, three months before she was killed."

"Why?"

"I've asked myself that too. She arrived unannounced. Near the end of the day—she knew from previous experience that I don't take patients after five o'clock. When I was ushering the last one out, she was standing there. I usually take ten minutes between each appointment so that patients don't bump into one another at the door, but there stood Anna."

"What did she say?" Henrik asked, lifting the glass of water with his left hand while he wiped the glass surface with his right. "What did she want, then?"

"To talk. It was as if she simply resumed the therapy sessions, without any further comment about having declined my help six months earlier. And without drawing any definite conclusions after a mere one-hour consultation, she had deteriorated considerably."

She lifted her left leg off the right and crossed her legs the opposite way.

"What makes you say that?" Henrik asked her.

Herdis Brattbakk moistened her lips and swallowed. She adjusted her blouse slightly—it fell in soft folds from her bust over what Henrik thought must be a remarkably firm stomach. A heart of white gold and diamonds glittered in the hollow of her neck, moving gently in rhythm with her pulse. She seemed much calmer than he was.

"Well, for a start, she looked far worse," she finally said. "Thinner. Her hair was lifeless and a bit too long. Her clothes were more haphazardly assembled. The dark rings under her eyes had become permanent, I think, and she had acquired that expression on her mouth . . ."

Shaking her head slowly, she ran her slim hand over her thigh a couple of times.

"After all these years, I can almost say that I can still see it," she said quietly.

"What do you see?"

"I see that they have given up."

"What?"

Henrik felt uncomfortably hot again. He held his breath to curb the blushing, but it was no use. "What do you mean by saying that they . . . had Anna given up? Given up what?"

"Life. She was in the process of giving up on living."

Again her hand slid over her pant leg, and she cast her eyes down.

"I was extremely concerned when she left me and asked her really earnestly to return. The very next day, in fact. She went along with that and agreed to come, but then she didn't turn up. I never saw her again. Tried to phone her a few times, but only reached her answering machine."

"Was she suicidal?" Henrik let slip, when he could no longer suppress the question.

Herdis Brattbakk's eyes narrowed. Her cheekbones seemed even more distinct now, and a sharp edge was clearly etched beneath each eye.

"I don't use the expression 'being suicidal.' At least not until someone has made a serious attempt to take his own life. Suicide can come like a bolt from the blue. To all appearances, anyway. Or else be . . . inevitable, in a way—to all intents and purposes, a calamity that has been flagged. In other words, 'being suicidal' is rather imprecise. But I was terribly worried."

She nodded deliberately and looked him straight in the eye. Hers were green, he noticed now for the first time, with brown, triangular flecks around the iris.

"Anna had begun to remove herself from her own life," she said softly. "It was as if she was preparing herself for death."

Henrik touched both sides of his nose at the same time and tapped his forehead.

"What do you mean?" he squeaked, before clearing his throat.

Herdis Brattbakk pondered this for some time. She fiddled with her wedding band, which besides the heart at her throat was the only jewelry she wore. She lifted her glass and sipped the water. When she replaced it on the table, Henrik noticed an almost imperceptible trembling in her hand. She ran her fingers slowly through her hair.

"She was disposing of things," she said in the end. "For example, she had made up her mind to divorce. Not that this was so terribly unexpected, for communication between her and Jonas had been dreadful since Dina died. But it was not just Jonas she was getting rid of. It was things. Dina's room had remained untouched for nearly two years. Jonas had refused to let her do anything with it, but on their divorce, she would keep the house and could do whatever she wanted. In the meantime, before Jonas moved out and they applied for a legal separation, she had cleared the room. Little by little, somehow. Things in the cabinets first, so that Jonas would not notice anything. Then photograph albums and—"

"Did she really throw out the photo albums? The ones with photos of Dina?"

"Yes, and her own, from when she herself was a young child. It was as if she somehow wanted to erase her own life. And worst of all was that she experienced great pain while doing this. It cost her a great deal. That was why she came to me."

A thousand questions filled Henrik's head, and he struggled to keep them all inside.

"Anna hadn't shed many tears at our earlier meetings," the psychologist continued. "I think she didn't have the energy. But on that last occasion, she was inconsolable. At times she quite simply had difficulty speaking. Every single object she removed from the house was like . . . cutting off part of her own soul."

The final part of the sentence was spoken as if reading from a document.

"That was exactly what she said. She was cutting off parts of her own soul. I was very worried about her. In some absurd way, she was looking forward to Jonas moving out so that she could continue with the task of 'packing herself away.'"

Her long fingers drew snappy quote marks in the air.

Henrik's mouth dropped open and, checking himself, he jerked it shut and coughed.

"Why . . . why did she come back to you?" he asked.

"I don't honestly know. A desperate need to talk, possibly. She did not have many people left. Her friends were gone. Her parents were dead. She had no more than a professional connection with her colleagues at that time. Jonas was on the way out, and she'd never had an especially close relationship with her sister. Not that they had fallen out or anything, but there was quite a big difference in age between them. Jonas and his sister-in-law got on well, but she and Anna were very different. Anna . . ."

Unexpectedly, she leaned across the table and held her hands out with palms turned down and fingers slightly splayed.

"You should have seen her hands," she said in an undertone. "They were dry and sore . . . she had been scouring and scrubbing. It's entirely possibly that at that time she had developed some kind of obsessive compulsive disorder."

Henrik quickly pushed both hands under his thighs.

"I can't be sure," Herdis Brattbakk said, with a sigh. "As I told you, she never came back."

"Were you not afraid she would . . . injure herself?"

"She had already done that!"

For the first time Henrik could detect a trace of irritation in her voice.

"It was obvious that she shouldn't dispose of everything that reminded her of Dina. Everything that reminded her of what her life had been when it was good to be alive, even long before she had her daughter. When she left, I caught myself fearing the moment when everything was gone."

"What do you mean?"

"I was afraid of what she would do when she had finished. When there was nothing left to eliminate. From what I'd understood, it was quite a slow process, getting rid of her dearest possessions, so it might take some time. But what would she do when everything was gone?"

She opened her arms wide as she asked the question.

Henrik did not answer.

"Why didn't you raise the alarm?" he asked instead.

"With whom? Her family? She really had nobody as the situation had evolved, and I couldn't see any reason to initiate involuntary hospitalization. I offered her help to find a voluntary place. I think I recall mentioning a clinic. Just for some breathing space. She rejected it out of hand."

"But when she died . . . did you never think that it might have been suicide and that Jonas was innocent? Didn't you ever consider speaking up about it?"

For the first time, Herdis Brattbakk looked at him in disapproval. "But, my dear, I had no reason to do so. It said in the newspapers that it was a case of murder. And with an obvious perpetrator!"

Henrik nodded. He had obtained what he had come here for. And a bit more besides. He felt unsteady when he rose from the deep armchair, and pain was stabbing at the small of his back. He glanced hurriedly at the clock.

"Many thanks," he said, lifting the towel roll from the table. "I'm very grateful you took the time to see me. And that you didn't make a fuss about . . ."

He hesitated. It was probably stupid to remind her that she had paid unusually scant attention to her duty to keep Anna Abrahamsen's mental state to herself.

"My duty of confidentiality?" Herdis Brattbakk said, with a smile. She had also stood up now. "Sooner or later you'd probably have got me released from that anyway. As I said, I'm too old to wait for that kind of bureaucracy. But may I ask . . ."

Approaching him, she placed a warm hand on his arm. Her breath smelled faintly of garlic and peppermint as she leaned in closer.

"Anna never got as far as taking her own life," she said in almost a whisper. "She was murdered. And the case is really old now. Dare I ask why a man like you has started digging into this again?"

Her eyes were sparkling. Henrik felt faint.

"Because," he began, and had to take a step back. "Because . . ."

Herdis Brattbakk released his arm.

"Unfortunately I'm not at liberty to tell you," he said, rapidly backtracking. "But thanks for your kindness. It's been an extremely useful conversation."

Then he made a dash for the door, racing downstairs from the sixth floor, out the main exit from the beautiful apartment building in Skillebekk, and on out into the wintry weather. He went on running along the sidewalk, cutting diagonally across roads jammed with honking cars and ill-tempered drivers. He jogged along the icy streets en route to Kruses gate, risking life and limb, until it suddenly dawned on him that he was no longer on speaking terms with Hanne Wilhelmsen.

And came to an abrupt halt.

"Hanne Wilhelmsen here," Hanne said as cheerfully as she could when the man at the other end had introduced himself. "From Oslo police. I'm in charge of the officer you spoke to yesterday, Henrik Holme."

"Yes, I see. Hello."

"Thanks for being so forthcoming with your answers to my officer's questions. We really appreciate cooperation from the public."

"It's the least I could do. All the same, I have to admit I couldn't quite see what the young man was after. We weren't exactly talking about any kind of crime. It was all actually so odd that I mentioned it to the pastor here, his name is—"

"Just to be brief," Hanne cut in. "The last thing I want is to take up too much of your time. We actually have just one more question, and then we'll leave Østre Gravlund in peace from the police for all eternity."

"Unless a body turns up," the chapel custodian said, laughing heartily before becoming serious again in short order. "I'd feel more comfortable if you spoke directly to the pastor. He was slightly concerned about—"

"I'm just wondering one thing," Hanne hurried to say. "And that is which company was responsible for Iselin Havørn's funeral. It's a shame to bother the pastor with such a minor detail."

She heard a door open and close in the background, and the chapel custodian's voice dropped a notch.

"I really can't," he began, speaking in almost a whisper. "The pastor, he says—"

"Was it Jølstad?" Hanne asked, staking everything on one card.

The minuscule pause before the man hung up was all the confirmation she needed. Hanne Wilhelmsen had never had a particular talent for calculating probabilities. Intuition and deduction were her forte. However, life had taught her that what was probable was not always right, but throwing out the name of by far the largest funeral directors in Norway turned out to have been a sensible ploy.

The chapel custodian's hesitation had given her the confirmation she required.

Jølstad had six offices in Oslo. The ones nearest the apartment in Tjuvholm must be Smestad and Kirkeveien. But the funeral had taken place at the Østre Gravlund cemetery, on the opposite side of the city. Of course, there could be any number of reasons for choosing a grave-yard far from home, with family connections being one of them. All the same, Hanne reckoned that the need for anonymity had been the decid-ing factor. Whoever organized the funeral had gone to great lengths to avoid the press, and Østre Gravlund was huge, impersonal, and sur-rounded by traffic interchanges. It was also one of only two graveyards in Oslo where you could be buried no matter where in Oslo you lived. If you were to make a guess based on Iselin Havørn's sizable ego, most people would have put their money on the Vår Frelsers graveyard in the city center. That was probably what the journalists had thought—the location where she would have shared eternal rest with Henrik Ibsen and other distinguished personages.

Jølstad had branches in Abildsø, Holtet, Grefsen, and Kalbakken, none of them particularly close to the Østre Gravlund cemetery, but they were closer than the others.

"Eeny, meeny," Hanne said sotto voce before calling the branch in Holtet.

A friendly, bright, and probably extremely young female voice answered at once.

"Hello," Hanne said mildly. "My name is Astri Selbekk."

Giving a false name came automatically, though she did not quite understand why. Fortunately she had a withheld number, and anyway, it would entail a convoluted rigmarole to discover her true identity via Telenor.

If anyone were to go to the trouble.

"My cousin has just buried her wife," she said, and found no difficulty sounding sympathetic. "Last week. Last Friday. And I just have one question in that regard, if it's possible to—"

"Unfortunately we can't answer third-party inquiries about forth-coming or past funeral arrangements," the woman interrupted her, no longer quite so friendly.

"But you see," Hanne said, lowering her voice to a confidential tone. "My cousin has had a terrible time, understandably—her wife was Iselin Havørn, you know—and only today she's discovered that she's lost her Filofax."

"Her Filofax?"

"Yes, it's a diary. A calendar. An appointment book, if you like. The sort of thing you—"

Hanne broke off for a moment to avoid sounding too upset.

"It was something we used in the past. And that some people still use. Losing it is like losing your . . . cell phone."

Yet another pause. The woman at the other end said nothing.

"Even worse," Hanne added. "It's not linked to the cloud, so it's impossible to restore it. And when I managed to tear her away from her grief for a moment or two, she thought she might have left it behind at the funeral."

Hanne gave a silent oath and grimaced at her own overkill.

"How awful," the woman said. "Losing something like that, I mean. Just a second."

The telephone went dead. Completely dead. No music while you wait. Hanne took the phone from her ear and looked at it. The call had not been disconnected.

"Hello?"

Still silence.

"Apologies," the voice returned at last. "I just had to do some checking. You've come to the wrong branch, you see. Maria Kvam . . . that's your cousin, isn't it?"

"That's right."

"She was at Abildsø. I can give you the number if—"

"No thanks. I'm sitting with your home page in front of me. Thanks very much for your help. Have a nice day."

Hanne hung up. She had found exactly what she was looking for.

For almost two weeks, she had believed Iselin Havørn was the person she had to examine more closely. For thirteen days, she had studied a life she knew only through the Internet, a woman she knew only as an Islamophobe and an eccentric.

Hanne may not have been personally harmed by having spent two years of her life scrutinizing extremism, as Henrik had hinted. Nevertheless, as she rolled out to the kitchen to put on the kettle, it struck her that she had become a bit shortsighted as a result.

Iselin Havørn had not merely been Tyrfing. Of course not, Hanne thought, really berating herself now. She had also been a wife, a friend, and a businesswoman. Maybe she had elderly parents. She might have had siblings as well, even though the unimpressive death notice had not mentioned any other relatives apart from Maria. Iselin was a rounded human being. She could have acquired enemies in areas other than the Internet and entirely different adversaries from the ones she herself described so contemptuously as the "multicultural mafia."

And they could be far closer to her, of course.

Hanne sat waiting for the kettle to boil.

Maria Kvam had made arrangements for the ceremony at which Iselin Havørn had been laid to rest. In a casket the chapel custodian had called a cardboard box, the cheapest possible. It was Maria who had decided that Iselin should be lowered into the earth, even though she must have known this was in direct opposition to the deceased's wishes. Maria had not even gone to the expense of a floral tribute for her wife of more than eight years.

The kettle shone with a blue light and gave off a little peep. Hanne picked out a teabag and dropped it into a cup before pouring in some water.

"Hostile treatment" was what Mauritz Bolle had called Maria's behavior.

Hanne sat lost in thought until her cup was empty.

Maybe Maria Kvam was the person she should take a closer look at, not Iselin Havørn or the racist blogger, Tyrfing.

If only Henrik had been here, Hanne thought, as she trundled back to her home office.

A long strip of gray paper had been added around Henrik Holme's tiny living room. It ran from wall to wall, divided in two along a thick line drawn with a broad marker pen. Here and there along the line, yellow sticky notes and printouts were attached, as well as a few pictures and individual copies of interviews. Henrik himself stood in the middle of the room studying it all and chewing on a pen.

The time line began on December 28, 2003, the point when Jonas had initially claimed to be the last time he saw Anna alive. It ended when court proceedings were initiated against him in July 2004. Since very little had happened from December 28 until New Year's Eve and from January 4 until summer, these periods were compressed into about twenty inches on either side of the preeminent New Year's Eve.

Henrik had not dared do this in his office. He was reluctant to risk having the Superintendent discover that the statistical work had taken only a few hours and that he was now spending all his time working on Bonsaksen's blue ring binder.

The time line looked like a gigantic children's drawing of a centipede. Its head was the killer indictment, and the tail a picture of Jonas that Henrik had taped to the gray paper.

The interesting part of the centipede lay in the middle.

At 10:30 a.m. on New Year's Eve, the neighbor, who was later in the day to have a house full of guests in party mood, exchanged a few words with Anna. She was seated in her car, on the way up their shared driveway. The neighbor had signaled that he wanted to talk to her to give her warning of the forthcoming party. Anna rolled down the window and seemed perfectly normal during their brief conversation, which meant, as the neighbor put it, reserved, serious, and polite. Then she drove up to the garbage cans, where she had left the car engine running for the few seconds it took her to dispose of something in the large communal containers.

The timing agreed with the statement from the Oslo Pistol Club.

At 11:00 a.m., a group of old competitive marksmen held their annual New Year get-together at Ekeberg. It came as a surprise to most of them when Anna turned up. Admittedly, she had resumed shooting earlier that autumn, but she had not shown any interest in returning to their social scene. Quite the opposite—she had firmly turned down a couple of friendly invitations.

She had shown no interest in chatting on New Year's Eve either. An introductory, informal competition was the traditional start to the meeting, with a bottle of champagne and a paper crown as the prize. After that, their guns were put away, and the subsequent fairly boozy party lasted until the participants wended their way onward to their own New Year's Eve parties.

Anna only wanted to fire a few shots.

She had completed five rounds before she put her Glock 17 back in its regular case and left. The club chairman, who had written the statement, had bumped into her on the way out and tried to persuade her to stay. She seemed down and very different from the time when she competed and they had known each other well. On the other hand, she had been like that all through the autumn, he wrote. When her daughter died, she had been really "wired," as he described it. She had wanted company all the time. Both he and several others from the club had visited her a lot. As 2002 progressed, it had tailed off, and Anna had become increasingly withdrawn. When she appeared at the firing range in September 2003, he had not seen her for at least a year. She seemed distant then and would hardly talk to anyone about anything other than the purely practical with regard to the shooting practice.

It was as if it had finally dawned on her that Dina was dead, Henrik read aloud to himself from the report. This certainly supported what Herdis Brattbakk had told him earlier that day.

Henrik would have to extend the time line.

With military precision, he cut off a yard or so of gray paper and fixed it behind the centipede's tail—it ended up at a 90 degree angle, jutting out to the next wall. He bit the lid off a marker pen and drew the midline all the way back to autumn 2001.

Monday, December 3, he jotted down after checking the papers.
Dina dies.

He had searched for the case in the archives without finding anything of note. It should have come up on the computer system. Although the police had struggled to digitize their records, most of them should have been transferred systematically as late as 2001. Judging by the sparse report of the accident in the criminal records, no crime had been committed. An accident, no less, a tragic chance encounter when the child was killed by a car while her father sorted through that day's Christmas mail at the mailbox. It seemed that the case had been left lying somewhere without being entered into the digital archives.

It probably wasn't important enough, Henrik thought, rubbing his forehead; the wretched case had been dropped because there was "no evidence of criminal conduct."

Just a dead child.

Above the date of Dina's death and through the entire ensuing autumn, he wrote: *Cheerful. Easygoing. Full of fun. Sociable. Lively. Self-deprecating. Super saleswoman.*

These were all characteristics he had found in the documents in which Anna Abrahamsen was described by colleagues and friends, by her sister, and by the chairman of the Oslo Pistol Club. She had quite simply been a woman other people liked—admired, even, for her approachable manner and her capacity for work. When Dina was born, she had taken only three months' maternity leave. She preferred working to staying at home, and Jonas had loved the idea of being a full-time dad for nine months. Very soon after, Anna had been promoted to the post of sales manager in Bilia. On this point, Bonsaksen's thorough ring binder also agreed with the psychologist's account.

Henrik pictured the family of three in his mind's eye. Attractive. Successful. Affluent. A perfect little family. If such a thing existed.

He drew back across the room to take in the whole time line. It struck him that Jonas and Anna had reacted to the calamity in totally different ways. He went back and began to write above the midline: *In shock. Withdrawn. Weeping. Lost weight. Rejected friends. Deep depression.*

That was how Jonas was described in the documents.

Below the line he wrote: *Sought contact, clinging, sought comfort, became religious, drank too much.*

This was Anna following her daughter's death.

Henrik knew little about grief. However, he did know a lot about loneliness. He had experienced pain and despair over always being the outsider, and he would prefer to forget his teenage years. Life had not always landed right-side-up.

But he did not complain.

At least not now. When, as an eight-year-old, he had come home from school in his stocking feet with his schoolbag turned inside out and a disgusting aftertaste of dog shit in his mouth, he had promised himself he would be a policeman. It became a goal that kept his spirits up throughout a school career he had later drawn a mental line under. Although his exam results were so outstanding that they would have enabled him to begin medical studies after high school, the physical entrance requirements for the police academy had almost cost him his childhood dream. Hard work and iron discipline had got him in all the same.

He was not only a policeman but also an exceptionally good policeman. He enjoyed it. He had his own little apartment. He had his mother, who could admittedly be a persistent nuisance at times but who loved him so dearly that it was almost enough.

He had that lovely, odd family in Kruses gate—if he could make friends with Hanne again. He probably could.

Henrik Holme was content with his life and knew little about real sorrow.

Sorrow such as this, he thought as he read the descriptions of Anna and Jonas over again.

Henrik could not imagine having his own children.

If it had been his child who had come home with his mouth full of dog shit, he would have been raging. He would have found the tormentors, shouted at them, complained to the school, informed the parents, reported them to the Child Welfare Service. To the police. Something along those lines, anyway: he would have been furious.

He would not have dumped the youngster in the bathtub and made hot chocolate with cream and put on a video. He would not have whispered to his child that he would have to take a roundabout route back from school, keep his head down, and maybe they would go to the circus over the weekend. Henrik Holme would most certainly not have told his son that it would have to stay between them, his mom and him, and that Dad probably wouldn't want to hear about all this tiresome stuff.

He would not have let it happen again, time after time.

Anyway, hot chocolate didn't help with anything whatsoever.

Henrik gulped.

He could not consider having children. The mere thought of having to protect a youngster scared him to death. Since he was now thirty and had never slept with anyone, the dilemma was extremely hypothetical anyway.

With a sigh, he forced all thought of the most painful aspect of his life out of his head.

They had grieved so differently, Jonas and Anna. Not strange that their marriage had fallen apart, Henrik thought, before once again acknowledging that he knew next to nothing about how a relationship worked.

Think like a policeman, he snarled through gritted teeth. *Don't think of yourself.*

Hanne always said that a case should be investigated without any biased theories. Instead you should discover the facts, indisputable facts, and use them to construct reality. Brick by brick. In this case, there were more than enough facts to build on. What was problematic was that someone else had already fixed them in place. All the information surrounding Anna Abrahamsen's death had been pieced together into a structure that made Jonas into the killer. When Henrik had drawn this time line, it was in an effort to deconstruct Bonsaksen's ring binder. Everything had to be broken down, every tiniest detail.

But it was extremely tempting to start at the opposite end. With a theory: Anna committed suicide.

Hanne Wilhelmsen was not here, so he cut off yet another yard of gray paper and hung it on the bathroom door. He used a red marker pen to divide the paper vertically.

Psyche, he wrote at the top of one column.

Even though he had never lost a child, he had read a great deal about human reactions. As Herdis Brattbakk had emphasized, Anna's reaction was far from atypical, Henrik thought as he wrote. In the initial phase, she had been in denial and filled her life with people, drink, and religion. She must have had a certain control over her drinking, since she had been at work throughout this period. In fact, she had spent only one week at home after Dina's death, something Henrik found less strange now that he had spoken to Herdis Brattbakk. Returning to work quickly could also tally with a kind of denial phase: Dina's death did not really sink in completely for her until much later.

That must have been in autumn 2002, he reasoned. It was nearly a year after the accident when she finally sought professional help.

Anna's first year of grief matched how she had been described prior to Dina's death. She was a distinctly sociable person, and it seemed natural that in catastrophe mode, she also turned to other people.

It was almost as obvious that this could not last.

In the first place, people have an unfortunate tendency to grow tired of other people's suffering. It must have been hard work for her friends to mix with Anna during this period, something that also emerged from some of the interviews if you read between the lines.

He bit the pen so hard that the metal cracked.

Anna had been in despair for almost a year, Henrik thought. Then she grew depressed.

Anna became so distraught that she had changed completely. Admittedly she had continued to go to work, had done what she had to do and more. Her colleagues said that she could still be the same old Anna in meetings with customers. Cheerful and lighthearted. Charming.

Once a contract was signed, however, she somehow went to pieces. She dropped out completely from the social side of work but performed her work duties as before, and with great success.

Jonas, however, struggled greatly at work.

He was on sick leave for an entire year. Then the benefit authorities began to make demands, and he chose to take the path of least resistance. He returned to his middle-management post in Statoil's Oslo office, but things did not go particularly well. Whereas Anna obviously still had the energy to make some kind of effort, Jonas was completely drained. From Henrik's reading of the police statements, it was exclusively thanks to his manager's leniency that he was not fired. His absences were frequent, and if Jonas was first to arrive in the office, he sat behind closed doors and accomplished very little. If Jonas had not been arrested one year later, he would have been fired anyway.

Henrik took a step back and peered at what he had written in the right-hand column.

Although Herdis Brattbakk had been reluctant to use the expression, it seemed clear to Henrik that Anna Abrahamsen could have been suicidal as early as the autumn before she died. She had experienced a great tragedy and seemed to be caught in a downward spiral.

The marriage was ailing. No new baby was on the way. Friends had disappeared, partly because she had pushed them away. The more he thought about the last two years of Anna's life, the more he could discern the contours of an impending danger of suicide. She had even spent her last Christmas entirely on her own. Nor had she any plans for New Year's Eve.

Apart from taking her own life.

Perhaps.

Henrik embarked on the left-hand column.

House immaculate, he wrote at the top.

Followed by: *Obviously deeply depressed.*

He could not think of anything further.

He replaced the lid on the pen and turned one of the armchairs to face the time line before he sat down.

At 5:30 p.m., Anna's sister, Benedicte, had visited her. For no more than twenty minutes, she had stated. That corresponded with her turning up for a party half an hour away at 6:20, as had been verified; she was to help with preparing the food.

Henrik had used a bracket to join the period between 10:30 p.m. and 11:30 p.m. Above the bracket he had hung a picture of Anna when alive, with a black cross in the corner.

The pathologists had confirmed that she had died around that time.

In the middle of the bracket, Henrik had attached a copy of the photograph taken from the neighbor's party. He had enlarged the part where Jonas Abrahamsen, a stooped figure jogging up the steep drive-way, could be seen behind the woman with the sparkler.

10:58, Henrik noted beneath the picture.

It was a deathly coincidence.

Discouraged, Henrik tossed the marker pen aside.

He still had a strong feeling that there was something here. It was just so difficult to know where exactly. Henrik's idea about suicide had cropped up when he noticed the extreme tidiness of the house. After his conversation with the psychologist, Herdis Brattbakk, much of the basis for his argument had caved in; Anna had already shown signs of a compulsive mania for cleaning several months prior to Christmas. The elation he had felt when he had confirmed that Anna might indeed have been suicidal was fading fast. Moreover, no matter how he twisted and turned things, he was faced with a problem so enormous and obvi-ous that he had not even started to give it any thought.

If this was a suicide, where on earth was the gun?

If only he could have discussed this with Hanne, he thought as he rapped his forehead three times in succession.

This time so hard it was actually painful.

THURSDAY, JANUARY 21, 2016

He knew her routines better than most.

That certainly wasn't the reason Jonas Abrahamsen had followed Christel Bengtson from a distance for all these years. In the beginning, from the first glimpse of an eight-year-old on her way home from school, he had failed to understand why he continued to keep an eye on her. It was simply an emotional hiatus, a brief moment when the sight of the little girl gave him a feeling different from his everlasting, guilt-ridden grief.

In prison, he had missed her. Speculated how she had changed and grown older without being able to watch the process. During his very first period of parole, he had spied on her for one entire day, fascinated by how quickly teenagers develop. In a way, watching her brought Dina closer, and for a long time, he had dwelled on whether Christel had become a substitute over the years.

No. No one could replace Dina.

He had no affection for Christel. She was merely an instrument, like a knife used by a self-harmer, cutting in order to make the pain inside easier to cope with. He could sometimes feel it physically: the dull, cramping pain in his gut that dissolved at the sight of the unknown child, later the teenager, and eventually the grown woman. The effect never lasted long, so he continued.

He had never been tempted to do anything to her.

Never.

Over the years, he had collected a number of her belongings. Worthless trash, such as an ice cream wrapper she had discarded or a shopping receipt left in the supermarket basket. A scarf she left behind on a bench in St. Hanshaugen last year. Once she had left her wallet in a city center coffee bar, but Jonas had handed it to an assistant in the hope that Christel would get it back.

He kept her driver's license, though: it lay in a shoebox together with the other items, looking the worse for wear.

When Christel established her blog, it was a real boon for Jonas. By collating the information she posted in her blog, on Instagram, Twitter, and Facebook, he had charted her life for years, down to the smallest detail. The advantage with celebrities was that they usually accepted friend requests from strangers, and he had several false, plausible accounts. As a rule he knew where she was, what she was doing, and what she was thinking—and, not least, who she was with.

Jonas knew Christel's routines. On Thursdays she dropped off and picked up Hedda at day care. That meant earlier drop-offs and later pickups than usual, and the toddler had her midday nap at day care rather than at home, as was the case when her grandfather collected her. So today too, Jonas had been there at quarter to eight to watch Hedda being dropped off.

It was now getting on to 12:30, and snow was in the air. Jonas had felt intense, unanticipated relief that morning when he noticed it was only 23 degrees outside. On really cold days, the children had to take their midday nap indoors. In this weather, they were sleeping outside as usual, well wrapped in blankets and sleeping bags, all in their respective strollers. To avoid the older children disturbing them unnecessarily with their high-spirited games and yells, the strollers were parked at the lower end of the day care area. Someone had cleared a narrow path from the main entrance on the other side of the building up there, just wide enough to accommodate a stroller. Now there were four of them parked beside the fence facing Geitmyrsveien, behind a gate that was not in use and secured with a chain and padlock.

The chain was not especially strong.

It took Jonas seconds to cut through it with wire cutters. He carefully placed both cutters and chain remnants in the snow and stepped inside the school grounds. Without as much as a glance at the children play-ing farther up the hill, he took Hedda's new red stroller. It was difficult to haul it across the snowdrifts between fence and road, where he also had to negotiate a bank of snow.

But he succeeded.

The child was still asleep, and he had remembered to shut the gate and retrieve the wire cutters. He had pushed them between the edge of the stroller and the thick blankets tucked around the little girl.

He turned left from Geitmyrsveien. It would be best to avoid the area around the synagogue across the road on the right, because it was probably well supplied with CCTV cameras. He walked at a rapid pace but avoided breaking into a run.

When he crossed Colletts gate, he still heard no sirens. He soon swung down past Lovisenberg Hospital. Since here too there was a danger of surveillance cameras usual for a health care facility, he had parked his car farther along the road. He had visited the stroller manufacturer's Internet site in advance, and it took him only thirty seconds to fold it. He lifted and pushed the detached bag with the upturned footplate on the rear seat and stowed the undercarriage in the trunk.

Hedda woke and began to cry, but by then Jonas had already started the engine and driven off. Bengt Bengtson would never see his beloved grandchild again.

It felt liberating—a gratifying void.

Hanne Wilhelmsen was in a bad mood.

She was banging her head against a brick wall. Even now that she had read all the newspaper articles written about Iselin Havørn in the past few weeks, she was not much wiser about the dead woman.

But she had learned a little.

For example, that Iselin Havørn was a close friend of Kari Thue.

Ever since the beginning of the 2000s, the by-now-nearly-fifty-year-old journalist Kari Thue had conducted a crusade against immigration from the Muslim world. Her involvement had begun commendably enough in the nineties, with a couple of prizewinning documentaries highlighting honor killings in the Norwegian-Pakistani community. This was followed by a book project about female genital mutilation that was less well received. The research she referenced was doubtful, and the numbers she quoted were never documented.

Hanne had always thought that somewhere along the line, something must have gone wrong. From being passionately concerned about the circumstances of immigrant women in both the family and working life, Kari Thue eventually became a home front soldier. Like Iselin Havørn, she saw her entire world threatened, and in the past year she had spoken up for state censorship of the Koran, the demolition of mosques, and the abolition of asylum provision for all Muslims. During the major refugee crisis in the summer and autumn of 2015, in a double-page feature in *VG*, she had demanded that the army be employed against the flood of asylum seekers making their way across the Storskog border station in Finnmark. They should shoot with live ammunition, she insisted, effectively putting a stopper in the vulnerable Norwegian border.

Despite the Defense Chief pointing out with a touch of irony that it was out of the question for Norway to declare war on Russia, Kari Thue was still taken seriously.

She received all the column space she wanted and avidly seized the opportunity.

All the same, it was not self-evident that she would be a friend of Iselin Havørn. Whereas Kari Thue fought fairly, under her full name and preferably on TV, Iselin Havørn had hidden away in cyberspace for a long time. And concealed herself well.

Hanne sat in the kitchen with a bowl of cornflakes.

She pushed it away, half eaten. The milk had become too sweet, and she was not really hungry. Her appetite was dreadful at the moment, though she did not fully understand why. They always had good food in the house. Increasingly often now, she halfheartedly crammed something simple and not particularly tasty into her mouth and then picked at her food at regular mealtimes.

Deep immersion in extremist waters during the past two years had definitely done something to her. When Henrik had dropped a hint about that last Wednesday, she had bitten his head off. In the week or so that had gone by since then, she had constantly returned to his comments. It felt equally uncomfortable every time.

It terrified her, the way the anti-immigrant brigade joined forces.

At times she was gripped by the same conspiracy theories as they espoused. She really hated the feeling, but there seemed to be so many of them. As if their numbers were constantly increasing. As if they were organized somehow rather than only forging alliances through Facebook and Twitter and God knew what else. People who had been poles apart politically seemed to be united in this single, relatively new refrain: we don't want to have them here. They are harming us. They are destroying what is ours.

The political landscape could no longer be described as linear, as an axis from the farthest right to the farthest left. It struck Hanne that politics had become a horseshoe, with the outer edges terrifyingly close to each other.

As Hanne scraped what was left of the unappetizing breakfast cereal into the sink, it sprang to mind that she had grown anxious. She put the bowl in the dishwasher and sat staring out the kitchen window, so huge and with such deep ledges that Ida was in the habit of sitting there to do her homework. Outside, it was snowing lightly and so calm that the winter-bare chestnut trees in the backyard seemed frozen stiff.

Hanne Wilhelmsen was afraid of what was happening. To Norway, not to put too fine a point on it, the country where her daughter, half-Turkish, mostly Norwegian, would grow up and live her life.

It was through an article in *VG* that Hanne had discovered the connection between Kari Thue and Iselin Havørn. A journalist had been given the rather thankless task of phoning Iselin's fellow partisans to gauge reactions to her death. Kari Thue had rejected the opportunity to comment. Probably for the first and last time in her life, Hanne assumed. It nevertheless emerged from the article that the two had been friends.

Close friends, was what was actually implied.

Hanne was not sure of the innuendo behind such a description.

Years ago, after an accident on the Bergen-Oslo railway line during the storm of the century, she had been extremely unwillingly stranded in the mountains with the rest of the passengers, among them Kari Thue. When the storm was over, Hanne had promised herself never, ever again to go anywhere near her scrawny frame: she had spent those days at the hotel, Finse 1222, spreading mistrust and doubt about Muslims.

Now, almost ten years later, she preached hate and agitated for their expulsion.

Hanne suddenly had a strong desire to talk to her.

It was out of the question, really. She would not be able to do it. It would turn into an unholy mess.

She could phone the journalist, of course. The next best thing.

Dag Beddington was his name, and before she could lay herself open to misgivings, she had located his number and keyed it in. Dag Beddington could not be very old because he greeted her with a brisk, "Hi there!"

"Hello," Hanne answered, considerably more subdued. "My name is Hanne Wilhelmsen. I'm a special advisor with the Oslo Police, and I—"

"Wilhelmsen! You're the one who broke the whole May 17 terrorist attack, of course!"

"Well, yes."

"You and that wimp . . . Henrik Holme, wasn't that his name?"

"Yes. I'm dealing with an entirely different case here, and in connection with that, I've come across an article you wrote ten days ago about Iselin Havørn. You had interviewed . . . you tried to obtain comments on the death from Iselin's fellow travelers. From Kari Thue, among others."

"What's your business with that case?"

A more guarded and considerably more mature tone had crept into his voice. Hanne imagined she heard a mechanical click. She quickly grabbed a pen and sticky notes from the basket beneath her seat and wrote REMEMBER HE IS TAPING THIS on a note. She attached it to the counter in front of her.

"Naturally, I can't tell you that," she said, unruffled. "However, it has to do with something quite peripheral. If you don't have time to talk, then I can wait until another time. If you don't want to answer my questions, then of course that's okay too."

The man at the other end hesitated. "What did you want to know?" he finally asked.

"Just a tiny detail. The way I read the article, you claimed that Kari Thue and Iselin Havørn were close friends. How do you know that?"

She could hear that he was smiling.

"I think you're well aware that I can't answer that," he said. "And this conversation's going to be a bit flat if we're to answer each other's questions by saying that we can't answer. Let's do a fair exchange."

"No."

"Yes, let's. You tell me what interest a member of Police Chief Sørensen's little supergroup has in Iselin Havørn's suicide. In exchange I can give you some more meat on the bone with reference to the relationship between Thue and Havørn."

"Was there a relationship?"

Now he laughed aloud. "*Something for something*, Wilhelmsen. You first."

"Iselin Havørn was married. Do you mean she was unfaithful?"

"I can answer that as soon as you have . . . wait a minute."

It sounded as if he had dropped his phone. In the background, she could hear voices all speaking at once, and hurried footsteps that disappeared into the distance. After more rasping and scraping, Dag Beddington was back on the line.

"Hello?" he said breathlessly.

"I'm still here."

"Sorry, but I have to run. It seems a child's been kidnapped. Properly kidnapped, I mean. By a stranger, seemingly. From a day care in the city center. Phone me later if you want to swap information about Iselin Havørn."

The phone was suddenly silent.

"A kidnapping?" Hanne murmured, opening her laptop. At present it told her nothing.

If only Henrik Holme had been here, she thought in desperation, then I could have sent him to see Kari Thue. If there was anyone in existence whom Hanne could palm off on the ill-tempered old bag in the hope of getting something out of her, then he was the one.

But she hadn't heard a word from him in three days, and it was Hanne's own fault.

FRIDAY, JANUARY 22, 2016

He had never seen anyone so like Dina.

Hedda had the same heart-shaped face. The tiny mouth with a distinct cupid's bow and winter-dry lips. The blue eyes and blond lashes that Anna had often said Dina had inherited from him and would cost her a fortune in mascara when that time came.

Jonas had loved those lashes: long and curled and almost white at the tips. *Little giraffe*, he had often called her, and she gave him butterfly kisses with her eyelashes on his cheekbones if he asked nicely.

Hedda didn't even know what a butterfly kiss was.

She had screamed like a banshee for roughly three hours. In the car on the way home. While he carried her from the Golf, parked as close to the front door as possible to minimize the risk of anyone hearing her howls. On the sofa where he laid her. At the table when he served her oatmeal just the way Dina had loved it, lightly cooked oats in a mixture of milk and apple juice with a pinch of cinnamon.

Cinnamon was not good for small children, he knew that, but after all, it was just a tiny amount, and it was delicious. He had eaten a generous helping himself while Hedda sat yelling on the opposite side of the little dining table by the window nearest to the kitchen sink. The little girl didn't want any. She just shrieked.

For Grampa and Mommy.

Mostly for Grampa.

He let her scream.

Dina could also be headstrong. Jonas's mother always said that it was simply a matter of treating them like dogs: ignore them until they find out it's not in their interest to behave like that. Anna had been shocked and pointed out that Dina was not a Dalmatian pup.

Jonas missed his mother: he had realized this for the very first time as he ate the oatmeal and put up with Hedda's earsplitting screams. His father had died in a work accident in the North Sea when Jonas was barely eight years old, and it had always been just him and his mother. She had died just prior to his release from prison. He was given permission to attend the funeral but turned it down. She had visited him only once in all the time he'd been inside, and that was immediately after sentence was passed. She had been fairly measured and in fact had come only to inform him of her intention to spend everything she possessed. By the time he was released, her estate would be drained dry. Since she had recently received a serious cancer diagnosis, she would speed up her spending plans. "Inter vivos disposition," she had declared triumphantly and left him without as much as a farewell handshake. His lawyer had advised him to go for the jugular with his mother because he did have rights to a share of his paternal inheritance, but Jonas had given up long ago.

His mother had always been cool and practical.

Before Jonas was convicted of killing his wife, though, his mother had never been nasty. Cynical perhaps, which meant she had a tendency to be ironic, sarcastic even. Jonas had never had anything against that, really. His mother was self-controlled, always restrained. She approached every difficulty as an arithmetic problem; there was always a solution. When Dina died, though, she had been really distraught and had wept at the funeral. Jonas had never witnessed anything like that before.

His mother would have known what he should do.

As for himself, he was feeling terribly worn out by all this shrieking. Dina had never been as bad as this.

Then, she had never been kidnapped either.

In the end Hedda had given in. She had eaten a portion of cold oatmeal, drunk two glasses of milk, and begun to draw cephalopods on the sheets of paper he gave her. He had no crayons, but he had offered her pencils and a red marker.

The night had passed surprisingly well. He had locked all the doors and propped chairs against them. Not because he was afraid anyone would break in, but because the little girl must not under any circumstances escape from the house at the edge of the woods. She had to sleep in his bed, and to be on the safe side, he had wound string between the bedroom door handle and a hook on the wall where a mirror had once hung.

She took only three minutes to fall asleep at 9:30 that evening, thoroughly exhausted. Before she was put into one of Jonas's old T-shirts and a diaper he had found in the stroller, she had been bathed in the tub in the old dining room.

She had not cried then and was uncomplaining when he carried her in to sleep.

When he was certain that she had journeyed far enough into the Land of Nod, he had risked sitting up in bed to check the Internet. He built a wall beside the little girl with pillows and part of her quilt so that the bluish glow from the screen would not disturb her. Within three minutes, he had ascertained what he had assumed in advance: Hedda's disappearance was front-page news everywhere.

He took no time to fall asleep.

Now morning had come.

The alarm clock's powder-blue numbers showed 5:10. Several seconds passed before it occurred to him that he was not alone. He carefully removed the downy wall between him and Hedda. Her mouth was open, and behind her eyelids he saw fast, flickering movements. She was dreaming. She was so beautiful it was difficult to restrain himself from stroking her cheek. She had perspired a little, and the hair on one side of her head was glued to her cheek. Maybe it was just drool.

The all-enveloping, pleasant emptiness was leaving him.

Now he was engulfed by a gnawing anxiety. Not for having stolen Hedda. Stealing Hedda was important and right. He had made a simple plan, he had executed it, and luck had been on his side. It was part two of the plan that was making him nervous. He had to accomplish something he had never had to do before. It was only a question of time before he was arrested, he was sure of that—so sure that he had assembled what he would need if police came to the door as early as tonight.

Everything was ready in the drawer of the bedside table.

It did not matter if they caught him. Nothing meant anything at all apart from this one thing: Bengt Bengtson would never see his granddaughter again. It was his turn now, Jonas determined, unable to resist bending close to the little girl and kissing her soft cheek. With infinite caution: she was still asleep when Jonas silently rose to check the Internet before Hedda woke.

Henrik had studied the time line so often and for such prolonged periods that he was unable to sleep. The last time he looked at the clock, it showed twenty-five to one. Now it was only half past five, and it was still impossible to fall asleep again when he returned to bed after a visit to the bathroom. He might as well get up.

The strips of gray paper were still displayed in the living room.

The centipede had acquired more feet, and Bonsaksen's ring binder had been pieced together again so many times that he had decided it would be a good idea to make a copy in the course of the day. That would take ages with his combined printer and photocopier. If he hurried, he could arrive so early at Police Headquarters that he could do it there without being seen. Anyway, he would have to show his face at work today. He was to deliver the violent crime statistics for Oslo Police District to Ulf Sandvik by noon.

He cracked two eggs into a frying pan on low heat and took a quick shower while they cooked. His hair was still damp when, already with his coat on, he stood with an egg sandwich, gobbling his breakfast as he gave the time line one more perusal.

Anna's sister had found her at around 11:00 a.m. on New Year's Day. She had called the police at once. Apart from the fact that, in her horror at finding her sister on the floor and covered in blood, Benedicte had trampled through all the mess to check whether she was still alive, she had behaved in exemplary fashion. She had phoned police emergency and given a good, if tearful, account. Thereafter she had stood quiet as a mouse outside the bathroom and not touched anything until the police arrived.

There was still nothing apart from the blasted tidiness to suggest anything other than that Jonas Abrahamsen had murdered his wife.

Maybe Anna was just an overly fastidious person. Maybe her depression had led to an obsessive-compulsive disorder, causing her to clean all the time. Who knew, it might be that the house at Stugguveien 2B was equally immaculate every single day, at every single hour of each day.

Kjell Bonsaksen could, of course, be mistaken. Jonas might well be guilty: he had been convicted and sent to jail. He had not even fought against it. Moreover, it was time to yield to the most obvious argument against a hopeless, flimsy theory: no gun had been found with which Anna Abrahamsen could have taken her own life.

Henrik made up his mind so unexpectedly that he dropped his egg on the floor. Leaving the mess, he wiped his mouth with his jacket sleeve and bolted for the door. Bonsaksen's ring binder was left behind on the coffee table.

Henrik Holme had decided to throw in the towel.

It was time to help Hanne Wilhelmsen. After all, she was the more experienced of the two, and he should have learned long ago that she was usually right.

To hell with Jonas Abrahamsen.

The pain was so severe that she had difficulty breathing. She had scratched her arms until they bled; it was as if a million ants were creeping around under her skin. A couple of times she had tried to look into Hedda's room, but nausea overcame her as soon as she smelled her daughter's sweet fragrance. The second time, she threw up.

Christel and her father had withdrawn into her bedroom. She could not stand any more of the police officers, the clergyman, and the couple from some crisis team or other who only made matters worse. Yesterday, when everything was chaotic and the unthinkable had happened, the police wanted them down at Grønland. Christel became hysterical. She was desperate to stay at home. To be where Hedda belonged and would probably turn up at any minute since it might all be some sort of misunderstanding. Another parent, someone who had the same kind of stroller and had made a mistake in a moment of stress. Or some kind of dare, a prank by high school students celebrating the end of the school year, and even though it was only January, perhaps things had changed since she was in school. There could be umpteen reasons for Hedda's disappearance, and no one was going to persuade Christel to set foot outside their apartment in Geitmyrsveien before this gruesome misunderstanding had been resolved.

It was now nineteen hours since Hedda had vanished.

"I don't know how many times I've told you that I never embark on an investigation with a theory in mind," Hanne Wilhelmsen said, crunching her teeth into an apple.

"Probably a hundred," Henrik replied. "But your thesis is undermined ever so slightly by the way you've become fixated on this particular case."

He nodded in the direction of Iselin Havørn's photograph.

They were seated in Hanne's home office again. She had greeted him with a quiet hello when he had let himself in after sending a text message requesting to pay her a visit. As if nothing had happened. As if he had not left her in a rage on Monday and failed to get in touch with her ever since then. Henrik had steeled himself for a real show-down all the way through the city. His worries had obviously been a waste of time.

He really did not understand her.

"I'm not fixated," she said with her mouth full of apple. "And I don't have a theory. I *know*, Henrik, and knowing is something completely different. People like Iselin Havørn just don't commit suicide, and I'm going to get to the bottom of what actually happened."

Swallowing, she added: "We. You and I. We're going to get to the bottom of what actually happened."

With a sigh, Henrik turned his gaze to the flat screen on the wall opposite the Las Vegas painting. It was exactly two o'clock, and the story of the missing child was still the main news on every broadcast.

"But since that's not your case," he said, nodding at the screen, "then maybe you could think aloud?"

"Money," she said tersely, tossing the apple core into the wastepaper basket. "Money's the root of a lot of evil, and it doesn't seem entirely coincidental that the child vanished into thin air just a few days after her grandfather won more than seven hundred million kroner on Lotto."

"EuroJackpot," Henrik corrected her before rushing to continue. "It's the money angle they're working on down at headquarters as far as I can gather from both the chat in the corridors and what they're saying in the media outlets. As a matter of fact, the grandfather seems more of a father to the child."

"I think he has been too. Or *is*, we should still say. Quite a vivacious sort, that daughter of his. Christel. A show-off name for someone who doesn't really seem too much of a show-off. I had a look at her blog last night. She's a go-getter, that one."

"She might not be so self-assured now," Henrik muttered.

They sat watching the broadcast in silence.

There were still no traces of three-year-old Hedda Bengtson. Of course, that was not the impression the police wanted to give, but both Hanne and Henrik were so familiar with the coded language that they could follow what was going on. At a press conference three hours earlier, the Police Chief had provided so few facts and been so earnest in her plea for assistance from the public that Hanne practically felt sorry for her. The police could not say whether they were searching for one

or several perpetrators. They would not answer as to whether the kidnappers had made contact, or if there was any truth in the persistent
rumors that the abduction had any connection with the huge prize the
child's grandfather had won only a week earlier.

"A child can't just vanish into thin air," Henrik exclaimed.

"No. Someone has taken her."

"But surely that can't be so easy? To break through a locked gate and
help yourself, so to speak?"

"Yes, I'm afraid so. It is as simple as that to steal a child in Norway.
With five minutes at my disposal and mobility in my legs, I could walk
out and bring three of them back to you. As a rule, you don't need to
force your way through a gate. Getting away with it is an entirely different matter. In the long term, I mean."

"We can't go on like this! They'll have to introduce new rules and—"

"No," Hanne cut in. "We have to keep things this way. Day care centers are not fortresses, and neither should they be. Any society is vulnerable. They are built on trust. In a schoolyard or a day care center, the
children can't be under constant, unremitting surveillance. It has to be
like this unless we want to barricade ourselves. Sit behind locked doors
and never venture outside."

Just like you, was the thought that ran through Henrik's mind, but he
did not say anything.

A grave newscaster indicated that an extended news bulletin would
be broadcast at four o'clock that afternoon.

"That was dreadful," Henrik said. "It's awful that a child's been stolen,
but . . . an extended broadcast?"

"This story has all the ingredients the media loves," Hanne said,
using the remote control to switch off the TV. "A gorgeous, successful,
and well-known mother. A defenseless little child disappears. An
updated, traditional family structure with three generations living idyl-
lically under the same roof. And staggering Lotto winnings that have
possibly set the whole mischief in train. A real Charles Lindbergh scenario, this one."

She slapped her hands lightly on the table. "But fortunately it's not
our case."

She glanced at the clock.

"I think you should go now," she said firmly. "Kari Thue's been struck
dumb ever since Iselin died. Not a single blog post, no comments

anywhere. I'll bet she's sitting at home wallowing in grief. Maybe Dag Badminton's right, that there was something going on between them."

"Beddington," Henrik quickly corrected her.

"Whatever. Pay the woman a visit. Try her home address first. Gain some impression. We've got masses of information about Tyrfing. Find out as much as you can about Iselin."

He rose obediently and headed for the door.

"*Please*," Hanne added swiftly to his retreating back. "Of course, I really did mean to say please!"

As he noticed she was smiling broadly, he decided against slamming the door.

The way he had done on Monday.

Killing a child wasn't easy.

It was probably extremely simple. When Jonas had decided what he had to do, in a hospital bed only five days ago, he had deliberately avoided thinking it all through. His energy had dissipated once he had secured the youngster. Taken her from day care without any immediate alarm being raised. Getting a slight head start, returning to the little house on the edge of the forest. Locking the doors. The plan's critical phase was the actual kidnapping: there was any number of methods of ensuring that a three-year-old girl weighing less than thirty-five pounds would never see her family again. Because he had not bothered considering what happened next, he had largely reached his goal. If only he could succeed in taking the final, unavoidable step.

It ought to be simple.

Hedda had eaten her dinner.

Fish fingers and mashed potato from a package, Dina's favorite meal. The three-year-old on the other side of the table wolfed it all down. Last night, while Hedda was drawing pictures, he had not noticed that she was a leftie too. Like Dina. Now she was sitting with the spoon in her left hand, about to attack fish finger number five. He had sliced them up into suitable pieces, mixed them into the mashed potato, and offered her ketchup.

She wanted that as well.

He smiled when she looked up from her food. Hedda smiled back. She smacked the spoon into the ketchup to make it splash.

"You mustn't do that," Jonas said. "You're making a mess of my kitchen."

The spoon slapped into the ketchup again.

Holding out both hands, Jonas took a firm grip of Hedda's left wrist and wrested the spoon from her.

"Now I think you must be full," he said, getting to his feet. "Do you want to draw?"

"Watch kids' TV."

"That hasn't started yet. In an hour or so you can watch it."

When Dina was little, children's TV had started at six o'clock. He had no idea whether that was still the case.

"Netfix?" Hedda asked, canting her head.

"I don't have Netflix. But we can play Picture Lotto."

"What's that?"

"It's fun."

When he had moved in, he had found a box of books, toys, and board games left behind by the previous tenant. It was still inside the closet beside the bedroom. He stood up and cleared the dishes from the table.

Although the curtains were closed at the window overlooking the yard, Jonas detected a movement at the corner of his eye as he approached the kitchen sink. Quick as a flash, he put down the plates and crept up to the window. He used his finger to open a chink between the window frame and the curtain.

Someone was approaching through the trees, on the path stretching from the house for a couple of hundred yards to the road, where Guttorm had lost his way.

It was his neighbor. The one who, according to the nurse, had found him last Saturday. She was barely a hundred yards away now, and she was carrying something. A gray dog with a curly tail scampered around her feet in the deep snow.

Jonas scanned the room. He opened the kitchen drawer, where everything lay ready. Hedda was still sitting on the kitchen chair, an expectant look on her ketchup-splattered face.

"Pictotto," she said, with a watchful smile.

Kari Thue looked as if she had not eaten for quite a long time.

For years, in fact.

She had barely opened the door more than ten inches. Nevertheless Henrik could see all of her. Middling height, with shoulders so angular they looked as if they could cut right through the gray cotton sweater at any moment. She was flat chested and slightly stooped, and her huge eyes dominated a face that could have belonged to a woman at least ten years older. Henrik had seen Kari Thue frequently on TV, but it was obvious she spent a long time in makeup prior to broadcast.

She was not very bonny, as his mother would have said.

But her hair was lovely. Chestnut brown and, in all likelihood, professionally colored, with thick, soft locks that reached far down her back.

Struggling with severe pangs of guilt, Henrik had identified himself as a police officer. However, Kari Thue was a woman who knew her rights. With bells on.

"No," she said for the third time. "You can't come in, and I've no interest whatsoever in talking to you. As far as I've understood, Iselin's death was not a crime of any kind."

She started to close the door. Henrik resisted the temptation to shove his foot into the gap.

"What if it was, though?"

The door stopped with a five-inch opening left. "What did you say?"

Henrik did not answer. Simply waited. The door slid open.

"Did someone help Iselin to commit suicide, is that what you mean?"

Her big eyes grew even larger. She reminded him increasingly of a Japanese manga drawing—if it hadn't been for all the wrinkles.

Henrik shrugged.

"I shouldn't have said anything," he told her, trying to seem disconcerted. That was easy in his case.

"But listen," he said, turning up his palms in a gesture of resignation and surrender, "I'm just a young, inexperienced policeman—"

"You solved the May 17 case in 2014," she broke in. "Along with Hanne Wilhelmsen. Not exactly inexperienced."

"I'm a young policeman," he began over again. "I've been given an assignment by a senior officer. And that was to speak to you. If you could just let me ask you a couple of questions, then I'll avoid getting a bucket load of abuse when I go back to . . . back."

"I've nothing to contribute," she said bluntly, but at least the door was open farther than it had been. "What sort . . . what sort of questions are we talking about?"

Henrik's eyes darted to both sides of the staircase. The elevator pinged on the floor below. Scratching the back of his head, he pulled a face.

"Could I come inside?"

"No."

"How did you get to know Iselin Havørn?" he rushed to ask when he saw she was about to close the door again; it felt like fighting a duel with a door.

"Through Benedicte. She's a childhood friend of my older brother."

"Benedicte?"

Henrik was so dumbfounded that he forgot to activate the recorder on his phone.

"Yes. Or Maria, you know. Maria Kvam. She was christened Benedicte Maria, but Iselin couldn't stand the name she went by when they first met. So it became Maria. I've never become entirely used to it."

For the first time, the suggestion of a smile crossed her face.

"I knew her as Benedicte Hansen until 2002. Then she married Roar and became Benedicte Kvam. Now she's called Maria Kvam."

The smile vanished just as quickly as it had come. "A psychiatrist would probably have something to say about that name-changing quest of hers."

It was as if a complicated clock movement began to tick inside Henrik's head, creaking and sluggish. He was so confused that he forgot to breathe, and he stood on tiptoe, knocking his heels together.

"But now you'll have to leave," Kari Thue said.

"Were you lovers? You and Iselin?"

She stiffened. Stared at him. He stared back. Refusing to relinquish contact with those eyes of hers, those extraordinarily immense orifices that now looked as if you could go for a swim in their blue pools. They stood like that, eyes locked together, hers increasingly moist, until all of a sudden she opened the door and slapped him hard across the face.

"Scumbag," she hissed, slamming the door shut with a bang that reverberated off the gray concrete walls of the stairwell.

Maria Kvam had at one time been called Benedicte Hansen.

His cheek smarted as if stung by an enormous wasp. He rubbed it gingerly as he stared at the shabby front door with its peeling brown paint.

Anna Abrahamsen's sister, who had visited her six hours before she died and found her dead body twelve hours later, was also called Benedicte Hansen.

They were both born in 1961, he recalled, and the clock inside his head stopped dead.

"Why is this case so important to you, Hammo?"

Ida Wilhelmsen, thirteen this summer, sat on the window seat in the kitchen eating bean salad from a bowl on her lap.

"Because I'm conceited," Hanne said.

Laughing, Ida cocked her head and peered at her mother while chewing chickpeas and red lentils. Hanne looked back at her above the lid of her laptop. The girl was growing more and more like her mom. Hanne had seen pictures of Nefis taken at the same age, and it was almost spooky. The same almond-shaped eyes. The same meandering eyetooth that would escape any effort to straighten it because it looked so charming. Even her hair fell in the same way, in a soft side parting from which the hair kept falling across her face, making her one-eyed. Ida was her mother all over again, except that her hair and complexion were a shade lighter.

"What do you mean by that?" Ida asked.

"Just what I said. I'm conceited. I've got a good opinion of myself. I think it's important to demonstrate that I'm fair, and can ignore the fact that the murder victim had views I don't only distance myself from but also believe to be harmful. To us all, and not least to people like your mom."

"Mom isn't bothered. I'm not either."

"Good. You have to turn your back on nasty people and walk away from them."

"Why don't you do that, then?"

Hanne closed the laptop and rolled forward to the window.

"Because I can't take it any longer," she said. "I've decided to do more, to become involved. I just don't really know how. It's a bit difficult when I"—she hesitated, letting her eyes slide around the room—"actually like best of all being here at home."

Ida smiled and chewed more slowly. "You're not conceited," she said.

"Yes I am. In areas such as this, I certainly am. Or maybe snobbish is a bit more accurate. I don't just think that I'm a better person than Iselin Havørn was. I actually look down on people like her. Sometimes, to be honest, I feel . . ."

She was going to say "contempt." She let it drop and smiled at her daughter instead.

"I don't really know. But I think somehow . . . just as Anders Behring Breivik was given a fair trial after being so horrendously evil, I believe that no one had the right to kill Iselin Havørn. Getting to the bottom of it has become somehow . . ."

Again she searched for words that would not be too difficult for a twelve-year-old.

"A way of showing that you're the best," Ida suggested. "By being kind to someone who is nasty, you show that you are better than them. A bit like Jesus, Hammo."

"Don't be sarcastic," Hanne said curtly, taking the empty salad bowl to convey it to the dishwasher. "Anyway, Jesus probably didn't mean that he was better than everybody else just because he turned the other cheek. As far as I'm concerned, it's a way of showing that our system functions."

"I like it when you tell me what you're working on," Ida said. "It's quite exciting, really."

"Earlier, you just got scared."

"Why can't you tell me about all your cases, Hammo?"

"Because I'm usually bound by confidentiality. The cases I receive from the Chief of Police are my official police investigations, and then I can't say anything. Not even to Mom. What I'm working on now is something I'm doing in my spare time. I take it for granted that I can trust you, and you won't talk to anyone else about what I'm telling you."

Ida looked slightly peeved and got up from the window seat. "As if I would," she said.

It had started to snow again, and she stood with her hands on her hips, looking out.

"I really like summer best."

"I agree. And spring. It won't be long now."

"I'm so awful at skiing. We're having a winter activity day on Wednesday, and all my friends are going to Grefsenkleiva to do slalom. I don't even have the gear."

"I've offered you both equipment and classes, Ida. Lots of times.

You've nothing to complain about. Mom hasn't ever had skis on her feet, and I can't teach you for obvious reasons. Anyway, skiing's not the most important thing in the world. I saw on the form that you could choose sledding as well."

Ida made no answer. She still stood there gazing out of the picture window. It was growing dark even though it was not yet four o'clock. The sound of police sirens penetrated the silence of the kitchen.

"Do you think those patrol cars are searching for the little girl?"

"They might be," Hanne answered.

"She was just stolen. My goodness. Just imagine being stolen, Hammo."

"Don't think about it, sweetheart."

"It's a bit difficult not to. Everybody's talking about it."

"But we don't need to. I'm going into my office for a while. If you need anything, just come in. Mom won't be late today, so she'll probably be back any minute."

Hanne tucked a bottle of water between her legs and rolled toward the living room.

"Hammo?"

"Yes?"

"When this handwriting analysis is done—"

"Yes?" Hanne stopped and turned the wheelchair around.

"What sort of thing do they compare it with?"

"What do you mean?" Hanne asked.

"You said that there were handwriting experts. Who can compare and discover if it was really the person who committed suicide who wrote the letter. What do they compare it with?"

Hanne, taken aback, gazed at her daughter.

"Another letter, of course! One they're absolutely certain was written by the person in question. They examine how the pen was held against the paper, how the pressure is distributed, and what the individual letters look like. Handwriting is extremely personal."

"But . . ." Ida had the same crooked furrow between her brows as Nefis had when she was doubtful. "We don't write much by hand anymore. Not once we've finished fourth grade anyway. At school, everything's on computers. The only thing I've written by hand in absolutely ages is a birthday card. And then I usually use big, colored letters. Mom doesn't even write shopping lists by hand. Just uses her cell phone. And then she texts them to me if she wants me to do the shopping."

"They probably found something," Hanne said distractedly; her cell phone was telling her she had received a text message. "We sign our passports, for instance. I'm sure Iselin Havørn would have had a passport."

"Isn't that too little to use for comparison purposes? And those signatures are often just squiggles, aren't they?"

Hanne did not reply—she was engrossed in her message.

I've visited Kari Thue. With really surprising results. Also, the message below has just come from A Foss.

Hi Henrik. Preliminary inquiries show that at least one of IH's social circle used antidepressants. Phone me. Amanda

I called her. This is quite astonishing. Can I come to see you? Henrik

Hanne wrote one word.

Yes.

When she looked up again, Ida had left the room.

"Enemies?" Bengt Bengtson asked, his eyes widening in an attempt to force moisture into his dry eyes that had no tears left. "No. I don't have any enemies."

The policewoman had put her notebook aside a long time ago. She was tall and well built, and her uniform jacket bulged open between the buttons on her chest. Her hair was gathered into a tight topknot that made her face look even rounder. Her face was bare of makeup. A delicate layer of perspiration reflected the ceiling light and made her cheeks shine.

"Why haven't the kidnappers made contact?" Bengt Bengtson demanded, slumping even farther into the sofa. "What is it they want?"

Chief Inspector Eva Grindheim gave an almost inaudible sigh.

"As I said, there could be lots of reasons for that. Anyway, we need to think along alternative lines."

"Alternative lines? I've just won more than seven hundred million kroner, and six days later, the dearest thing I have is stolen from me in broad daylight! From a purely professional point of view, it looks as if you don't have a clue what happened! *In broad daylight!*"

He slammed his fist down on the table. The policewoman glanced at the window, where the January gloom was forcing its way through, despite the workday being far from over.

"There really must be some connection," Bengt groaned, putting his face in his hands. "And they can have everything I've got. But hell, they have to get in touch!"

A low, deep sound, almost a growl, grew louder and louder and changed into a monotonous, wailing howl that made the far younger woman who was looking after Christel pop her head out of the bedroom to see what was going on.

"What do you know, then?" he virtually screamed before subsiding into the cushions.

"We can go through it one more time if you like," the Chief Inspector said patiently, adjusting her skirt. "Unfortunately, it took nearly twenty minutes for anyone to discover that Hedda's stroller was no longer parked where it should be. At that time it had been snowing heavily, but the footprints were still visible, out of the day care grounds and through the broken gate. It's also clear that there was only one person who carried out the actual . . ."

She cleared her throat quietly with a clenched fist in front of her mouth.

". . . abduction. And that the person in question walked east along Geitmyrsveien. We don't know whether anyone was waiting to help at the bottom of the road. Whether someone drove along there in a vehicle, we don't know that either."

"Is there anything at all you do know?" Bengt hammered his fists on the sofa cushions. "Other than that Hedda is gone, I mean! DNA? Don't you have any ideas, or what? It's surely possible to find DNA in the snow, damnit!"

"Yes, we do," Eva Grindheim said, nodding. "It's entirely possible. But I should remind you that it's only been just over twenty-four hours since Hedda disappeared. We do, of course, have a large number of samples to analyze, but . . ."

She tried to find a more comfortable sitting position but eventually gave up. Her skirt kept sliding above her knees, and she sat holding the edge of the hem. Bengt could not remember the last time he had seen a uniformed police officer in a skirt, and he felt an absurd impulse to laugh. To cry. To do something that didn't drive him absolutely crazy, such as sitting in the apartment waiting for something that never happened. He snatched up his phone, glanced at it, raised his arm, and was on the point of hurling it across the room when it suddenly dawned on him that it would be difficult for anyone to call him if he was no longer in possession of a phone. His arm dropped into his lap, and his head fell forward.

"I do really understand that this is a terribly difficult situation for both you and your daughter," Eva Grindheim said softly. "And, of course, we're working on the possibility that there's some connection between your Lotto win and—"

"EuroJackpot!" Bengt barked at her. "What is it you lot get up to in the police? Don't you know anything? How can we depend on . . ."

He tossed the cell phone aside on the sofa cushions and leaned forward with his elbows on his knees.

"Help us," he said, and broke into sobs.

"That's what we're trying to do. But we must also explore other possibilities. That's why it's important to know if there could be anyone who . . . wishes you harm."

"Why would anyone wish me harm?" Bengt said in a muffled voice; he had grabbed a cushion and was holding it in front of his face. "I'm a former bank employee who worked on house purchases and mortgages. Of course I've turned down one or two loans in my time, but you don't steal a child from a bank clerk for that reason!"

Now he was clutching the cushion to his chest. "I don't have any enemies."

"I see."

Bengt stared at the policewoman, who got to her feet and brutally pulled the tight skirt down before resuming her seat.

"No one who wishes you any harm," she declared, nodding.

An abrupt thought caused Bengt's grip on the cushion to stiffen.

There *was* one person he had harmed. Really seriously. Not with a scathing comment, of which there had necessarily been a few over the years, both at work and in his personal life. Not by refusing a house loan, even though some people could get furious and be on the verge of tears at having their deficient credit score shoved in their faces. Not by a rejection, though he had turned his back on more than one woman, and not always with great gallantry.

There was one person he had robbed of a child. Bengt could not remember what he was called. He had deliberately forgotten it. He couldn't even remember the name of the child. It was so many years ago.

The girl wore a pink hat.

The man was wearing a green quilted jacket.

It was more than fifteen years ago.

Inconceivable, he decided.

No one would have waited fifteen years to inflict this atrocity on him. At least not the grief-stricken father of a young child in the neighborhood. The idea was absurd. The little girl's death had been a catastrophic accident, for which no one was to blame. Neither he nor the poor father. The police had said that when they returned his driver's license with a comforting pat on his shoulder: Bengt Bengtson had not killed anyone.

Even the father had said so. He had yelled it through his tears: *It wasn't your fault.*

The child's dad had shouted it out, over and over again, and that was more than fifteen years ago.

Bengt had not even been given a fine. There couldn't possibly be any record of the episode anywhere in the police's computer files. The accident had been horrific, but it had never been a real police case, Bengt thought.

If he told this plump woman about the incident that he normally managed to forget, the police would waste a lot of time on it. Hedda's abduction had been effected in such haste, leaving no traces, that it must have been executed by a gang. Russians, for example. Former Yugoslavs. A mafia-like organization like the ones he had often read about: they put the authorities to shame and were a threat to everyone and everything. It was increasingly obvious that the police had minimal evidence to go on, and a blind alley such as the poor man in the green quilted jacket from an almost wiped-out, ancient memory would be seized with enthusiasm.

Someone out there wanted Bengt's winnings. That was the truth of it. Stealing Hedda was not a matter of outdated, twisted revenge, but of money. He would soon hear from the kidnappers. He was going to pay them whatever they asked; they could have all of it. They could have all the money if only his world could return to the way things had been before Turid from Hamar had phoned and forced on him a sum of money so huge that no good could possibly come of winning it.

The police had to concentrate on the money—on gangsters who wanted 763 million kroner in exchange for Hedda.

Those were the ones they had to find. He let his perpetual aversion to being reminded of that dreadful December morning in 2001 slide back to where it belonged. It had not been his fault, and the father of the little girl had been in complete agreement.

"No," he said hoarsely, clearing his throat before he went on: "I can't think of anyone who would wish me any harm."

"Did she slap you?"

Hanne made big eyes.

"Yes. And really hard too. Look!"

Henrik leaned across Hanne's office desk and turned his left cheek to her. She thought she could make out a reddish shadow on the pale, boyish skin.

"Good grief," she exclaimed. "Did you hit her back?"

"Of course not. Anyway, she went straight back into the apartment and slammed the door behind her. But I didn't leave empty-handed!"

In an unfamiliar, almost childish gesture, he put two thumbs up in the air.

"You were right," he said, lifting a glass of red wine, then looking at it and putting it down again without tasting it. "These cases somehow fit together. In their own, bizarre way."

Hanne let the red wine swirl around her glass. Sniffed it and tasted.

"This means that Maria Kvam too has experienced an overdose of suffering," she said pensively. "First, her sister was killed, and thirteen years later, her wife commits suicide."

"Quite apart from us thinking it's the other way around, though."

"What?" She gazed at him absentmindedly, as if she had been lost in thought about something else.

"You believe her wife was murdered," Henrik said. "And I believe her sister committed suicide. The other way around, you see."

"The Book of Job," Hanne said, staring into the distance.

"What about it?"

"Have you read it since the last time we talked about it?"

"Yes."

"What do you think it means?"

Henrik's fingers drummed on the pale wood of Hanne's desk.

"Please stop doing that," she said in an undertone.

He quickly thrust his hands under his thighs after tapping both sides of his nose.

"About God," he said in a loud voice. "Job's book is about how God moves in mysterious ways. And that he doesn't necessarily reward the good with good things and penalize the bad with bad things, as we humans tend to see it. It's beyond Job's comprehension why he's being punished so hard, since he has always done the right thing. His friends claim he must have done something wrong because God strikes only the unjust. They beg him to confess his sins, but—"

"You don't need to repeat the whole story," she interrupted him. "I've read it many times. Most recently last night."

"The Book of Job is about the difference between God and human beings," Henrik said hurriedly. "When God delivers his thundering speech to Job and his friends after hearing them out for a while, he makes clear that they comprehend none of it. That the universe is so complicated and God himself so mighty that they have no possibility of understanding. Only he, God, fathoms the great mystery of the world. We humans can complain all we like, as Job also did, but we can never place ourselves in judgment over God's actions. We have no competence to make sense of them."

Hanne smiled, with an almost imperceptible nod.

"Job suffered so dreadfully, entirely without having done anything wrong," Henrik went on, more eagerly now. "I interpret this as meaning that there isn't always a reason for good and evil. That suffering some-times just . . . comes about, so to speak. That we humans simply have to endure it."

"Shit happens."

"What?"

"That's how I interpret the Book of Job. God tells Job and his friends quite bluntly that shit happens. And he's absolutely right about that. Just look at me."

Lethargically, she opened out her hands and looked herself up and down.

"And when Job submitted himself to this great truth and expressed regret for having tried to understand God's ways in any shape or form, he was given back everything he had lost. It's at that point the writer of the Book of Job and I part company. I don't believe in that sort of thing. But it's a beautiful piece of writing all the same, don't you think?"

"Yes, I suppose so."

Henrik sat with his mouth half open. His back was slightly curved, as it always was when he sat on his hands like this. Hanne had grown used to all these strange tics of his, the twitches and bad habits and occasional somewhat noisy rituals. They seldom embarrassed her, and with time she had learned to regard them as part of his whole personality. She thought she had found a kind of pattern in the involuntary movements. Some came about through excitement, others through attacks of worry or anxiety. The knocking on the doorframe on his way into a room was of relatively recent origin and grew more marked with stress.

The drum rolls were the only aspect she really could not stand.

Probably none of his bad habits would disappear, because from time to time new ones appeared. It was a shame, she had often thought. They got in his way. As for herself, she had come to terms with her antisocial predisposition years before. Life had become so much easier after she had crept into hibernation. The first few years had been boring but necessary. She had also found a sense of peace, and that came from staying away from other people. After the demanding affair at Finse 1222 nearly ten years ago, she had nevertheless realized that police work was a greater part of her than she had previously wanted to admit. When the Oslo Police Chief had contacted her with a request to look at cold cases, if she wished from her inner exile and without an office at Police Headquarters, she had accepted by phone and opened a bottle of champagne that evening. The past two years had been the best of Hanne's life. Many days had passed since she had realized that her eagerness to investigate Iselin Havørn's death was due just as much to the lack of new cases allocated by officialdom as the desire to prove that she was right. It mattered not a jot. She was back doing what she did best: investigating.

Finding answers where others had not even caught sight of the question.

Now she had everything in the world she wanted.

Henrik also deserved to be like this.

Henrik Holme was something rare: a person who was good through and through. He would be a fantastic boyfriend for someone who could see past his clumsy tics. All the same, Hanne was fairly sure that he had never been in any real relationship. On a couple of occasions she had started to broach the subject, but he blushed so fiercely that she always stopped in time.

"The Book of Job," she said softly. "The Book of Job teaches us that we should not curse our fate. Life comes with neither instructions nor guarantees. When we strive to behave well, it should not be in hope of reward. We should be good because it is the right thing to do. Because it's good, regardless. Whether chance punishes or rewards us is random. We have to play the cards we've been dealt. That's how I read the Book of Job."

"I like listening to you," Henrik said just as softly, with a smile. "Every single night, I thank God that I met you. In my prayers."

There was an awkward silence.

For once, Hanne felt she was the one who was blushing. She'd had no idea that Henrik was on speaking terms with God. In fact, there was still a great deal she did not know about the slim, insecure, fantastic man on the opposite side of the desk.

"Kari Thue," she finally said, tucking her hair behind her ears. "So it was *her* medication that Iselin Havørn ingested?"

"We don't know that for sure, of course. But Amanda Foss has clarified that Kari Thue is the only one of the Kvam-Havørn couple's friends and acquaintances who actually takes antidepressants. The medication's called Anafranil. Which may well match the preliminary analyses of what Iselin took."

Hanne's fingers raced over her laptop keyboard. "Medical dictionary," she mumbled, reading for a few seconds. "Tastes disgusting, it says here."

"What?"

"Anafranil is sugar-coated, and it says here that the tablets should be swallowed whole because of the horrible taste. It also looks as if . . ."

She read on in silence for almost a minute.

"Shit scary medication," she said in the end. "Reading the medical dictionary can terrify the sickest person into getting well again on the spot. Listen to this: considerable danger of intoxication. Side effects are everything from tinnitus through impotence problems to irregular heartbeat and increased danger of suicide. Heavens above. You'd have to be really down in the dumps to dare take this pill. I think I'd give it a miss."

"If you were struggling with severe depression, I think you'd be willing to take a chance," Henrik said. "And those side effects are probably rare."

Hanne glanced at him over her glasses. "Why did she crush the tablets, do you think?"

"Who?"

"Iselin, if we're to believe the police. She died of cardiac arrest following an overdose of Anafranil, but she apparently chose to pulverize them, despite their tasting like shit. Why?"

"Er . . . that vegetable smoothie was pretty grotesque," Henrik said, pulling a face. "Maybe the taste was camouflaged by the spinach, broccoli, and cabbage."

"But why? Why not just swallow the pills and avoid the taste altogether?"

"Some people can't manage to swallow pills."

"Or someone knew they tasted foul and so concocted an extra yucky smoothie to make sure that Iselin wouldn't notice that she was taking medication."

"Or maybe a slightly horrible taste doesn't matter too much when you're intent on dying in a few minutes."

"Touché. But you see that I have a point? A tiny one?"

Henrik nodded, apparently with reluctance.

"Yes, of course. If we begin with the assumption that Iselin didn't commit suicide, then it would be a good idea to camouflage the pills in an obnoxious drink. But if something like that happened, the circle of possible suspects suddenly grows quite large. A fair number of people could have done something like that. And then we're faced with a megaproblem with both our cases."

He put one hand on Iselin's slim folder and the other on Bonsaksen's ring binder, which he had gone home to retrieve before paying Hanne a visit.

"They're not ours. As I've said several times before. And the more suspects we have, the more active our investigation has to be. And we can't do that. Investigate anything much, I mean."

"Yes, we can. Accept a challenge, Henrik."

"Do you know what they say about you at Police Headquarters?"

"I can guess."

"They say quite a lot, even though the people who worked with you are getting thin on the ground. But one of the rumors is that you were someone who always went by the book. That what was most impressive about you was that you cleared up so many cases despite never taking shortcuts. Never did anything at all borderline."

"That was a long time ago," she said, smiling. "I've become more pragmatic with age."

With a sigh, Henrik used both hands to rap his forehead.

"That double rapping is new," Hanne said, lifting her wineglass. "Do you think Kari Thue and Iselin had a relationship?"

"Impossible to say. As I said, she flew off the handle when I asked and slapped my face. It's difficult to put any definite interpretation on that. She might have been affronted because it wasn't true or angry because I'd unmasked them. Who knows? But, Hanne . . ."

Henrik slid the two folders closer until they lay in the middle of the desk.

"What if we start all over again? These cases turn out to have a common denominator. Maria Kvam."

"Or Benedicte Hansen."

"Let's stick with the name she uses today. It's a bit odd that she has a completely different name now than when she was younger, as a matter of fact."

"Not really," Hanne said, taking a mouthful of wine. "Double first names are extremely common. Oddly enough, it's become a tradition again for Norwegian women to take their husband's surname. That she chose to drop Hansen in favor of Kvam is understandable anyway. The only striking thing here is that she gave in to Iselin's wishes when it came to deciding which of her first names she should use. My own name is Hanne Dorthe, and if Nefis had asked me to—"

"Are you really called Dorthe?" Henrik jerked his hands from under his legs and opened out his arms. "*Hanne Dorthe*?"

"Yes, and if you tell anyone, I'll kill you. I've never used it and should have applied to have it removed from my passport years ago. Since I haven't been abroad for more than fifteen years, I no longer have a valid passport anyway."

Henrik tried not to laugh. She could see it, and he buttoned his mouth so hard that his lips disappeared.

"In other words it's not so strange that Benedicte Hansen became Maria Kvam," Hanne pointed out, putting a stopper on the discussion of names. "Just suggests that she was a bit docile. Possibly head over heels in love."

"Dorthe," Henrik repeated in disbelief.

"Stop it. What's that there?"

Hanne pointed at a roll of gray paper protruding from a black trash bag.

"A time line," Henrik replied. "I'd given up the whole investigation, in fact, and this was going in the trash. But then I learned that Maria Kvam is involved in both cases, so I decided to bring it with me."

"Hang it up."

"Where?"

"Here, for heaven's sake!"

Hanne pointed at the wall where the expensive painting of Las Vegas took up a couple of square yards.

Henrik got to his feet, looking uncertain.

"Take down the picture," Hanne commanded. "Hang up the time line."

She pushed a tape dispenser toward him. It took him only a minute or two to fix the gray paper in place. The wall was long enough for the entire roll, and he stepped back a couple of paces. They studied the collage in silence.

"One thing hits me," Hanne said at last. "Each of these deaths in a sense is encircled by Maria."

"What do you mean?"

"The day Iselin died, Maria traveled to Bergen in the morning. Away from home and so away from Iselin. The next day she came home and found Iselin dead. In the case of Anna Abrahamsen, her sister called in at around 5:30 on New Year's Eve, before heading off to a party. It is emphatically established that she was actually at that party until 4:30 the next morning. At eleven the following day, she went back to Stugguveien, and by then her sister was dead."

"And the time of death is stipulated at one hour prior to midnight," Henrik said, nodding.

"On what grounds?"

"The usual," Henrik said, opening the ring binder and leafing rapidly through to the appropriate document. "Death stiffness had occurred and was possibly just starting to diminish. The variables with rigor mortis, as you know, are so extensive that it only provides a rough estimate, but anyway there was nothing to contradict the time of death being before midnight. The core temperature, measured in both the brain and rectally, carried most weight."

He picked up his glass for the second time, raised it, and then set it down again without drinking.

"Unfortunately we didn't have the expertise to analyze hypoxanthine from ocular fluid as early as 2003."

"What's that?" Hanne asked.

"Hypoxanthine analysis. Of the eye. The vitreous humors."

He stared at her, incredulous, before his face broke into a reassuring smile.

"It came about long after your time. If the test is taken within twenty-four hours of death, the tolerance is far less than by using these nomograms for brain and rectal temperature. Halved, at least. And in fact you can use this method on corpses that are up to four days old. The rectal temperature gives a certain indication for up to twenty-four hours, the brain temperature only twelve. In that respect, the hypoxanthine method is a huge improvement in legal precision."

"Thanks for the lecture," Hanne muttered before raising her voice: "But in this case, it was the good old brain temperature that was used."

She dramatically propelled her pen closer to her left nostril.

"Yes. And rectal. As we agreed ages ago, this case was very thoroughly investigated. The relationship between Anna's body temperature and the ambient temperature in the bathroom, taking her clothing and the position of the body into consideration, as well as other evidence, provided a basis for the estimated time of death. Between 10:30 and 11:30. Approximately."

Hanne was staring intently at Henrik's time line. "And this is the time when Jonas was spotted and photographed on his way from the house," she said slowly. "And Maria was verifiably at a party. Henrik?"

"Yes?"

"What was it Anna threw out? In the trash bins, I mean?"

"Er . . . there's nothing in the case notes about it, Hanne."

"She went to those bins twice." Hanne pointed at the centipede: "On December 26 and early in the morning of New Year's Eve."

"She was doing a lot of clearing out," Henrik said. "Probably it was leftover food. Something like that. After all, the house was absolutely immaculate. According to Herdis Brattbakk, it could just be a matter of compulsive behavior."

Hanne nodded. "The house was pretty spotless, true enough. And along with the fact that the woman was really depressed, as we said, this is the only aspect, in a pinch, that might suggest a suicide. Though to put it mildly, it is incredibly far-fetched."

"So you say! You're the one who's rooting around in an obvious case of suicide based on a notion that fanatics never take their own lives! As if . . . as if there was no such thing as hara-kiri, for heaven's sake! There are any number of specific suicide rituals for fanatics, Hanne. I haven't mentioned this before out of respect for . . . Besides, I don't only have this unusually clean and tidy house to build on. Super-intendent Kjell Bonsaksen, an outstanding police officer ever since the sixties, has a really bad gut feeling about this case. It has niggled at him for years, Hanne. And the gut feelings of experienced police officers should be—"

"Relax."

Hanne raised her palms in a mollifying gesture before skirting around the end of the desk and placing her wheelchair in front of the center of Henrik's by now somewhat colorful time line.

"Are you staying for supper?" she asked, with her back turned.

"Yes, please" was his mumbled answer.

"You have to find out what Anna threw out."

"What Anna . . . do you expect me to find out what a woman put in her trash more than twelve years ago?"

"Yes."

"Why on earth should I do that?"

"Because . . ." Hanne looked over her shoulder. "You need something more, Henrik. A tidy house isn't enough. Even though it was virtually sterilized. You've twisted and turned all the details in this case for days on end now, and you still haven't come any further than this, in reality fairly weak, point. Plus the fact that the woman was on a downer, yes. But the police were aware of that at the time too."

"Only in general terms! They didn't even speak to Herdis Brattbakk."

"No. Why should they? It was a homicide investigation, Henrik. The victim's frame of mind may be of interest in certain instances, of course, but hardly when the murderer's name lands out of the blue as in this case."

He was about to protest again, but she waved him aside.

"But if you're right . . ."

She began to move to the door, where the smell of pizza was wafting into the office.

"If Anna really did take her own life after putting her house in order, it would be interesting to know what it was she got rid of. What was the very last thing she no longer wanted to hold on to? Maybe it was one thing that was the most difficult of all to say goodbye to. Herdis Brattbakk talked about Anna removing herself from her own life and feared what would happen once everything was gone."

"And how on earth am I going to find out something like that?"

"Use your imagination," Hanne said, opening the door. "Use the little gray cells, Henrik."

Trundling out the doorway, she could hear he had remained behind.

"Putting her house in order?" he murmured before finally trotting after her.

"I was clever," Hedda said, beaming.

"You were really clever," Jonas said, lying down in bed beside her.

He had only one quilt, and it was tucked around the little girl. He had stuffed a double woolen blanket into a clean quilt cover and pulled this over himself. He put two pillows behind his neck and opened one of the children's books he had found in the box of belongings left behind by the previous tenant.

"I said nothing," Hedda said. "Quiet as a mouse."

"You were quiet as a mouse in the bathroom," Jonas said. "We played hide and seek."

"Hide and seek with the woman. She didn't find me. But you found me."

"Well, I was the one who had hidden you, after all. Shall I read?"

"Grampa's coming tomorrow."

"We'll see."

"And Mommy."

"Shall we read? This book is good, I think. You've been really, really good and haven't needed a diaper all day. I'm sure you'll manage tonight too."

"Mommy," Hedda whimpered, thrusting out her bottom lip. "I want to go to Mommy now. To Mommy and Grampa."

"You can't. Mommy's busy. Making that film, you know."

Hedda began to cry. "I want them to come for me," she sobbed.

"Maybe tomorrow. Would you rather sleep instead of reading?"

The moon hung round and heavy above the dark silhouettes of the trees at the edge of the forest. The way Jonas was lying, he could see the driveway from the house to the main road. It had snowed again since yesterday. There were no visible tire tracks, and to be on the safe side, he had parked the Golf behind the woodshed. Not that it mattered too much. He had checked the Internet numerous times during the day, always while Hedda was occupied with something else. Pictures of her smiled out at readers from the headlines of every online Norwegian newspaper and a number of foreign ones as well: the story had spread across many parts of the world. British and American journalists focused on the famous young mother, the grandfather who had recently come into money, as well as the absurd, uniquely Norwegian practice of letting small children sleep outside in the middle of winter.

There had been no mention of any particular vehicle being sought.

The woman, his neighbor, had brought some food.

A dish of freshly made lasagna. She had been solicitous and full of concern and eager to come inside. Jonas had blamed a terribly sore throat, not so strange after his lengthy sojourn in the snow less than a week earlier. He made his voice sound as rasping as he could and managed to see the woman off before Hedda's patience ran out, beneath the towel in the makeshift bathtub.

It crossed his mind that he had completely forgotten to thank his neighbor, as he followed her with his eyes when she walked back to the path. Her dog lurched from side to side in the deep snow. When they were finally out of sight, he gave Hedda chocolate and milk.

Jonas felt no gratitude for being saved. All the same, he should have thanked her.

Fortunately his neighbor had disappeared, and he hoped she would never come back. He would decide later what to do with the empty lasagna dish. When it was all over, and then nothing would matter any more.

"Mommy," Hedda mumbled through her tears. "Want Mommy. Now."

"This book is all about the Gruffalo," Jonas told her. "He's a monster, but a very nice one in the end. He makes friends with a mouse."

"I want to go home."

"*Soon it will be night, in barn and in stable.*"

He sang softly. It amazed him that he still remembered the words. *Amalie's Christmas* had been one of Dina's favorites on video, and he must have seen all twenty-four episodes of the TV Advent calendar at least five times.

"And now all Christmas elves must go to sleep!"

He saw that she was struggling to keep her swollen eyes open.

"Our dear and gentle Moon . . ."

He tenderly drew her close and pointed at the moon's pale face hanging low in the sky outside. Hedda stopped crying and put her thumb in her mouth.

". . . shine on all who have no bed, and all who have no home . . ."

Her eyelashes were so long. So blond, almost white at the tips, and he was sure they could give him butterfly kisses if he showed her how.

". . . all the children of the world must sleep tonight, no one must cry and no one left behind."

She was asleep. Jonas warily laid her down on her side of the bed and tucked the quilt around her. For a few minutes, he lay in silence by her side to make sure she did not stir. Her thumb was still halfway into her mouth, but her lips had only a slack hold on it. When he held his breath, he could hear hers, even and slow, and its fragrance was sweet, with a hint of toothpaste.

He had lain like this so often in the past.

He closed his eyes and saw Dina's room in his mind's eye. The bed he had built for her when she turned one, painted lilac and with big golden stars on the headboard. He had even sewn the curtains, and Dina had been allowed to choose the fabric sprigged with tiny flowers.

It struck him that little children smelled so alike.

He was out of diapers; only two had been left in the stroller. Hedda had told him she didn't need any—she was a big girl now. He had made sure to remind her to go to the bathroom, the way he had with Dina in the last few weeks of her life. "A helping hand," he said with a smile every time he put one on her, for safety's sake, as he had done on the day when everything had fallen into ruins.

Up until now Hedda had managed without any problem, even though she was still a bit doubtful about the chemical toilet in the makeshift bathroom. However, Jonas would soon need to do some shopping. For instance, he had run out of milk. The little girl drank at least a quart a day, and that evening he had been forced to give her water to save a glass for her breakfast in the morning.

This was not what he had planned, and even though the police seemed to have strayed off course, it was only a question of time before they would arrive at his door. He had helped himself to a child in broad daylight, leaving a distance of several hundred yards behind him and the red stroller. Someone must have seen him. He had encountered any number of people. When he had folded the stroller, opened the door, and placed Hedda inside the car, a red Opel had almost knocked him down. It had braked hard, and the angry young woman behind the wheel had given him the finger.

It was all a question of time.

"Tomorrow," he thought, as he rose gingerly from the bed.

Tomorrow he'd go through with it all.

SATURDAY, JANUARY 23, 2016

Henrik had tried to use those little gray cells as best he could. As soon as the vast recycling center at Haraldrud opened, he had phoned them. After some back and forth, he had managed to speak to a manager of some kind, though Henrik didn't entirely understand what his title signified. However, the man had a good grasp of garbage, and when Henrik asked if there was any possibility at all that trash from a particular address on a given date in 2003 could be traced today, the manager laughed so loudly that he was overcome by a coughing fit.

That conversation was extremely brief.

Sometimes the simplest way was the best way, and Henrik soon realized there was only one possibility of discovering what Anna Abrahamsen had disposed of twelve hours before she died.

Her neighbor.

A man by the name of Heikki Pettersen—a hasty search showed that he still lived at Stugguveien 2A in Nordberg. The walk took Henrik almost an hour and a half. En route, he stopped off at Damplassen and treated himself to a cup of coffee and a cinnamon bun, mostly because he dreaded carrying out the somewhat absurd assignment. As he passed Ullevål stadium and began to cross the pedestrian bridge above the Ring 3 motorway, he felt a strong urge to turn back.

But Hanne was right. The clinically clean house belonging to Anna Abrahamsen was consistent with a planned suicide but a world away from providing proof. His visit to Herdis Brattbakk had certainly confirmed that Anna was an obvious suicide candidate during the period leading up to her death, but even that was insufficient to alter Jonas's conviction. Since today was his day off and Henrik had no other plans anyway, he might as well fire off a shot in the dark and talk to one of the last people to see Anna Abrahamsen alive. If the neighbor could not remember what Anna had thrown out, he might possibly have noticed something else—something that had not emerged in the comprehensive interview he had undergone only days after Anna's death.

The utter improbability that the neighbor's recollection might be sharper twelve years later rather than two days after the murder made Henrik want to turn back yet again. Just as he was about to pass the allotment gardens in Sogn, he slowed his pace. Walking was proving difficult. Milder weather had set in around midnight, and the pavement was covered in deep, heavy snow.

It would not take him more than fifteen minutes to reach Stugguveien.

To avoid the temptation to abandon his journey yet again, he jumped over the snowdrift onto the road and began to jog. The asphalt was bare in the tire tracks, and traffic was sparse. Ten minutes later, he stood, out of breath, beside a low, brown fence, peering into Stugguveien 2B, the house where the Abrahamsen family had once lived. It was painted brown with glazed tiles on the roof. A big Mercedes was parked in the courtyard in front of a double garage. Henrik noticed it had CD plates, indicating membership of the diplomatic corps. The drive had been de-iced all the way down to the paving stones, with extremely sharp edges along the snow on either side. At the top, beside the entrance into the short street, wedged between a streetlamp and a tall conifer hedge, was a row of four garbage cans.

Number 2A, presumably the original main residence, was a red box. Henrik guessed it dated from the thirties. All the windows were small except the one facing southeast, where a large picture window had been installed at a much later date with patio doors leading to an extensive terrace. The entrance was at the top, level with the road, and Henrik began to approach the open gate. And came to a sudden halt.

This was where it had happened. Exactly here. A green mailbox with three names written in both Cyrillic and Latin letters was attached to the fence just in front of an enormous spruce tree. It was here that Dina Abrahamsen had been killed by a convergence of tragic coincidences for which no one had later been held accountable.

Henrik regretted the mislaying of the police file with details of the accident.

Dragging himself away, he walked farther along the fence, in through the gate, and on to the front door. A sign beside the doorbell confirmed that he had arrived at Heikki Pettersen's house. Henrik knew the man had just turned fifty—that certainly tallied with the figure who opened the door only seconds after Henrik had rung the bell.

"Hello there," the man said in a hesitant voice.

"Hello," Henrik replied, holding up his police ID. "My name's Henrik Holme. Could I come in for a moment?"

The man looked doubtful, verging on worried. "What's it about?"

"An old case. A very old case in which a couple of questions have cropped up."

Heikki Pettersen's eyes narrowed before he gave a broad smile and opened the door wide.

"But it's you!" he exclaimed. "You're the one who led the investigation into those terrible May 17 terrorists!"

"Sort of," Henrik mumbled.

At Kari Thue's apartment, being recognized had been a disadvantage, but here it was obviously an asset.

"Come in, come on in."

Henrik stepped inside the hallway and closed the door before taking off his shoes. The house was totally silent, and he took time to arrange his boots to perfection.

Mathematically precise, side by side on the almost empty shoe shelf, and with the laces pulled forward in parallel lines.

"I live on my own," Heikki Pettersen called out from the living room—Henrik followed the sound. "So you're not disturbing me. Can I offer you anything?"

"Just water, please. That would be great."

Henrik moved into the small living room, which struck him as pleasant, though he could not quite explain why. The furnishings were old-fashioned, more or less antiques, and they didn't really match the owner. Heikki Pettersen was a good-looking man who had kept all his hair. Admittedly, it was graying at the temples, and his complexion looked as if it had been exposed to too much sun for too many years. His forehead was marked with deep furrows, and when he smiled, what had once been dimples became two deep gashes on his cheeks. Nevertheless, he carried himself like a young man, with flexibility in his movements that suggested a lot of exercise.

Heikki Pettersen looked like a guy who liked steel and concrete and leather furniture, not rococo chairs and dark oak. The view across the city was stupendous, though that was of no interest to

Henrik. He stood at the window, studying the house farther down the sloping terrain, where Anna Abrahamsen had once both lived and died.

"Here you are," Heikki Pettersen said, placing a bottle of water on the heavy, varnished oak coffee table. "Drink it from the bottle, and then you can take it with you when you leave. How can I help you?"

He sat down on the sofa and pointed out the solitary armchair to Henrik.

"Russians," he said when he saw that Henrik could not tear himself away from the view of Anna's house. "From the embassy. They come and go, but they're good enough neighbors. Don't see much of them normally. Except in summer, when they hold the occasional barbecue. Very good at keeping the driveway clear of snow; I hardly ever manage to get it done before some caretaker from the embassy turns up and gets the snowblower going."

Henrik moved away and sat down. "I've come because of Anna Abrahamsen," he said.

"Thought it might be that," Heikki Pettersen answered. He sat with his feet wide apart, both arms resting on the back of the sofa. "The only time I've had anything to do with the police was when Anna was murdered. Apart from a couple of speeding tickets, that is, but I expect that would be too insignificant for a big guy like you."

The chair Henrik sat on was so narrow and the armrests so high that he could not get his hands under his thighs. As he became increasingly stressed, he pushed them between his thighs, like a little girl.

"It's about the last conversation you had with her," he said.

The man nodded his head. "New Year's Eve. In the morning. The day she was killed."

"Yes. Can you tell me exactly what happened?"

"It's a whole lifetime ago."

"Twelve years. And it must have been a day that made a deep impression on you. Try."

Several seconds passed. Heikki Pettersen shifted uncomfortably on the sofa.

"I was having a party," he began somewhat tentatively. "My wife and I had separated that summer, and it was the first time I'd held a party on my own. I was pretty stressed out. I'd forgotten to warn the neighbors. Here in the street . . ."

A lock of hair fell over his forehead, and he used his fingers to comb it back in place.

"It's a very good, friendly area. We have summer parties and share ownership of power saws. Take on voluntary work at the playground. That sort of thing. We have an unwritten rule that the nearest neighbors should be alerted if there's going to be a party. At least in summer when socializing takes place outdoors. New Year's Eve is really an exception to the rule. Everybody up here has parties then, in fact."

He nodded at the huge window with the outdoor terrace. "Because of the view. Fireworks. They make a brilliant show from up here. But since Anna lives so close by . . . lived, I mean . . ."

He abruptly got to his feet and crossed to the window.

"She was so alone," he said in a hushed voice. "After the little one died, things went from bad to worse down there. I'd had my own troubles that year. My divorce was far from an enjoyable experience, but all the same I noticed it wasn't exactly a happy household down there either. Jonas had moved out. I damn well think . . ."

He puffed out his cheeks and let the air slowly trickle out again.

"She was alone at Christmas. At Christmas! Even my ex-wife and I managed to have some sort of family Christmas since both our children were still living at home at that time. We couldn't stand the sight of each other, but at Christmas, you have to pull yourself together. Anna, however, was completely on her own. We should have invited her in."

"I think she would have turned you down."

Heikki looked at him. "Did you know her?"

"No. But I know a bit about her now. What did you talk about?"

"I saw her come driving up while I was stacking cases of beer in the basement."

He pointed at the decking on the terrace outside the window.

"There's a carport underneath that, with a door into the house. Anna had opened her gate and came driving up to the road. I thought I should at least give her some notice, since the terrace is so close to her property. I waved, and she stopped in the middle of the slope."

His eyes narrowed, as if trying to picture the scene. "She rolled the window halfway down. I told her about the party and asked her to let me know if we were making too much noise. And wished her a Happy New Year."

He returned to the sofa and sat down again. He picked up a cushion, punched it gently, and put it back down.

"I should have invited her, of course," he murmured.

"She would probably have turned that down too. Did she say anything?"

"Say anything? Well. She probably said something or other. Not much. She never said much. Not after Dina died. From a purely technical point of view, that damn accident took place on my property. Did you know that?"

"No."

"My plot of land extends six feet out into the street. She fucking died on my land."

"What did Anna say?"

"I really don't remember," Heikki said, and now a touch of irritation had crept into his voice. "It happened an eternity ago. She probably said Happy New Year. Thanked me for telling her about the party. Something along those lines. I don't honestly remember."

"How did she seem?"

"Fed up. As usual. Very . . . off, in a sense. She'd been like that for a long time. Flat. Uninterested."

Now, running both hands through his hair, he scratched the back of his head in exasperation.

"I honestly don't really know whether I remember this or am just assuming something on the basis of how she'd been behaving for a long time."

"In your police interview, you said that Anna drove farther up to the top of the hill, where she stopped and disposed of some trash."

For the first time, a shadow of uncertainty crossed the face of the self-assured man with straddled legs. He blinked repeatedly and used his tongue to moisten his lips.

"Yes, she did."

"Do you know what she threw out?"

Henrik could feel his pulse racing. The urge to tap his forehead was almost irresistible. He squeezed his legs together as hard as he could. Heikki Pettersen seemed at least as uncomfortable. He stood up unexpectedly and walked halfway around the sofa. Leaning forward, he supported himself on the sofa back and all of a sudden dashed to get something from the kitchen. Halfway across the room, he stopped.

"Well," he began, with his back turned. "There's one thing I have to explain as far as Anna Abrahamsen and trash are concerned."

"Please do."

A faint, piping sound whistled in his ears.

"It's just that it was so fucking annoying," Heikki said, sounding dismayed, and he turned around slowly. "All that trash of hers. You should really take it all to the recycling station, you know? Clothes and shoes and toys and God knows what, all stuffed into those bins that autumn: they should have been taken to the recycling station! Garbage pickup is only once a week, and if they're overfilled, they refuse to touch them. Only household waste should go in those containers up there. There must have been . . ."

His hair had fallen across his forehead again. This time he left it dangling there.

"We hadn't yet started to sort out our waste at that time," he said, mulling it over yet again. "There was no system of green and blue bags, at least. Only paper and cardboard had a separate container. But Anna sometimes put pieces of furniture in there."

"Furniture? What kind of furniture can a garbage container hold?"

"Well, I once found a child's chair in it. In fact, I didn't say anything about that at the time, it was so . . ."

Looking down at the floor, he shrugged his broad shoulders.

". . . sad, really. I tossed it in my car and took it down to the dump the next time I was going there myself. But all the other stuff! She crammed all sorts of things into black plastic bags that filled up the bins as soon as they'd been emptied. I had to mention it, in the end. On more than one occasion, actually, even though I felt really fucking sorry for that family."

"And?"

"Can you blame me? I mean, we share trash bins, and it got totally chaotic when she just ignored the rules and . . ."

He broke off to rub the underside of his nose with the back of his hand.

"So I just wanted to check," he added, in a mumble.

"You wanted to check," Henrik repeated in a louder voice: the ringing in his ears had worsened. "You wanted to check what Anna Abrahamsen had thrown out on the day she died?"

"Yes."

"You didn't mention this to the police earlier."

"They never asked. It seemed completely irrelevant. Besides, it was . . . it was a bit embarrassing to admit to rummaging around in your neighbor's trash, especially when she'd been killed and all that. So I was pleased that nobody asked. Hell, there was total chaos in the street here at that time. People talked of nothing but that murder, and when Jonas was arrested a short time later, the atmosphere in the street wasn't exactly euphoric either, if I can put it that way. Who knows what effect that kind of thing might have on house prices? A year or more passed before anyone here dared to put their house on the market. Number 13."

He pointed vaguely to the west.

"What did you find in the garbage?"

Heikki Pettersen finally sat down again. "A black trash bag, as usual. With clothes inside."

He opened out his arms and hunched his shoulders up to his ears.

"Anna had a car and a driver's license at that time! Beautiful, huge Volvos, a new one every six months! Why couldn't she drive to the recycling station like the rest of us? I got damned annoyed. Until I saw what it was. Then I actually felt a bit . . ."

He dragged it out. Adjusted a couple of cushions and opened his own bottle of water.

". . . embarrassed," he completed his sentence at last. "Sorry for Anna and Jonas."

"Why?"

"They were Dina's clothes," Heikki said softly. "I'd found lots of her things in the trash that autumn, both clothes and toys. And as I said, a lot of small items of furniture. But these were . . ."

He took a gulp of water, set the bottle down on a coaster, and put his face in his hands with his elbows on his thighs.

"They were the clothes she was wearing when she died," Henrik was sure he heard the man say.

"What?"

Heikki removed his hands and stared straight at him.

"They were Dina's clothes," he repeated slowly. "The ones she was wearing when she died. A pink hat, a blue snowsuit, and a few indoor clothes. A pair of boots. And a school bag."

Henrik's fingers found the tabletop of their own volition and beat a lightning-fast drum roll. Heikki stared at them with an expression of surprise that changed to something reminiscent of disgust.

"Sorry," Henrik rushed to say. "It's a compulsive action. Just ignore it. How did you know they were the clothes she was wearing at the time of the accident? Were they covered in blood?"

"No, not at all. They looked freshly laundered. Not that it would have been really necessary, I think. Dina died of internal injuries. From the pictures, you couldn't see that she had bled at all. Just a little trickle from her nose, I seem to recall."

"Pictures? What pictures?"

His fingers took on a life of their own. They drummed on the table and tapped the sides of his nose at top speed, with the occasional rap on his forehead in between. His heels knocked so fast against each other underneath the table that he counted himself lucky he had taken off his boots. At least it was quiet down there on the floor.

"My daughter took photographs," Heikki said in an undertone. "From her room. Her window looks out on to Stugguveien. She was . . ."

He did a rapid calculation.

". . . twelve at the time. Fortunately she didn't see the actual accident. She was ill and had to stay home from school that day. She'd been given a new camera for her birthday in November. This was long before smartphones. Cameras were still popular."

"Fortunately, it was before social media too. Twelve-year-olds can show relatively poor judgment when it comes to posting on Instagram."

Heikki turned distinctly pale at the thought.

"Good God," he exclaimed, and gulped. "As soon as she showed me the photos, I deleted them. They were absolutely . . . they were absolutely . . ."

He grabbed the bottle, unscrewed the lid, and drank half the contents.

"The worst thing was that the pictures were so good," he said. "Technically speaking, that is. Crystal clear, despite the local council having already come up with the idiotic idea of putting yellow lightbulbs in the streetlamps. And despite the foul weather on that particular day. Gray, rainy, and dark."

"What did the photos show?"

Heikki's shoulders sank. He put his slack hands in his lap, opened out, as if waiting to be given something. He stared at them for a long time before he said anything.

Henrik now had his hands and feet under control.

"They showed such terrible anguish that even my daughter understood it," Heikki finally said. "Astri, that's her name. She cried when she showed them to me. Jonas had picked Dina up. Her bag was lying on the ground. Whether Dina was dead or dying, I can't really say, but she was lying completely limp in her dad's arms. And his face . . ."

He shook his head vigorously and clasped his hands. Tightly, Henrik noticed: his knuckles were white.

"I remember thinking: What if it had been me! Imagine if I were the one standing there with Astri or Bendik in my arms! They really affected me, those photographs. They were fucking horrendous. Jonas's face . . . My God."

He used his forefinger to wipe his eyes as he forced out a rueful smile.

"It's such a long time ago. All the same, I can still see those pictures as crystal clear as ever. Of course, we went to the funeral. It was totally . . . totally—"

"Fucking ghastly," Henrik suggested to his own great surprise.

"Yes. Fucking ghastly. Anna just sat there. Like a zombie. Chalk white and silent, with tears running down her face even though she didn't make a sound. Jonas broke down completely. He was taken away in an ambulance, in fact, but was brought home that same evening. That casket . . ."

He measured out a yard with his hands. "It was not much bigger than that."

Silence ensued. Henrik could hear the monotonous barking of a dog in a garden somewhere in the vicinity. He became aware of a sudden vibration from the basement, as if a washing machine had reached its spin cycle. The ringing in his ears had stopped.

"Do you know who the driver was?" he asked.

Heikki glanced up, clearly taken aback by the sudden change of subject.

"Oh . . . no. He wasn't in the picture, and I've never heard anything about that here in the street. Just some guy. In a BMW, I think. He was never charged or anything, as far as I know. It was obviously just an accident. The sort of thing that sometimes happens."

"And you're quite sure the clothes Anna threw away that day were the same ones that Dina was wearing on the day she died?"

"If they weren't the same ones, then they were exact copies. The same hat, the same bag. The same blue snowsuit and little boots. I honestly thought it was strange that they had kept them all. Anna had been busy, clearing things out all through that autumn. If I'd been her, those clothes would have been what I threw out first. The death clothes."

He picked up a cushion. This time he clasped it to his stomach and wrapped his arms around it. His smile was still strained.

"Or maybe it would have been the other way around," he said. "Maybe those would have been the clothes I got rid of last of all."

"I think that's how it was," Henrik said, getting up from the chair. "I think Anna threw away the very last traces of Dina that very morning. That was the day, New Year's Eve 2003, that she finished packing her daughter away. And her own life too."

"The day she died?" Heikki Pettersen said, almost startled. "What an odd coincidence. Do you really think so?"

"More milk."

"We don't have any more, sorry."

Hedda thumped the glass on the table and pushed away the plate and half-eaten slice of bread.

"Want more milk!" she cried, defiantly jutting out her bottom lip.

"A fizzy drink," Jonas said hurriedly. "You can have a fizzy drink, if you like."

Hedda's pout was transformed into a broad smile.

"Cola?"

"Yes, you can have cola with lunch. That'll be good, won't it?"

He opened the fridge and took out a can that he opened as he crossed the room. When the froth threatened to spill over, he grabbed the milk glass and poured it in.

"Milk cola," he said and put the glass in front of her. "Really good. Eat up the rest of your bread, please, my pet."

He really had to do some shopping.

They were running out of fresh food. Also, the kid needed more clothes. Last night he had washed the pants she had been wearing since he snatched her. There had only been one extra pair in the bag beneath the stroller. Her sweater was splattered with ketchup stains and milk splashes. Even though she was bathed every evening, she was beginning to smell disgusting because of her clothes.

He had to do some shopping, but he couldn't leave the little girl. And he certainly couldn't take her with him.

This was not the plan, he thought, as he gazed at Hedda. She had already drunk half of the disgusting milky cola and had her mouth full of bread. A one-armed Barbie doll lay on the table before her, and she was busy wrapping it in a pink baby blanket. The boxes the previous tenant had left behind turned out to be a treasure trove for the toddler. She had not made a fuss about other toys since she had been permitted to empty it all out on the living room floor and found the blond doll with the bizarre body shape among all the games and books, LEGO bricks, toy cars, and a blind, brown teddy bear.

This definitely wasn't the plan, and now he had to take some action.

Of course, he needed to go shopping. If he simply did what he had to do, then he could sit down and wait for the police. Sooner or later they would turn up, and if he hesitated any longer, he might land back in prison with unfinished business on his mind. There was more than enough canned food in the house for him to hold out here for a long time. But only if he didn't have to look after the little girl.

She was so lovely.

This morning, he had woken up when she kicked him in the side. Hedda slept like a helicopter, spinning around in the bed all night long. At about 2:00 a.m., he had gotten up for a piss, and she had been lying on her back with her head at the footboard, her arms and legs spread out, like a little star. She took up all the space in the bed. Quite naturally, just as Dina had so often forced him to the edge of the bed and sometimes even to wake with a start when he fell on the floor.

Anna had never been there on those nights.

When Dina crawled into their bed during the night, Anna moved into the guest bedroom and stayed there until morning. Jonas was the one who grew accustomed to having a helicopter in the bed.

Anna thought she was a bad mother. It wasn't true. She had never said anything of the kind before Dina died. On the contrary—they were both happy with their existence at Stugguveien 2B. Anna had both time and space to outshine all the others at selling cars and to meet all the friends she found so important. For exercise and shooting. As for himself, he had wanted a child for as long as he could remember, and spending far more time with Dina than her mother did was his own choice. The best choice in his life.

His choice of life.

Anna was so pleased with him that she had grown receptive to the idea of making a sister for Dina. Or a brother. Another child.

She was a good mother. She had loved Dina and been kind to her. Caring and firm and perhaps a little stricter than Jonas. It had been good for Dina, and Jonas had shrieked it at her one night in an endless series of horrendous nights: *You were a good mother, Anna!*

It had not helped. Nothing had helped when Dina died, and now he must soon take the life of the child who looked so terribly like her that it was simply impossible.

"Pictotto?" Hedda asked, looking up at him.

He had opened the laptop on the kitchen counter, turning it away so that she could not glimpse the screen. *VG Nett* was set as the default home page, and the headline screamed at him.

Police Search for Dark-Colored Golf, Probably Blue

Jonas felt a cramp in his groin. His car was dark green, but it was close. His throat tightened, and, opening his mouth to breathe more easily, he forced himself to read on.

> *In connection with the abduction of Hedda Bengtson (3), police seek information about a dark-colored Golf, probably an older model, which was parked in Lovisenberggata on Thursday morning. It was driven by a man aged between 50 and possibly of foreign origin. The police emphasize that this is only one of many tips from the public, and that in the first instance they wish only to speak to the owner of the vehicle.*

Jonas struggled to breathe more deeply. He felt dizzy, and to be on the safe side, he used the kitchen counter for support.

Jonas Abrahamsen was forty-seven years old and extremely pale. He was Norwegian and blue-eyed, with sparse gray hair and almost completely bald. Admittedly, the witness could not know that, because he had pulled his black cap so far down his forehead that he had to push it out of his eyes now and again during his walk from the day care center to the undoubtedly rather elderly Golf.

They had made a lot of mistakes, but some of it was correct. They were closing in.

"Pictotto?" Hedda repeated impatiently.

"Not now," Jonas said, forcing out a smile for the toddler. "Not just yet, my lamb."

Henrik Holme had not walked farther than two minutes from Stugguveien 2A when he stopped short. As he fished his cell phone from his pocket, he noticed his hands were shaking. A car drove past him far too fast, and three children about the age of ten who were approaching him on foot took off their mittens and gave the driver the finger. It had started to rain. The north wind was so biting that Henrik crossed the road and sought refuge beside a garage wall.

"Bonsaksen here," barked a voice at the other end of the line.

"Hello. This is Henrik Holme here."

"Hello there! You should be here, you know! Brilliant sunshine and warm—59 degrees, and it'll soon be time for a beer."

"Sounds great. It's raining cats and dogs here. I'd just like—"

"What's this about?"

Either the connection was bad, or else Kjell Bonsaksen was standing beside a roaring waterfall. Henrik had the distinct impression that there weren't many of them in Provence, so he asked to be allowed to call back.

The new line was better.

"Have you made any progress?" Bonsaksen asked. "With my ring binder, I mean?"

"Well, I'm still working on it."

"Let me hear!"

Henrik's fingers were already growing numb, and he pressed closer to the eaves of the gray garage.

"I'm not very well placed at the moment, so if we could do that later, it'd—"

"Next week I'll be back in Norway to sort out some paperwork. I'm arriving on Sunday night. We can meet for a coffee or even dinner? Everyone needs to eat!"

"That sounds good. Right now I've just got one brief question."

"Fire away!"

Kjell Bonsaksen was obviously reveling in his new life. His speech was punctuated with exclamation marks and he had a smile in his voice. In the background, Henrik could hear glasses clinking and the buzz of chatter and traffic. It sounded as if he was seated at a sidewalk café.

"Photos were taken of nearly all the rooms in Anna's house," he said. "Even the storeroom was included in the bundle of photographs."

"That's right! As I hope you've seen for yourself, we were incredibly thorough. Not a stone was left unturned in that case. It's been some kind of consolation to me, you know, whenever I've had this niggling feeling that Jonas Abrahamsen might be innocent. We did everything we should and could, and then some."

"Yes, of course," Henrik said patiently. "But there are no pictures of the daughter's room."

"The daughter?"

"Yes, Dina. The three-year-old who died two years earlier."

"But she was dead!"

"Yes, but—"

"There was no child's room there. Definitely not! Not a trace of a youngster anywhere."

Henrik had to shift the phone to his left hand and push the right one into his pocket.

"But the room," he insisted. "There must have been a room in the house that had once been Dina's?"

"Yes, I suppose so. Sounds logical, anyway. But they must have gotten rid of it. Converted it into . . ."

The retired superintendent suddenly fell silent. Henrik heard a tinkling sound, as if a tray of glasses had been dropped on the floor. He knocked his legs together in an effort to stay warm.

"Hello?" he said. "Are you there?"

"One of the rooms was totally empty," Bonsaksen replied, more slowly now. "And by that, I mean really empty. No furniture. Empty closets. The wallpaper had been stripped off the walls, as far as I remember. I may be wrong, of course, but I . . ."

The sound of footsteps. Engine noise. Henrik could hear a child crying, and then everything went completely quiet.

"Is that better?" Bonsaksen asked. "I'm in the restroom!"

"Much better."

"I thought it was to be redecorated. The door was locked, but the key was in the lock. The technicians also went in there, of course, so it surprises me that there are no pictures of the room in the ring binder. Are you sure?"

"Yes. I know the case inside out by now."

"The only explanation I can think of is that the room was of no interest. Just about to be redecorated. And locked to the bargain. But you know, I really need to get back to the table. My wife's busy making us new friends, and she gets really tetchy when I just up and leave. I'll phone you when I get home to Norway, okay? A cup of coffee or . . ."

Henrik was no longer listening.

The photographs in Bonsaksen's ring binder agreed with Herdis Brattbakk's theory. There was no trace of the child in any of them. No old framed drawings. No photographs, and certainly no sign of any little nook dedicated to her memory, with Dina in a silver frame beside the perpetual flame of a wax candle.

The empty room at Stugguveien 2B was not going to be redecorated.

Far from it—it had been stowed away completely, at last. Exactly as the psychologist had feared, Henrik thought as he began to trudge back to the city.

The apartment in Geitmyrsveien had been totally transformed.

Bengt Bengtson had been so proud of the place. He had renovated it room by room, almost entirely by himself. An electrician and a plumber had contributed exactly as much as they needed to in order to comply with regulations, but that was all. Bengt had personally revamped the spacious residence from an acceptable apartment into a beautiful home in the course of three months. Christel had been eager to help, but she was not allowed because of her pregnancy. She explained to him about modern, water-based, nontoxic types of paint, to no avail. For half a semester, she came home from school to an airy, cool apartment that looked better and better by the day. And she got to choose most of the textiles, furnishings, and colors.

They had both loved that apartment so much.

One of the first things Christel had said just over a week ago when Turid from Hamar had phoned to offer congratulations on the preposterous prize money was that the little family should stay where they were. She wished for nothing other than that. This was where they belonged and were happy, and it was in St. Hanshaugen that Hedda should grow up. No money in the world could possibly create a better home for the three of them than the one they already had.

Now that apartment was dead.

The police had turned the living room into the center of operations. At least that was how it seemed to Bengt. Computers and telecommunications equipment were strewn all over the place, and you had to take care not to trip over all the cables that stretched from wherever outlets were situated in the room. Bengt had asked if it was necessary to have so many, but it made no difference. People kept coming and going. He had entirely given up trying to tell them all apart. Sometimes he had the impression that he had only himself to blame, as he and Christel had refused point-blank to leave the apartment ever since Thursday afternoon.

The bedrooms were their places of refuge.

Christel mostly wanted to be left alone. Some office offering crisis help—Bengt had no idea which one—had stationed a woman in the apartment. She alternated with an older man who had introduced himself as a pastor. The woman took the mornings and the clergyman the afternoons and evenings. When Christel and Bengt had been unwilling to talk to them, something they eventually made no attempt to do at all, they took turns sitting on a chair they had moved from the kitchen to the hallway. There they sat, still and silent, but always with a sympathetic look every time Bengt walked by.

"We're here if you need us," was all she said from time to time. "Remember we're here if you need us, Bengt."

He could not abide her.

He and Christel were left in peace only at night. The police retained a presence: one person, but only one. Last night it had been a woman, and she had slept for a few hours on the sofa in full uniform.

She was the one who had knocked on his door and asked to speak to him three minutes ago. Now she was sitting on one of the kitchen chairs that she had brought with her into the bedroom. He sat on the bed, with his laptop by his side and a cup of tea on the bedside table.

"That's right," she said, nodding. "We have every reason to raise our hopes with this tip. Unfortunately, the witness had been working around the clock on an exam at home and barely checked the news until yesterday evening. Then she made contact with us right away."

"Exam? Who has exams in January?"

"Lots of people," the policewoman said brusquely. "And the information is profoundly interesting."

"Why do you say that? There's next to nothing here!"

He lightly slapped the laptop screen with the back of his hand.

"An old, dark-colored Golf and a foreigner, you mean? How much does that tell you?"

"Now we don't know for sure that we're talking about a foreigner. The witness wasn't certain. He was at least dressed in dark clothes."

"Just like about 90 percent of all men in the fifty-to-sixty age group at this time of year," Bengt said, smacking the laptop again. "Don't you have anything more than that?"

"Yes, we do," she said calmly. "We have more. That's all we can mention at the moment. To the media, I mean. The witness says that the man with the blue . . . with the dark-colored Golf had just folded up a red stroller. He had removed the undercarriage and was putting the bag on the backseat. From the way he was holding it, she definitely thought there was a child inside. He lost his balance, and the car door suddenly opened farther into the road just as the witness was driving past. She had to brake suddenly. She was angry and gave him . . . she made an obscene gesture as she passed him."

Bengt closed his eyes. Christel's room was still completely silent. Maybe she had fallen asleep. He hoped so. He had nearly blacked out and lost consciousness for an hour or so around three o'clock last night, but that was all the rest he had managed since Thursday morning.

"One man," he said softly. "Are you saying that one person has been able to steal a child, take her several hundred yards in her stroller, drive away with her, and still not be caught, more than forty-eight hours later? Without you knowing anything more than that it was an old, dark-colored Golf and a driver who might not be Norwegian? What is he then? Russian? Ex-Yugoslav? What can you . . ."

He punched the pillow with his fist and opened his eyes wide. His eyes nailed the slightly built Superintendent. "*What are you doing about it?*"

"A great deal. Loads. We're doing a lot of cross-checking of the information we do nevertheless have. It's time-consuming, but this may in fact bring us closer to a solution. We're still getting new tips from the public, but as you understand, it's a major task to sort the wheat from the chaff, so to speak."

Bengt shook his head.

"Why don't they call?" he complained feebly. "They can have everything they want. They can have all the winnings. If only they'd please phone."

He grabbed the pillow and buried his face in it. His shoulders were shaking. He drew up his knees and wrapped his arms around them, with the pillow caught up in the midst of it all.

"Since they haven't phoned, we must consider the possibility that this is not about money at all. That's it's not a matter of a regular . . . kidnapping. Both you and Christel must be willing to talk to us about other possibilities, about whether there might be . . ."

He could not hear her, she realized. At least he was not listening. That was okay, she thought with a touch of resignation, and she stood up without making a sound. Then she could avoid telling him any more. For another few hours, Bengt Bengtson would escape knowing that the police were now concentrating on pedophile sex offenders living in the Østland region.

With the main focus on owners of old, dark-colored Golfs.

Fifty-three hours had now elapsed since Hedda's disappearance, and all their experience suggested that the situation was urgent now.

Hanne Wilhelmsen had spent Saturday studying Benedicte Maria Kvam, née Hansen, far more exhaustively than she had done before. It was far more excruciatingly boring than taking a close look at Iselin Havørn.

Whereas Iselin had taken the fascinating political round-trip from the far left as an AKP adherent to the nationalist far right in the guise of an Islamophobic conspiracy theorist, Maria seemed to have been a fairly ordinary opportunist. While Iselin had definitely possessed her own highly original style when it came to both hair and clothes, Maria appeared to be a rather dull, blond Norwegian woman in relatively good shape. At least as far as you could tell from her Facebook profile.

She was born in 1961, seven years before her sister, Anna. Following an apparently idyllic childhood in Nordberg, she failed two subjects in her final high school exams. This was mostly due to wild partying: she was vice president of the Oslo High School Student Organization in 1980, and parties and high jinks have always formed an important part of the final year of high school life in Norway. That kind of official position often led to the holder having to repeat the final high school year. From LinkedIn, however, it emerged that she had subsequently attended the Norwegian School of Economics in Bergen, even though there was much to suggest that she had never passed her final examination to allow her to graduate from high school.

As well as her Facebook profile, which had been regularly updated until Iselin's exposure, Maria had her own blog. It was very different from Iselin's. The graphic design was attractive and meticulously executed, but the content was mundane. Tyrfing's blog showed signs of the writer having too much on her mind to bother about layout, presentation, and grammar. The important thing for Iselin was to reach out with her message without having her identity revealed, not that it should all be wrapped up in trailing roses and painfully correct orthography.

Maria's blog was all about nothing—more accurately, about health food.

Hanne had never read so much claptrap about the alleged magic of nature. She suspected that the blog was an idea dreamed up by the marketing department of VitaeBrass. The company's website had links to Maria's blog in three different places, and the graphic layouts were so similar that the same designer was probably behind them both.

Maria wrote about the effects of honey on the female libido, the amazing impact of walnuts on acne, and the unbeatable effect of blueberries on the immune system. It was hinted in several places that the unique tree extract VitaeBrass sold could have a limiting, and sometimes even arresting, effect on several types of cancer.

Hanne already knew that vitamin C was beneficial for the body, that honey had a mild antiseptic effect, and that a handful of nuts each day was healthy for most people—like the rest of the adult population, she assumed. It was something entirely different to drop these ingredients into jars and bottles along with a large dollop of hocus-pocus and sell it all for a fortune. What's more, it was downright objectionable to entice people with what purported to be a cure for cancer, cunningly formulated and only just within the boundaries designed to exclude quack medicine.

Though that was not the reason Hanne felt so provoked.

She could no longer be bothered. The world was eager to be duped, and if she were to form a picture of Maria Kvam, she would have to read everything available about her on the Internet. After five articles on her blog, one about the company's indisputable bestseller, BrassCure, she began to suspect that Maria had not written any of this at all. She had merely put her name to it as the founder of the company and still one of the majority owners. It was true that the blog came across as personal, peppered as it was with minor incidents from everyday life and photographs of Maria, but deep down, it was nothing but a marketing ploy all the same.

Hanne read all of it regardless, and when she had spent nearly five hours on locating, printing, and reading all the material about Maria to be found on the Internet, she read Bonsaksen's documents on Anna's sister one last time.

And then put them all together in a neatly stacked bundle. Maria Kvam did not seem especially sympathetic, she concluded. Instead, she was superficial, superstitious, and somewhat self-centered. But, above all, pretty dull. On social media she was one of the characters who never surprised. She was especially wary of flagging controversial opinions. From the material available on the Internet, it was impossible to discern any agreement with Iselin as far as Muslims or any other groups of immigrants were concerned. Only after the events in Cologne, when gangs of alleged asylum seekers had molested a large number of German women on New Year's Eve, had she let slip a tweet on the subject. Hanne agreed completely with the sentiment.

Taharrush gamea has no place in Europe #cologne

Group sexual harassment had no place anywhere, and, of course, not here either. The tweet was retweeted twice and had also been marked with a heart by 4 of Maria's just over 3,200 followers.

If Maria had agreed with her wife on the topic of immigrants in general and Muslims in particular, she had hidden it well, at least in public. It was beyond Hanne how it might be possible for spouses to disagree on such fundamental questions as the intrinsic value of other human beings. Iselin Havørn was not only skeptical about immigration and critical of Islam. She hated the very idea of both.

Intensely.

In order to live with Iselin, Maria Kvam must either be in agreement, completely ignorant, or perhaps extremely cynical. Hanne guessed at a combination of the first and last. It would be unfortunate for the business to publicize a clear standpoint about such an exceptionally controversial subject. Hazy photographs of Maria with bouquets of Saint-John's-wort at her country cottage were far safer to show the public than tart comments about drowning refugees in the Mediterranean. The image of a well-manicured hand filled with hazelnuts, held out to the camera, was probably far more effective than aggressive overtures about the tyranny of goodness and dysfunctional parasites. Just like the picture taken from the mountain peak of Galdhøpiggen in glorious weather with a bottle of blueberry extract shown to the photographer. That was how Maria Kvam chose to stage her own life, for the benefit of those who went to the trouble of following it.

However, there were a few obvious holes in the lifeline Hanne had pieced together.

First of all, it was unclear what Maria had actually been doing in the period from when she finished at the School of Economics until she set up PureHerb, as VitaeBrass was then known. Somewhere in the papers it was hinted that she had spent time studying in Bali, and elsewhere there was mention of an around-the-world trip in 1998. At the end of the eighties, she had worked in her parents' firm for three years. Her father, a wholesaler of home appliances, had been quite successful financially. That was brought to an end by the introduction of major chain stores, and the business was quietly wound up in 1991. Her father had obviously been a frugal man, and when both he and Maria's mother died within a short time of each other in 1993, their daughters were left a tidy sum.

It struck Hanne that she might not have been working at all. It could be that she was living on her inherited wealth. That would chime with the stay in Bali and travels around the world, both of which had taken place in the wake of the deaths of her parents.

Hanne glanced at the time. It was almost 4:30, and Nefis and Ida would soon be home. Unfortunately they were expecting guests— friends of Nefis, who were nice enough people, but it would mean a late night. Too much noise. Too many questions and raking over the coals of the May 17 terrorist attack and what it had been like to stand face-to-face with Kirsten Ranvik in the witness box.

For one fleeting moment, Hanne considered fabricating an excuse about a stomachache and spending the whole evening in her bedroom. Nefis was so kind that she was easily fooled.

But not Ida, as she was only too well aware, and so she dismissed the idea.

She rolled out of the office to put the veal roast in the oven, as she had promised Nefis she would do promptly at three o'clock. It was to be slow-cooked. One and a half hours late meant she would have to fiddle a little with the temperature in the hope that the others would be late arriving from the equestrian event on Bygdøy.

Something about the PureHerb start-up did not tally. Some sources stated that the company was set up in August 2001. Others, such as the VitaeBrass home pages, gave 2004 as the date of establishment. Between those two dates, a lot of dramatic events had taken place with reference to Maria's sister and her family, to put it mildly, and a sudden impulse made Hanne trundle back to her home office to log into the company registry at Brønnøysund.

Twenty minutes and several searches later, she understood the connection.

PureHerb was originally Anna Abrahamsen's company.

It was correct that she had registered the business in August 2001, only four months before Dina died. As a wholly owned, limited company, with thirty thousand kroner in share capital and, incidentally, no other visible activity. Other than that, PureHerb had secured an agency for a range of health food products from the Aloewonder company in Hawaii, as well as sole rights in Scandinavia for BrassCure, the ancient Inca remedy from Peru, at that time totally unknown, but by 2016 the bestselling health food supplement in Northern Europe.

So at its very beginning, Maria's flourishing business had belonged to her sister. When it had been passed on as part of her inheritance, the value of the company had initially been confined to the amount of share capital deposited, but in time the agencies had proved a gold mine.

Hanne sat deep in thought. It was no sin to inherit something. No crime either.

At the turn of the year between 2003 and 2004, the rights to both Aloewonder and BrassCure were purely hypothetical in value. Maria could not possibly have known that the company would later take off. Nevertheless, she had chosen to take a stab at what Anna would in all probability have done had the tragedy not struck. Her colleagues had characterized Anna as a super saleswoman. Whether cars or health food, it all probably depended on the same thing. The establishment of the company might suggest plans to feather her nest rather than using her talents for the benefit of the Volvo Group. When Dina died, the agencies were left dormant for nearly three years, until six months or so after her sister's death, Maria breathed new life into the company. Later, with help from Iselin Havørn, she won the Gazelle Prize, awarded by the *Dagens Næringsliv* business newspaper, under the new name VitaeBrass.

They won on two occasions, the only company in history ever to do so.

There was certainly nothing wrong with inheriting something.

All the same, there could be something very wrong in making sure you inherited it.

But Maria could not have killed Anna, Hanne knew that. When Anna was shot, Maria was at a party along with almost sixty other people. Not only had a whole string of them confirmed that she had never left the house, she had also had ongoing responsibility for topping up the drinks. Abandoning your post behind the bar on New Year's Eve would have been noticed, without a doubt.

Hanne reached out to the printer and pulled out a sheet of paper. Using a blue marker, she drew a horizontal line across the page.

Maria's life was unbroken until now.

Prior to Anna's death, she had been unemployed for some time, at least according to the sources Hanne had discovered on the Internet. Perhaps it had been the legacy from her parents that had given her the opportunity to see the world instead of working, and maybe she had been running out of money near the end. However you looked at it, twisting and turning the facts, Maria was the only person who gained from Anna's death.

She inherited her childhood home at Stugguveien 2B. She inherited a cottage in Hemsedal and a share in an old small farm near Arendal that she had subsequently sold to distant relatives in the summer of 2004 for a good sum, if not exactly a fortune.

And she had inherited PureHerb.

Hanne broke the long line with a vertical stroke in red marker pen several inches across the paper.

Anna's death.

Snatching up the blue marker again, she doubled the thickness of Maria's lifeline up to another red streak.

Iselin's death.

Hanne tripled Maria's lifeline all the way to the edge of the paper.

Maria had not only benefited from her sister's murder. According to an extensive article in *Dagens Næringsliv* last week, she had gained even more by Iselin's passing. When they married, Maria had presented her wife with half of her 80 percent holding in VitaeBrass, a transaction the business newspaper described as lovesick idiocy. No conditions were attached to the agreement.

None apart from that they both had mutual inheritance rights.

In other words, 80 percent of VitaeBrass was back in Maria's hands, and she was now wealthier than ever before. On the long road from life as a beachcombing deadbeat in 2001 to becoming a rich and successful businesswoman in 2016, her niece had died, her sister murdered, her brother-in-law condemned to prison and eternal suffering, and her wife had died by her own hand after being exposed as one of the Internet's worst propagandists against the Muslim population of Europe.

It sounded like a novel. A terribly bad novel that no one would want to read.

"Hammo!" she heard Ida call from the hallway. "We're home!"

"Shit," Hanne spluttered, logging out of her computer at lightning speed.

It was long past five o'clock, and the veal roast was still on the kitchen counter.

SUNDAY, JANUARY 24, 2016

Henrik Holme woke with a sore ear.

Several seconds passed before he discovered that he had fallen asleep using his laptop as a pillow. He had no idea why he had closed it up in his sleep and pushed it under his head. He had been watching a film on Netflix, he remembered, a sci-fi effort about a gang of teenagers making a zombie movie. The last thing he had taken in was when a train veered off the track in an inferno of flames and explosions.

He wasn't likely to watch the rest of it.

His body felt stiff and exhausted as he struggled up to a sitting position and stuffed a couple of pillows behind his back. His left knee had started to ache again. Just less than two years ago, soon after the bombs had gone off on May 17, his habitual walking had led to an infection that had persisted for several weeks. The previous day's lengthy trip to and from Heikki Pettersen's house in the pouring rain and biting north wind had probably been too much. Henrik carefully massaged both sides of his knee, though it did not help in the least.

But the trip had been well worth it.

Henrik opened the laptop and perched it on his knee. Last night he had scanned the entire contents of Bonsaksen's ring binder and organized it all on the computer, something he should have done ages ago. Hanne had commandeered her own copy, and now the original ring binder was finally installed on the bookshelf in the living room.

It had mostly been the autopsy report that had engrossed him after his visit to Heikki Pettersen at Stugguveien 2A. He clicked his way into the document and read it once again.

Anna had bled to death.

She had been shot in the lower part of her face at close range. The bullet had entered beneath her chin, just to the left of the midpoint. It had shattered her lower jaw, struck her teeth on the left side of her

232

mouth, leaving behind an exit wound just below the eye that Henrik still could not bear to look at for more than a second or two.

According to the report, Anna Abrahamsen had been five foot eight and weighed 154 pounds. She had not sustained any other injuries apart from the ones to her face. The report stated that she had an appendectomy scar; something Henrik guessed meant that she had had her appendix removed. There was nothing of note about her lungs and heart, which had both been of normal weight.

Henrik did not like the thought of organs being weighed. It necessarily entailed removing them from the body. Even now, after five years on the police force, he found it difficult to be anywhere near a corpse. In no way did he find them repulsive—instead, the problem was that he became so unspeakably sad at the sight of dead human beings. He was overcome by a feeling of tenderness. Of respect. He still couldn't, even after five years filled to overflowing with dead bodies, stop thinking about who they had been. What kind of life they had led, and who had been fond of them.

Or hadn't been fond of them. Six years ago, he had been forced to break into an apartment in Brobekk. It was located on the sixth floor, and the neighbor below had noticed a strange, rosette-shaped stain spreading across the ceiling. When the door was smashed open, Henrik's colleagues had initially reacted to the unbearable stench inside, whereas Henrik had been overwhelmed by a strong sense of sorrow. The man on the living room floor was sixty-six years old, and it turned out that he had lain there for three weeks without anyone raising the alarm. No one had reported him missing. Even though a mountain of copies of *Aftenposten* had piled up at his door, not a single soul had bothered to check that everything was okay.

Henrik had wept that evening and still remembered the old man in his nightly prayers.

Which he had not got around to saying last night, it crossed his mind, and he struggled to concentrate on the autopsy report.

None of Anna's vital organs was damaged. Admittedly, the bullet had virtually destroyed the lower left part of her face, but the brain was untouched. Unless the intense pain had knocked her out, she could have remained conscious as she slowly bled to death.

The thought was almost intolerable.

Henrik searched for something that might tell him how quickly it had all gone but found nothing. However, what emerged clearly was that both of Anna's hands had distinct traces of gunshot residue. Since she had shot five rounds at the firing range on the morning of New Year's Eve, the pathologist's findings had not been questioned elsewhere in Bonsaksen's papers.

Henrik logged out of the digital folder he had created and placed the laptop on the bedside table. It was only 5:30. He knew he could forget the idea of going back to sleep and instead padded out to the bathroom, had a pee, washed his face in ice-cold water, and stood looking at his reflection in the mirror.

The harsh bathroom lighting made him look even paler than usual.

He tried to hunch his shoulders, but paradoxically enough, this made them look even narrower. He lifted his chin and studied the scar that ran so precisely along the fold of skin where his chin met his neck. It was fading. By summer it would have almost disappeared. This year he would make a serious effort to acquire a suntan, something he had never done before. He never took his shirt off around others; his rib cage had always reminded him of a scrawny bird. Until now his legs had been like sticks, and since the age of eleven, he had greeted every summer fully dressed from head to toe.

Henrik Holme had barely been able to swim when, as an eighteen-year-old, he had launched himself into rigorous training to gain admittance to the police academy.

But it dawned on him that he looked better now. His weight training was beginning to show results. He ran his fingers over his rib cage and felt that he could flex his muscles. It was as if the reddish-blond hairs that etched the outline of a letter "T" across his chest had become thicker. It must be his imagination, but Henrik tensed and jutted his chin forward. His mother had always insisted he use factor 50 sunscreen, but now that would stop. This summer he would find himself a girlfriend. Tinder, he had thought. Or Bumble, where only women could initiate a conversation. Henrik had read that this was a precaution to restrict sleaziness, and he certainly had no wish to appear suspect.

This summer, when the scar was completely gone and he had turned brown.

He brushed his teeth.

Anna Abrahamsen had been attractive. She could certainly have had any man she wanted. A sporty type, tall and athletic, and an excellent markswoman. Jonas had once been a lucky man. There must be an Anna Abrahamsen for Henrik too, somewhere out there, and soon he would find her.

He spat and rinsed his mouth, staring once again into his own eyes.

Jonas could well have been telling the truth.

After the first lie when he claimed he had not been to Stugguveien since December 28, he had asserted that no one had opened the door on New Year's Eve, one hour before midnight, when he had visited her to ask for forgiveness. To beg Anna for a fresh start. To try to live together without Dina instead of separate lives. The door was locked, and he had considered using his own key, the interview transcripts revealed. He had decided not to. He hadn't wanted to be provocative: after all, he was looking for a second chance.

No one had believed Jonas. Except perhaps Kjell Bonsaksen. And Henrik Holme.

He wanted to believe Jonas. He really wanted to believe that Jonas had never stepped inside Anna's house that night. If he had done so, could he have saved her? Was she lying there bleeding to death at that very moment while the neighbors partied and Jonas stood at a loss outside the door? Was there another killer inside, someone no one had seen any sign of, either during the intensive, painstaking investigation in the early months of 2004 or now, when both he and Hanne had gone through the entire set of papers one more time?

In that case, it must be a perpetrator who had moved completely under the radar, hidden from the police and all of Anna's acquaintances, with no motive, someone who had not stolen anything and not raped her either. Someone who had entered and exited the locked house unseen, without leaving behind as much as a microscopic speck.

A ghost, in other words. But ghosts don't exist.

If Jonas was telling the truth, as Bonsaksen had always suspected, there could not possibly be another perpetrator. It must be suicide. The only thing that could unravel the puzzle.

Dina's death, the marriage on the rocks, Anna's depression that was gradually worsening. The pristine house, purged of every personal belonging, clinically cleaned as if for a house showing, and, in addition, Dina's dismantled room. The clothes Dina had been wearing when she died and thrown out last of all so that Anna could finally choose to die.

It would solve the mystery if it hadn't been for the confounded unknown variable.

The gun.

Henrik wondered whether to have a shower, but decided on a fast wash instead. While the basin was filling with hot water, it struck him that Jonas was the only conceivable candidate to have removed the Glock after the suicide. However, it would have been completely illogical. No matter how hard Henrik tried, he could not find a single plausible reason for Jonas to have let himself in, found his estranged wife either dead or dying, picked up the gun, taken it with him, and then gone home.

Henrik attacked his armpits with two soapy hands and rubbed energetically.

It would have been senseless for Jonas to remove the gun. Anyway, Henrik believed him. He had made up his mind to trust Bonsaksen's gut feeling, and that meant Jonas had not let himself in.

He toweled himself dry and headed into the bedroom for clean clothes. He opened the closet and ran his eyes over his shirts, all freshly ironed and hung in order of color, the white ones on the left and then all the way through red, green, and blue to the two black ones on the extreme right. Underpants, also ironed and neatly folded, were stored in a wire basket.

Guns did not disappear by themselves. If it were a case of suicide, someone must have removed the gun.

Someone must have been in the house when it was clear that no one had been there. A recently fired Glock 17 had vanished without trace from an empty house that was closed and locked.

Henrik snatched at a green flannel shirt and froze. For several minutes, he stood thinking with one hand on the clothes hanger and the other loosely holding the closet door. A thought had struck him, only just and almost imperceptibly, and he concentrated hard on not letting it slip away. It felt as if, in a sudden flash, he had glimpsed the value of the unknown variable, the piece of the jigsaw that could solve the puzzle and make everything fall neatly into place.

"Of course," he said aloud all of a sudden—he had seized hold of the fleeting thought and held it firmly in his grasp. "If Mohammad won't come to the mountain, then the mountain must go to Mohammad—of course!"

There was something wrong with the timing, and he knew the very person he needed to speak to about that.

The shopping expedition had gone well.

Since Jonas did not dare use the car and also lacked the energy to clear away the thick, soaking wet snow that covered the track leading to the road, he had taken the bus to Storo. It did not run very often, and he had to walk a half mile to the bus stop, but transport had not been the greatest challenge.

Somehow he had needed to get Hedda to sleep during his absence.

The solution was Cosylan, a prescription cough medicine.

He had a bottle in the fridge from a bad chest infection he had suffered in November. He had refused to call in sick for work, and the cough medicine contained morphine, so the bottle was almost full. It had been tricky to work out how much to administer to the little girl, and the liquid must taste horrible too. He had wheedled and coaxed to no avail, and in the end he had mixed four tablespoons into a cherry yogurt that Hedda readily gobbled up with a hearty appetite.

It took only fifteen minutes for her to fall asleep. He had laid her in the double bed, tucked her cozily into the quilt, and wound steel wire around the window catches. Then he barricaded the bedroom door with a heavy chest of drawers that a three-year-old would have no chance of budging.

Jonas's shopping trip to the Storo center had taken two hours and fifteen minutes.

When he returned with his backpack crammed with food, diapers, children's clothing, and a brand-new Barbie doll, Hedda was still sleeping heavily. She had wet the bed without noticing and didn't even wake when he carried her into the living room to change the bedsheets.

Clothes had presented the biggest problem.

The whole of Norway was preoccupied with Hedda Bengtson's disappearance. The advertising on the digital displays at the Storo center had been replaced by pictures of the three-year-old, four different ones shown in continuous rotation. Although there was nothing intrinsically criminal about buying children's clothes, he was so afraid of anyone raising the alarm that he had bought boy's clothing. The woman behind the counter had asked with a smile if the numerous garments were a gift. He had nodded and let her wrap them in dark green paper decorated with blue teddy bears. Because he feared that Hedda would refuse point-blank to put on underpants with a fly front, he had risked throwing two packs of pink underpants into his shopping basket at the supermarket, where he had filled his bag with fresh groceries.

He had not been scared to buy a Barbie doll. Three-year-olds shouldn't really like Barbie. Dina had been given one by her aunt when she was two, and it had gone straight into the trash on Anna's instructions.

Hedda had slept all through the night. Jonas had hardly closed an eye.

She seemed so peaceful as she lay there. Her breath was regular and she smelled so sweet. She lay facing him, halfway over on her side, and she had kicked off the quilt. If he put his own pillow over her face and held it tight, it would all be over. It would not take more than a few minutes. It would be so easy. Merciful, even, because she would barely be aware of what was happening before she was no longer alive.

"Hungry," Hedda said in a sleepy voice, opening her eyes. "Jonas!"

She crept close to him, boring her head into the crook of his neck and putting her stubby, warm hand on his cheek.

"Fuzzy beard," she mumbled. "I'm hungry, Jonas."

"I'll make pancakes for breakfast," he whispered and kissed her hair. "And then I've got a present for you."

He pushed her away discreetly and got up from the bed.

He would have to do it today, and he could not for the life of him work out why he had not gotten rid of Hedda as early as Thursday. It was lunacy to keep the toddler here. Absolutely crazy. He could not fathom why he had jeopardized his whole plan by doping her up to the eyeballs in order to buy a Barbie doll and new clothes when she was soon to die.

Today.

Today he would have to pull himself together and complete the undertaking he had embarked on. But first he would make the best pancakes in the world.

Dina's favorite dish.

"Here," Hanne said, pointing at an apartment building on Trondheim-sveien. "Drop me off as close as possible to that door over there."

Nefis was a hopeless driver. Like most other hopeless drivers, she

could not really bear driving. Hanne had frequently wondered why
they had a car at all, since it was used only on a handful of occasions a
year. Nefis had become expert at arranging rides from other parents for
Ida's many riding lessons and shows and school activities, and she herself preferred to take a taxi.

However, taxis were one of the worst things Hanne had ever experienced.

Taxi drivers with foreign backgrounds—and they were in the
majority—insisted as if their lives depended on it on helping her with
everything. As soon as they spotted her waiting on the sidewalk, they
leaped from their cabs to lift her onto the backseat, fold up her wheelchair, and fasten her seat belt. These moves involved being touched so
many times by total strangers that Hanne felt exhausted for days afterward.

Almost worse were the Norwegian drivers, who wanted to quiz her
and delve into what it was like to be confined to a wheelchair. About
what had happened to her, what problems she had experienced with
disability benefits, and how politicians were driving the welfare state to
rack and ruin by peering through their fingers at the tricks and fakery
of worthless bums and work-shy scroungers. Especially of "our new
countrymen," as they normally expressed it, in the ironic and forlorn
hope of not offending their passenger.

When Hanne had decided there was no possibility of avoiding a conversation with Kari Thue, she had asked Nefis to drive her. Now the six-
year-old Audi was parked diagonally across the tram tracks in
Trondheimsveien. Hanne wisely kept her own counsel as Nefis swore
loudly at the tram honking angrily behind them, while she craned over
the steering wheel in an effort to see whether it was legal to drive into
Conradis gate.

"I think this'll be okay, Hanna!"

She stalled the engine. How it was possible to stall a car with automatic gears was beyond Hanne's comprehension. The tram was making
an infernal racket. A truck approached, blinking its headlights before
the driver let loose on the horn. Nefis reeled off a string of Turkish
words Hanne had heard many times before without ever finding out
what they meant. She shut her eyes.

"No one died," she mouthed silently.

Now Nefis was cursing in Norwegian, but fortunately she managed to start the car. It lurched ahead into Conradis gate, where it came to a sudden halt again.

Halfway across the sidewalk this time.

Hanne sat in silence waiting until Nefis had heaved the wheelchair out of the trunk and set it down just outside the passenger seat. It took her only seconds to transfer into the chair, and when Nefis closed the car door, she mumbled a few words of thanks as she surveyed the grayish-yellow apartment building where Kari Thue lived.

"How long will this take?" Nefis asked.

"Maybe only a minute," Hanne said. "I have my doubts whether she'll want to talk to me at all. At best it might take some time. Can I call you when I want to be picked up?"

"Of course!"

Nefis gave her a fleeting kiss on the mouth and quickly stroked her hair. Hanne reacted by mussing it up again, using the fingers of both hands.

"Just phone," Nefis said. "I can do some shopping in the meantime."

"It's Sunday, don't forget."

"That doesn't matter. Just take whatever time you need. Shall I help you in?"

"No thanks. Henrik said there was an elevator here. But wait for five minutes before you drive off. It's far from certain that she'll be at home."

Hanne approached the entrance, where a panel mounted with door-bells confirmed that Kari Thue lived on the third floor. Ringing the bell would probably be a bad idea. If Hanne were to have the tiniest chance of at least initiating a conversation, she would have to depend on con-fronting Thue face-to-face. So she fished out her cell phone and immersed herself in Wordfeud just long enough to spot an elderly man closing in at the corner of her eye. He had already taken out his keys. When, as expected, he turned onto the slushy path leading to the dou-ble entrance doors, Hanne began to maneuver her wheelchair in the same direction.

She did not even need to say anything. The wheelchair worked its magic.

"Let me help you," the old man offered cheerfully and held the heavy door open, obviously pleased he was not the one with mobility prob-lems. "Are you using the elevator?"

Hanne nodded.

"Third," she said tersely when the man had summoned the elevator and stepped politely aside to let her in first. "Thanks very much."

The man got off on the second floor, and when the doors opened again one floor up, Hanne trundled out into the center of a deserted stairwell. She glanced to the right, where a large hand-painted porcelain plaque decorated with meadow flowers announced that the apartment belonged to A. and B. Strømstad. Hanne moved to the left. Kari Thue had chosen a more modern variation, a transparent acrylic sign giving her full name in black letters.

She had become more courageous in the end, Hanne thought. She would grant Kari Thue that, if nothing else. While at Finse 1222 she had sneaked around in the dark like Gollum with vile whispers and innuendo, but over the years she had become both more visible and considerably more vociferous. Hanne knew that revealing her address must have brought about a great deal of unpleasantness, as the paintwork on the door also indicated. It had obviously been scrubbed down a number of times. Perhaps Thue had finally grown tired of repainting every time someone attacked her apartment with marker pens, spray paint, and abuse. Hanne thought she could just make out the pale shadow of *Racist cunt!!!* diagonally across the upper part of the door.

She rang the doorbell. The silence continued.

Fortunately the door was not fitted with a peephole. Kari would have to open the door if she wanted to find out what this was about. At last Hanne could hear footsteps. The door opened a crack, with the security chain still fastened.

"Hello," Hanne said.

"Hanne Wilhelmsen," Kari Thue replied tonelessly with her face pressed to the gap.

"Yes. I'd appreciate a chance to talk to you. It won't take long."

"Sorry, but I've no interest in talking to you."

"It's not about Iselin. It's about Maria. Benedicte."

Kari Thue did not respond, but at least she did not shut the door.

"I don't believe that Iselin committed suicide," Hanne added, staking everything on one card.

The door was still only slightly opened.

"What do you mean?" Kari Thue asked after such a lengthy pause that Hanne began to think something was seriously amiss.

"If you'd let me come in, I can explain."

"But surely she took her own life?"

"I don't think so."

"Why not?"

"Because . . . Could I just come in for a minute?"

"No. Why do you think she didn't take her own life?"

Her wan face looked almost greenish in the light given off by the fluorescent tubes in the ancient fixture in the stairwell. Her mouth was broad, with thin lips bombarded from above by an arrow shower of fine wrinkles.

"I don't think Iselin was ashamed," Hanne said, unruffled. "It was unpleasant, being exposed, just as it must be extremely unpleasant for you to have this door . . ."

She glanced up at the barely visible abuse.

". . . repeatedly vandalized. It must be disturbing and awkward and shouldn't happen, of course. But it doesn't make you change your mind, does it? Far from it—it makes you even more convinced of the importance of the battle you're fighting."

No reaction. Not a nod, not a word.

"Iselin wasn't ashamed," Hanne repeated. "Being unmasked as Tyrfing was distasteful, but it didn't involve any social disgrace. Quite the opposite, in fact—she was defended by her supporters. Praised to the skies by many of them. And after all, when push comes to shove, it's our own people who mean the most to us in this world."

Still no reaction.

"But as I said, it's primarily Maria I'd like to talk to you about. Could I come in?"

"No."

Hanne made a face. She felt a stab of pain in the small of her back: it had grown more troublesome in the past few weeks. A cold draft from a broken leaded window in the stairwell did not improve matters.

"You've been struggling with depression," Hanne plucked up the courage to say. "You're taking antidepressants. Anafranil. I'm willing to place a large bet on some of your medication having been stolen."

Now at last, Kari Thue's facial expression altered. Her eyes narrowed and a sharp, V-shaped furrow appeared between her eyebrows.

"Wait," she said abruptly and slammed the door shut.

Hanne was happy to shift position in the wheelchair, but now her right arm had begun to ache. It gave way when she tried to hoist herself up, and her shoulder twisted painfully.

"Shit," she murmured, tugging her jacket more snugly around her.

A minute passed, then two, and nearly three. She heard fumbling with the chain on the inside of the door.

"You were right," Kari Thue said, opening the door wide. "Someone has stolen my pills."

She ran her hand over her face in a gesture of helplessness.

"Come in," she said, as she disappeared into the apartment.

"I knew you would make something of yourself, Henrik."

Professor Emeritus Carsten Bru laid a colossal hand on Henrik Holme's slim shoulder as he ushered him into his home office.

The room was spacious and had originally been one of the enormous villa's many living rooms. Facing south, bay windows overhung what Henrik knew was an old apple orchard. On good days you could enjoy the sight of a beautiful copper beech by the fence skirting the neighbor's garden at the foot of the sloping ground. Now it was impossible to see anything except grayish-white snowflakes dancing in the light cast by an outdoor lamp; it had turned cold again. Henrik had taken the bus to spare his knee.

The massive tiled Swedish stove in the corner was lit. Professor Bru opened the door and tossed a log on the fire before sitting down at his desk in the center of the room. The walls were lined with bookshelves crammed full of books, both vertical and perpendicular. Professional textbooks and novels, travel books and atlases and poetry collections. Henrik had been here once before, and it was one of the most impressive rooms he had ever set eyes on. The ceiling was decorated as a pale-blue summer sky, with birds, butterflies, and vine branches so detailed that they looked as if they needed watering. A polar-bear-skin rug covered the floor in front of the stove, with a gaping mouth and terrifying teeth. Professor Bru claimed it had been shot in self-defense on Svalbard in 1963 after it had killed two expedition members, but Henrik did not always place much trust in the old professor's stories about his many travels and experiences. He was not even sure that the man had ever been to Svalbard.

When it came to professional topics, however, he was first-class and could always be relied on.

Carsten Bru was Norway's grand old man of forensic medicine. Henrik had come across him in autumn 2011, when the country was still struggling to recover from that brutal summer, and Henrik's only friend was dead. In an attack of loneliness and despair, Henrik had applied for a postgraduate course in the forensic investigation of homicide and violent crime. He gained a place on the course, even though he had just finished his elementary training.

Professor Bru had paid him so much attention from the very first class that for a few months, Henrik had thought they might become friends. When he finally realized that the seventy-year-old man had absolutely no wish to extend his social circle and the professor merely kept an eye open for talented students, he was so embarrassed that he hardly looked up from his notes for the remainder of the course.

When he needed advice in an old murder case that Hanne and he had solved a year or so ago, he had swallowed his pride and paid a visit to Professor Bru. The man, who had retired on full pension, was in great form on all fronts. He gave lectures and edited textbooks and in addition sat on the board of Oslo University Hospital. His delight at being visited by a former student seemed so genuine at that time that Henrik had now steeled himself to do it again.

"Do you think they'll be found guilty? All of them?"

Carsten Bru pointed at one of the two wing chairs in front of his desk.

"We'll have to wait and see," Henrik replied, sitting down. "Hanne Wilhelmsen is convinced. As for myself, I'm a bit doubtful as far as the more peripheral accused are concerned. I think judgment will be passed fairly soon. That's what the rumors say, anyway."

"Quite a story," the old man said, shaking his head. "Quite a story. But how can I help you today, Henrik?"

His eyes glittered under his trimmed, wiry eyebrows. His head was shaved, but he had acquired a well-tended, pepper-and-salt beard since last they'd met. He must weigh well over two hundred pounds, but carried his bulk with the authority bestowed by a long career as a self-assured star academic.

"A time of death," Henrik said, with a gulp. "I'm unsure of a time of death. In a case from 2004. Or . . ."

He gulped again and looked around for something to drink. The professor had not offered him anything, and he did not dare ask.

"The death occurred in 2003," he corrected himself. "On New Year's Eve, just before midnight. Or . . ."

He lifted his bag from the floor and opened it. He pulled out a bottle of water and unscrewed the lid.

"Excuse me," he said, and took a drink.

"My wife will be here with coffee in a minute," Professor Bru said with a smile.

"The point was that I wonder whether the police might have been mistaken at that time. They found the body on January 1, 2004, even though the death itself took place the previous year, on—"

"I understand it now. Why do you think they were wrong? If the corpse was found within twenty-four hours, it should have been possible to arrive at a fairly good estimate. That was possible even in 2004."

Henrik replaced the lid on the bottle and returned it to his bag. "Do you really have time to hear me out?" he asked.

"I've all the time in the world," Carsten Bru answered.

"It's about a murder for which a man was sentenced to twelve years' imprisonment," Henrik began hesitantly. "But I think it may have been a miscarriage of justice. Actually, I think this woman took her own life. The problem is that no weapon was found at the crime scene. That's why I really need your help. To place a weapon there somehow."

Professor Bru stretched out his arms before leaning across the massive, solid desk.

"Then I'm damn glad you came," he said, chuckling, and began to roll up his shirtsleeves. "Now we're going to have some fun, Henrik. We'll have a damn brilliant time, the two of us."

"I stopped taking them a few weeks ago," Kari Thue said. "That's why I didn't notice they were gone."

"How many are you missing?"

"Eleven. The ones that were left. And you're mistaken. I'm not depressed. I have a panic disorder."

That was how she looked, Hanne thought. The guarded eyes never lingered anywhere for longer than a second or two at a time. Her eyes were unnaturally wide, as if she were constantly shocked about something or other. Her hands were never at peace. Kari Thue was fiddling with a silver ring, then scratching her arms and pulling her sleeves up and down. Her left leg was shaking slightly and had done so ever since she sat down.

"What a shame," Hanne said, hoping that she sounded sincere. "Didn't the medicine help?"

Kari Thue's eyes looked accusingly at Hanne's for all of three seconds.

"As you've stopped using them, I mean?"

"Side effects" was Kari Thue's curt reply. "Anyway, it's none of your business. Do you think you know who stole my pills?"

"No. I can't claim that. But I do have a theory. Do you see much of Iselin and Maria?"

"Iselin's dead. I haven't seen Benedicte . . . Maria since then. I wasn't even told about the funeral."

Hanne noticed a faint quiver in Kari Thue's voice. Sorrow or anger—it was difficult to tell.

"Yes, of course," she said patiently. "But earlier, I mean. Before Iselin died. Did you socialize much with them?"

Kari Thue stood up abruptly. At Finse 1222, she had been slim but not skinny. Since then Hanne had seen her only in the media, and then she obviously had help to look better than she did in reality. The contrast now between the dour, scrawny figure and her flowing, well-groomed hair was almost comical. As if someone had placed a highly inappropriate wig on her head.

"I've known Maria since I was little," Kari Thue said. "She was called Benedicte then, as I told your colleague when he was here. She was in my brother's class and lived not far from us. I got to know Iselin through her. And yes . . ."

She walked to the kitchen and disappeared inside. "Yes," she repeated from beyond the doorway. "We've seen a lot of one another, all three of us."

Hanne heard a tap being turned on. She looked around the small living room. If Hanne had counted the total number of doors in the hallway correctly, there were two apartments with kitchen and bathroom. It was pleasant in here, she grudgingly admitted. A seating arrangement in grayish blue; Ida loved the color and had a feature wall in her bedroom painted the same. There were houseplants everywhere: Kari

Thue obviously had a green thumb. On an abundantly filled bookshelf sat a TV with a cathode ray tube; Hanne could not remember having seen one like that in years.

The walls were adorned with lithographs of the type the Norwegian Book Club used to give away as recruitment gifts in their heyday: acceptable, worthless, and reasonably decorative.

"I assumed you'd want some," Kari Thue said, putting down two glasses of water with ice cubes on the coffee table.

"Thanks."

"Was it my tablets that killed Iselin? Had she taken them from here?"

Hanne thought she could detect tears in the woman's big eyes. However, Kari Thue had been red-eyed before, and it could be that she was suffering from conjunctivitis.

"That's not what I believe," Hanne said calmly. "I don't think Iselin committed suicide, so it's beyond me what she would have wanted with your tablets."

"Do you mean that someone has . . . killed her? With my pills?"

"Yes, that's my opinion. But for the present I can't prove any of it. That's why I've come. Here. To you."

Her phone vibrated in the pocket of her leather jacket; she had not taken off her outdoor clothes. She glanced at the display. Nefis was wondering if she could drive off. Hanne texted a hasty *OK*.

"Apologies," she said. "An important message, that's all."

"I don't know who could have taken my pills," Kari Thue said.

"No. But you know who might have had the opportunity."

"My brother. He's here often and has his own key. I can assure you it wasn't him."

She lifted her glass of water. The ice cubes betrayed her nervousness.

"My mother."

Kari Thue drank half the glass of water.

"As a matter of fact," she corrected herself, "she hasn't been here since I decided to try life without Anafranil. That was seven weeks ago. So it wasn't her either."

"Anyone else?"

"Friends," she said, mulling it over. "But I haven't been very sociable recently. The side effects from the medicine have gone, but . . ."

She clasped her arms around herself, as if she were freezing.

"The positive effects disappear too, of course. It's quite difficult. To tell the truth, I'm not really in good shape."

For the first time Hanne felt some sympathy for her. She resembled a mournful bird as she sat there in her mustard-yellow clothes and with her bony hands that were never at rest. A children's rhyme that Ida had loved entered Hanne's head. It was about a sad yellow bird that was depressed because he didn't really exist.

Here and now it was as if Kari Thue had also disappeared. Even though she could obviously take care of herself despite her panic disorder, it was as if there was something indescribably bewildered about her as she appeared now. The stiff-necked behavior when she had answered the door was gone, as was her well-known fury in countless TV debates. It was inconceivable that this half-dead creature in a knitted sweater several sizes too big was the same woman who had suggested in *VG* that the refugees in Storskog should be shot with live ammunition.

"Could Iselin or Maria have taken the pills?" Hanne probed.

Kari Thue nodded almost imperceptibly, as if the effort of moving was too much for her.

"Well, they've been here three times since I stopped," she said softly.

"Both of them?"

The hesitation was precisely a fraction too long.

"Yes."

Hanne leaned back in her wheelchair. She had a strong urge to move into an armchair, but did not want to spoil what she thought she was succeeding in achieving. Instead she put her hands quietly on her lap and made an effort to catch Kari Thue's eye.

"But not always?"

"What . . . what do you mean?"

"They didn't always come together?"

"Yes, they did."

"I don't think so. I think that Iselin came on her own when Maria didn't know about it."

"I think you should leave now."

There was no power in her voice, and she made no move to get up. She did not even look in Hanne's direction.

"I will, of course, if that's what you really want. First of all, though, I want to reassure you that . . ."

Hesitating, she rolled her chair closer to the other woman, who did not react at all.

"Whatever you tell me will remain between the two of us. You don't like me, and quite honestly I've never been a great fan of yours either. None of that matters a bit right now. What does matter, and I'm sure we're in total agreement about this, is that no one should be able to murder other people here in this country of ours. Far less get away with it."

They were sitting so close that Hanne could see that Kari's dry lips had cracked open into tiny cold sores.

"But the police," Kari Thue began, and now she was twirling one hand around and around on her sweater. "The police said right away that it was a case of suicide. You could read that between the lines in the online press only hours after it happened."

"Yes. Mostly because there was a suicide note. When you find a letter like that and the circumstances also seem to fit the inference that the person has taken his or her own life, then a rapid conclusion is usually drawn. Sometimes too rapid, unfortunately."

"A suicide letter . . ." Sniffing, she wiped her nose with the dirty-yellow angora sleeve. "Then it must have been an old one."

"What?"

"If there was a suicide letter there, it must have been an old one."

"Why is that?"

Kari Thue swallowed, picked up the water glass, and drained it in one gulp.

"She suffered from electrosensitivity."

"Elec . . . what are you talking about?"

"Iselin was allergic to electricity. She discovered that years ago. Hypersensitive. She had a box made . . ."

Kari Thue used her hands to outline a square about the size of a laptop.

". . . that prevented the electromagnetism from getting out. Something like that. It fell apart the day after she was . . . outed. Three weeks before she died. She wrote nothing after that. She couldn't write without that box."

When she looked up, she seemed almost self-conscious.

"I don't know very much about that sort of thing. Iselin knew such a lot. She was impressive—she knew so much about everything. She had a device around her cell phone too. That was okay, as far as I know. But she didn't write the suicide letter on her cell phone, did she?"

Hanne let her chair roll back, as she straightened her spine and gave a stiff smile.

"The letter was handwritten," she said. "If a suicide letter is typed, then it certainly wouldn't have the same effect. On the police, I mean. Then it would always be examined with care. Even more carefully, you know. Then someone else may be behind it. But this one was handwritten in Iselin's own writing. So the fact that her ... anti-electricity-allergy gizmo was broken is of no significance."

"Iselin didn't write by hand."

"What?"

"Iselin never writes by hand. She hasn't handwritten anything for a very, very long time. Several decades, in fact."

It was as if a fork was being slowly drawn down Hanne's spine. She shivered, and her back ached insanely.

"Of course she must have written some things by hand," Hanne said, trying to smile.

It was difficult—she felt hot and as if her chest was being crushed.

"As we all do," she added. "Shopping lists, at the very least. Christmas cards. Little things like that."

Hanne had never written Christmas cards in all her life. She suddenly thought of the conversation she'd had with Ida the other day, about how little the modern person actually used handwriting. She greatly regretted not having paid more attention to her daughter.

"And passports!" she came up with. "After all, you have to sign your passport. And contracts. Iselin Havørn was a businesswoman. She must have signed loads of documents. Frequently."

"Yes, she did sign things. But that was all she did. You see ..."

Now she looked around the apartment and lowered her voice, as if she and Hanne were old confidantes guarding against hidden microphones.

"Do you really think someone killed her?"

Her eyes were as big as saucers. A tiny drop of clear snot had attached itself to the fine hairs inside one nostril. She was still twisting her hands around the front of her sweater. It would start to unravel soon.

"Why didn't she write by hand?" Hanne asked.

"Because," Kari Thue launched into an explanation. She stood up abruptly and began to pace around the room.

"Iselin was dyslexic. Quite badly affected."

"Dys . . . but she's worked as a journalist!"

"Yes, it was fucking awful. As it was all through school too. And when she was studying law. Iselin had greater problems writing than reading, but in the end, she found the intricate legal language impenetrable. She dropped out and started working in a factory."

"I thought that was to acquire proletarian credentials?" Hanne said.

Kari Thue shrugged. "That too, I suppose. But it suited her to stop, if I can put it that way. Do you really think somebody killed Iselin?"

Then the tears began. Genuine, grief-stricken weeping. Hanne breathed more easily and rolled her chair all the way to the other side of the coffee table to allow the brokenhearted woman more air and space.

"I promised Iselin that I wouldn't tell anyone," she managed to confess through her sobs. "That dyslexia . . . she had struggled with it all her life. Why on earth she chose to be a journalist when . . . I can't understand it."

She cupped her hands around her face, as if trying to console herself.

"The first few years at *Dagbladet* she worked night and day. It took her five times as long as anyone else to write an article. The text was littered with mistakes anyway, but luckily newspapers then could still afford to employ proofreaders. When she began writing features, she secretly hired a student. To help her, no less. It was a huge relief when she started working on TV with NRK, even though she still had to tackle written material there too, of course. It's crossed my mind that this was why she became ill at the end of the eighties. She was worn out, to tell the truth. Both because of the dyslexia itself and having to keep it hidden. Then computers and advanced correction programs came along. Some of them are specially designed for dyslexics. Iselin could start to write again. Even though there are still a few mistakes in what she produces. Produced, I should say."

She dried her tears, but it looked as if there was still plenty where they came from.

Hanne was no longer listening properly.

It was difficult to process the consequences of what she had just learned. Her brain was working overtime. She had already started to think of what she would have to do once she could leave Kari Thue's apartment. It had begun to feel cramped, and most of all, she wanted to ask Nefis to come and pick her up at once.

"You don't need to say any more," she said. "I'm taking your word for it that she didn't use handwriting. Fortunately nowadays we have a lot more expertise about reading and writing problems. In the fifties and sixties, it was different. I understand that this has been difficult for you."

Kari Thue stopped crying all of a sudden. "People like you have no idea how difficult it is to be like us. About how it feels to be ridiculed and browbeaten. Bullied and called an idiot down through the years. When it comes to immigration, for example, who was right?"

Kari Thue left the question hanging in the air. Hanne clenched her teeth to avoid falling for the temptation to come up with an answer. The other woman seized the opportunity to do it for her.

"We," she said, pointing both forefingers at herself. "We're the ones who were right. For years I've been warning against what's happening now. Iselin too. We've seen them coming. Parallel societies that breed terror and hate. Brussels, Paris, and Rinkeby. Everywhere. Enclaves of wickedness in a landscape of naive, freedom-loving Europeans who until recently have closed their eyes to the catastrophic destruction we're facing. The annihilation of the European way of life. Of every-thing that belongs to us."

Hanne picked up the glass of water. Now it was her hands that were shaking.

"I think we'll drop that subject," she said in an undertone.

"You've never seen the major connections," Kari Thue persevered as she continued to circle the floor. "You don't see how everything hangs together with everything else. How what is happening is in the interests of Israel and the United States. It's in their interests to have a weakened Europe invaded by Muslims, just as the CIA, ever since World War II, has manipulated the regimes in the Middle East in order to create pre-cisely that instability in the area to their benefit. As long as they were dependent on oil from Saudi Arabia."

It was as if she had regained her strength in a split second. Now she was drained again, and she slumped back in her chair.

"Iselin saw all that. She knew so much. You understand none of it. And we're the ones who have to assume the burden. The persecution.

The ridicule. But now, fortunately, people have begun to see the light. It's only to be hoped that it's not too late."

Silence ensued. Hanne could hardly hear the other woman breathing. A magpie had settled on the window ledge. It cocked its head against the light streaming from the apartment and tapped on the glass before giving a muffled screech and flying off.

A tram rattled past in Trondheimsveien.

"How many people knew about it?" Hanne asked.

"About what?"

"That Iselin only ever used a computer to write because she was dyslexic."

"Not many. She's always worked hard to conceal it. Maria must know about it, of course. Sometimes when it wasn't possible to write on the computer, Iselin let Maria do it for her. Condolence cards, for instance. I know of at least one example of that. One of Iselin's childhood friends died of cancer last summer. She was married and had children, and her husband received a letter that Maria had written for Iselin."

She was crying again. Quiet sobs accompanied by snot and tears.

"That student from her *Dagbladet* days must know about it too," she whispered. "But I've no idea who that was. I don't know about anyone else."

"Did Maria know that you knew?"

Kari Thue did not answer. Her shoulders were so angular and bony it looked as if her sweater were suspended on a clothes hanger.

"I don't think so," she finally whispered.

"But she knows you had a relationship? That you and Iselin were having an affair?"

"I thought maybe she did. Now I do believe so. But I don't know for sure."

"How long were you . . . involved?"

"For eight months. You see . . ."

She was really struggling to compose herself. She straightened up, lifted her chin, and used her sweater to wipe her nose. Folded her hands and put them on her lap.

"Maria's not political. She hasn't been a . . . spiritual partner for Iselin. They could never really discuss anything. She always agreed with what Iselin said and has always admired her hugely. When Iselin proved to have a good head for business, the pedestal she put her on grew higher and higher. But Iselin wasn't comfortable there, on that pedestal. She and I, we were on a more . . . equal footing, you might say. We shared an outlook on life, you see. A common determination to fight for what we believe in."

Hanne gritted her teeth so hard that her jaw creaked.

"What kind of future did you imagine for yourselves?" she asked as quietly as she could.

"Iselin was going to tell Maria everything. She was here four days before she died. She hadn't yet said anything at that point. But she intended to, you know. She promised. We were going to live together here . . ."

Her gaze swept over the bookshelves, the furniture, and stopped at the windows facing the little balcony where a whole family of magpies was now ensconced.

". . . until we found something bigger. After all, Iselin owned 40 percent of VitaeBrass. She wouldn't be left high and dry, not by any means. We could have had a comfortable life from that point of view."

If Hanne had been granted the use of her legs, she would have stood up right now. She would have walked to the hallway without a word, exited the door, run down the stairs and all the way home, and then taken a long, hot shower.

"When was the last time Maria was here?" she asked instead.

The other woman got to her feet and headed into the kitchen again. When she returned, she was carrying a wall calendar.

"Just before Christmas," she said. "December 18."

"Did she know that you were taking antidepressants?"

"Yes. Panic attacks are easier to cope with when people around you are aware of the disorder."

"Where did you keep your pills?"

"In the bathroom. I have a sort of cabinet that is also a mirror."

"Locked?"

"No."

"Then I won't detain you any longer," Hanne said.

She began to trundle to the hallway and stopped at the door, where she turned the chair around and gazed at Kari Thue. She opened her mouth to say something, but then closed it again.

"What is it?" Kari Thue said when the silence threatened to become awkward.

"Love letters," Hanne said.

"What?"

"I've had a few in the course of my life. Not many, but a few. Believe it or not, I've even written one or two myself."

"Well?"

"None of them was machine written. Far too impersonal, wouldn't you agree?"

The woman in the yellow sweater did not answer.

"If Iselin ever wrote a letter of that kind to you," Hanne continued, "then I'd really appreciate seeing it."

She was still talking to apparently deaf ears.

"As I said, I believe Iselin was murdered. For a long time, I was of the opinion that it all had something to do with Tyrfing. With her views. Your views, the views you shared with Iselin. Now I'm convinced it's all about something else entirely."

If Kari Thue didn't find it worth responding, she nevertheless followed her words carefully. Her hands were quietly clasped on her lap, and her eyes were no longer flickering and flitting about so much.

"If you *do* have a handwritten letter from Iselin, then I'd be incredibly grateful to be allowed to see it. It might be of really crucial—"

She broke off when Kari Thue suddenly rose from her seat. "Who killed Iselin?" she asked, taking a few steps closer.

"I don't know, but I can help the police find out."

"Was it Maria?"

Hanne did not answer. She could not answer. She had paid this visit to Conradis gate with no authority other than her own irrepressible obstinacy. This was not her case. Until this very moment there had been no investigation at all, and Iselin Havørn's suicide was about to be closed and sealed as "no case to answer; no crime committed." That would now change. But not at this very second. Amanda Foss had to be informed. It would take days, if not weeks, to substantiate Kari Thue's assertions. Until that could happen, it was important that Hanne did not muddy the waters. That she did not diminish the value of the most significant testimony in the case by letting Kari Thue know too much.

Hanne could not give an answer, but she must get her hands on the letter she was sure existed.

"Yes," she said. "That's what I think. I believe Maria killed Iselin. And if I'm to have any chance of proving that, then I really must have a look at Iselin's own handwriting. I think you have a sample of that. You see, falling in love is actually . . ."

She put on a smile and this time it felt genuine.

". . . a pretty universal experience."

Kari Thue walked into the hallway without hesitation. As she passed Hanne, she paused for a moment and looked as if she was about to say something. She changed her mind and disappeared through a doorway directly opposite the entrance. Seconds later she was back.

"Here," she said, handing Hanne an envelope. "I received this from Iselin a month ago. I promised to burn it as soon as I'd read it. But I haven't had the heart to do that. It's been . . . I didn't even get a chance to go to the funeral."

She rubbed her arm slowly over her eyes.

"I just sat here waiting. She promised so many times to leave Maria. This letter has been a . . . comfort. A ray of hope. I could never bring myself to destroy it."

"That's how it goes. We don't burn love letters until love has died. Could you open the envelope and put the letter in a transparent plastic bag for me?"

Kari stared at her in bewilderment for a moment, before doing as Hanne requested. She had placed the envelope behind the letter and used tape to seal the bag.

The letter was legible.

It was a love letter. Quite a clumsy one, and with so many grammar and spelling mistakes that it could have been written by a teenager. And far too full of politics to boot.

But definitely a love letter, signed by Iselin with a heart instead of a dot above the *i*.

And all in handwriting Hanne had never seen before. Despite having spent hours scrutinizing the same woman's allegedly handwritten suicide letter.

The only part that was similar was the signature.

"Thanatos," Professor Carsten Bru said dramatically, "was the son of Nyx and twin brother of Hypnos."

His fingers gently caressed the figure he had brought from one of the jam-packed bookshelves. The bronze sculpture was around ten inches high and depicted a handsome naked man with angel wings holding a skull in his hands.

"Are you familiar with Greek mythology?"

Henrik gave an almost undetectable shrug, a gesture that could mean anything at all.

"Thanatos is the god of death. His father was Night and his brother Sleep. So appropriate, don't you think? Death being closely related to night and sleep?"

He smacked his lips in satisfaction and picked up a porcelain cup that seemed vanishingly small in his thick hands. The professor's wife had, as anticipated, brought both tea and coffee, and a tray of cookies that Henrik had soon scarfed up.

"Why is he so handsome?" Henrik asked with his mouth full of crumbs.

"Because he was the god of nonviolent death—the natural end of life, in other words. The touch of Thanatos was mild and gentle, just like that of his brother, Hypnos. Most often Thanatos is presented as an old, bearded man. I prefer this variant. Just a stripling."

He cautiously sipped the scalding-hot tea.

"And from this young man we have the most thrilling branch of science of them all. Thanatology. The study of dying, quite simply. The science of death. It goes without saying that such a comprehensive subject must have a multidisciplinary approach. Sociology and psychology, anthropology and philosophy, as well as medicine, of course, and a lot more besides."

"What would make a doctor choose death as a subject?"

The professor looked at him in astonishment.

"Death's all about life! It's through death that we learn most of what it is to live. For most of us, life is fundamentally all about postponing death for as long as we can. You know what they say about us pathologists? We're the ones who know everything, but by then it's sadly too late."

His laughter was feeble and reedy, contrasting strangely with his ample body.

"As far as I understand, you want help from me not to postpone death but to hasten it. Was that it?"

Henrik nodded.

"A woman," Carsten Bru said, encapsulating what Henrik had told him up till now. "Born in 1967, so around the age of thirty-six when she died. Physically fit, but mental state extremely low. She has lost her child and is recently separated. It was documented by a psychology specialist that as early as four months prior to her death, she was a suicide risk. This frame of mind is confirmed by witnesses in contact with her right up until the day she died. Devastated, alone, and with access to her own gun."

He glanced up from his notes. "Is that right?"

"Absolutely."

"Women rarely use guns to take their own lives."

"All the same it does happen. Anna was an expert with guns and, as you know, had access to a pistol."

"Yes. But one odd fact remains: she didn't kill herself! Not directly, at least. It emerges from the autopsy report that she bled to death. In other words, that she died as a result of wounds that were not treated quickly enough, not actually of a fatal shot to the head. If we are going to be painfully precise, and we are. From this . . ."

He waved the report.

". . . I'm convinced that she would have survived if she'd received prompt attention."

Henrik tried to swallow the dry crumbs from the rest of Mrs. Bru's Christmas cookies. He picked up his cup and drank while he mulled this over.

"What about a para-suicide?" he ventured deferentially.

The old professor raised his eyebrows.

"Now you're disappointing me deeply," he said reprovingly. "In the first place, para-suicide is a relatively controversial concept. As a rule, it describes a suicide attempt where a genuine desire to die does not really exist. Merely a wish to force some change in circumstances, be it other people's attitudes or social conditions. There's absolutely nothing in this poor woman's life cycle to suggest that she wanted anything of the kind."

"Sorry," Henrik let slip.

"On the other hand, if we're talking about a suicide *attempt*," Carsten Bru said with extreme emphasis on the last word, "then you might be on to something. Anna Abrahamsen might have sincerely wanted to end her own life. Pointed the pistol like so . . ."

His right hand became a gun, with his index finger as the barrel on the underside of his chin. He used his middle finger to pull the trigger.

"Bang. I'm dead. Most definitely and beyond any redemption, in such a short space of time that it's virtually impossible to measure it. Besides . . ."

He snatched up the autopsy report again, shoved his glasses farther up his nose, and read.

"The shot was fired at short range, it says here. There's no sign of contact between the muzzle and the skin. Okay, then. So . . ."

He repeated the experiment, using his own hand as a pistol close to his skin.

"Now I'm going to shoot. I'm totally determined. There's nothing more to live for. But then . . ."

He drew his finger slowly an inch or two away from his chin.

"Some people have second thoughts," he said. "Not because they miraculously emerge from their depression then and there. Not because they actually change their minds either, but because the sanctity of life is so deeply embedded within us. And I don't mean that in a religious sense."

His voice became a touch distorted because he was leaning his head back.

"Fundamental evolutionary theory," he said, still staring up at the exquisite ceiling. "The fight for existence. If all living things didn't have a really strong will to live, we would never endure this world's vale of tears. Just think of the Jews in concentration camps. The slaves in American cotton fields."

He suddenly removed his hand and looked Henrik straight in the eye.

"Losing a child," he said deliberately. "An experience I've been spared. But it's easy to imagine the pain, if you were ever minded to make the attempt. Why don't we take our own lives, Henrik, not even when the greatest pain is inflicted on us?"

Henrik was almost certain the question was rhetorical. Instead of responding, he lifted the elegant porcelain cup to his mouth and drank.

He had interpreted him correctly.

"The will to live," the professor said, raising his voice. "It is embedded deep within us. Lying deep within all of what combines to create the incredibly complicated human psyche is this one, all-important element: our desperate will to go on living. And then . . ."

Yet again he raised the mock pistol to his chin. Drew it terribly slowly a few inches down and to one side. The muzzle was now pointing diagonally to the left.

"She could have been struggling with herself," he said. "Won't. Will. And then the shot was fired. Bang."

Once again he pulled the trigger. Henrik could see exactly where the bullet would have gone. Into the chin and through the tongue. It would have shattered the teeth in the upper jaw before exiting through a crater just beneath the eye.

"Not dead," the pathologist said, with a broad smile. "More tea?"

"Yes please."

"It's also possible that the won't side won. And that the gun quite simply fired by accident. After all, if it was a competition gun she used, their triggers are easy to fire."

Henrik watched the golden stream as Carsten Bru poured tea from a blue-patterned pot. He felt oddly numb. These were thoughts he had never entertained. He clicked his heels together and tapped both sides of his nose.

"Have you read Albert Camus?" the old man asked. "'The Myth of Sisyphus'?"

"No, never."

"Do. It's exceptionally interesting, but quite depressing reading, I must say. Very briefly summarized, he claims that the only truly philosophical problem is whether we choose to commit suicide or not. Here . . ."

He pushed the sugar bowl closer to Henrik, who helped himself to four cubes. He stirred them into his tea and listened with half an ear to the professor's not particularly cheerful discourse on Camus, Kierkegaard, and Jean-Paul Sartre.

It was of no interest to him. Henrik felt ashamed of himself. He struggled against his blushes and possibly also against tears. He had been so terribly caught up with Anna's clinically clean and tidy house. In her depression. In all the losses she had suffered. And not least in the dismantling of Dina's little life, that had ended with the clothes she had been wearing on the day she died disappearing into the garbage can at Stugguveien 2B.

His visit to Herdis Brattbakk had reinforced his belief that Anna herself had chosen to depart from life. Kjell Bonsaksen's gut instinct and the experienced Superintendent's confidence that Henrik could get to the bottom of something that had eluded him had made him think in a restricted and presumptuous fashion. He had taken such a limited view that he had never reflected that Anna, if it really had been a case of suicide, in reality had not succeeded. She had not died of the gunshot wound. It was the absence of medical attention that had killed her.

". . . modernism's great breakthrough," Professor Bru concluded, slapping both hands down on the desktop. "But we had a completely different problem, Henrik, didn't we? The time of death!"

Henrik tapped the teaspoon lightly on the rim of the cup and laid it aside.

"Between 10:30 and 11:30?" Carsten Bru asked, leafing through the documents he had borrowed from Henrik. "Was that when she was killed, according to the pathologist?"

"Yes."

"Have you lost heart, Henrik? Buck up, boy!"

Henrik tried to straighten up. He smiled weakly and drew back his shoulders. The tea smelled of flowers, and without giving it another thought, he dropped another two sugar cubes into his cup.

"I'm sure you know how we arrive at the time of death," Carsten Bru said in a gratified tone; he seemed to be enjoying himself more than he had in ages. "Or more correctly, how we *try* to establish it."

His cheeks were flushed behind the gray beard, and his eyes were smiling no matter what he was talking about.

"Body temperature," Henrik said when the old man looked at him encouragingly. "The relationship between the temperature of the surroundings and the rectal and brain temperature. Rigor mortis and livor mortis, death stiffness and postmortem lividity. Subsequently decomposition and the presence of insects. Entomology. And God knows what else. All with reference to the size of the body, any possible fever, what the body is lying on, whether the corpse has been outdoors or inside. Atmospheric humidity. And now, in recent years, the vitreous humors of the eye. Potassium and hypoxanthine analysis. Which are more precise methods, even though we still rely mainly on the good old temperature tables. At least when the corpse is relatively fresh, that is."

"Yes of course," the professor replied, nodding. "You keep up to date, I see. But in this case . . ."

He glanced at the papers and raised his cup with a slight nod, as if proposing a toast.

"In this case, we'll go back to basics."

He opened one of the massive desk drawers and rummaged around for a few seconds.

"Here it is," he said, sounding pleased. "Henssge's nomogram. You must remember this."

The paper he pushed across to Henrik was a folded ledger sheet. Henrik opened it out. The nomogram had seemed completely incomprehensible the first time Henrik had seen it, but when he had participated in the postgraduate course run by Professor Bru, he had finally seen the light. A quarter circle was filled with sectors and numbers, with a scale for rectal temperature on the one side. A corresponding line with specifications for the ambient temperature was drawn on the other side, farther down than the first. Completely asymmetrical in the image, aslant and close to the hub of the quarter circle, was something that looked like a bull's eye. From the marking for normal body temperature, 98.6 degrees, a line was extended downward at a relatively sharp angle. It ended at a great void.

"I didn't understand the significance of that illustration in your course," Henrik said, tapping a swift drumroll with his fingers.

"Yes, you did. When I explained it, all of you understood."

"We no longer need to use it."

"You're right there. Everything's done on computer nowadays, but it can be useful to see what the table looks like when it's not entered into a machine that produces answers without us having to think for ourselves. What did you say Anna's rectal temperature was when she was found?"

"It was 89.6 degrees. She was lying on a bathroom floor with radiant heating installed, though it wasn't switched on, and she was fully clothed. The temperature in the room was exactly 68 degrees. An adjustment factor of 1.3 was put in for the clothes and flooring."

"So it was 1.3 times 154 pounds," the professor rattled off. "That was what she weighed: 154 pounds?"

Henrik nodded.

"Then we have an adjusted weight of two hundred. To tell the truth, this is one of the most enjoyable things I know."

From another of the drawers, he pulled out a ruler. It was large and painstakingly made, with a fixed handle mounted in the middle. He closed one eye and calibrated the ruler between 89.6 degrees on the one side of the diagram and 68 on the other. Grabbing a pen, he drew a line from one point to the other.

"Like so," he said, sounding satisfied, before placing the ruler at a different angle.

Another line.

"There," he said, evidently pleased with himself, as he pointed at one of the numbers spread out across the semicircle. "The rectal temperature was taken at noon the next day. The table shows that death occurred approximately thirteen hours earlier. But what happens if we do this?"

His experienced hands performed the whole operation one more time.

"Voilà," he said, pointing to a different number. "If the temperature in the bathroom had been 86 degrees, then the time of death you'd arrive at would be around eighteen hours earlier. All other variables being the same. That is to say around six the previous evening. Give or take an hour."

That specific time caused Henrik to feel a strong impulse to snatch up Henssge's nomogram and rush out the door. Instead he slapped the back of his head and said, "Stupid!"

A brand-new tic, but Carsten Bru pretended not to notice.

"Can I take that away with me?" Henrik asked, pointing at the large sheet of paper.

"Yes, of course! But the problem isn't solved."

"What do you mean?"

"The police measured the temperature in the bathroom at 68 degrees, not 86. We haven't yet managed to shift the time of death. And we still haven't located a weapon."

Henrik picked up his cup of tea and drank it all down so quickly that he burned his mouth.

"You're absolutely right," he said with a sharp intake of breath, rolling up the broad sheet of paper before cramming it into his bag. "But if I can prove that the police were mistaken about the temperature in

Anna's bathroom, then I may solve the problem of Anna's gun at the same time. Thanks a million for your help, Professor Bru. Thank you so much."

He proffered his hand. The old man stood up and held it firmly.

"Are you claiming that the police crime scene technicians can't do a good job of reading a thermometer in a serious case of homicide, Henrik?"

"No," Henrik answered. "But I might be able to find evidence that they were tricked."

Maria Kvam was forging ahead, building a new life for herself at the age of almost fifty-five.

She had done it before, and she would succeed yet again.

The apartment was almost empty. Working in conjunction with an interior designer, she had chosen new furniture to suit the apartment in Tjuvholm for as long as she lived there, but would also be appropriate for the house at Stugguveien 2B. Maria had already sent notice of termination to the Russian embassy. By summer it would all be done and dusted, and she would be back where it all began.

In her own childhood home.

The real estate agent had been over the moon about the apartment.

The new colors were perfect, he had said, and as soon as the furniture on order was installed, he would send a photographer. The prospectus would be stylish, but not overly high-flown. Elegant and minimalist, but not pretentious. He predicted a sale within twenty-four hours of listing the property.

Maria was startled when the doorbell rang. She waited for a moment or two. She and Iselin had prided themselves on an abundance of friends, and scarcely a weekend had gone by without some kind of social occasion in the diary. That had all come to an end when Tyrfing was exposed. In the weeks before she died, Iselin had mainly isolated herself at home, apart from the three times she had sneaked out at night, refusing to say where she had been when she returned at the crack of dawn.

"Meetings," she had explained crisply, as if Maria was a complete idiot.

Admittedly, she knew that Iselin sometimes had meetings at peculiar hours, in peculiar places, because of the danger of surveillance. You could never be too careful, especially after July 22. All the same, it was inconceivable that she should spend time on political assignations while engulfed in a catastrophic media crisis.

Maria knew where Iselin had been, but she couldn't bear to dwell on it.

She was never going to think about it again. Instead she went to open the door.

"Hello," Halvor Stenskar said. "May I come in?"

Maria did not answer, but left the front door open when she returned to the living room. He followed behind her.

"My goodness," he said, surveying the room.

Six pots of paint were lined up along one wall beside a stepladder. A fat roll of thick cardboard and three rolls of masking tape were lying beside the window. The flat-screen TV was still mounted on the opposite wall, and a beanbag chair was placed there so that Maria could watch TV.

Apart from that, the living room was bare.

"You're not wasting any time!" he said. "When do you move out?"

"In three months. All that's needed at Stugguveien is a fresh coat of paint. The Russians have taken good care of the property. I'll stay here in the meantime."

"That'll be dismal."

"The furniture will be here soon. Would you like anything?"

"Well, maybe a chair?"

Without a word, she disappeared farther into the apartment and came back with a bright-green folding chair in each hand. She tried to assemble them but didn't have the knack. Halvor Stenskar watched her for sixty seconds or so before he intervened irritably, folded them out, and placed them a couple of feet apart by the window.

"You haven't been to the office since the funeral," he said, sitting down on one of the chairs. "When do you plan to come back?"

"It's only been a week."

"Nine days."

"It's Sunday, for God's sake! I'll come in sometime during the week."

"Things have to be attended to, Maria. We need to appoint a new chairman of the board, among other things. Bjørg Vatne has stepped in until further notice, but she has let me know privately that it's out of the question for her to take over Iselin's post on a permanent basis. And since Iselin was the executive chairman, it may be tricky to find a replacement. Unless we discontinue that particular arrangement."

"And make you the chief executive?"

"*I already am in all but name!*" he barked in annoyance. "I'm the general manager of VitaeBrass, as I have been ever since you and I met. That Iselin had a sort of . . . roving commission suited me fine, but I think the time is ripe to appoint an absolutely ordinary chairman of the board. Iselin's terms were contingent on her . . . special skills."

"Along with the fact that she and I together owned 80 percent of the company," Maria retorted. "Which means that I'm now the one who owns the same 80 percent. And accordingly should have a suitable position."

"Don't put on airs and graces! With the greatest respect, Maria, you have next to no qualifications for heading up VitaeBrass. Neither as a chairman nor as a chief executive."

"Strictly speaking, I'm the one to decide that."

Halvor Stenskar stood up so abruptly that the chair toppled.

"Now I think you should have a really good think before you say anything more," he snarled, holding a trembling finger out right underneath her nose. "If I hadn't discovered that you were sitting on an empty, dead company with hidden assets in the form of agencies, you'd still be wandering around, unemployed and idle. Besides . . ."

Adjusting his tie, he cleared his throat and righted the chair.

"You'd be flat broke if it hadn't been for me," he said in a strained voice, and sat down again. "The way you were when Anna died. I'm the one who saw what gold you possessed when you inherited from her, and I'm the one who should take the credit for PureHerb becoming such a success."

"It was only with Iselin's arrival and the name change that we became successful," Maria said in a monotone.

She realized now that she really couldn't stand the man. For years on end, she had treated him well. Did as he said, in the first few years, before Iselin came on the scene, and put up with him ever since then. It was as if Iselin's demise had released her, making her more complete and sure of herself. Halvor was no more than an arrogant wannabe in a far too expensive suit. When he had looked her up in the summer of 2004, she had completely forgotten about the company Anna had left her. It was merely a piece of paper. The money she had inherited from Anna made it possible for her to live a globe-trotting life for a while longer, and the house in Stugguveien had been easy to rent out. Then Halvor had discovered that she was sitting on the rights to Aloewonder and the Peruvian remedy, already becoming a bestseller in countries with less restrictive health authorities than Norway.

She had let herself be coaxed into giving him 20 percent of the shares in exchange for his labor and entrepreneurship.

"Iselin created VitaeBrass," she said, gazing out to the terrace, where the outdoor furniture was stowed away in a corner under a tarpaulin. "You just did the preliminary work. PureHerb was a seed that would never have blossomed if Iselin hadn't come along."

Halvor got to his feet again, this time quietly and without knocking over the chair.

"You're completely incompetent," he said slowly. "But you've had incredible luck. First, you inherited from your parents. Then you inherited from your sister, and then you met me. Or the other way around. Eventually Iselin came along. Through sheer good fortune or other people's efforts—or death—you've grown rich. You haven't lifted a fucking finger yourself, Maria. Just tagged along. Played along. Spent money. You're fit for nothing. You can't even manage to attend to that blog of yours without help. It's sad that Iselin's dead, but that's the way it is. We have to get a grip. And if you won't let me take charge of VitaeBrass, then I'll buy myself out. That is an ultimatum."

He gave a brief nod and headed out to the hallway. "I must have an answer this week," he yelled back at her once he had opened the front door. "By Friday at four. Understood?"

The door slammed with such force that the living room window shook.

His sore knee forced Henrik to take a taxi. It was all the same to him—he had a lot to do before he could report to Hanne. Now he was sitting in the backseat of a Mercedes with pale-brown leather seats, making lightning-fast notes on his phone while he attempted to gather his thoughts.

It was not easy.

Suicide? Murder?

He kept writing.

Maria, Anna's sister, originally called Benedicte, had apparently been to Stugguveien 2B at around 5:30 on New Year's Eve. The police's temperature measurement, based on an average temperature of 68 degrees in the room, had calculated that death would have occurred just prior to midnight. If the bathroom had been 18 degrees warmer, Anna could have passed away shortly after her sister's admitted visit.

His thumb could not keep up with his stream of thoughts as he keyed in his notes at breakneck speed. Autocorrect went bananas, and he would probably find it difficult later to make out what he had written.

Had she slipped away peacefully? Did she go to her death screaming, with a shattered jaw and the knowledge that her sister wished her such misfortune?

His phone rang. Henrik flinched, and the taxi made such a sharp turn that his phone dropped on the floor. He had to unfasten his seat belt to retrieve it—it had slid underneath the driver's seat—and he was afraid the call had already been transferred to voicemail when he was finally able to put the phone to his cheek with a breathless hello.

"Hello there," said the voice at the other end. "This is Herdis Brattbakk calling. We spoke the other day, and I—"

"Hello," Henrik said, practically euphoric. "It was a very useful conversation. Thank you."

"That's good. It roused a lot of thoughts in me as well. I had an extra good look through my records when you left, and there was one piece of information there I thought you should have."

"Yes?"

"When Anna came back, in September 2003, she was, as I said, pretty down. As you'll recall, I offered her further follow-up, which she accepted."

"But she never turned up again," Henrik said, nodding as he struggled to re-fasten his seat belt. "You told me."

"Exactly. But what I also said to her was that I thought she could benefit from taking antidepressants. That's not something I usually recommend to my patients, but—"

"You're a psychologist," Henrik broke in. "Not a psychiatrist."

"That's correct. And I didn't offer to write out a prescription: I don't have authority to do that. But her GP does. I earnestly advised her to make an appointment with her. In fact, I sent an email to Dr. Sivesind about it, but I didn't get a reply from her either."

"I see."

Henrik could not imagine that the information gave him anything at all. He had already known that Anna was extremely depressed, and whether she was taking prescription medicines was of little interest.

"Thanks," he said, disappointed. "If you think of anything else, I'd appreciate a call to let me know."

"There really was so little. Anna's fate . . . I'd almost forgotten her, but after our discussion it's been on my mind—"

"By the way," Henrik said, "just one tiny detail. Wait!"

The taxi was about to drive the wrong way to Advokat Dehlis plass, and he had to give directions to the driver.

"Are you there?" he asked a few seconds later.

"Yes."

"You told me Anna had begun to brood. When she was attending regularly from September to March. About religion. She was 'looking for God,' I think you said."

"That's right. Not unusual, considering her situation."

"Was there any particular passage in the Bible that interested her?"

"What do you mean?"

"Er . . . the Sermon on the Mount, for instance?"

"Now I've no idea where you're going with this. She was searching in a more general sense, I seem to recall. She was trying to find some sort of meaning in all the pain inflicted on her. Struggling to see God's will in her life having turned out as it had. I don't know if she really . . ."

She was silent for so long that Henrik worried that the call had been disconnected.

"Hello?"

"I'm still here. Now that you mention it, there was actually something she was particularly obsessed about. Not when she was coming here regularly but when she came back, in September."

"What was it?"

"That story in the Old Testament," she said. "The one about the rich man who has all the sufferings in the world inflicted on him and yet still doesn't deny God. Uh—"

"The Book of Job," Henrik suggested.

"Yes, the Book of Job. Anna could not fathom how God could let so many terrible things happen to him, a person who . . ."

Henrik let the phone sink onto his lap.

He had been confused enough when he had boarded the cab, but now he understood nothing whatsoever.

Anna was the one who was obsessed by the Book of Job.

Not Iselin.

Yet another day would soon be over. Yet another day with Hedda.

Jonas Abrahamsen had begun to think stupid thoughts. About fleeing the country. About moving somewhere else, to a completely different life. About taking Hedda with him, traveling far away and becoming a family.

He and Dina.

Hedda.

She was sleeping now: in his bed, where he would soon turn in for the night himself. They had played Picture Lotto and had fun with Barbie. Jonas was given the old, one-armed, almost hairless doll. Hedda had been delighted with the new one, which had come in a pack with a bikini and a surfboard. He had filled the tub in the bathroom with water, and the one-armed doll had to go for a swim while the new one surfed back and forth, sometimes screaming in terror when Jonas threatened her with the fish slice that was really a tiger shark.

Of course he couldn't run away. In the first place, the whole of Norway was hunting for him. The Golf was now the right color. He was no longer a foreigner, but a white man wearing a black cap pulled well down on his forehead. With each hour that passed, the descriptions on the Internet grew increasingly precise.

And second, they had no passport, neither one of them.

It was only a matter of a short time now. Maybe they would come tomorrow. The only thing he could think of that might delay them was that they were now searching for a sex offender.

It was not stated in black and white, but it was easy to work out that this was what they were looking for. No ransom demand had arrived for any of Bengt's huge fortune. The kidnappers had not been in touch at all, even though the desperate grandfather had promised everything he owned to whoever brought his grandchild home again.

Jonas was no sex offender. He was not a criminal of any kind, even though he had been treated like one for eight years. A whole lifetime. If anyone, just one person, could have looked him in the eye and said that they believed him, that he was innocent and had never done anything wrong, he would never have stolen Hedda. He would have handed her back. He could go to prison for abducting her, but he had taken good care of the little girl and would at least have known that someone knew. Who he was. What he had done. What he had never done, and that was to kill someone. One single person was all he needed, a fellow human being who would sit down and listen to Jonas's story about how he had lost everything without having done anything wrong.

And who believed in him.

It had never happened and never would.

Bengt Bengtson would never see Hedda again.

Jonas would have to steel himself. He had to keep a tight hold of the pain, of all the years of guilt and sorrow and the microscopic glimmers of hatred that made it possible to go on.

After brushing his teeth, he stripped off his clothes and pulled on the striped pajamas he had never used before Hedda arrived and became a helicopter in his bed.

One more night, and then it would be over.

One more night, and now he knew exactly how he was going to accomplish it.

"You know I can't tell you that, Wilhelmsen."

Hanne shut her eyes and swore under her breath.

"Not if I swear on my honor to keep you out of it? And if at the same time I promise you the juiciest story on earth before the week is out? Maybe as early as Tuesday, and I promise you'll be the very first to know. It's a story of such dimensions that you'd cut off your right arm to get it."

VG journalist Dag Beddington gave a demonstrative sigh at the other end of the line.

"I thought you'd know better after all these years," he complained. "Revealing a source would be the same as signing my own resignation. Not only from *VG*, but also from any future as a journalist. We simply don't give away our sources, Wilhelmsen. I can't tell you who tipped us off that Iselin Havørn was behind the Tyrfing alias. I can't. I won't. Read my lips?"

She made no response as she shifted the phone from one hand to the other.

"But what's this story about?" he added.

"*Something for something*, Beddington. That was what you said to me the last time we spoke."

She could hear him grinning broadly as he continued.

"Well, I must be allowed to try. Can't you give me a hint at least?"

"What's the point of that? After all, you've already said it's downright impossible for you to tell me who exposed Tyrfing's identity."

Neither of them uttered a word. Neither of them hung up.

"Listen," Hanne said sotto voce once almost a minute had elapsed. "We can sit here and play chicken all night long with nothing to show for it. For either of us."

"I've got plenty of time. And I'm absolutely open to listening to you if you've got something exciting to tell me. The best thing would be—"

"Here's the deal," she interrupted him. "I promise you first dibs at a juicy story in the course of a few days. The only thing you have to do in return is to act appropriately when I ask you a question."

"Act approp—"

"Shut up. Listen to me. You'll get a story if you do exactly as I say. I'm going to ask you a question in a few seconds. It will give you a hint about the subject matter of my story. If the answer to the question is no, then you can answer whatever the hell you like. If, on the other hand, the answer is yes, all you have to do is disconnect the call. In that way you'll have nothing to worry about."

He roared with laughter at the other end. Hanne had to hold her phone away from her ear.

"I certainly can't do that!" he said. "I think you've seen too many movies, Wilhelmsen. My duty of confidentiality is absolute and can't be compromised by that kind of hocus pocus. But if I could just hear what kind of story you're talking about, then I can—"

"Was it Maria Kvam who tipped you off about Tyrfing's true identity?"

His laughter was suddenly silenced. Hanne feared for a moment that he had already hung up before she had asked the question. Then she heard his breathing. Heaving breaths, lasting several seconds, before silence fell.

Dag Beddington had put down the receiver.

Hanne and Henrik were sitting in the living room, even though Ida and Nefis were at home. Hanne's family had gone to bed ages ago, and it was now almost 11:30. It had only been an hour or so since Henrik had arrived. He was no longer lugging folders around and had left his usual bag of case documents and notes in Grünerløkka. The first thing he had done when he arrived in Kruses gate was to enter Hanne's home office without asking permission. The temptation to rip the whole time line to shreds was pressing, but Hanne had trundled after him and persuaded him to leave it. Reluctantly he had rolled up the centipede before flinging it into a corner and sauntering back to the living room. It had taken Hanne ten minutes to tell him what she had learned that day, which was a great deal, in fact. Henrik had spent almost an hour, and he had only become more confused.

"I don't understand any of it," he said, sinking even farther into the armchair in front of the fire. "And I can't prove anything either. Which isn't the slightest bit strange, since it's impossible to prove anything you don't understand yourself. A vicious circle, really."

"Don't take it so hard," Hanne said. "We've got Maria for Iselin's murder."

Henrik leaned forward and tossed a log into the flames. A shower of sparks lit up the darkened room, and he threw on another.

"I was aiming to help Jonas," he said in an undertone. "All these weeks I've been falling asleep to the thought of how he would take it. When I came to tell him that we had got to the bottom of it all. That he's a victim of a miscarriage of justice. That he would receive redress. Primarily moral, but perhaps also in the form of financial compensation. For sure. Don't you think so?"

"Yes he would. But you shouldn't give up. You've still a lot to go on."

Henrik tapped the back of his head three times and said, "Stupid, stupid, stupid!" Hanne looked at him in astonishment.

"I don't have shit to go on," he said so loudly that he immediately blushed and touched his mouth with his hand. "Sorry!"

Hanne put her forefinger to her lips and smiled.

"In Iselin's suicide letter," he began, in almost a whisper, "which we now believe Maria wrote, it's clear—"

"Which we now *know* Maria wrote."

"We don't *know* anything, Hanne. Everything has to be scrutinized more closely. But it's extremely likely. In that letter there are clear references to the Book of Job. Almost a transcription, at the beginning. We also know Anna was obsessed with the Book of Job, something that is by no means strange. But Anna died twelve years ago, and there was no letter found at her house."

He pushed forward to the edge of the chair and began to gesticulate.

"It started with a vague suspicion that Anna had taken her own life. That suspicion has been strengthened on a daily basis. The tidying. The disposal of Dina's clothes. Her depression and grief that increasingly pulled her down. If she really did take her own life, Hanne, it would quite simply have been the story of a predictable suicide. But then there's this business of the gun . . ."

He sank back into the chair and sat staring into the flames. Hanne gave him time to think. Most of all she wanted to open a bottle of champagne to celebrate her own success. Maria Kvam would languish behind bars, and all credit was due to Hanne.

And, it struck her all of a sudden, Henrik.

"I thought I could shift the time of death," Henrik grumbled. "If I could just find something to indicate that the police had made some mistake with their measurements. That they were tricked somehow. If only that bathroom had been 18 degrees warmer—"

"Eighteen really is a lot, Henrik. If it's 68 degrees outside on a summer's day, then it's a bit cool in the shade. If it's 86 degrees, we go about panting and sweating. I honestly do think the crime scene technicians would be able to tell the difference. But . . ."

She was suddenly a million miles away. Henrik looked at her. She sat with her mouth half-open and her head canted, as if rooted to the spot. She had sat down in the other armchair and drawn a blanket over her stick legs. The blaze in the open fireplace cast an orange shadow play over her face, and yet she did not blink.

"Who found Anna?" she finally said without taking her eyes from the flames.

"You know that. It was Maria. She came to Stugguveien at about eleven o'clock the next day."

"Isn't that strange?"

"Strange?"

Hanne used her arms to raise herself and find a more comfortable sitting position. Leaning closer to him across the armrest, she lifted her index finger.

"Let's say that her alibi holds water," she said softly and slowly. "She was at a New Year's party from six in the evening until five the following morning. For eleven hours, in other words. She had responsibility for the bar. There's no mention anywhere that Maria was teetotal, so she's probably had quite a bit to drink herself in the course of the night. The earliest she could have gone to bed would be . . . do you remember where she was living at that time?"

"With a female friend in Frogner. She'd been traveling extensively and didn't have her own place."

"And the party was in Årvoll. Even if she was super-lucky and managed to hail a cab on a night when it's virtually impossible, she couldn't have gone to sleep before 6:00 a.m. at the earliest anyway. What was she doing, then, at her sister's at eleven o'clock, only five hours later? Watching the Vienna New Year Concert with a hangover?"

Henrik said nothing. The cogs in his brain had started turning again.

"It doesn't say anything about it anywhere," Hanne went on, her voice so low that he had to lean in closer. "No one asked the question: Why did a sister who wasn't especially close to Anna visit her twice in twenty-four hours?"

"Before and after her death."

"Yes. Or when she died and the following day. To report to the police that her sister was dead. Something she'd been aware of all night long. Could be."

Henrik launched into a series of tics that continued for so long that in the end Hanne had to tell him to stop. He rounded them off with a muffled drumroll on the soft armrest.

"Sorry," he said. "Do you really mean that Maria killed Anna?"

She did not answer. Once again she had withdrawn into herself. Henrik waited for her to share her thoughts, but knew he was waiting in vain. In a few seconds, she would ask him to go. With a sigh, he tapped his forehead.

"Would you like to stay the night?" she asked quietly. "The bed's made in the guestroom and Nefis has a store of toiletry bags from her trips on business class."

"Er . . . yes, please. But shouldn't we let Amanda Foss know? About the Iselin business, I mean?"

"No. That airhead isn't going to root around in this investigation any more than she already has done. When I hand it over, which is going to happen tomorrow, it's going to be so crystal clear that nothing can be screwed up. To be on the safe side, I'll give it to Silje."

She pulled up the sleeve of her sweater.

"It's nearly midnight," she said. "I'm going to sit in my office and draw up a synopsis of everything we know. You can take my copies of the crime scene in Stugguveien to bed with you and see if there's anything we've missed. Something we didn't notice before because until now, we hadn't considered how manipulation of the bathroom temperature could result in an inaccurate time of death."

She pulled the wheelchair toward her and hoisted herself across.

"It could be quite a long night. If you want to use the bathroom first, you'll find Nefis's toiletry bags in the tall cabinet on the right. The ones from Qatar Airways are the best."

"Thanks. I need . . . I need an iPad or something."

"Take mine. It's lying in the kitchen. You'll find the pictures from the crime scene in my office. I need to use the bathroom first. If you don't find anything of interest, then try to have a good sleep anyway. Otherwise, I'll be in my office for at least a couple of hours. We'll go together to Police Headquarters tomorrow morning. Night night."

"Goodnight, Hanne."

He had a sudden, strong impulse to give her a hug. Fortunately he swiftly came to his senses and padded out to get the bundle of photographs he had already studied in so much detail that he knew them by heart.

The three-year-old awoke and was afraid. From where she lay, she could no longer see the lovely, gentle moon at the window. The man's back was so high, and she sat up in bed. The moon was gone. Everything was dark out there, and she began to cry.

"Jonas," she said in a loud whisper. "I want Mommy now."

He did not answer. He pushed her carefully down again without turning around. She didn't want to sleep. She wanted to go home.

"I want to go home," she said, sobbing. "I want picked up now. Take Barbie with me and Pictotto and go home."

Jonas did not lose his temper. He never got angry, and he played with her. There were sharks in that weird bathtub, but Jonas looked out for them.

"You have to sleep," he said, and all of a sudden his voice was a bit scary. "Lie down again."

"Home," Hedda whimpered. "I want Mommy."

Finally Jonas turned around.

"I don't want to stay here anymore," the toddler said.

"And you're not going to."

"Home. I want to sleep in my own bed."

"You won't have to stay here any longer than tomorrow, Hedda. I promise. Lie down, pet."

Tomorrow meant after the man had slept. Tomorrow was brushing teeth and putting on pajamas, listening to stories and two songs and then falling asleep. When you woke up, it was tomorrow.

"Tomorrow," she repeated and lay down. "Going home tomorrow. Home to Mommy and Grampa."

Without saying a word, Jonas tucked the quilt comfortably around her. He sang a lullaby twice over and kissed her on the forehead.

The three-year-old was no longer scared. Tomorrow she wouldn't be here anymore, Jonas had said so, and soon she was sleeping soundly again.

MONDAY, JANUARY 25, 2016

I t was 2:00 a.m.

A short time ago, Henrik had heard Hanne leave her office. She had gone into the kitchen before disappearing into the inner recesses of the apartment where the bedrooms were situated. As for him, he didn't feel tired in the slightest. He was worn out, and his knee was throbbing with pain, but he was wide awake inside his head. He regretted not having asked for a couple of aspirin and wondered whether it would be brazen of him to creep into the bathroom and look for a bottle.

Very impolite, he heard his mother's voice in his ear.

He decided not to bother and instead placed a pillow under his knee to see if that would help.

He had not found anything at all.

The pictures from the house where Anna Abrahamsen died told him nothing he did not already know. It was still just as clean and tidy everywhere. Photos from Dina's old room were still missing, a room that according to Bonsaksen had been so bare and insignificant that there had been no reason to take any pictures in there. The bathroom was still covered in bloodstains, both in the photographs with Anna's body lying prone on the floor, as well as the ones taken when she had been removed and you could make out the outline of her head in the red pool of blood. Close-ups of the blood spatter on the shower wall were the same as before. There was nothing whatsoever to tell him whether the temperature in the bathroom had originally been higher than the police calculations.

When he discovered that the heated towel rack had a separate thermostat, he grew fleetingly enthusiastic. The technical quality of the image was good, but he had to use the app that transformed his phone into a magnifying glass to see the thermostat setting.

Sixty-eight degrees, he saw, feeling disappointed again.

He felt glum.

He leafed through the pictures one last time.

The towel rack was attached to the wall beneath a high, rectangular wall recess. Two glass candlesticks were displayed there, each with a slim, amber-yellow candle inserted. They had never been lit, he noticed. The wicks were white and would need to be trimmed before use.

The candlesticks were also included in two of the other photographs, snapped from different angles. When he looked more closely at the third photograph, he found exactly what he was searching for.

The candles were bent.

Not by very much, but beyond doubt all the same. One in particular was obviously bowed from top to bottom. Henrik sat up in bed and, without giving a damn about his sore knee, he stuffed all the pillows behind his back. He swiftly googled "melting point stearin wax" and came up with 788 hits. He went straight to the most reliable encyclopedia:

Stearin is a triglyceride derived from stearic acid with the formula $(C17H35COO)3C3H5$, and a melting point of 161 degrees F (72 degrees C).

"Good grief," he mumbled, and went on typing.

It crossed his mind that some tall candles were made of paraffin wax.

The encyclopedia told him that the melting point lay between 122 and 140 degrees.

"Good heavens," he muttered.

But the candles had not melted. They were bent. Had just lost their shape, something that might possibly occur at lower temperatures. Although he eagerly continued with Google, it did not make him much wiser. Some manufacturers warned against high temperatures and strong sunlight because both could affect the shape and color of the candles.

None of them stated what they meant by "high temperatures."

Again he scrutinized the best of the images.

The candles were amber-yellow. Or perhaps honey-yellow. Honey. Beeswax.

Henrik almost dropped the iPad on the floor as he recalled his mother's annual Christmas workshop when he had lived at home. They had sat at the kitchen table, Henrik and his mother and nobody else, and rolled honeycomb beeswax around wicks she had made. Some of the honeycombs were melted in a bain-marie and made into tea lights and tall candles he wasn't allowed to touch. He might burn himself, his mother said, even once he was well into his teenage years.

He typed "beeswax melting point" in the search field.

Beeswax has a melting point of 143–149 degrees F (62–65 degrees C) and softens at 89–95 degrees F (32–35 degrees C).

He punched the quilt with his fists and smothered a roar of triumph. Leaning his head back, he closed his eyes and let his hand run over his blessedly normal Adam's apple. He made soundless grimaces of pleasure and felt an uncontrollable impulse to wake everybody in the amazing little family in Kruses gate that had almost become his own.

At least to some extent.

Two drooping beeswax candles in a twelve-year-old photo would not acquit Jonas Abrahamsen of his wife's murder. Nevertheless, the candles were the first palpable sign that there could be something in Henrik's theory. No candle became deformed at a temperature of 68 degrees. But few people would feel comfortable in a temperature of more than 86 degrees in their bathroom.

No one, in fact, unless with a deliberate intention to wreck a police investigation.

Henrik must have been mistaken. Anna had not killed herself. Someone had taken her life earlier that evening, turned all the heating sources to max in the bathroom, and closed the door. At eleven o'clock the next day, it would take only a matter of minutes to bring the temperature down again. It was the middle of winter, and the bathroom had two windows.

One person had been at Anna's both late in the afternoon and at eleven o'clock the next morning. Only one person could have killed Anna.

Maria.

But it was still impossible to prove.

"So you think this woman has committed two murders? First her sister and then her wife twelve years later?"

Chief of Police Silje Sørensen looked from Hanne to Henrik and back again. Amanda Foss sat beside them, tugging nervously at her uniform shirt every other minute. Until now she had not uttered a word. She had been summoned into the Police Chief's office at five minutes' notice without forewarning of what it was about and had thought it best to turn up in uniform. Now she appeared to regret that.

The Police Chief herself was dressed in jeans and a sweater. She had come straight from her cottage at Hafjell and had given up on the idea of taking a detour home to change when Hanne had called her at half past six to request a meeting.

"Well," Hanne Wilhelmsen commented, with a shrug. "Henrik's case isn't quite ready for firm conclusions to be drawn. A hundred signs point in one single direction, but there's not a scrap of firm evidence. Yet. As far as Iselin Havørn's killing is concerned, on the other hand, there can be no doubt of at least grounds for arrest and a search of her apartment. What kind . . ."

She turned to the fair-haired Chief Inspector in the freshly ironed uniform and asked: "What on earth did you give the handwriting analyst to use for comparison?"

"Er . . . a condolence card from last year, a shopping list, and a letter to a friend in Sandefjord. It was only four weeks old. Signed and everything."

"And it never entered your head to investigate whether Iselin Havørn was in the habit of sending letters to friends in Sandefjord? Or anywhere else for that matter? Do people even send *letters* to one another any longer? Didn't it cross your mind at all—"

Henrik cleared his throat noisily.

"The signature was really only a squiggle," he said, with an apologetic smile at Amanda Foss. "A squiggle and a dash and a dot over the last *i*. Easy to forge."

Hanne gave a histrionic sigh.

"Has this force not learned anything at all from other cases, even recent ones? Before we dismiss a death as a suicide, in the name of heaven, we need to . . ."

With two speedy wheel movements she turned her chair so that she now sat with her back half-turned to an increasingly red-cheeked Amanda Foss.

"Get a grip, Hanne. Put a lid on it." Silje Sørensen emphasized her authority by rising from her chair. She was only five foot three and dressed for hiking outdoors, and her hair was tied back in two pony-tails.

It helped, all the same.

"Sorry," Hanne said, far more meekly. "But it's a pretty serious business that none of the investigators asked the most obvious question of them all: Did Iselin Havørn have any reason at all to want to die? I think my daughter who'll soon be thirteen would have the brains to answer that in the negative."

Silje raised both hands in a pacifying gesture.

"Naturally, the handling of the case will be subject to internal investigation later. The important thing now is to get it on the right track. So, we have . . ."

Swallowing, she started again.

"So *you* have uncovered that the suicide letter is a forgery. And that Iselin was extremely reluctant to write anything whatsoever by hand. You believe that Maria Kvam had a motive for murder . . ."

She let her sentence hang like a question in the air and fixed her eye on Henrik.

"Stupid, stupid," he said, slapping himself on the back of the head. "Money. Jealousy. For some reason, love; perhaps . . ."

He blushed at the very mention of the word.

". . . Maria transferred half her shares to Iselin when they married. Unconditionally. On divorce, she had a lot to lose. She must have discovered Iselin's infidelity quite a while ago. We have little reason to believe that Iselin had told her about it. The letter to this friend in Sandefjord . . ."

He smiled as encouragingly as he could at Amanda Foss.

". . . must of necessity have been written by Maria. It's one thing that she helped Iselin on the rare occasions when it was considered most appropriate to use handwriting. It seems totally unnecessary that she should have sent an ordinary letter when she could have used email. That suggests Maria had planned the murder for some time. And planned it well, I must add."

"You can say that again," Hanne said tartly. "So well planned that she was about to get away with it."

"And then we have the tip," Henrik said, shooting another smile in Amanda Foss's direction. "It was Maria who tipped *VG* off about Tyrfing. By doing that, she created a media storm that would persuade the police to draw rather . . . hasty conclusions, you might say."

"How do you know that? That the tip came from Maria?"

Silje Sørensen was still on her feet. She had moved in front of the desk and was leaning against it with her arms crossed.

"I can't tell you that," Hanne said. "Not yet, at least. You'll have to trust me for the moment. And by the way . . ."

She lifted the coffee cup she had taken from a fancy machine at the door when she arrived and drained it dry.

". . . it's absolutely clear she had ample opportunity to get hold of the pills she needed to kill Iselin. She crushed them and prepared a horrible vegetable smoothie that perhaps Iselin drank every evening. And then headed off to Bergen to secure an alibi. Something of that sort. What do I know? Only that all this is enough for both a search warrant and an arrest warrant. Then time will tell what we can prove."

Silje Sørensen gazed at her for several seconds.

"Amanda, you may go now."

Amanda Foss looked baffled for a moment before she got to her feet, dashed to the door, and disappeared.

"She'll get her just deserts," the Police Chief said as soon as the door was closed. "But to tell the truth, so will both of *you*. How *dare* you poke around in cases you haven't been allocated by me? As if I didn't have enough on my plate with this dreadful Hedda investigation, the two of you . . ."

Clutching her hands to her head, she groaned. The fury had come on her so suddenly—as if a switch had been flicked the minute the door closed behind Amanda Foss. Angry roses were etched on her cheeks, and now she hovered almost threateningly above Hanne Wilhelmsen.

"This will have consequences. I guarantee that this will have consequences. For you both."

"I haven't done anything other than read the newspaper and think for myself," Hanne said, shrugging her shoulders nonchalantly. "And as far as Henrik's case is concerned, Ulf Sandvik gave him the green light to take a closer look at it."

"Well," Henrik said, forcing yet another smile. He noticed they had soon lost their impact. "I might not exactly call it a green light; it was more of a—"

There was an angry knock at the door. Silje Sørensen rolled her eyes and shouted, "Come in."

"The verdict will be delivered shortly," her secretary said in almost reverential tones. "The verdict in the May 17 terrorism trial. It is to be read out in court at ten o'clock, but Oslo District Court has sent us a copy already. In confidence. Highly confidential! I haven't seen it, though. Not even a tiny peek. This is really extremely irregular. Highly irregular!"

He approached the Police Chief carrying a thick document that he held outstretched, eyes averted, as if it were a well-filled baby's diaper.

"My God," Hanne said.

"Heavens above," said Henrik.

"Let me see!" Hanne said.

But the room fell silent for what seemed an eternity. Silje Sørensen read a bit here and a bit there, without batting an eyelid. Hanne, frantically yearning for a chance to flick through to the conclusion, wisely kept her own counsel. Until now she had not divulged that she had only had four hours sleep before her alarm clock had gone off. The silence in the spacious office and the barely audible hum of the computer on the desk made her eyes slide shut. She thought of Maria Kvam and Iselin Havørn. And of Kari Thue, who, despite seeming so exhausted and pathetic, was still impossible to like.

Hanne's thoughts turned to Jonas Abrahamsen, and she sent up a silent prayer that they would be able to prove what she and Henrik were already convinced of.

Without a doubt, Jonas was a modern Job.

"They were all found guilty," the Police Chief finally announced. "Six jailed for life, among them Kirsten Ranvik and her son Peder. Congratulations. To you both. They'll all appeal, of course, but congratulations all the same. Good work."

She made no move to show them the document.

"Don't mention this to anyone until the verdict has been formally announced," she said, resuming her seat behind the desk.

Taking two forms from a drawer, she picked up a pen and filled out both warrants at top speed. When the final period was banged down, she handed the papers to Henrik, who stood up uncertainly to accept them.

"There are still a few of us who write things out by hand," the Police Chief said with a faint smile. "Now and again. And don't think I'm finished with you. But it'll have to wait. Go. Liaise with Amanda on a house search and arrest. And off you go."

Hanne moved to the door. Henrik stood hesitantly by the Police Chief's desk. He had rolled up the forms and was twisting them around and around in his hand.

"Can I continue working on the Jonas case?" he pleaded falteringly. "Please?"

Silje gazed at him with a resigned look, shaking her head gently and leaning back into her chair, holding both armrests with grim determination.

"A bit late to ask, Henrik. But yes. Find out if this poor man was wrongly convicted."

"I'll do that," Henrik said, flashing a broad smile before abruptly turning deadly serious again. "Thanks a million. And . . . apologies."

"This is all I've found that's of interest," the young detective said, slightly embarrassed, as he put a half-filled brown carton on the floor between Amanda Foss and Hanne Wilhelmsen.

Hanne leaned down from her wheelchair and peered into it. She could see an iMac Mini, two iPads, one cell phone, and a few credit card readers. A big stack of papers and documents. Three blister packs of seemingly innocuous medicines. And a book she lifted out and examined more closely: *Beauty and the Beast: Poisonous Plants in the City Garden*.

"She certainly didn't use foxglove and laburnum to kill anyone," she murmured, recklessly flinging the book back before removing her latex gloves and staring at the young police officer. "Give it one more sweep. Minimum."

Maria Kvam had been led away some time ago. Even though it was a very long time since Hanne had been present at an ordinary arrest, she recognized the ashen woman's reactions. First, she went two shades paler. Then came the protests, which grew increasingly vociferous. After a few minutes, these changed to demands for a lawyer, combined with veiled and eventually pretty direct threats of outrageous consequences for the six police representatives if they did not leave her apartment at once.

That had been over an hour ago, and now Maria Kvam was ensconced in the backyard at Police Headquarters in an incredibly uncomfortable holding cell.

"Money," Hanne said softly. "Money, sex, or revenge. Or a combination of all three. That's usually how it goes."

"What?"

Amanda stared at her nervously. She had seemed jittery ever since they had left Grønlandsleiret 44 together and made their way to a stripped luxury apartment in Tjuvholm.

"I should have realized," Hanne said. "Prejudices are dangerous. You're not alone in drawing hasty conclusions, Amanda."

The blond woman gave a perplexed smile.

"I was so sure that Iselin was killed because of her opinions," Hanne explained. "Probably because I find her opinions so objectionable that I could have murdered her myself."

Amanda Foss's smile morphed into a stiff grimace.

"Figuratively speaking, of course," Hanne added dolefully. "But actually it was only about money, jealousy, and revenge and all the good old sins. Maria was furious that Iselin had found someone else. Terrified that she would take off with half of VitaeBrass. In addition, I assume, Henrik tells me that Maria did not have sole ownership of anything."

She held the cell phone display up to Amanda, but pulled it back again so quickly that it was impossible for her to read the message.

"The house in Stugguveien. The cottage. The money and this apartment. Everything would have to be split down the middle if Iselin left her for another woman. On Iselin's death, everything reverted to Maria. Wow."

She smacked her lips and shook her head. "We humans are so banal. Hello! Hello there!"

She waved the young officer over. He was busy opening pots of paint to check if there was anything of relevance to the murder case hidden in eight gallons of white emulsion.

"The safe," Hanne said as he approached. "Was there anything of value inside it?"

"Not particularly. A photo album. That just held old childhood photos, so I didn't take it. A lot of jewelry. Papers. They're in here." He nodded at the carton on the floor.

"Is the safe empty now?"

"Yes."

"Let's see," Hanne said, rolling in the direction of the apartment's bedroom.

Although most of the rooms were virtually stripped of contents, the vast wardrobe was well filled, on one side at least. Hanne immediately assumed that Maria had found it difficult to remove what remained of Iselin. In the middle, between the empty and the chock-full sections of the capacious wardrobe, she could see a pale-gray safe about five feet high. Despite noisy protests, Maria had agreed to open it before she was escorted off the premises, once Hanne had delivered threats she could only hope none of the other police officers present had recorded.

The door was open and the safe empty. On the floor beside it, the detective had placed everything he had not considered of sufficient interest to seize as evidence.

Hanne gazed at the safe. Amanda was trailing behind her.

"Are you looking for anything in particular?" Amanda ventured to ask.

"No. But that safe is quite unusual in itself."

"Oh . . . is it?"

"Fairly hefty, don't you think?"

"Yes, maybe. We don't need a safe, so I don't really know what—"

"Right. You don't need a safe. At least not one as big and bulky as that one. Was your name Finnerud?" She raised her voice for the final sentence.

"Yes," called the young man from the living room.

"Come here!"

He took only two seconds.

"Check that safe for me," Hanne said, pointing. "Feel along all the sides and edges. Top and bottom. Press and push and scratch. Just with your hands to start with, but use gloves."

Finnerud held his hands up to show that he was already wearing gloves, but discovered they were both stained with paint. Blushing furiously, he tore them off and put on a new pair he produced from his pocket. Crouching on all fours, he put his head under the safe's lower shelf.

"What am I looking for?" he asked through his contortions.

"Irregularities. Depressions. Something that gives. Clicks. Anything at all that's not smooth, regular, and silent."

He groaned, moved his hand, and swore when he hit his head on the metal shelf.

Amanda Foss said nothing. She had started to perspire, Hanne noticed, and a fine film of moisture had appeared on her forehead and upper lip.

"There's something here," the young man on the floor panted. "It's just as if . . ."

A little click, almost inaudible.

"A . . . it's a . . ."

He backed out of the safe, straightened his back, and remained kneeling on the floor. His hair was damp.

"A little platform," he said, using the thumb and forefinger of both hands to describe a narrow rectangle. "It slid open when I rubbed along the edges. There are eight tiny keys underneath. Black, I think: it's difficult to see in there."

Hanne smiled.

"Well done, Finnerud. Your next task is to find out who sells these safes. Get one of their men here as fast as you can and tell him what we want him to do. And if that takes more than . . ."

She glanced at her wristwatch.

". . . an hour, then get hold of one of our people with a blowtorch instead."

Finnerud nodded and gave the safe a skeptical look.

"It'd have to be a big blowtorch," he said, standing upright. "A damned big, powerful blowtorch!"

"I once killed a child."

Nearly four days and nights had passed since Hedda Bengtson had been abducted while she slept in a red stroller in the day care near her home.

Ninety-six hours and seven minutes, to be exact, as Bengt was well aware; he kept count minute by minute. It couldn't be about the money. No one had made any demands, and no one had contacted him to request 763 million kroner in exchange for a three-year-old with long, blond eyelashes and soft, downy hair.

"You have not killed anyone," Christel said listlessly. She had finally accepted the offer of something to help her sleep.

In the past few hours, she had slipped in and out of a kind of doze but had just been woken by thirst. She drained her glass and held it out to her father for a refill.

"Yes, I did," Bengt Bengtson said quietly without taking it. "I once killed a child."

Christel heaved herself up into a sitting position.

"What's that you're saying?" she mumbled. "I need some water."

He gave her his own bottle.

"You have to believe me," he said. "It's important that you listen to me and believe what I'm telling you. I should have mentioned this to you before now."

"What are you talking about?" she yelled, drawing back from him. "Dad! Don't talk like that!"

"I killed a three-year-old," Bengt said. "She was called Dina."

He thought he had forgotten her name. He had forced himself to forget her, to forget all about her and that poor father of hers. It was impossible to forget the little girl whose name was Dina Abrahamsen, but until now, he had thought he had succeeded. Made up his mind that it was all in the past and forgotten.

"What are you talking about?" Christel shrieked.

"You were so little yourself. Eight years old. Mom had left only a couple of years earlier. There were just the two of us, Christel. You were too young to know anything about it. It was an accident. A sheer accident. The police said I couldn't be blamed, I hadn't . . ."

He suddenly held back as she got out of bed and retreated to a corner of the room where a white wall met pastel-colored wallpaper decorated with huge flowers. She held her hands up as if to fend him off.

"Stop!" she snarled. "Dad, stop. Hedda's not dead."

He put his face in his hands. "No, she's not dead."

"So why are you tormenting me with this, then? Why are you telling me about dead children and that you've killed somebody and . . ."

Bengt rose stiffly from the bed. The room was spinning: he had to find his sea legs. Once he regained his balance, he opened out his arms and closed his eyes, fearing that Christel would not come to embrace him.

But she did.

He had to hold them both up. He could only just manage to stand himself, but Christel was so small in his arms, so fragile and exhausted that he lifted her up and laid her on the bed. He tucked a blanket around her, straight and tight; she crept into a fetal position and would soon have no more tears left to cry.

"You should never have won that money, Dad. We have to tell the police about this. Maybe it's the little girl's family that wants it."

Her voice was so weak that he had to lower his face all the way down to hers.

"They're probably after the money," she whimpered. "But why haven't they been in touch? Dad, why don't they tell us anything?"

She was terrifyingly pale. She folded her hands and sank her teeth into them, so hard that they made red indentations on her skin.

"Don't do that," he whispered, trying to hold her hands in his.

Eventually she looked up.

Pleading, incredulity, and desperation: something seemed to be falling apart in Christel's eyes. Bengt had seen this before, only once, more than fourteen years earlier. He had knocked down a child. A three-year-old, and he remembered only too vividly that her name was Dina.

The police had come. And an ambulance, driving full tilt with all sirens blaring. When it left, it had set off in somber silence, and on the stretcher inside the vehicle lay a tiny little body now beyond all help.

He remembered he had wept.

He remembered the schoolchildren, shocked and curious, held back by the police whose numbers had swelled and who took the driver's license that was returned to him only two weeks later. Bengt remembered the biting wind. The weather had been dismal and rainy, and his body grew so frozen to the bone that it took a long time to thaw out. A solitary streetlamp cast a nauseous, yellow light over the chalk-white child with half-open eyes and a thin trickle of blood running from her nose.

That was all. A tiny trickle of blood from the left nostril, but the little girl was dead.

It was not Bengt's fault. He was aware of that there and then, and in the weeks that followed—that was how he had managed to live with what had happened. It had been an accident. The sort of thing that now and again just happens. A chance incident with a catastrophic result.

The police arrived at the same conclusion. He had been driving well under the speed limit. The reconstruction had also shown that it had been impossible for him to catch sight of the child before she suddenly ran out in front of his car. Her father blocked his view: he was standing with his back to the road, poking around in a mailbox.

It was quite simply no one's fault.

That had been a difficult Christmas, but he had kept up appearances out of consideration for Christel. He had visited the child's parents a few weeks later, but the father refused to meet him. The mother seemed upset and tear-stained, but had thanked him nicely for the white roses he had sent to the funeral.

In time, the circumstances surrounding Dina's death were reduced to a tender spot in Bengt Bengtson's personal history. Something he would really prefer to be without, but something that did not bother him unduly. In recent years, he had hardly spared the victim a moment's thought.

But he had not forgotten. None of it was completely erased. And the most difficult detail to banish was the look in the eyes of the man in the green quilted jacket. He had just stood there with his dying daughter in his arms while he screamed at the lowering, blue-gray skies until he suddenly stopped and stared at Bengt and said: *It wasn't your fault.*

Jonas Abrahamsen was his name, and now Christel reminded him of that man.

Their eyes were distressingly similar, and it was unbearable.

"Yes," Bengt whispered to his daughter. "I'll tell the police that there is one man who probably harbors ill will against me. Who has probably wished me ill for fifteen years, in fact. I'll go to the living room and tell them right now."

Maria Kvam sat in a cell trying to shut out the harsh light.

It was no use closing her eyes. Then everything went white, with gray specks dancing over her retinas, making her headache even worse. She was sitting on a hard bunk. They had not given her a mattress. No blankets either, but that didn't matter. It was far too warm in here anyway. The toilet in the corner stank of urine. The contraption for defecating in was a molded unit and had no lid. Maria tugged at her sweater with her eyes squeezed tightly shut: this light was driving her mad.

She did not think of Iselin.

She certainly did not want to spare a single thought for Iselin, who had betrayed her despite Maria having given her everything. Maria had even renounced her own original first name because that's what Iselin had wanted. When they met, Iselin Havørn was barely more than a bad blog and a heap of colorful clothes. She was on long-term sick leave and flat broke. It was true that she was highly regarded on the alternative scene and its related splendors, but essentially, as things turned out, she was only a damn fortune hunter.

Maria was not thinking about Iselin, because it had been just as easy to start hating someone as it had once been to fall head over heels in love and let her have everything she possessed. Iselin had to die because she deserved it, and she no longer warranted as much as a passing thought.

It was Anna who forced her way into her thoughts.

The little sister who had always been best at everything.

The prettiest. The sweetest. The cleverest, of course, and Daddy's little sweetheart. When they were children, Maria had not given it too much thought. After all, the age difference was so great. Even Maria had to admit that Anna was beautiful as a three-year-old in her inherited regional costume for the National Day celebrations on May 17 when she still couldn't pronounce either *h* or *r*.

"Ullah, ullah, ullah!" Anna had cheered as she marched around the garden, looking good enough to eat. "Ipp, ipp ulaaah!"

In time, it grew far worse.

Maria tried to stretch out on the bunk. The light only grew even more insistent, and it hurt her shoulder blades. She hauled herself up again and began to pace the floor.

There were so many noises in here. Loud shouts. Ferocious swearing from some man or other with a rough voice and increasingly obscene requests for attention from the custody officers. She could hear some people crying, followed by keys rattling, and for a moment she stood at attention, listening intently: it seemed as if someone was about to open her door.

And let her out perhaps.

Tell her that it had all been a misunderstanding and let her go home.

Anna forced her way into her head. When Maria sat down on the bunk again with her eyes closed, she saw her sister in her mind's eye, lying on the bathroom floor in a pool of blood, with half her face blown away. She had raised her right hand to her, the hand that had held the pistol when she shot herself; it could not have been anything else, since her last will and testament was lying open on the kitchen counter.

Now Anna held out a blood-soaked cell phone: a text message had summoned Maria to Stugguveien 2B. She could still recall the bizarre message.

Come comenow Soon. Warfare.

If the message had conveyed a more run-of-the-mill message, Maria probably wouldn't have gone to the bother of turning up at Stugguveien.

Anna had been increasingly depressed after Dina's tragic death. The first year, her sister had drawn closer to Maria. Anna wanted to surround herself with people all the time, and it felt good to have her make persistent contact. Maria was in Australia when her niece had died, but Anna sent a fully paid return ticket and earnestly entreated her to come home for the funeral.

Her sister had needed her for the very first time.

As weeks and months passed, she no longer needed anyone at all.

Anna buried herself more and more in what Maria realized was an extremely serious depression. It was tiresome, in Maria's opinion. A real drag, to be honest. Although at first Anna had hugged her every time she came, and usually sobbed in her arms after the loads of food and wine they had delivered to the door, she eventually became completely sober. And more aloof. Maria in the meantime had married Roar, and they had gone back to Australia in summer 2003. The only reason she had come back to Norway just before Christmas was that her money had run out.

Roar stayed behind down under, and they didn't get around to divorce until 2006.

He had at least given her a more attractive surname than the one her sister had acquired through marriage. Hansen, the name they had both been born with, was one neither of them could bear.

She had called on Anna in the hope of getting some help at the end of November. It was only fair that she should. When their parents had died within only six weeks of each other in 1993, it was clear to everyone how the old dears had felt about their offspring. The sale of Hansen White Goods had raised a tidy sum of money. Their father had run the family business as his own private savings bank, more miserly than Scrooge McDuck. So a lucrative estate had been wound up after their mother's funeral, and Maria had thought that the sisters would receive equal shares.

But Anna was the one their parents had favored. She inherited their childhood home, the cottage, and the share in the family farm belonging to their father's relatives near Arendal. Plus 6 million kroner. Maria received 4 million kroner, and nothing more. In a state of shock, she had visited a lawyer, an arrogant bastard. Strictly speaking, Maria was not entitled to any more than her basic legal entitlement, he had curtly explained, and challenging her parents' will through the courts would be a waste of both time and money. The next lawyer said exactly the same.

Four million had lasted for a few years. She had eked it out with the occasional casual job, but Maria Kvam did not much enjoy working. She had other fish to fry. Traveling. Meeting new people, experiencing new countries. While Anna was a prudish slave to bourgeois conventions, Maria was a free spirit.

It had all been so unfair, and 4 million did not last very long. It had been advantageous to get married, but that too had been like wetting your pants to keep warm.

In November, Anna had seemed indifferent to Maria's pleas. She wrote a check for 10,000 kroner and then went to bed. As if a sum like that would help in the least. Anna had inherited her father's miserliness, and Maria had avoided her for three weeks after that.

The text message had been very odd. When it arrived, Maria was in her car en route to Årvoll to help set things up for a New Year's party at her friend's house. It would take only a few minutes to reach Stugguveien, and she was, to tell the truth, slightly curious about why her sister had sent her a message that contained the word *warfare*.

Not until many years later, and then by sheer accident, had she discovered that the spell checker on the Nokia phone was the culprit: *I'm dying* in Norwegian turned into *warfare* if you forgot the space between the two short words.

I'm dying was what Anna had typed in.

And she was.

Maria had first rung the doorbell, more from sheer laziness than good manners. She had left her keys in the car. When no one opened the door, she had decided she would not give a damn, but her curiosity had gained the upper hand. She got her keys and let herself in.

It seemed so quiet inside that she caught herself creeping around like a mouse. She kicked off her winter shoes and hung up her coat in the hallway before sneaking into the vast kitchen where she usually liked to sit. It was deserted. And unusually clean and tidy.

Anna always kept things tidy. Even when they were little, she was always the one who was praised to the skies for keeping her room in order even though she was seven years younger. This past year, her tidiness had become an obsession. Everything was always in place, and you couldn't even put down an empty water glass before Anna was on the spot, rinsing it out and stacking it in the dishwasher.

But this was absurd. It must be the result of some obsessive-compulsive disorder.

Maria stood surveying the room with her mouth open. The kitchen was approximately square, fitted out in a horseshoe shape along three of the walls. In the center of the spacious room, a kitchen island had been installed with a sink and two bar stools on the opposite side.

All the surfaces were bare. Not even the kettle was on view. The dishcloth that usually hung neatly folded over the tap was nowhere to be seen. Neither was the sponge that always sat in a metal soap dish beside the sink.

A faint smell of bleach hung in the air. The room was in semidarkness, and Maria switched on all the lights. In the glass cabinet on one wall, she could now see that even the glasses were arranged in very straight lines and recently sorted according to size. Beer glasses at the bottom, through assorted wine glasses, and little liqueur glasses on the top shelf.

To be honest, it looked as if no one lived there. It would have looked like a catalog photograph if it weren't for the fact that the obligatory basket laden with fruit was missing.

Maria grew slightly worried.

She opened the fridge, which was virtually empty. The stench of chlorine was stronger now, and not even in the vegetable drawer was there the slightest trace of grime. Three bottles of water were lined up on a shelf in the door, and that was all.

It was not until she closed the fridge door that she caught sight of the letters.

"No," Maria said, opening her eyes.

The light was an assault. It could not be legal to torment people in prison in this way. What's more, she was thirsty, and her headache was worsening by the minute. She crossed to the door. The bellowing man had finally kept his mouth shut, but the sobbing of whoever was in the adjacent cell had not yet been stilled.

"I need water!" Maria Kvam shouted, hammering on the metal door.

She refused to entertain any more thoughts about Anna.

The man with the blowtorch arrived at Maria Kvam's apartment at exactly the same moment as the representative from SafeGuard, the importer and seller of home and office security equipment. The policeman seemed disappointed that the woman in her forties with a tight skirt and high heels was to open the safe and that he would have to leave the business unfinished when it turned out that SafeGuard had complete control of its products. And its employees. It took the red-haired woman six minutes flat to override Maria Kvam's combination lock, all while hunkered down smartly with her feet together in their Jimmy Choo shoes.

Hanne was impressed.

The woman carefully lifted the metal plate concealing the secret compartment in the base of the safe. She laid it on the floor and stood up in a single elegant movement.

"I'll take a back seat now," she said, with a brief nod in Hanne's direction. "I'll wait in the living room in case you have any further need of me."

She left the room.

"What the hell?"

Ove Finnerud stared in disbelief at the small compartment that now lay open.

"That there," Hanne Wilhelmsen said, bending down and picking up a piece of paper, "is what I'd call an interesting find. An extremely interesting find."

No one brought Maria Kvam any water. She hammered on the door until her hands were throbbing and gave up.

When she got home, she would send a complaint to Amnesty International.

At the time of Iselin's death, Maria had been in Bergen, and no one could prove anything at all. The police had probably left her apartment ages ago. There was nothing there for them to find. There was nothing of interest in the safe.

Except for the secret compartment.

The secret compartment was impossible to discover, however, and soon someone would come and let her out. Maria lay down again on the bunk to concentrate on not thinking about either Iselin or Anna.

Two letters had been left lying on Anna's gleaming kitchen counter.

One was a folded copy of the separation agreement. Jonas and Anna had now legally parted.

The other was a sealed white envelope. Anna had written "Jonas" by hand on the front. Nothing else. Maria was tempted to open it but resisted. Anna would be annoyed. More sulky and sullen than ever.

"Anna?"

Maria left the kitchen. She still could not hear anything other than the occasional shout from the neighboring property: they seemed to be preparing for a party. When she switched on the living room lights, she saw that Anna's compulsive cleaning had left its mark here too. The room seemed absolutely dead. Not as much as a coffee cup or a newspaper to be seen. No sign of a flower or a potted plant, no knitting or unfinished crossword. The books on the bookshelves stood erect as soldiers on parade, sorted according to color and size and at precisely the same distance from the edges of the shelves.

By this point, Maria was growing terribly anxious, mainly because she had no idea what this was all about.

"Anna?"

A sound, she definitely thought. She tiptoed hesitantly upstairs. The bathroom door was open and a cone of light illuminated the gloom of the hallway.

"Anna," Maria said yet again, daring to move step by step closer to the open door.

Anna's eyes were the most difficult to forget.

Her left hand was pressed to her face, which looked as if it had collapsed inward. Or else was gone. Blood oozed out through her fingers. Anna was holding her cell phone in her right hand and she held it out to Maria as she struggled to say something.

There was no mouth left to say anything with, Maria could see that. No mouth to phone for an ambulance. No voice to call police emergency or any other place, and she had sent Maria a message instead.

Anna was trying to sit up without success.

A pistol lay on the floor.

Anna dropped the cell phone and reached out for the gun. Was she going to shoot herself again?

Maybe she was going to shoot Maria.

Quick as a flash, she crouched down and grabbed the pistol. She stared at it in fright and dropped it on the floor as if she had burned herself. Now at least it was beyond Anna's reach.

Anna gurgled something incomprehensible and tried to wriggle closer to the door. Maria jerked two steps back, but it was unnecessary. Anna was no longer able to move.

It might be possible to save her sister.

If Anna died, though, Maria would inherit everything. The separation formalities had been completed, and Maria knew someone who had been through something similar. His wife had died only four weeks after authorization had come through, and he was left with nothing at all.

Maria had nothing either.

She could call the police emergency number. It looked as if Anna had managed to stanch the worst of the bleeding by holding her hand pressed against the wound. Slow it, at least.

She withdrew slowly, out of Anna's sight. She went downstairs, through the living room, out into the hallway, and then into the kitchen. With hands that trembled only ever so slightly, she ripped open the envelope that Anna had left for Jonas.

A suicide letter, she quickly ascertained.

And a last will and testament.

Jonas was to inherit everything from Anna.

Maria was raging. She swore loudly and tore the will into as many tiny pieces as she could. She put them in her mouth, chewed them, and spat them out again, threw them about, cursing and screaming, finally pulling herself together so abruptly that she stopped breathing.

She had to find every single scrap of paper.

She was methodical. Took plenty of time. In the end, the kitchen was immaculate again.

Maria stuffed the suicide letter into her back pocket, put the separation agreement in a kitchen drawer, and scanned the room. Everything was exactly as it had been when she arrived.

Apart from two letters that had now vanished.

She had to return to the bathroom again, no matter how much she wanted to run. She could just leave. Anna was going to die anyway. If she left the suicide letter behind, then everything would go smoothly.

Or would it, really?

She could not leave Anna's letter to Jonas. Not without also leaving the will, which the letter mentioned at one point. And that had now been reduced to minuscule wet scraps in her pants pocket.

It struck her as she climbed the stairs that not everyone who committed suicide left a letter. She could run out to the car and phone for an ambulance; maybe it would still be possible to save Anna's life. But if she died, Maria would be rich. She would be the one to inherit this house. The cottage. All of Anna's money.

She slowed down as she approached the bathroom.

The problem was that she had been there so long. She glanced at her wristwatch. It was twenty minutes since she had arrived. Someone in the neighbor's house might have spotted her. They could have done what she did when she parked up on the street: glanced at the time.

She had no good explanation for not having phoned ages ago. She would not have the chance to get rid of the chewed-up will and the letter to Jonas if she called now.

Maria began to cry. Quietly, and not over Anna, who extended her hand to her again and gurgled something unintelligible. Her eyes were dying. Probably it was too late. Everything was too late. She could not be saved, Maria decided, shedding bitter tears at her own fate.

No one must ever see the weird message she had received. The police would find out through Telenor that the cell phone had been used, but not the contents of the message. Not if they didn't have the phone. She leaned into the bathroom and picked it up.

The pistol too, she thought, as panic set in. She had already touched it. While fingerprints elsewhere in the house could be explained by saying she was here often, a print on a bloody gun would be far more difficult to get away with.

Impossible.

She had no idea what she should do, and so she took it with her. She wrapped both the pistol and the cell phone in toilet paper before she put both inside her waistband. For a second, because she had to step aside to avoid losing her balance when she stood up, she touched Anna's hand. It was still warm.

Warm, Maria thought. Heat delayed the death process. Anna was bleeding to death, but it mustn't happen around six o'clock. Death must take place later than that. Maria had no idea how much later the result would have to be, but she turned the thermostat to the maximum setting. On both the heated floor and the towel rail, which she could reach easily without stepping in all the blood.

Maria closed the door and left her sister to die.

She already knew what she would have to do the next morning, and it would be easy, given the weather outside. The windows could be reached without coming into contact with as much as a drop of blood.

And so Maria was the one who inherited everything from Anna.

"It was only fair," Maria said to herself as she screwed up her eyes against the light on the ceiling. "It was the only fair thing to do, and Anna's life probably couldn't have been saved."

She had never regretted it. In fact, she had not done anything wrong. If Anna, contrary to expectation, had survived, she would have looked dreadful. She had wanted to die, but not managed to do it cleanly. Maria had simply helped her along, and as for getting back her childhood home and everything that was hers by right—no one could gainsay any of that.

Maria could not be reproached because it had entered Jonas's head to pay a visit to Anna in the middle of the night and then become enmeshed in a net of idiotic lies. Far from it. He only had himself to blame. As far as Maria was concerned, Jonas's visit to Stugguveien 2B was a stroke of luck. Or maybe a sign that fate wished her well.

She regretted none of it and sat up quickly to resume hammering on the cell door again. Her tongue felt like sandpaper.

She had smashed Anna's cell phone to smithereens on New Year's Day before returning to Stugguveien and thrown it into a random garbage can. She had considered tossing the pistol in the sea, but it was a long time before the opportunity arose. She had been terrified for the first few days of 2004 when she had spent hours on end with the police. The gun was still lying under the seat in her car, and she almost had a heart attack every time someone knocked on the interview room door. Fortunately she was treated as a deeply sorrowing sister: any interruptions were normally due to offers of more coffee and water. When Jonas was arrested, she breathed considerably more easily, and later that spring she took a trip on the Danish ferry.

The pistol had disappeared into the Skagerrak.

But she had needed the suicide letter.

It was impossible to burn that.

She had read it probably a hundred times during that first year.

It gave her such comfort, that letter. Anna had wanted to die, more than anything else, and Maria had helped her to depart from life. Leaving Anna on the bathroom floor had been an act of compassion. The only right thing to do, and the letter brought her peace and reassurance that she had done the correct thing.

It was a beautiful letter, and she kept it so that she could have regular confirmation that she had not done anything wrong that evening when her sister had made up her mind to die.

Besides, the letter had come in useful later and was now hidden in a compartment in the double-bottomed safe that no one had any idea existed.

"Hello!" Maria yelled, slapping both hands on the metal door. "I'm dying of thirst!"

No one came to give her water. Not for hours yet.

"Convictions for the whole gang of them," Kjell Bonsaksen said, clapping his hands as he entered Henrik's office without knocking. "Congratulations!"

Henrik looked up from his computer screen and smiled at the retired superintendent.

"Well, really we shouldn't congratulate each other on achieving convictions," he answered. "But thanks. No one was found unfit to plead either. How's it going down in France?"

"Brilliant, thanks," Bonsaksen said, sounding pleased, as he sat down in the empty chair. "We've ordered three breeding animals now. Australian cobberdogs—one from Australia and two from the Netherlands. It's going well. And then there's the weather! If it's not exactly summer at the moment, at least it's a vast improvement on the deplorable weather here."

He pointed apathetically at the gray light outside and fished out a cigar butt from his breast pocket. Henrik could swear that it was the same one as last time.

It was just after eleven o'clock.

"You're very capable, Holme. Really smart. Thanks to you, twenty-two convicted terrorists are now under lock and key and you're due much of the credit. Take it while you can."

He rubbed his face with his right hand and shook his head, as if struggling to stay awake.

"Have you been equally clever with the Abrahamsen case?" he asked, looking around.

"The ring binder's at home," Henrik reassured him. "Safe and sound. We've actually taken a really good look at it, both Hanne Wilhelmsen and me. And we've made quite a bit of progress. We've come a good distance, in fact."

"And what do you think you've found? Was I right? Is the poor guy innocent after all?"

Henrik gave a faint smile and slammed his heels together under the desk.

"I think so. I really do think so. At first I thought it was a case of suicide, but eventually I arrived at—"

His phone rang.

"Excuse me," Henrik said to Kjell Bonsaksen before answering the phone. "Hello, Hanne."

The conversation lasted six and a half minutes, though Henrik did not contribute anything other than a brief *yes* now and again and a *what?* on a couple of occasions. Bonsaksen helped himself to a cup of coffee from the coffee machine and scrolled through his own cell phone for news, without making any move to leave Henrik to take the call in peace.

Finally it ended, and Henrik got to his feet.

"You look very pale!" Kjell Bonsaksen glanced up at him with an anxious expression as he returned the cigar to his pocket. "Is something wrong?"

Henrik crossed to a hook by the door and grabbed his leather jacket.

"I need to find out where Jonas Abrahamsen lives," he said quietly as he tapped the back of his head. *Stupid, stupid.*

"He lives in Maridalen. I checked it out after I bumped into him at the gas station here at the beginning of the month. Why do you ask?"

"Hanne's asked me to bring him in for interview as quickly as I can. He's innocent, Bonsaksen. It really does look to me as if you were absolutely right. Hanne wants him in before the story leaks to the media."

"What the hell . . ." The retired policeman leaped up faster than anyone would have thought possible. "I'm coming with you," he said firmly. "Then you can tell me the whole story on the way."

Henrik hesitated for a few seconds before pulling on his jacket and winding his scarf around his neck.

"Okay," he said, nodding. "It's probably best if you tag along."

"Today I'm not going to stay here anymore," Hedda said happily and took a big bite of her apple. "Today I'm getting picked up!"

"Yes, today you won't have to stay here any longer," Jonas said, with a nod, and he held her under her chin as he looked into her eyes. "But are you sure you don't want to stay here, then? Stay with Jonas?"

Hedda laughed. Her gleaming white milk teeth sparkled in the light from the shoemaker's lamp above the kitchen table.

"Nooo," she whined. "I want to go home to Mommy and Grampa. Oh!"

She pulled away from his grasp and ran to the window.

"Police!" she yelled with delight. "Maybe they're looking for burglars!"

Jonas walked calmly across and peered out.

In the distance, on the other side of the field at the bottom of the road, two police cars were driving, approaching quietly, but with blue lights pulsing in the gray morning darkness. The snow that had fallen in such quantities last week was now almost entirely gone. Clumps were dotted here and there across the field, and dirty gray snowdrifts still flanked the roads here in the valley.

"They're probably hunting for burglars, right enough," Jonas told her. "And now you and I will just go back to the bedroom."

"No," the three-year-old complained. "I want to watch. I want to go out. Why can't we go out, Jonas?"

"Because I've got something important to do," Jonas said. "Come on now, sweetheart. We'll go into the bedroom."

"Well, that's certainly some crazy story," Bonsaksen said, indicating left up Sandermosveien. "The worst one I've ever heard. Poor, poor Jonas. And did Maria Kvam really use the introduction to Anna's genuine suicide letter as a template for the one she forged?"

"Yes. She wanted to make it . . . more authentic? In any case, the first four sentences were identical, word for word. I've read them before. Very religious, and obviously influenced by the Book of Job."

"But did Anna take her own life, or was she murdered by Maria?"

"That remains to be seen. Anyway, at least there can no longer be any doubt that Anna planned to commit suicide. Whether Maria beat her to it or whether something else happened, it's impossible to say. In the meantime it's clear, though, that Maria is involved in some way or another. She had the suicide letter hidden in her safe."

"Incredible," Kjell Bonsaksen murmured. "But maybe not, all the same. History is too full of such stories. Anna took care of her inheritance. Maria frittered it away and was never satisfied. Do you know . . ."

He had slowed down. They were driving in his personal vehicle, which was to be sold in the course of that week.

"Maria Kvam was nothing but a fucking drifter," he said, running the fingers of his left hand over the bridge of his nose. "All her life. Never passed her exams. Spent all the money she inherited. Got rich when her sister died. Squandered money when she had it, and when Iselin was about to leave her and keep a small fortune, she made damn sure she kept that as well."

"More of an out-and-out criminal than just a drifter," Henrik said. "I think we have some colleagues behind us."

He peered out through the side window. Two patrol cars with blue lights flashing, without sirens. Suddenly the blue lights were switched off.

"We do a lot of emergency squad training out on these roads," Bonsaksen said. "Here we are! Nearly there. Henrik—"

"Yes?"

"I should have looked more closely at Maria Kvam. What a fucking slipup. But you know, when not even Jonas's lawyer did that, and—"

"She had an alibi. A watertight alibi. Seemingly. And Jonas lied, in addition to being verifiably at the crime scene at the worst possible time. For him, I mean. And you."

Bonsaksen turned into a narrow road leading to a farmyard. The windows in the small farmhouse were brightly lit. The track was icy and rutted. The snow had not been cleared when it was dry and had subsequently melted before freezing again.

"I'm looking forward to this," Bonsaksen said softly, switching off the engine. "Think what it must be like to hear . . . after all these years. After having lost everything."

He sniffed noisily and unfastened his seat belt.

"Could I lead the way?" he asked, seeming almost disconcerted. "You see, after I met him on New Year's Day, I've sometimes dreamed about . . . I've thought that—"

"Of course you can," Henrik said. "But you're an experienced policeman. Don't promise too much. Stick to the main point."

"Which is that we're convinced of his innocence," Kjell Bonsaksen said, smiling. "I'm looking forward to it like a child to his birthday! Thanks very much."

They stepped out of the car. The farmyard was covered in ice. Henrik hopped from one bare patch to another in the direction of the front door. Kjell Bonsaksen wobbled unsteadily with his legs splayed, moving across the ice in the same direction.

"Are they coming here?" Henrik called out in surprise, pointing.

One of the police cars had stopped with its hood turned into the driveway, less than a hundred yards away.

"They're probably just turning," Bonsaksen shouted back. "Wait for me, and then we'll knock on the door."

He laughed, so excited he almost couldn't bear to wait.

They had arrived, just as it had been decreed by fate that they would, sooner or later. Four days and nights was what it had taken. Jonas had spent four days and nights with a child who looked like Dina, and they were the best days of his life since he lost her.

He had smiled. Even laughed sometimes. They had played and eaten meals together. At night she had snuggled up beside him, just as daughters creep up behind their fathers, shielded from everything evil and wicked.

Of course they had come. It was only strange that it had taken them so long.

Someone was knocking on the door of the little unlocked porch.

Jonas opened the door and recognized Kjell Bonsaksen. The other man was slim and looked bashful. They asked if they could come in. Bonsaksen was smiling. Jonas had never seen him smile before, but now he was grinning so broadly that Jonas backed away. Both men stepped into the room that was Jonas Abrahamsen's living room and kitchen combined.

Bonsaksen was talking. Jonas could not properly hear what he was saying. It was as if someone had slipped a glass jar over his head, and it was so cold inside there. Cold and incredibly silent. He looked at the policeman's mouth. Tried to see all the words streaming out that he could suddenly hear, but that did not convey any meaning.

"Would you like to sit down?" the other man said.

He had kind eyes. Jonas did not know his name. Maybe he had mentioned it to him when they arrived. He could not remember. He hadn't heard, and he put both hands over his ears as he sank down onto the sofa.

He caught the words "miscarriage of justice."

The stout policeman kept talking and now there was something that might be about Anna. Or about Maria.

No one was talking about Dina, though, and Jonas rocked from side to side on the sofa as he clutched his hands tightly to his ears.

He did not quite follow what Bonsaksen was talking about, and he didn't dare listen. Not even when he began to hear. The policeman said that he was innocent. He said that Jonas had spent eight years in prison for something he hadn't done, but Jonas did not want to hear it. It was too late now.

There was another knock at the door.

The men turned around in astonishment, and Jonas rose from the sofa.

"She's lying in there," he said hoarsely, pointing at the low, shabby wooden door leading into a bedroom with a bed he had built himself. "She's lying in there and she's dead, and I'm really sorry."

The door crashed open. Policemen poured in and now there was noise everywhere. Loud, piercing, shouting, murderous sounds, and Jonas covered his ears.

"I'm sorry," he repeated, though no one could hear him.

The slim man with the kind eyes rushed to the bedroom door.

"It's too late," Jonas said, bowing his head. "Everything is too late."

Henrik forced a finger beneath the tight belt. He screamed furious commands at the two uniformed men who had followed him, *keep away, open that window, call for an ambulance*, as he tugged and tugged at the brown leather strap around the neck of the child in Jonas's bed. Henrik could neither pull his finger out nor push it in. He shrieked so loudly that everything fell silent, and he growled and snarled as he tugged at the leather, but the child was still dead.

A knife appeared out of nowhere. Grabbing it, Henrik sliced along his own finger, where a few millimeters of air between the child's skin and the coarse leather had opened up. He cut himself as he twisted the blade into the leather, but the belt was now starting to give.

He was bleeding copiously by the time the leather snapped.

He kissed the little girl with deep breaths, and applied his stiff fingers with rhythmic brutality to her heart. Kissed and pressed and prayed to God.

"It's no use," Bonsaksen said, placing a hand on his back as he attempted to breathe life into her for perhaps the tenth time. "It's too late."

Hedda would not wake. She was spattered with Henrik's blood, the gash on his finger was gaping right down to the bone, and he could hear a man weep in the living room.

"No," Henrik snarled, striking the child's chest with his fist as he uttered one syllable at a time: Noth-ing. Is. Ev-er. Too. Late.

Once again he leaned over her. Covered the girl's mouth with his own and blew. Then he straightened his back, ready to thump; he would never stop, there was always some hope; and he refused point-blank when Bonsaksen tried to drag him away.

"That's enough now, Henrik. She's dead."

Eventually Henrik let his arms fall. The uniformed policemen withdrew silently from the room.

"No one could have done more," Bonsaksen told him. "You did everything you could."

Henrik Holme did not answer. He slowly crouched down. With his good hand on the three-year-old's forehead, he was whispering words of comfort, almost a lullaby, as if the child might be his very own.

Hedda Bengtson opened her eyes.

About the Author

Anne Holt has worked as a journalist and a news anchor, and she spent two years working for the Oslo Police Department before founding her own law firm and serving as Norway's minister for justice from 1996 to 1997. Since her first book in 1993, Holt's work has been published in thirty languages and sold more than seven million copies. She is the recipient of several awards, including the Riverton Prize and the Norwegian Booksellers' Prize, and she was short-listed for an Edgar Award in 2012. She was also short-listed for the 2012 Shamus Award and a 2012 Macavity Award. In October 2012, Anne Holt was awarded the Great Calibre Award of Honor in Poland for her entire authorship. She lives in Oslo with her family.